PRAISE FO

"The author of the Dra... trilogies, as well as the urban fantasies *Spellbinder* and *Fire Raiser*, returns to high fantasy with a captivating tale of magic, theater, politics, and love. She sets her story in a Renaissance-like world, a place recovering from a devastating war that resulted in the stringent regulation of potentially harmful magic. Rawn's storytelling mastery, ability to create unforgettable characters, and fresh approaches to world-building and magic theory make this a must-read for an audience that extends well beyond her fans."

—*Library Journal* (starred review)

"This first in a new series introduces a world full of people of mixed magical heritage and a love of magical theater. Nineteen-year-old Cayden wants nothing more than to be a famous playwright, but in order for his group to succeed, they need a fourth member. When young, beautiful, mercurial Elven Mieka joins in a performance, he transforms the group and gives them a shot at becoming one of the few troupes to travel the Kingdom. . . . With a fully realized world and magical system, as well as a character-driven plot, this will appeal to fans of traditional fantasies like *Warbreaker* by Brandon Sanderson or Michael J. Sullivan's Riyria series. Highly recommended."

—*Booklist*

"Rawn takes heroic fantasy to its logical conclusion, creating a lived-in world where the scars from magical wars still linger and pure blood is a thing of the distant past. . . . This strong, heartfelt, and familiar performer's tale is full of astonishing promise, powerful but codependent friendships, insecurity, and addiction, and it will appeal to fantasy fans and theater lovers alike." —*Publishers Weekly*

"I've been talking mostly about story, and an imaginatively detailed yet never overdrawn fantasy background. But what impresses me most about *Touchstone* proves to be its unexpected sense of realism. These are the personal adventures of brash, foulmouthed young people, where maturation is still a work in progress. Professional or moral failures could lie ahead—for their best and brightest?—yet hope lingers while they find their own strange way to success." —*Locus*

"Rawn knows what makes people tick and how to create and present rich, complex characters the reader cares deeply about. *Touchstone* is a fascinating mix of character choreography, magic, and a refreshingly new fantasy backdrop." —Jennifer Roberson

"Melanie Rawn is in her usual fine form with a vivid world and thoroughly captivating characters. A masterful blend of plot, character, and setting makes reading seem effortless in this tale of four young men devoted to the magical theater of their world. Rawn's skill as a writer brings you right onto the stage with them." —Kate Elliott

MELANIE RAWN

Touchstone

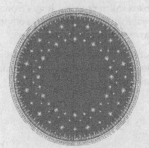

Book One of The Glass Thorns

A TOM DOHERTY ASSOCIATES BOOK
NEW YORK

This is a work of fiction. All of the characters, organizations, and events portrayed in this novel are either products of the author's imagination or are used fictitiously.

TOUCHSTONE

Copyright © 2012 by Melanie Rawn

A Tor Book
Published by Tom Doherty Associates, LLC
175 Fifth Avenue
New York, NY 10010

www.tor-forge.com

Tor® is a registered trademark of Tom Doherty Associates, LLC.

ISBN 978-0-7653-6347-3

First Edition: February 2012
First Mass Market Edition: January 2013

Printed in the United States of America

0 9 8 7 6 5 4 3 2 1

Touchstone

One

PREDICTABLY, THE GIRL was willing to draw the pint only when the coin was glinting on the bar. Cayden stretched his lips in a parody of a smile as she scooped up the money with one hand and pulled the tap with the other. No glass for him, oh no; leather tankard instead, sealed with tar and riveted with brass and bound to taste of both.

Well, it was alcohol, and that was all that mattered. But if that fool who'd had the bollocks to claim himself a glisker had been any good, Cade would be knocking back whiskey right now, and plenty of it—from a real glass, and with coin to spare for something to eat. Decent drink and his supper had walked out of the tavern a little while ago, jingling in the incompetent's purse. Glisker, he'd termed himself. Experienced, even. Cade snorted. Probably had about as much Elfenblood in him as the dirty rag the girl was using to mop up the bar. At least he was paid off and gone, and nobody was any the worse for the performance.

Yet when Cade thought about what might have been, if he had the right glisker, one with real talent and real magic—

"Wuzna too gude, wuzzee?"

The accent was excruciating—especially as Cayden

had worked so hard to soften his own, distorted during years of schooling not twenty miles from here. Eyeing the young man beside him at the bar, he noted a confusion of features that proclaimed an ancestry so diverse that probably even he didn't know what to call himself.

"No, he wasn't too good." He had to admit it. Honesty was the hallmark of a real artist, or so his Sagemaster had told him. Or maybe it was "truth" that mattered most. They weren't the same.

"Gotz me a chum c'n do ooshuns better," the rough voice continued.

"Do you?" Cayden smiled politely and returned his attention to his ale.

"Domn near purely breeded Elferblud, an' tha's fact. Givvem withies next show, whyn't ya?"

Yet another aspiring glisker. Splendid. What was he, the audition manager for every amateur in the Kingdom?

Still . . . they'd gone through four gliskers this year alone, not counting the idiot tonight, never finding the right mix, never finding anyone Cayden could trust with his visions and Jeschenar could trust with his skin and Rafcadion could trust with his sanity. They weren't anywhere near good enough even to seek Trials, and it was all because they didn't have the right glisker.

What would it be like, he wondered, to experience that effortless balance of talent and energy and magic that this was supposed to be? It was what all the greatest players had known, what he sensed was going on with the Shadowshapers now that they'd hired Chattim Czillag away from his old group. That nobody had ever heard a name so outrageous, nobody knew where he'd come from or his lineage or the name of his clan—if any—or indeed aught about him mattered not at all. Chattim *fit*. With the right glisker, a performance became an event, a distinction.

Hells, what was one more tryout, anyway? It wasn't

as if anyone would ever hear about yet another botched playlet, not in this rickety old tavern only half a step inside civilization.

Cade shrugged to himself and glanced down—way down—at the youth beside him. "All right, send him up for the next show."

Breath hissed between ragged teeth—a sign of delight in a Troll, and of an impending brawl in a Gnome. As he hurried off to find his friend, he moved with the rolling shoulders and splayed knees peculiar to the former, thereby settling the question of his primary ancestry as surely as Cayden's long-boned height proclaimed his. Watching the little man, recalling the quirks of his accent, for an instant Cade felt a twinge of longing for home. Not for his parents; a bit for his little brother; mostly for their Trollwife, Mistress Mirdley. She'd been strict and kind to him, when all his mother knew how to be was neglectful and harsh.

"*Oh, pity the poor little Wizardling!*" jeered the Sagemaster's voice in his head. "*How horrid to be you!*"

A small commotion behind him jostled him into the bar, and he turned his head to snarl. One more trite old playlet tonight for this unsophisticated crowd, and they could get out of here, get some sleep in the hayloft, and then tomorrow be gone entirely from this village of sour ale and foul manners. And really lousy trimmings, he thought with a gloomy sigh; two nights of this, and they'd barely made enough for the coach fare home. He thought with longing of the brand-new private coach his friend (and rival, though nobody but Cayden knew that yet) Rauel Kevelock had so gleefully described last month, painted in swirling colors like a demented prism, with SHADOWSHAPERS in stark black on both sides. It had bunk beds for when they got tired, and a firepocket for when they got cold. True, the group still had to hire horses from the post stations, but at least they were no longer at the mercy of worn-out springs and a coachman who drank his wages in full before clambering up to take the reins, and—

Someone bumped into him again, knocking his hand against his leather flask of ale. He half-turned and shoved right back. Spindle-boned Cade might be, but Jeska had taught him how to use his fists efficiently rather than his magic haphazardly, and he was just frustrated enough right now to relish the prospect of a punch-up.

Then he saw what had knocked into him.

Even for someone with plenty of Wizardly blood, Cayden was tall. The man whose chest was on a level with his eyes—this man was at least half Giant. Maybe more than half; there was very little mitigating intellect visible in the red-rimmed eyes glaring down on him.

"Uh—sorry," Cade managed. "Thought you were somebody else."

"Did 'ee, now?" The depth of his rumble rattled the bottles on the shelves.

Oh, shit.

"Yazz!" exclaimed a light, cheerful voice. "Don't break him! He's me new Quill, he is! It's rich an' famed he and me will be—but only if ye leave him all his wits an' bones!"

A slow, fond smile gentled the massive face. Cade turned, wondering if he was more grateful for the rescue or annoyed by the glisker's arrogance. Because a glisker this had to be, the one promised by the Troll. For an Elf, however, this boy had peculiar taste in friends.

And then all speculation—indeed, all thought—fled Cade's brain, except for the sure knowledge that he would remember for the rest of his life the instant those huge, melting eyes looked up at him from beneath a shock of coal-black hair.

Those eyes: sparkling with what his Sagemaster called "front and effrontery," a combination of awful nervousness and awe-inspiring conceit. Cade had been accused of it himself on occasion, but hard lessoning in the brutal school of his own family had taught him to hide any fear behind all the arrogance he could possibly project. This boy was too young yet to have perfected his mask.

Those eyes: a bit too bright with the alcohol downed to get his courage up, trying to hide apprehension that Cade wouldn't think he was good enough, but not trying at all to disguise that he thought any group of players would be colossally lucky to get him.

Those eyes: full of anxiety and arrogance, innocence and cunning, and a dozen other conflicting things that dizzied Cade for a moment.

There was a low growling in his ears that he hoped was Yazz agreeing to let him live. A burst of bright laughter followed from the Elf. His new glisker.

Those eyes were directed at him again, calculating, challenging. "Mieka say-it-five-times-fast Windthistle."

"Dare 'ee t'try!" The Giant nudged Cade with an elbow strongly reminiscent of a roof joist, and he staggered against the bar.

"Did I tell ye or did I not, Yazz? *Don't* damage him!"

"Much beholden," Cade said, taking refuge in the stock phrases of civility. "You're the glisker wants a chance?"

"You need me, and here I am. Thought I'd introduce meself afore we start work." Thick black brows arched an invitation to share his name.

"Cayden Silversun, Falcon Clan," he said.

To his annoyance, the Elf didn't look as impressed as he ought to have done. But there was an odd sort of approval in his eyes, and perhaps relief, as he said, "Falcon, not Hawk? Good. Such a harsh, cruel word, innit? Typical of that tongue—and that clan. Always makes me think of claws with blood drippin' off 'em. Met any foreign kin?"

"No. Are you ready to work?" He cast an eloquent glance at the whiskey in Windthistle's hand.

"Almost." He slugged back the remainder of his drink, slapped the glass onto the bar, wiped his mouth with the back of his hand, belched delicately, and gave Cade a dazzling smile. "*Now* I'm ready."

Yazz reached out a finger and tapped a carefully gentle admonishment on the Elf's head. "Rich un' famed, Miek," he rasped, and Cade had the irrelevant thought that *meek* was precisely the wrong word for any Elf, particularly this one.

"Oh, certain sure," the boy laughed, and scampered off towards the tavern's pathetic excuse for a stage.

"Givvem simple t'do," said Yazz. "Makes everythin' from nothin', Miek does."

"Is that so?" Hearing the sharp skepticism in his own voice, he dredged up a smile meant to mollify the Giant. "I'm looking forward to it."

* * *

THE TROUBLE WITH being the tregetour, Cayden thought for possibly the millionth time, was that after you were done with your part of the piece, you were helpless. Superfluous. At times, a nuisance.

No, that was wrong, he thought morosely as he crouched before his glass baskets of crystalline withies. The worst part of it was having to trust.

Rafcadion and Jeschenar, them he trusted. It wasn't their fault they'd never found a glisker who really knew what he was doing—or, more to the purpose, knew what to do with Cade's magic. Jeska was a good masquer, and getting better—and Cade knew that a lot of the reason they'd gotten as far as they had was that Jeska really could make much out of practically nothing. Rafe was just plain brilliant: steady, calm, powerful, everything a fettler ought to be and more. But Cayden couldn't help wondering what it would be like when Rafe didn't have to use up so much of himself keeping the performance together because the glisker was lazy or erratic or reckless; when he could fine-tune things, work *with* the man instead of guarding against excesses, correcting failures, glossing over incompetences.

Given a glisker who could not only perform the piece but also enhance it, Jeska and Rafcadion would be free to develop their gifts to their fullest, to provide Cayden's work with the nuances he craved. And they would no longer end each evening so wrung out they could hardly stand.

Despite Yazz's affectionate confidence in this new glisker, Cade had no hopes for him. He'd never known of any Elf from that kin line who even aspired to what the Troll and the Giant claimed this one could do. All Elves were maddeningly insubordinate, but the Air lineages added a wicked capriciousness to the mix, just as the Earths were devious and greedy, the Waters were sullen, and the Fires were downright malicious. Cade doubted that this Elf could sit still long enough for a performance.

Things definitely ran in families; he knew that for a fact. His mother's great-grandfather—the one without a title, the one she never talked about—had been a noteworthy poet. His father's father had been a Master Fettler who'd performed on the Ducal Circuit. Some of Cade's cousins participated in amateur theatrics—though none of them would dream of making it a profession, for more money and status were to be had in other Wizardcraftings. His uncle had begun a promising career as a fettler before being called up into the army for that despicable experiment that had killed so many—and left others drooling imbeciles, like Uncle Dennet. It was a grudge Wizards had against Elfenkind, that they had flatly refused to participate in the Archduke's scheme to use magic as a method of war, and had thus escaped tragedy.

That this Mieka Windthistle had no ancestors Cayden knew of who'd ever worked in theater boded ill. Then again, maybe his circumstances were like Cayden's: a talent that simply would not be stifled, a restless need to create that could not be channeled into more respectable ways of making a living. Maybe he had chafed and rebelled as Cayden had, until finally his parents gave their unwilling consent to let him try.

And if that was indeed the case, he wondered if, like his own parents, they expected him to fail.

The claim to "purebred" he dismissed as absurd. How many centuries since the last truebloods of *any* race had died? He could trace his own ancestry back seven generations in his father's line, and fully twelve in his mother's. In their long, long history had been some genuine oddities, but his mother considered him the oddest of all. "Something must not be quite right on your father's side," she'd mused more than once. "*My* people never threw such a mongrel as you." He knew by the names alone that he had Wizard and Elf (two Water, one Fire), Piksey and Sprite, and even that rarest of all bloods, Fae, in him. And Troll, he'd heard his mad great-granny say, because where else could he have got a face like this? Hook-beak nose and long jaw, cheekbones that could cut glass, wide mouth—granted, he was tall and gangly, not short and stout, but the byword for ugliness had stuck to him like pine sap, and every nickname he'd ever been inflicted with and every insult ever flung his way incorporated *troll* amongst its syllables. Never mind that his eyes were the fundamental truth about him: a clear, luminous gray, like the moonstones in Queen Roshien's crown. They were Elfen eyes, inheritance of Mistbind and Watersmith, just as his long bones and thin, strong hands proclaimed Wizard, and his straight white teeth were entirely Human.

But it was the gift he never spoke about that was proof

positive he was Fae. How all these things had combined to create him, he neither knew nor cared. He was what he was, and he knew what he could someday be. He'd seen it.

But . . . trueblood Elf? Not damned likely. Usually the bit remaining showed only in the coloring—the very dark, the very pale. Black hair, and eyes brown as tree bark or green like a forest pool, and skin the golden brown of fallen leaves. White-blond hair, with eyes blue as ice or gray as snow clouds, and translucent milky skin. The other features—delicate little hands and feet, sharp teeth, pointed ears—those things seemed to have faded first from the bloodlines.

If they reappeared, they were quite often hidden somehow. There were chirurgeons who did a brisk business in mutilating a newborn's ears (as had been done to Jeska at the orders of a grandfather frantic to be thought entirely Human), and grinding down or knocking out and replacing any suspect teeth. Hands could not be hidden, but feet could be broken at the instep to flatten the telltale high arch. There were dyes for the hair and cosmetics for the skin, and specialists who retrained the lilting voice—or broke the willful spirit.

Nothing had been done to disguise this boy. Nothing. He was Elfen from his thick hair to his small, high-arched feet. Moreover, he had inherited the most attractive aspects of both major Kins. No Dark Elf would have skin as purely white as his, with no brown freckles or brick-red mottling, and no Light Elf would have hair that black. Those eyes confirmed it: neither gray nor blue, neither green nor brown, but an almost opalescent combination of all those colors, with an elusive golden spark in the iris of the left eye. It just wasn't right that anything male, even Elfen male, should have eyes that beautiful, with such long, thick lashes. The teeth were small and regular and entirely Human; the ears, peeking shyly from the heavy silk hair, were entirely Elfen. It was a quick, wick-edly nimble little body, and the fine bones were long enough to give him Human height. His voice was soft and lively, deeper than a young Elf's treble. And his spirit was untamed—and, Cayden suspected, completely un-tamable.

He was the most beautiful thing Cayden had ever seen in his life. And he was asking to be given a chance.

So: should Cade give him something simple, as the Giant had suggested, something to ease him into it, give him the opportunity to succeed? Or something complex, difficult, to challenge the arrogance in those eyes? For Cayden realized that Mieka Windthistle wasn't *asking* for anything, any more than Cayden had ever *asked* his parents' permission to become a player. He was *demanding* control of Cayden's glass withies, and Jeschenar's absolute trust, and the entirety of Rafcadion's supportive skill. Arrogant little Elf.

Cayden crouched down beside the glass baskets, his lips softening in a smile. Woven of ropes made of clear glass, there were two sets of four baskets each, the smooth curved rims tincted in sequential rainbow colors. Within were distributed almost three dozen hollow glass twigs varying in length from half a foot to nearly thrice that, crimped at one end and stamped there with the glass-crafter's hallmark, their colors more delicate. The withies trembled with random sparks, reacting to the proximity of the one who had imbued them with magic.

He and Rafe and Jeska had thought to do another classic tonight, a cloying sentimental piece about a sailor coming home rich from his voyages to find his girl be-spoken to another man. It was simple enough, requiring a masquer to shift only twice, from the sailor to the girl and back to the sailor again. There was magic and more than enough in the withies already primed. Simple magic for a simple story. Had he been forced to do the glisking, as he would have had to after the departure of the talent-less idiot if Mieka Windthistle hadn't shown up, these withies would have been sufficient. He had enough Elf-enblood for the work, but a restrained magic was all he could handle on his own. It wasn't that he was incapable, he told himself, it was just that he was so much better at the creating than the working. But he had to be honest inside his own head: He was clumsy at best, his hands too big and his fingers too long for the delicate manipu-lations required. With a quick glance at Mieka, who was over in a corner sharing a laugh with his Giant and Troll friends, he decided that the magic inside the slender glass twigs was *too* simple. On impulse he grasped a handful from the far basket, the indigo one. A few moments' con-centration imbued them with fresh spells. A second bas-ket, and a third, and he breathed deeply before rising to his feet again. Let the snooty little Elf give *this* a try, he told himself, and went to talk to Jeschenar and Rafca-dion.

"You really want to?" Jeska asked, frowning all over his gorgeous golden face. "I'm game, of course I am, but—"

"You've Elf enough in you to supplement whatever he can't do. I've watched you work this one when you're so drunk, you can't hardly see straight." To Rafe, he added, "I'll tell him he'll have more than the usual to work with on this piece, but if you catch him messing about, slap him back down."

The fettler shrugged powerful shoulders and nodded. "I'll keep him in line. No flourishes."

"Oh, you can tease him a bit. Just don't let him get away with anything silly."

Ten minutes later, watching from his hiding place be-neath the stairs—hiding not to avoid seeing the audi-ence's reactions but to avoid their seeing him—he clenched his jaw and his fists and prayed to the good Lord and

Lady to protect his friends if this new glisker should
prove not just arrogant but dangerous. Still, their long
search for the right glisker had taught them to deal swiftly
with the inconsistent and the incompetent, the nervous
and the confused. Jeschenar was strong, with great instincts; Rafcadion was capable of throttling any flawed
or frantic magic. And if needs must, Cayden could summon up his own skills and help his friends.

Expecting the boy to wait politely beside the glass baskets while Jeska readied himself and Rafe took a position at far stage left, Cade was startled when the glisker
charmingly persuaded a couple of patrons out of their
chairs and dragged the furniture to the back of the stage.
Then he began rearranging baskets. Quick hands switched
green with blue, yellow with violet, perched the black
and white onto chair seats and balanced the orange on
their slick rims. Then he seemed to be looking for something. Not finding it, he shrugged—and picked out two
withies from the red basket to balance across the blue.
It was a configuration that made no sense to Cade at all,
who always used the classic prism pattern. Then, rather
than seat himself on the glisker's bench within easy reach
of all the baskets, he remained standing. When Jeska
nodded to Rafe that he was ready, and Rafe began the
foundation work—steady and solid as always, the best
fettler Cade had ever encountered—the glisker bounced
a few times on his heels, laughing soundlessly to himself.

Magic began to radiate through the tavern. Usually
Cade spent a few moments watching the audience, marking those who resisted and those who instinctively
fought, just in case his help might be needed. It never
was. Rafe was too good at control. But vigilance was
another duty a tregetour owed his group. Tonight,
though, he completely forgot. The Elf did something he'd
never seen a glisker do before, not even the Winterly or
Ducal or Royal Circuit professionals.

He made his work into a dance.

Instead of sitting where he could reach for one withie at a time to have it ready in the left hand for the switch to the right when needed, he twisted and curled his whole body, swaying from one basket to another, grabbing up glass twigs in both hands and waving them like a Good Brother censing parishioners at High Chapel. Cayden bit back a despairing moan. If the boy was this wild just setting up the scene, who knew what he'd do with the piece itself?

Mieka played it straight for the Sailor's homecoming. A mast and a white backdrop sail, and a wooden deck below Jeska's feet: all these things were usual. The hint of salt air, the touch of a breeze, even the dim ring of ship's bells calling the hour—all were subtle touches usually found only on the Circuits. But when the Sailor set foot on land and caught sight of his beloved in the company of another man, instead of the outrage and pain and betrayal the piece called for, Mieka projected shocked amazement without letting the audience—or poor Jeska— in on why.

What he had in mind became apparent when Jeska made his shift to the persona of the Sweetheart. At first she was as the Sailor had remembered and described her: a lovely, dainty little thing with blond curls and a winsome smile. But quickly the demure blue gown deepened to a vile purple; the shawl turning from leaf to livid green; the gold hair brassy; and the petal-pink lips blood-crimson as the glisker conjured the painted face and blowsy figure of a seasoned whore. She lamented how hard she had to work, how difficult her life was—all with Jeska behaving physically as if he wore the usual pretty face and graceful form. The audience howled with laughter and pounded tables with fists and flagons. As she bemoaned the fact that she'd had to accept the other man's proposal because it just wasn't possible for her to go on any longer alone and unprotected, Jeska did what he always did at this point—what, by tradition, every masquer did at this point: sank to his knees. A pitiable gesture for a young girl, it now looked as if she was kneeling to perform certain services.

Jeska held the pose, then got to his feet almost as if pulled upright by powerful, unseen hands on his shoulders. By the time he was standing, the shift back to the Sailor had been made. Cayden swallowed a gasp of shock at the glisker's skill—and nearly strangled on an exclamation when he sensed Rafe loosen his stringent hold on the flux of magic. The Sailor told his former girlfriend that it was breaking his heart but he understood, he'd been gone a long time, it was only natural that she'd grown tired of waiting—and all the while the Elf emanated waves of gleeful relief at this lucky escape that washed over the eagerly receptive audience. At the end, the Sailor was supposed to slump into a tavern to drown his sorrows, dejection in every line of him as he dropped coins on the bar and bought drinks all round so he'd have company in his despair. By now Jeska had adapted—oh, had he ever adapted. Jaunty and carefree, whistling in between his lines, he dug deep in pockets and flung coins high in the air as he invited everyone to toast his freedom. The imaginary coins were one of Cade's best feats of magic, something very few tregetours his age could do; their cheery chiming was all Mieka, and something no other glisker had ever managed to do for Cade before.

It was funny, it was brilliant, it was completely outrageous, and it had the patrons flinging real coins onto the stage.

The Elf had one more trick. As Jeska bent to retrieve the money, he suddenly wore once again the Sweetheart's garish gown and brassy curls. Startled, he nearly tripped on his own feet. Cayden heard Mieka chortling behind the glass baskets. Jeska again reacted swiftly, changing the crouches to curtseys, blowing kisses to the audience. And the trimmings piled up in his swift, snatching hands.

It was a while before Cayden felt ready to leave the darkness beneath the stairs and shoulder his way through the crowd to the bar. The whole village was congratulating the Elf, buying him and Rafe and Jeska drinks, roaring out the stale old lines that Mieka had turned from histrionic to hilarious. When Cade at last ventured out, he was swept up in the general celebration of the glisker's triumph.

He had never been so furious in his life.

He wasn't so furious that he turned down the chance to get drunk for free.

Neither was he so drunk by the end of the night that he neglected his duty to himself and his friends by making it easy for the tavern keeper to hire them for another night. Guessing that the coins would keep coming from the audience, Cade demanded not money but decent beds—*including* tonight—and three meals tomorrow instead of one, plus a full supper before they went to bed tonight and breakfast on the day they left. By the time he got what he wanted, the minster chimes had rung curfew and the place was nearly empty. Both he and the landlord knew that tomorrow night, from opening bell until closing, there would scarcely be room in the tavern to stand. He spread his hands wide open in the Wizardly gesture that meant *You may trust my word, I use no magic* and concluded the deal, then returned to the bar.

Rafe was superbly drunk, lids drooping over his blue-gray eyes, a silly smile curving his lips beneath the heavy beard he was very proud of being able to grow at the ripe old age of nineteen. Jeska was a little more sober, but only a little; the tavern keeper's daughter might or might not get the full benefits of his attention later on. Cade wondered whether he ought to mention they'd be in real beds tonight, not in the hayloft, then shrugged to himself. Jeska always found a way.

As for the glisker—Mieka Windthistle couldn't have said his own name once, slowly, let alone five times fast, without hopelessly tangling his tongue.

Cayden didn't wait to be noticed. He poked the Elf in the ribs and demanded, "What the fuck was *that*?"

Big, innocent, very drunk eyes—almost entirely green at the moment—blinked up at him. "Ye dinnit like it?" Before Cade could reply, he turned to Jeska. "Sorry for that bit at the end, mate, but it were such a fetchin' little Sweetheart, I just couldn't resist."

"You're a shithead," Jeska remarked amiably, sorting coins on the bar. "You want your share now, or after the show tomorrow night?"

"Tomorrow night?" Cade sucked in an outraged breath. How dare they decide such things without him? "Have I said yet that there's gonna be a next show with this—this—"

Rafcadion interrupted. "This best glisker you or me or Jeska or anybody else in this shit-pit of a town ever saw? Yeh, there'll be a next show." He grinned, white teeth flashing in his dark beard. "And a next, and a next, and a next—all the way to Trials." Raising his glass—they'd all been given the real thing in place of the leather—he announced, "Trials, and the Winterly Circuit!"

Mieka laughed and raised his glass to his lips—but his gaze was sharp and watchful, and suddenly he appeared considerably more sober. Cade looked into those eyes, discovered he was unable to look away. When at last he nodded, and drank the toast, the Elf nodded back, satisfied.

"Much beholden, Quill," he murmured. "Very much beholden."

Two

EVEN THOUGH HE'D long since learned not to anticipate, Cayden wasn't too surprised when he didn't dream that night. He had both expected to and expected not to; that was the particular glorious hell of what his Fae heritage had done to him. His Sagemaster had explained it once.

"*There are things that occur which are important, and things that are not. There are things that are essential, things that* must *happen—and things that are so trivial, they make no difference at all. The difficulty is discerning which is which. Now, what may seem obviously important—a death in the family, moving from one village to another, falling in love—might not be important after all. And things such as choosing to wear the red tunic instead of the blue, this might be absolutely vital. Simply put, you will never, ever know.*

"*It would be logical to assume that events, people, interior realizations that you know at once will change your life—these will be pivots from which visions will come. Assume nothing of the kind. Some of these things are simply fated. They must happen for every other thing to happen. You have no choices to make and therefore you will dream no futures. You cannot unmeet your future wife, for example. So the day you meet her, you probably won't dream. But if you bring her daisies instead of roses, if you wear that red tunic instead of the blue, these things may very well trigger more dreams than you can keep track of—for these are the things that often determine what shape the future will take.*

"*So the lesson must be that there is no predicting what will set off a foretelling. What seems important may be trivial, and what seems insignificant may be critical. You cannot control your gift. You are at the mercy of fate.*"

Which was why, as Cade knew very well, he enjoyed his work so much. For, during the time he spent devising his tales, he *was* in control.

Once his part was done, once he'd written or rewritten the lines and employed his own special ciphers that signaled the sensory underlays, he had to give everything over to Jeska and Rafe and now, apparently, Mieka. But for those hours and days of the creative process, the work was entirely his. He supposed he could learn to trust the Elf the way he trusted his two other partners.

At least—unlike their last couple of gliskers—Mieka told them the truth, that next afternoon when they met to discuss what they would perform that night. When Rafe asked a polite question about where in the village he lived, he laughed.

"Don't live here at all! I'm as much a Gallybanker as you three." When they stared at him, he shrugged. "Saw you last year, didn't I, at that tavern over on Beekbacks. With a glisker not worth a splintered withie—nor the one I saw you with next, or next as well. The one last month wasn't *bad*, but . . ."

"A cullion, he was," Jeska commented. "Wish him good morrow, and he'd say, 'I take it you're planning to die before then? Lovely!' Mean of spirit and meaner of pocket. But I don't understand why everyone here seems to know you."

"My auntie's house is out on the edge of town. She's the one as brews the whiskey." He winked; those eyes were blue with flecks of green this afternoon. "I'd be popular and indeed beloved even if I weren't adorable all on me own."

"And modest, I see," Rafe drawled.

Mieka nodded genially. "When I heard you were booked here, I decided to make a visit to Auntie Brishen."

"You followed us," Cade accused.

"And aren't you glad I did?"

He sat back in his chair, rolling his eyes. "When His Gracious Majesty gives you the silver sword and golden spurs, Sir Mieka, you'll be sure to spare a nod for us petty quidams, won't you?"

"Don't condemn yourself to wretched obscurity so soon," Mieka shot back. "Tell me what you want to do for tonight, and then tell me what your thinking is for Trials."

"That's almost three months away," Rafe observed. "We've the first of two shows in three hours."

"Only one show tonight." The boy burst out laughing when they stared at him. "Thunderin' hells, I hope what's between your legs is more use to you than what's between your ears! They expect us at eight. We come on near nine. They expect a good giggle, and we give it to 'em—but instead of an interval, we go right into what makes 'em weep. I know this lot. They're surly outside and mushy inside—and once they've worn themselves out laughing, they won't have energy to resist a good long cry. Which is what they really want anyway, drunk as they'll be by then."

Cayden had the feeling this would not be the last time he'd have to struggle for control of his own group. "If they expect us at eight and we come on at nine, they'll be so impatient and angry that Jeska will have to work twice as hard to win them over."

"Not with *me* doing the glisking." He tapped a finger down the list Rafe had given him of the works in their folio. "No . . . no . . . no—Gods and Angels, not that one!—and not that one, neither, not if you held a sword to me throat—"

"Do you ever stay still long enough for anyone to give it a try?" Jeska asked.

"Not often, and certainly not when I'm working. Not this one—but I think the sons-and-fathers dialogue would be just the thing."

Rafe actually recoiled. "We don't hardly ever do that one."

"Nobody does," Mieka responded with a shrug. "But it's perfect tonight, and here's why. There's a reason this village is near empty of old men—hadn't you noticed?"

With a suddenness that set his heart pounding too hard, Cade knew everything. "We're on the Archduke's old domains, aren't we?"

"And full marks with shooting star clusters for the scion of the Falcon Clan." Mieka crooked a finger at the tavern keeper's daughter. "Another round here, if you would, please, darlin'," he called, and gave her a beguiling smile.

"Not for me," Jeska told him. "Not until after."

Mieka shrugged. "As you will. I'll have yours, then. What Cayden knows and you haven't yet guessed—"

"Almost every man of military age either died or was crippled by the Archduke's War," Rafe said flatly. "You don't yet know me, boy, but there's no advantage in routinely assuming everyone you meet isn't near as smart as you."

Mieka had the grace to look abashed—for all of three heartbeats. "Won't happen again. Anyway, the piece may be about the loss of three fathers in a collapsed silver mine, but that's neither here nor there nor anywhere else for our purpose. There's no man will be present tonight who'll not have lost a father or a grandsir, an uncle or older brother. They'll weep oceans. And we'll be up to our necks in trimmings."

Cade accepted his glass of ale before the maid could spill it—her attention was dangerously divided between Jeska and Mieka—and took a long swallow. It wasn't polite to ask, but previous experience had made him cautious about a glisker's willingness to work the really wrenching pieces, the ones that demanded a fettler's iron control but a glisker's near-total abandonment to emotion. Uninhibited expression of joy or sorrow, love or fear, was the reason no one not substantially Elfenblood could function effectively as a glisker. Elves were creatures of unabashed emotion; unruly as a rule, even the best of them were unpredictable. The worst of them . . . *self-indulgent* was a nice way of putting it.

As for the best of them . . . perhaps Mieka was one, though from his enthusiastic consumption of alcohol, he appeared to have fully mastered the *self-indulgent* part. Cade slumped back in his chair again and sipped his ale, listening as the other three discussed the proposed performance of "The Silver Mine." There was a wild glint in those changeable eyes, granted—but there was also an intensity of purpose as Mieka plotted out the changes with Jeska and made notes with Rafe on when he'd have to exert most control. Skepticism turned to cautious admiration as it became plain that the glisker knew what he was doing.

It was odd, Cade reflected, that he'd never once had a dream—waking or sleeping—about anyone even vaguely resembling this Elf. Jeschenar had been glimpsed several times, so when they'd finally met almost two years ago, Cade felt reasonably comfortable with him from the start. Getting used to his occasionally belligerent ways had been another matter, but at least Cade knew not to challenge him physically: Jeska was effectively king of about a square mile of Gallantrybanks, with a bagful of souvenir teeth he'd knocked out to prove it. The roster of his defeated rivals had stopped growing only because these days nobody was fool enough to confront him and add another name to the list, or tooth to the collection.

Cade had known Rafe since littleschool, so the foretelling dreams about him had no power to surprise him. He was still waiting for the squat little Gnomelike man he'd seen more and more often this last year. Those dreams were comparatively forceful, the kind that flashed through his waking consciousness as well as invaded his sleeping mind. There were several other people who populated his foretellings with more or less frequency and importance. But he'd never caught even a hint of this Elf, and it confused him.

Did it mean Mieka was insignificant? Cade would never believe that. What he'd seen and experienced last night, what he presumed would happen again this evening, argued for a powerful presence in his life. But why had he never seen the boy before?

"The worst mistake you can make is to believe that you are the sole arbiter of your existence. Put another way—do you really have the arrogance to think that nothing anyone else does has any effect on you? That if you don't envision it in advance, it can't possibly be real? That you make all the choices?"

Mieka must be one of those people whose caprices ruled his own life so thoroughly that Cayden's prescience was of no use at all in predicting his sudden arrival. Now that he was here, however, Cade found it equally unsettling that there had been no dream last night, not even a vague impression upon waking that something in life had changed forever.

In fact, now that he considered it, last night he'd slept better than he had in a long time. Worry usually kept him awake until sheer physical exhaustion dragged him down into sleep. He'd attributed the swift and untroubled slumber of last night to good liquor and a blissfully soft bed. But now, watching his group thrash out the details of the night's performance, he wondered if something else might be at work here.

"Cade? Cayden!"

"Oh—sorry," he said as Jeska's impatience finally penetrated his self-absorption. "Have you decided, then?"

Mieka was giving him a sidelong glitter of a smile. "Remind me—why do we need you?"

Cade grinned back, set down his empty glass, and flexed his fingers. "Without me, you'd all be nothing. Are you ready to make your choices, then, Mieka? Come on."

Together they went into the kitchen, where a large cupboard was unlocked by the glowering Trollwife who vastly resented this interruption from her bread-making—until the Elf gave her a sweetly innocent smile. Without the slightest twinge of a dreaming, Cade foresaw infinite doors being opened for them by that smile.

They took the glass baskets outside to the enclosed porch, trying to ignore the stench of uncovered rubbish bins as they sorted through for what Mieka would be using tonight.

"Who made these for you?" he asked, fingers caressing the graceful curvature of the blue basket.

"Friend of mine," Cade answered.

Another sidelong glance, this time speculative, and a moment later Mieka said, "You'll have to introduce me to her."

Cade stared. "How did you know—?"

"I didn't!" He crowed with triumphant laughter. "Quill, you really do need to guard those eyes of yours! You can turn down your mouth and knot up your eyebrows all you like, but the eyes will always give you away! Does she make the withies as well?"

"Some of them," he admitted grudgingly. "Most of them are her father's castoffs. I have terrible trouble priming some of them."

"I felt that, last night." He selected a glass twig and inspected it. "This is one of hers?"

"Yes. Even her best aren't quite as supple as her father's culls, but she knows me better."

"Let's pick out the ones he made," Mieka instructed, "and return them for credit. Whatever skill she lacks, I can make up for. I didn't much like the feel of some of those from last night. They fought me."

Bemused, he helped to sort as required. Mieka made no mistakes in choosing which had been Blye's work and which her father's. Those quick little fingers were exquisitely sensitive.

"Bleedin' indecent, if you ask me," the boy muttered, tossing a withie onto the discard pile, "trying to pass off mottles like these as usable. And you were a fool to buy them, I don't care how much of a discount he gave you. Look at the warp in this!" He held up a foot-long twig of glass tinted faint blue, and pointed to a distortion halfway down. "It's a tribute to your skill that these do what you want them to do—but they make you work much too hard. From now on, we use only the best, right? What's your glasscrafter girl's name?"

"Blye Cindercliff."

"A rare and lovely Goblin name," he approved. "We'll make her as rich as us—but on what she'll charge *other* people," he added with a grin, "once we've made her famous!"

"We can't use her name. No Guild allows women to use a hallmark." And thus their wares went for much less than Guild-sanctioned items, and foreign trade was forbidden to them—"inferior" goods might ruin the Kingdom's reputation. Never mind that what Blye made was far beyond apprentice work, approaching that of Master. She, and the hundreds of women crafters like her, would never receive Guild-level prices or Guild rights.

"This is her father's, then?" He ran a finger over the symbol stamped into the crimp end of a withie.

"Yes. You don't seem upset that she's a girl."

"A knack's a knack, no matter if it comes wearing trousers or a skirt. You say she knows you, and that's a very good thing. Once she gets to know *me,* it'll be even better." He paused, head tilting to one side, hair shifting to reveal one pointed ear. "Forgot to ask—how well do you know her? Meaning—"

"—would I be upset if you bedded her?" Cade laughed, genuinely amused. "I'd like to see you try, to be honest."

"Oh. Likes girls, does she?"

"Not that I've ever noticed. It's not something we discuss. No, it's just that I've never seen her with anybody—she works too hard, being her father's only child and determined to learn all she can from him before he dies. After, she'll hire another glasscrafter, to keep the Guild happy and everything looking legal. But she wants to know everything about the work so the new man doesn't swindle her." He rolled one of Blye's better efforts between his palms. There was only one barely discernible bump near the crimp to mark it as apprentice work. But no bubbles, no rutilations. Blye knew what she was about, and would only get better. As the chill glass warmed to his skin, the warmth within it seemed to stir and stretch like a cat recognizing a familiar caress.

"I like her more and more," Mieka announced. "What's ailing her father, can I ask?"

"Lungs. He was in the war."

Mieka shivered. "No wonder his hand slips and his breath's unsteady, then. Is he at the blood stage yet?"

"Not quite. A year or so, the physicker says."

Anger made him look years older as he snarled, "Damn the Archduke, and damn the Wizards he corrupted!"

It was a typical attitude for Elfenkind, but there was a subtlety of loathing that differed from what Cayden had come to expect. It was a lack of contempt, he decided as he searched Mieka's face, and a sincere compassion for the victims. But to hear an Elf count Wizards amongst those victims . . . perhaps Mieka wasn't just the better sort of Elf. Perhaps he was one of the best.

"You'll have to change up your ciphering," Mieka said all at once. "These codes and colors—no, none of this will work at all."

"Are you insane? Do you know how long it took me to put that together?"

"And how many gliskers have you explained it to?" He tapped the page of performance notes. "I don't want anyone stealing and copying. So there'll have to be a new cipher. I'll help."

"Kindly of you," Cade snapped.

"Not at all," Mieka replied blithely. "We see things in the same colors, you know. It's alike to the quality as makes Chattim so good with Vered's work—but with Rauel's, not as much."

"How do you know that? And how do you know the Shadowshapers, anyway?"

"And that's *another* thing. We need a name, and a good one. But I'll help with that, too. Anyway, all you and I need do is settle on a color arch, organize the subtleties, and code everything so just the four of us understand it. A night's work, if the whiskey's good enough for inspiration." He smiled. "I'll ask me auntie to contribute to the cause, shall I?"

"Anything else about our lives you'd care to rearrange?"

"Well . . ." Critically, gaze flickering down and up Cade's frame. "The clothes could use a tweak. Yellow just isn't your color. You ought to wear something silver or gray, always, to play on your name and play up your eyes. And do stop trying to grow a beard, Quill, you're only embarrassing yourself."

Had he really just speculated that this Elf might be one of the best sort?

"You know I'm right," Mieka added with a cajoling smile. "I always am. But if you won't admit it now, you will after tonight."

It turned out he *was* right—about the performance, anyway. The tavern's patrons laughed themselves silly over "The Sailor's Sweetheart," just as Mieka had predicted, soon forgetting that the show had begun almost an hour late. They had barely recovered their breath when "The Silver Mine" began. And they wept unashamed, also as Mieka had predicted. For all that Cade himself had been the one to supply the magic for the withies used tonight, he was hard-pressed to keep tears from his own eyes as he watched from beneath the stairs. Across Jeska's features the anguished faces of the dying fathers melted one by one, with heartrending subtlety, into the younger, grief-stricken faces of their sons; the elusive sensations of physical pain in broken legs, ribs, fingers were diffused by Rafe carefully, gently, gliding into the emotional pain of loss as the boys bade their fathers farewell. The changes from the sunlit hill where the sons stood to the dark depths of the silver mine, with a single candle glinting that turned veins of ore to threads of light, were accomplished with breathtaking grace. The dialogue was traditional to the piece, except for a dozen or so lines Cade had changed within each section, adding and subtracting words as he sensed them needed or unnecessary. For all the familiarity of the story, there was nothing mawkish about the performance, nothing squirmy. All of it was honest. All of it was real.

He wondered what Mieka was using to produce such effects, what he was quarrying inside himself that created this art. Surely he was too young to have experienced that intensity of emotion. As the last echoes faded and Rafe allowed the magic to drain quietly away, Cade found himself doing something he never did: He joined his masquer, fettler, and glisker onstage to share, as their tregetour, in the applause.

Jeska's arched brows conveyed his astonishment at this break with Cade's introverted habits. Rafe's wry smile of understanding wasn't quite hidden in his beard. Mieka, breathing hard, damp with sweat, grinned brightly up at him and shouted over the tumult, "Free ale tonight!"

He was right about that, too. Ale there was, and the best, in tall green glasses the landlord brought out from his wife's own shelves. When Cade finally staggered upstairs to bed—oh, the delight of a real bed with a real mattress and real sheets, and all to himself besides—he had to work hard at it to remember how buttons and lacings worked as he got out of his clothes and slid between those real sheets, naked so he could fully enjoy them. He was asleep before he had time to do more than stretch in the luxurious little cocoon. For the second night in a row, he had no dreams. And when he woke in the morning, surprisingly free of a hangover, considering the amount of ale he'd drained down his throat the night before, he was actually happy.

Their ride home was in the back of one of Mieka's aunt's whiskey wagons. It was chilly, but it was free—and it became a lot less chilly when Mieka tugged the bung from a half-size barrel snugged in beneath the driver's bench and handed out tin cups.

"She always puts this one in for me," he said, patting the barrel fondly.

By the milestone that marked halfway home, all four of them were roaring drunk—or, rather, warbling drunk, because Jeska had issued a singing challenge for Most Obscene Ballad. The black sky overhead, dappled with stars, was treated to Rafe's touching rendition of "Whistlecock and Biggerstaff" and Jeska's contribution of "The Wizard's Wondrous Wand." Cade gave them a mercifully truncated version of the thirty-three stanza "What a Lady Needs," mainly because he was too drunk to recall the middle fifteen requirements. But before Mieka could offer a contender, he passed out. By the Presence Lamps of a lonesome countryside chapel Cade saw him do it, marveling at the transition from full, laughing consciousness to absolute oblivion between one eyeblink and the next. He slumped against a barrel of whiskey, his jaw dropped open, and he began to snore. Jeska prodded him in the side with a toe of his boot; there was no reaction.

"Will somebody for the love of the Lord shut him up?" Rafe growled.

"Lay him down on his side," said the driver, with a glance over his shoulder.

They tried, tugging and cursing, until Mieka grunted, pulled away, and—still sitting up, more or less—curled with his cheek to one of the padded crates containing Cade's glass baskets and withies.

"He'll sleep it off by daybreak," the driver continued. "Now, tell me again, where am I setting you boys down?"

"He won't be sick, will he?" Cade asked. He'd stitched the feather-filled cushioning himself, each nest specific to the basket it held.

"Never that I've seen it." He paused for thought. "Always a first time, though."

"Wonderful," Cade muttered, and yanked the boy away from the padded crate with scant sympathy for any bruises he might be giving. Mieka grunted again, shifted, and this time curled on the floor of the wagon with his head on Cade's knee. He snuffled like a puppy and settled back into sleep.

Jeska sniggered. "At least if he yarks, it'll be on *you*."

"I'm washable." Shrugging, he addressed the back of the driver's head. "Let them off at Beekbacks Lane." Rafe lived a block north, Jeska four blocks east. "And me at Criddow Close, if you would." He had all his baskets to carry, and his partners helped him when they took the public coach, but he was certain that Blye would be readying the glassworks by the time the wagon got them home, and be on the lookout for him—he was returning a day later than planned. That she would help him with the crates was secondary, though; he wanted her to get a look at his new glisker.

It was nearly daybreak, and the city traffic had not

quite snarled the streets yet, when the wagon stopped at the top of Beekbacks Lane. Mieka didn't stir as Jeska and Rafe jumped off. Cade threw their satchels down to them and reminded them of rehearsal at Rafe's the following afternoon. The fettler's parents were most obliging when it came to giving over their sitting room to their son and his friends. Jeska's widowed mother allowed them the use of her cellar, but strictly in the summer months; she worried about the damp. Cade's parents didn't want that rubbish in their house at all. He wondered suddenly what sort of attitude Mieka's family had towards his work, his ambitions, his determination to live the unpredictable life of a traveling player. As the horses began their weary clopping over the pavement again, he looked down at the head still resting on his knee. Shaggy black hair hid most of the face, and Cade was tempted to brush it back, wake him up, ask the thousand questions he should have been asking all day yesterday and all night last night. What held him back was the memory of another bit of advice from the Sage who had taught him.

"*Sometimes, you know, it's best just to let things happen. There are places and moments and people meant to be savored. You can force flowers to a quicker bloom in a hothouse, but they only fade all the faster. What your mind can do to you, Cayden, means that all too often you're skipping ahead in a book to the last few pages, and you find out how it ends—but you have no idea how you got there, how it happened the way it did. In brief, there are times when you simply have to sit back, relax, and enjoy the show.*"

The driver brought the horses to a halt at the bottom of Criddow Close, tucked up onto the cobbled footway to avoid carts and coaches now clogging the morning. The city had woken up; Mieka hadn't. Cade stacked the crates handed down to him by the driver, who also did him the favor of yelling at a Trollwife as she prepared to slosh her slops bucket down to the drainage runnel right next to Cade's feet. By the time the last of the gear was unloaded, Blye had been distracted from her kiln, as Cade had known she would be. She stood in the middle of the lane, absently smacking fireproof dragon-gut gloves against her thigh. He waved, and she tossed the gloves back into the shop and started towards him.

"Until another time then, lad," the driver said. Cade nodded and began to express his gratitude, but he interrupted with, "Last night? I was watching. You'd do well to keep him, in spite of the trouble he'll be to you."

He would have asked how much trouble, and what kind, but Blye was beside him, cuffing him affectionately on the shoulder, and he smiled down at her. No one would ever know it to look at her, because the more obvious traits of the bloodline had been more or less overcome by Human and Wizard, Piksey and even some Elf, but like all those who worked with fire or forge, she was primarily of Goblin descent. It showed in how short she was, and her wiry build, and her slightly crooked teeth, but only if you were looking for Goblin traits. Her beauty was in the silvery blond hair that any other woman would have slit her own throat rather than cut; Blye kept it scythed off to barely neck length, to keep it out of her way when she worked. Cade hadn't seen her in a skirt for any occasion other than Chapel since they were children. She was exactly five days older than he, and they had known each other all their lives.

"Yes," he told her before she could say anything, "I made it home in one piece. Yes, I have the money you lent me for the trip, plus enough to take you out for a drink tonight. Yes, we were good, and he's why." He pointed to the slumbering Elf curled between whiskey barrels. "Introductions will have to wait for when he's conscious, but that's our new glisker."

Placing a foot on a wheel spoke, she hoisted herself up to peer over the side of the wagon. "You're hiring children now?"

"He's eighteen. Well, probably. But it doesn't matter, Blye, he's *good*." Then, shrewdly, knowing she'd be caught even if she didn't want to admit it, he added, "He only wants to use your work from now on."

"So I'll be getting to know him whether I like it or not?" Blye looked for a moment more, then jumped down. "I'd *better* like it, Cade," she warned. "Come on, let's get your things inside and you can tell me all about it."

They were arranging the crates between them with the ease of long practice, and the wagon had just set off again, when a voice rang out.

"Tell her she'll adore me, Quill—everyone does!"

Blye slanted a look at Cade, dark eyes not quite amused. "Adorable, is he?"

"To hear him tell it." He shrugged. "Me, I don't much care what he says or does offstage. When he's on . . ."

"Jeska and Rafe agree with you?"

"They agreed with me before *I* did!" They reached the back door of Cade's parents' house, and he paused. "We'll be at the Downstreet tomorrow night, Blye, I wish you'd come and see."

"P'rhaps I will. Is he really that good?"

Reluctant as he was to admit this, still he had never been anything less than honest with her. "Y'know, I think he might be better."

Three

TIME AFTER TIME it happened, and every time it happened, it was different.

Sometimes there was a setting, just as if he'd planned it all out for a performance: a backdrop as clear and tangible as if he could walk into the room and pull the curtains open to the sunshine, or stride up the hill and feel the wind on his face as it rustled the trees. There were smells and sensations, he could hear chirring birds and mothers calling their children inside for supper. He even knew what clothes he wore by the feel of linen or wool or leather against his skin. He was *there*, in that place and time, and if he was lucky, a glance around would show him a broadsheet thrown on a table or left open across a chair arm, and a glimpse of its date would tell him precisely *when* he was.

But sometimes there were only vague shadows. Glimpses. Fleeting sensations. Unrecognized, unclear voices. Being a crafter of words, a designer of specific magic, he was both annoyed and frightened by the imprecision. He never knew if the blurred dreams were blurred because that particular future was as yet unresolved, unset, uncaused. He did know that the crisply real futures could be changed, in spite of their detailed authenticity, because he'd done it. He had done it when he was twelve years old.

⟨His mother turned her back on him and stepped lightly from the drawing room, the satisfied smile on her face seeming to linger in the mirror above the hearth. He felt Mistress Mirdley's warm, powerful arms around his waist as she hugged him, but she let go very quickly and hurried for the kitchen. He thought she might be crying. He hoisted his satchel up onto a shoulder and turned,

catching sight of himself in the huge gold-flecked mirror
that had long since been drained of its magic. Very tall,
very thin, the merest shadow of a beard on his jaw, he
could not have been more than sixteen. His fist clenched
around parchment, and he looked down at the letter
with loathing.

> *Master Remey Honeycoil*
> *Fine Imported Wines*
> *72 Tullyhowe Lane*
> *Vintners and Victuallers Guild*

How pleased Master Honeycoil was to accept so clever a
boy as his clerk—and how relieved his mother was that
selling her son into servitude would cancel out the family's liquor bills for the last two years and the next three
besides. Shoving open the door to the vestibule, grabbing up his father's old blue cloak, not pausing to don it
against the snow-swirled night outside, he unlatched the
front door and left his parents' house for what he knew
was the last time.

   It had all felt so real. So appallingly real. He'd woken,
shivering as desperately as if he really had been outside
in the bitterest cold, rather than sweating with the midsummer heat in his own bedroom high above Redpebble
Square. But what had awakened him had not been the
lingering chill of his dream. As he lay there, trying to
catch his breath, he heard his mother cry out, and then
the quick heavy stomping of Mistress Mirdley's feet up
the wrought iron staircase, and knew the baby was finally about to be born. Pillows over his head to muffle
the awful sounds from two floors below, he reviewed the
dream and concluded the obvious: that this new baby
would be a boy, and healthy, and as good-looking as his
handsome parents, and therefore Cade would no longer
be required to enhance the family repute. But something

would have to be done with him, something would have
to be found for him to do with his life. When the bills
came in for little Derien's Namingday party a month
later, he saw the note from Master Honeycoil, and chills
shook him once again.

That he was not tending the wine shop at 72 Tullyhowe
Lane was his own doing. It had not been as simple as
stealing his father's new blue woolen cloak and stuffing
it into the glassworks kiln, although that was the very
first thing he'd done. In retrospect, he was ashamed of
himself for it. Not for stealing and destroying the cloak (a
household mystery ever after), but for having panicked.
One had to think these things through, he decided. So he
thought, and found that it was even simpler than it had
at first appeared, for what it all came down to was money.
So for the rest of that summer and on into the autumn,
he ran errands for the Trollwives who served the other
houses in Redpebble Square, using the coins earned to
pay Master Honeycoil on the sly. It wasn't until the beginning of winter that he had his inspiration: to work *for*
Master Honeycoil after school each day. During a month
of sweeping floors and lugging crates, he learned quite
a lot about wine—at secondhand, of course, being not
quite thirteen years old. And then one day his employer
mentioned that when the current apprentice went to
open his own shop, another boy would be needed. So
Cayden—who only the previous night had woken from a
slightly different version of the same dreadful dream, still
featuring his departure from home to become Master
Honeycoil's apprentice—made the "mistake" that cost
him his job. A shipment of twenty-year-old wine to a
very important client for a very important Wintering party
in the Spillwater district somehow was switched with two
dozen bottles of rumbullion lately arrived from the Islands. Master Honeycoil sacked him and refused to have
anything to do with the Silversun household again.

There had been other dreams, of course, where he saw himself walking out the front door to become anything from an office clerk to a bookseller. (That wouldn't have been too bad, but it wasn't his choice any more than the wine shop.) There were also visions of being summarily thrown out the back door and slinking along to Blye's or Rafe's because he had nowhere else to go. As each dream occurred, he made plans to show himself incompetent at the proposed work, or to offend the master whose apprentice he might have become. It seemed to him that just thinking about how to avoid a particular future must change things enough to cancel those possibilities for all time. Yet it remained that *he* had done it, *he* had made certain that he would never be trapped into any life he didn't want. Now, at nearly nineteen, he was what he had always yearned to be: a tregetour, an *artist*. And when he finally walked out his parents' front door for good, it would be to lodgings of his own, paid for with his own money, and he would be answerable to no one and live exactly as he pleased.

But for the time being, he still slept in the smallest and highest of the bedrooms, and mostly avoided his family—though it had turned out that he and Derien liked each other. The little boy was old enough now to understand that he was the important one, not Cade, and it was beginning to be clear to him that the responsibility was a burden Cade was more than happy to surrender. It remained to be seen if Derien would choose to shoulder their parents' hopes or shrug them aside. Cade thought it could go either way. He spent as much time with Derien as he could, bespelling silly voices into stuffed animals and creating Fae lights that danced to make him laugh. He liked Dery for his affectionate heart and inquisitive mind; but even if he hadn't, Cade would have been benevolence personified to anybody who freed him of his parents' ambitions.

Those ambitions were emphasized by their address. Criddow Close was the back entrance. Their front door opened on the infinitely more stylish Redpebble Square. It had been the pretty conceit of the long-dead nobleman who had ordered the town houses constructed to use dark red sandstone from his own quarries. He had, regrettably, started a trend; Gallantrybanks was here and there inflicted with buildings made of stone in shades of sunshine yellow, seaweed green, clover blue, and a frightful shade of orange. Any color other than white or gray made it easy to date a block of houses to that period. The Silversun residence was the smallest and narrowest on the Square, having originally housed a collection of upper servants who worked in the more lavish homes. Cade's great-great-great-grandfather had purchased the five-floors-plus-attic house from the founding noble's impoverished descendant, and by now Cade's mother had almost everyone convinced that it had never been servants' quarters at all, but the elegant little town mansion of the nobleman's widowed mother. Not that anyone but Lady Jaspiela cared. Cade certainly didn't. The tall, thin house had felt constricted to him ever since he could remember—as if it were a coat too tight in the shoulders, that wouldn't allow him to stretch without ripping a seam. His mother glided with perfect composure up and down the delicate wrought iron staircase, serenely approving the tricks she had herself arranged—mirrors, pale walls, sparse but supremely elegant furniture—to make the rooms look bigger. All of it illusion, especially the big gilt-framed looking-glass over the hearth. Long ago that mirror had been the dwelling of no one quite knew who or what. But there was no magic left in it now.

The glassworks down Criddow Close had been established by Cade's grandfather, a Master Fettler who had performed on the Royal Circuit. He had set up his favorite glasscrafter a few steps away from his own back door.

This artisan had been Blye's great-grandfather. The families got along splendidly until Cade's father brought Lady Jaspiela home as his bride. Arrogant about her heritage, she had no time for anyone tainted by even a trace of Goblin blood. The Lord and Lady and all the Angels help anyone who failed to address her by her title—even though their title was all her family had retained after championing the losing side in the Archduke's War. She had condescended to marry Cade's father for two reasons: his descent from some long-ago princess nobody else cared about, and the fact that he was the only undamaged son of a wealthy Master Fettler with plenty of Court connections. She hadn't counted on his being a shiftless quiddler who was forever promising the world . . . tomorrow. Or surely the day after. Perhaps next week. Certainly by the end of the month . . .

But he was charming and handsome, was Zekien Silversun, and she forgave him everything so long as he treated her with the deference that was her due, and called her *Lady,* and brought a few Court nobles to dine every so often.

Cade wondered sometimes if he was so good at what he did, at making up scenes and stories, because he'd inherited his mother's gift for pretending.

At least he wasn't self-delusional. Sagemaster Emmot had crushed that out of him by the time he turned fourteen. His parents, however, were of the opinion that Cade was deceiving himself about his life's work. If so, he intended to go on deceiving himself—and everyone who saw his work—until the day he died.

But accompanying the Wizardly magic that he was positive would make his name and his fortune onstage was the bequest of the Fae within him. The dreams were not delusions. They were real. Worse, they might *become* real.

Blye always knew when the visions had come. When

he met her at his parents' back door the evening of his return from Gowerion, she saw it in his face at once. She said nothing, though, until they were well away from Criddow Close and walking up the cobbled slope of Beekbacks to the only tavern within a mile that allowed decent women inside—even the eccentric ones who wore trousers.

"What was it this time?" she asked quietly.

He shrugged.

"You looked tired this morning when you got home. You look about ready for the burn and the urn now. Did you get any rest this afternoon?"

"Not much." That morning, he'd begged off telling her the tale of the last few days and gone up to his bed. He'd slept, but he hadn't rested. Not at all.

"We don't have to do this tonight," she insisted. "Why don't we go back to the works, and I'll get out that bottle my da keeps for important customers? He won't miss it," she added bitterly. "Word's got round. There aren't many customers, important or otherwise."

"You should have told me." He detoured down a side street, nipped into a shop, and emerged a few minutes later with a distinctive long-necked bottle. "Colvado brandy," he said. "I can afford it."

"Because of the new glisker. I've been fretting myself to splinters all day," she admitted as they retraced their steps back to the glassworks. "You have to tell me everything, Cade. Especially if I'm to be making all the withies from now on."

He grinned down at her. "I knew you wouldn't be able to stop thinking about that part of it! And he's serious, he truly is. Picked out yours from your father's without a single mistake. What's more, he said that while he was working, he could sense how well you knew me from how they felt in his hands."

"Hands?" She looked up sharply. "Both hands?"

"I know it's odd," he said. "But he does, he works with both. And doesn't just sit there, either. It's—it's a dance, what he does. You *have* to come see us tomorrow night, Blye, you just have to."

She unlocked the door of the glassworks and gestured him inside. "P'rhaps I will," she allowed.

"I wish you'd let me spell that for you," he said suddenly, gesturing to the lock. "So nobody but you and your father can get in."

She shook her head. The silvery hair, loose from its band and neatly combed, shifted around her cheeks. "Beholden, Cade, but I can always feel additional magic, and it distracts me when I work." She led him through to the little shop, and he made a casual gesture that lit the overhead lamp with a mellow bluish light: Wizardfire in its gentlest form. Shelf on shelf of vases, goblets, bowls, and baskets gleamed the full spectrum of colors. In a special display case atop a wooden plinth was a sampling of a full suite of tableware, plate to chalice to eggcup. Cade walked over to investigate.

"This is new," he remarked. "Yours, right?"

"Some of it," she admitted. "As much of each piece as the Guild allows, so we can legally sell it with Da's hallmark. But it's my design."

"It looks like you," he said. When he saw her brows arch, he smiled. "Silver and gold round the edges, dark accents. Unpretentious. And threatening to become elegant any moment now."

"Elegant!" Blye snorted. "Lady forefend! Open the bottle and tell me about the glisker." From the assortment on the shelves she selected a pair of round-bellied snifters swirled with green, eyeing him sidelong as she appended shrewdly, "Or maybe I should say, tell me the dream you had today that was about the glisker."

He supposed it was a measure of how much he'd learned while bargaining with tavern keepers that not a flicker of reaction crossed his face. As Blye held out the glasses, he was ashamed of himself. Of all the people in his life—including Rafe and Jeska and even Mistress Mirdley—he trusted Blye alone with most of himself. Most; not all.

"I know you remember it," she went on sympathetically. "Sage Emmot taught you how to remember every single detail. If you don't want to talk about it, fine. But you *did* dream today."

He poured brandy, set the bottle aside, and cradled the glass in his hands to warm the liquor. "I'm not sure I want to talk about it yet. But wait till you hear what happened in Gowerion."

He talked, she listened, and they got through half the bottle. Yet even as he described what Mieka had done, and how the audiences had reacted, the boundary line separating his waking mind from the insistent dreaming began to smudge. Yes, he remembered it; all of it; Sage Emmot had taught him so well that he could never *not* remember.

Perhaps the tavern had once been fashionable and popular. Not anymore. The chairs were rickety, the tables stained and scarred. Instead of fragrant wood in the huge hearth, finances compelled the burning of turfs, and not very good ones at that. The stink was unmistakable.

Over in a back corner two men sat opposite each other, leather tankards between them. One man stared into his ale; the other stared with calculating intent, paper and pen and ink at the ready.

The first man spoke, his voice raspy, one hand suddenly raking lank brown hair from his face, fingers shaking a little. "I must've written a dozen pieces about them through the years. I don't think anybody ever realized how good they really were." He drained his ale down his throat, coughed, wiped his mouth with his sleeve, and glanced at his companion.

The hint was not taken. The second man smiled blandly and rendered ink onto paper with a delicacy unsuspected in such thick fingers. "You said you first met them after their rather sensational appearance at Trials."

"I didn't see the performance, but I knew somebody who did, and he tipped me that they might be something very special. They were, of course. But no one ever really understood until he was gone."

"Did they ever admit to it?"

"Rafcadion came closest, two or three years ago. Said he missed him." He reached over and appropriated the other man's ale, took a swig. "But a week or two later, he gave another interview saying he didn't miss him at all, when it came to the performing. As a friend, yes. Not as an artist, a partner onstage."

"He was lying," the other man suggested.

"Oh, yes. Jeschenar's never said anything about him at all, but I've spoken with Cayden a few times since it happened."

"And—?"

"Full of himself, he is. The meaning of this and the significance of that, what art must do and artists must be in society, all sorts of bilge. But he's a cold unfeeling bastard and it's no wonder his wife finally left him."

"Unfeeling? Forgive me, Tobalt, but—"

"I know. He emotes all over everything, doesn't he, in his work. But the only feelings that matter are his, you see. It's only important if *he* feels it—and he expects unconditional compassion that he's feeling that way. Not that he expects understanding, because nobody could possibly understand him, he's unique, and an artist, and all that rot. And he'd never let anyone help him find his way out of whatever mood he happens to be wallowing in." Tobalt leaned forward. "What isn't readily obvious in the work is that although he does feel these things right enough, he also stands apart from them so he can slice them up like feast-day mutton and then use them. His mind's cold, but his heart's colder."

"He wasn't always like that, was he?"

The rest of the ale was swallowed, the tankard slammed down onto the table. "He has to be that way, now. Got no choice, has he? He'd go mad, otherwise. Because he knows. He'll never admit it, but he knows. When the Cornerstones lost their Elf, they lost their soul."

"Cade."

The snifter almost dropped from his hand. Blye was looking at him as if she'd been looking at him for quite some time—waiting for him to rouse from whatever vision was playing itself out inside his head. "Sorry," he muttered.

"Stop apologizing! I'm not your mother." She held out her near-empty glass. "Might as well finish it."

He thoroughly agreed. They sat quietly for a time, sipping fine liquor that tasted of oak and golden apples. At last he made an effort. "How's your da? You haven't said."

"No better, no worse. He got in a few hours of work today, actually."

"Anything usable?" He regretted the words as soon as he spoke them. Her dark eyes flashed angrily, and then her face became a mask quite as good as any he'd ever worn himself, or magicked into a withie for Jeska to wear. But he knew better than to apologize again; she'd only snap at him again. Instead, he asked, "Want something to eat? Mistress Mirdley was making dumplings earlier."

"No, I'm fine. I know better than to drink on an empty stomach—which is more than can be said for you."

"I've had practice. Say you'll come tomorrow night."

"So I can meet him and adore him?"

The image of the Elf came into his head. He flinched.

Their soul, the man had said, he had been their soul, and when they'd lost him—

"That bad, was it?" Blye murmured. "I think it'll take more than half a bottle of brandy to get you to sleep tonight."

"I slept fine in Gowerion," he heard himself say.

"Was she pretty?"

"Was who pretty?" Then he tumbled to what she was saying, and saw the teasing glint in her eyes, and groaned. "Don't, Blye! You know Jeska always has first pick—and in Gowerion, there wasn't a second pick, nor a third."

"We need to find you a girl, Cade." She swallowed the remaining brandy and set the glass on the counter. "Somebody to warm your bed and keep her mouth shut—oh, except when you *want* her to open it, that is!"

"Blye!" he exclaimed, scandalized.

"You're always so intimidated by Jeska's looks," she went on, shaking her head with disapproval. "Rafe has a nice, smooth line of chatter when he takes the trouble, and when Crisiant isn't around to hear, and *that* daunts you, too. As for this Elf—Lord and Lady save us, he's gorgeous even when he's passed out. Or pretending to be passed out, now that I think on it," she finished broodingly. "So he'll be yet another excuse for you not to try, even if a girl does look thrice at you." All at once she made a face at him. "I know, I know!" In the high-pitched, die-away tones of the upper classes, she said, "The most they evah mahnage is twice—just to make sure they've seen what they've seen, dontchaknow."

"Now you do sound like my mother." Then something occurred to him, and he asked, "Blye, is there anything wrong with my clothes?"

He ought to have guessed that she'd make the connection. She knew him very well indeed. She laughed at him as she took the two glasses into the back room for a wash.

"The Elf thinks so, is that it? He'll be turning you into

a prancing peacock inside of a month, I see it now! A shirt first, a tunic thereafter, and then a coat with embroidered sleeves—you'll be frustling your pretty new feathers every chance you get!"

Picking up a clean towel from the stack beside the sink, he agreed amiably, "So now we really *do* have to find me a girl—preferably one who can sew!"

Blye started listing the girls they'd known at school and the girls who worked in various nearby shops, but when she got to the daughters of his mother's friends, he growled a playful warning.

"And how would you know any of those useless little twitchies, anyway?" he demanded.

"They come in and break the glassware, don't they? And say it jumped off the shelves all by itself, and leave me to explain to Da why a set of eight goblets now has to be sold as a set of six. But all's not lost, oh not a bit of it, for we can send out the seventh as a sample."

The seven could not be made eight again, because her father wasn't capable of making a new glass to match the old anymore. It was one reason custom had fallen off at the shop lately: no one really wanted to buy a suite of highly breakable objects if replacements were out of the question.

"But we'll be wanting scores of withies," he burst out, "and once people learn that it's you as made them for us—"

"Sweet Angels of Mercy, don't even whisper it!" she exclaimed. "Don't you know what the Guild would do to me if they found out?"

"It's not fair. Why should it matter that you're a girl?"

"Same reason it matters if I try to walk openly into a tavern where you're working, or board the public coach on my own, or attempt any profession but weaver or seamstress. No good reason at all." She returned to the shop front to replace the snifters.

Following her, he said, "You know I don't think that way."

"That and a penny and my hair hidden under a hat will get me a drink tomorrow night at the Downstreet to watch you perform. Get the light, won't you? I don't want to come down tomorrow morning and have to clean up after your magic."

He waited until she had gone back into the glass-works, and doused the lamp with a tired gesture. She was waiting for him by the door, arms folded, fingers drumming.

"Blye—Mieka says we'll make you rich, and he's right. It *will* happen—Guild or no Guild. We're using only your withies from now on, and when everyone else wants to know where we got them—"

"Just so long as you don't mention who made them," she muttered. Then: "Wait a moment—did you say Mieka? The Windthistle boy?"

"Yes. Didn't I say his name before? He's my glisker."

"Everybody's glisker, you sapskull! He's worked with more players than you've got teeth—for all of a week at the most! I heard last year that he even approached the Shadowshapers and asked if he could join them! *He's* your new glisker?"

So that was how he knew Vered and Rauel, Cade thought. "Yes," he repeated. "My new glisker." He heard the voice again, from his dream of that morning: *"You said you first met them after their rather sensational appearance at Trials."* Mieka would be with them through Trials at least—three months from now. But then that other voice echoed in his head, the bleak and bitter one: *"When the Cornerstones lost their Elf, they lost their soul."*

Blye touched his arm lightly, hesitantly. "Cade?"

"Mine he is, and mine he'll stay," he said without thinking, heard his own words, and amended swiftly, "*Ours*, I mean. He's *our* glisker now."

{Mieka was laughing, young laughter in an older face: lines framing his mouth and crossing his forehead and his black hair going silvery, but those eyes were bright with the joy unique to him, and he was still the mad little Elf of all those years ago, gazing up at Cade and laughing—}

He blinked, and saw Blye's frown. Before she could voice the worry in her eyes, he nodded a good night and headed for his parents' back door, and the warmth of Mistress Mirdley's kitchen, where no dreams had ever touched him, not since the dreaming began. It was the only place in the world, including his own private bed-chamber, where he felt truly safe.

Four

EVENTUALLY MIEKA SHOWED up for rehearsal, and blamed his lateness on Cade.

"Didn't tell me where Rafe lives, now, did you? I've been wandering like a stray breeze, asking after anyone who knows anything about anybody in the fettling way." He stripped off a pair of very fine and very flash gold-embroidered gloves, shoving them into a pocket of his cloak. This, too, was eye-catching, woven with a dark green warp and a black weft, with crosswise threads of blue and gold, so that every time he moved, the material seemed to change colors. Cade, wearing old brown wool trousers, a plain white shirt, and a black tunic with a frayed hem, began to understand what he'd meant about the clothes. "I'd still be drifting round Beekbacks if I hadn't bethought me of the delightful Mistress Blye, who not only gave me directions but the pleasure of her company."

He stepped lightly from the vestibule doorway, removing the cloak with a flourish as if drawing aside a stage curtain, to reveal Blye hanging up a shabby gray coat. It was the ankle-length one she always borrowed from her father when she didn't want to be bothered with the jeers and insults that always assaulted any girl past age twelve who wore trousers. She half-turned, startled, and shrugged as she recognized the annoyance in Cade's eyes. Not that he entirely understood why he was annoyed, but it had something to do with the pair of them walking over here, talking about only they knew what.

"I brought a cap," she said. "We can just go from here to the Downstreet, can't we?" A cap to hide her hair and enough of her face so that when she removed the coat people would think her a boy. "The nice one," she added.

Cade knew the cap she meant. Blye had made a half-dozen child-sized pretend withies for Derien, and he had insisted on giving her his best cap in return, the sapphire velvet one with the puffy black feather. Being a shrewd little boy as well as a generous one, he'd told Lady Jaspiela that the wind had blown the cap into the river. As her ladyship was in company with Blye perhaps five times a year, and never deigned to notice her anyway, the chance of her seeing and recognizing the cap was nonexistent. That Dery so easily lied to their mother bothered Cade a little, but he shrugged it aside, knowing that if the boy was to have any kind of life of his own, he'd have to learn how to lie to her, and lie convincingly. That Dery had begged Cade for the withies, even if they were just pretend, after Lady Jaspiela reacted with horror to his request, told Cade that there was a nice streak of rebellion in his baby brother. And he grinned to himself every time he glimpsed Dery in his big bedroom on the third floor, solemnly declaiming "magical words" to bespell the glass twigs or waving them gently as imagination turned him into a Master Glisker. After twelve years of being the only child, pinched and pushed to fit a mold of his mother's devising, Cade was rather wickedly looking forward to watching Derien stand up to her the way he himself had done. She deserved it.

"Blye, dearling!" Rafe's mother, large and stout and loud, held out her arms to welcome the girl. Overwhelmed by a cinnamon-scented embrace—as Cade had been half an hour earlier—Blye hugged back. "You'll be going with the boys tonight? Sweet Angels, I do wish I still had the figure to do the same! But that's what being a baker's wife will do, and it's a fact not to be argued with. Come, leave the boys to their plotting. You and I will go into the kitchen and make their tea, and you can tell me how your dear father is these days. And don't let me forget to send you home with a dozen of those little seedy cakes he likes."

Even as she bustled with Blye through the kitchen door, her eyes sought the Elf with a look more suited to a woman half her age. Surely she was promising herself a much longer look later on. Rafe had noticed his mother's sidelong glance; his jaw dropped slightly and his grayblue eyes blinked wide. Cade hid a grin by turning his back and pretending to examine the magnificent inlaid chessboard hanging above the hearth. He'd learned to play on that board. Master Threadchaser's pride and joy, it had been handed down from father to son for five generations, and an offer to take it down for a game was a signal that he liked you. As Cade examined for the hundredth time the delicate spiderweb patterns decorating its wide border, he had the thought that it was rather emblematic of the two families—that above this hearth was a symbol of intellectual skill, and above his mother's was an empty looking-glass drained of magic, in which one could look only at oneself.

"Jeska, please tell me your house is easier to locate," Mieka whined, and Cade decided it would waste too much time to remind the Elf that he'd been very clear about the location. Even if he hadn't, all anyone had to do was ask about for a door with a spiderweb carved above it, proclaiming the family's clan.

"Middle of the block, right after Marketty Round, can't miss it," the masquer replied absently as he scanned the evening's performance charts. He was agonizingly meticulous, for he'd always had difficulty reading, which made him work all the harder at memorizing his lines. But he'd rarely got a word wrong in the year Cade had worked with him. "I think I've got this now, Cade, but I'd like to run through the whole thing at least once, just to make sure."

Seating himself on a ladder-back chair with a glass basket of withies at his feet, Cade said, "As many times as you need, Jeska. We'll be doing the 'Sailor' again tonight, and then 'The Princess and the Deep Dark Well'—how are you at echoes, Mieka?"

"Excellent. But don't you have something original? That's such a boring old drudge of a thing." He sprawled in one of the overstuffed chairs, looking disgruntled.

Still without glancing up, Jeska asked, "Hadn't you noticed? Cade puts in things of his own all the time."

"But not enough to make people *realize* it!"

"We'll make a splash some other night," Cade said. "We made this booking with another glisker, you know—somebody who works traditional."

"They don't know I'm coming? Get ready for a drenching, then, because it's no mere splash we'll make. The Downstreet is almost a real theater, you know. The stage was specially built, not just nailed together with spare planks. Big enough so I can really work!"

Rafe caught Cade's glance and rolled his eyes. Was there no limit to Mieka's arrogance? But what Rafe said had nothing to do with stemming the boy's vanity. "You've played the Downstreet before?"

Incautiously, still caught up in his vision of their triumph, the Elf said, "Sat in with Vered and Rauel and Sakary one night, when Chattim took ill."

"You *what?*" Jeska exclaimed.

"Good reason to think well of yourself, then, have you?" Rafe snarled. "Quite a downcoming, playing with quidams like us!"

Stricken, Mieka stammered, "I'm sorry—I didn't mean to say that—I mean, I'm not hiding anything, it was just one show and—" He looked an appeal at Cade. "Quill, it's not like it sounds!"

So *that* was how he knew the Shadowshapers. Blye had mentioned that he knew them, but it turned out that Vered and Rauel had trusted him with their work. Only because their own glisker had been ill, but—Mieka had actually played a show with the Shadowshapers. Cade was all for interrogating him about what it had been like, and the pieces they'd done, and a hundred other things. But anger touched his tongue first, and he demanded, "Why so bloody eager to join up with *us,* then?"

"Sakary couldn't cope with me, all right? I can't help it when I don't like the taste of someone's magic, and he had a stranglehold on me and—and I fought him, I couldn't help it! We got through the show and he hasn't spoken to me since! He's a good fettler, one of the best, but I couldn't work with him—"

"Because he couldn't *cope* with you?"

"Leave him be," Rafe said suddenly. "You know the trouble they had finding a glisker, before Chattim. Like us. Just like us, Cade. Call it the taste or the feel of the magic, or puzzle pieces locking into place, or instinct, but you and me and Jeska worked strong together from the first. We fit." Pointing a long finger at Mieka, he finished, "And so does he. With us. Not with them, nor anybody else. *Us.*"

Mieka cast him a grateful glance, then turned back to

Cade with his shoulders slightly hunched, as if he was anticipating a fist to the jaw. "Cade?" he ventured. "I'm sorry I didn't say anything earlier. But Rafe's right, isn't he?"

They were all looking at him now, waiting for his concurrence. How did he explain to them that knowing Mieka had worked with the absolute best, had done the glisking for two of the most innovative minds in the theater, had shaken his confidence on the very night when a successful booking at the Downstreet could assure their future?

"Please don't be cross," Mieka said softly.

"He's not," Rafe said with the certainty of long friendship. "He's comparing himself to Vered and Rauel again, that's all. He does it all the time. The good thing is that it always makes him work harder." Eyeing Cade with wry understanding, he added, "If you're through being over-awed by the thought of *your* glisker working with the illustrious Shadowshapers, can we get down to it now?"

"Mine he is, and mine he'll stay." He heard his own voice saying it just last evening. He nodded sharply.

"Right, then," Rafe said. "What can you tell me about the Downstreet, Mieka? We've never played a place that big before."

With a last wary glance at Cade, Mieka made a grimace that was half relief and half apology. "Nothing to it, really."

"No, nothing at all," Cade muttered, but when he caught the nervous flicker of those big eyes—dark now with apprehension, plain brown and murky—he shrugged and gestured for him to start talking.

The Downstreet was, as Mieka had mentioned, a real venue, not just a tavern with a rickety makeshift platform. The stage was actually divided for a performance: a solidly made wooden riser for the glisker, a lectern for the fettler, with the masquer given plenty of room. It was so big, in fact, that a glisker could add more than just the usual impressions of a landscape, buildings, a room's interior: he could really paint a whole scene for the masquer to act against.

But there was a problem with this large a venue, as well, because the fettler had to make sure the people in the cheap seats could feel things, sense things, just as well as the people up front and in the middle. Rafe was nervous about exactly how and where to direct everything.

"How did Sakary do it?" he asked.

"Played to the middle, and just slightly to the right. The roof timbers aren't evenly spaced on that side of the room. There's an extra row crosswise, put in to support the Lady Shrine upstairs. The wife and daughters insisted, once there was coin enough for it. They've a stone plinth, and a little fountain—remind me to flick some extra magic up there. It's only polite to give them a nice little cascade for their evening devotions."

"Plinth *and* fountain?" Jeska asked, amazed. "Most noble ladies make do with molded plaster and a bowl!"

Mieka snorted. "'Make do' isn't a thing the mistress would recognize if it introduced itself and paid for the privilege. She has plans for her girls, she does. The elder is to make a noble marriage, the younger will be consigned to whichever minster's influence matches up with their money." He paused, then resumed pensively, "Why is it that mothers lacking a son reach even higher than those with?"

"You've never met Lady Jaspiela," Cade said before either of the other two could.

"Really?" Those eyes were lighter now, the shine back in them. "What did she want you to be, before you told her you'd be a tregetour or nothing?"

"His father's at Court," Rafe said quite casually, and Cade silently blessed him. "Her Ladyship was seeing Cayden there in a few years when Prince Ashgar takes a bride, and then a rich marriage, and by the time the grandchildren come, everybody'd forget that Herself married middle for the money and not upper for the glory."

Mieka whistled softly between his teeth. "Sounds grim. Prince Ashgar is nobody's pattern of perfection, is he? Lovely of your little brother to oblige you by being born. But if he's anything like you, I'd imagine your lady mother will be thwarted a second time." Shifting in the wide chair, drawing both legs up and wrapping his arms around his shins, he rested his chin on his knees. "Bless the good Gods for giving my parents four sets of twins! There's enough of us to drive them stark staring mad, and they know it, so they let us do what we please!"

"Must be nice," Jeska said. "Can we get on with the rehearsal now?"

"Yes," Rafe said, "and I'd like to get there a bit early, and have a look at this ceiling. Extra timbers, and a big stone plinth above—it'll be tricky, no doubt of it. How did you know about the Lady Shrine?"

"Showed it to me, didn't she? Old ladies, they like me," he confided with a smirk. "They think I'm sweet. Anyhow, the support timbers deflect things a bit odd, but if you play to the right, everything bounces just like it should, all the way back to the bar."

An hour later they were all more than ready for their tea. In some ways, containing even the minimal magic used in rehearsal was harder on Rafe than an entire show. A few years ago, when they finally confessed to each other that they had the same ambitions regarding the theater and were learning their crafts, Cade had tried to impart as much as he recalled of what his grandsir the Master Fettler had taught him when he was little. Lady Jaspiela had not been pleased, having decided there were more distinguished uses for her son's magic than stage-craft. But she hadn't dared speak against it while the old man was still alive. Cade had tried to feel disappointed that he had no talent for his grandsir's specialty; a restless imagination impelled him instead towards the creative process of the tregetour. But even years later, he remembered most of what he'd been taught, even if he didn't really understand it, and had shared it all with Rafe. On one memorable occasion, up in Rafe's big, airy bedchamber that occupied the whole of the attic high above the bakery, Cade's attempted demonstration of how to expand and contract control had burst every piece of glass and ceramic in the room, including the mirror, and warped the chamber door into the bargain. It had never closed properly since, or so Rafe's mother avowed with a wink at Cade every time she said it. She treasured the memory of that afternoon, for as it turned out, her son's instincts had kicked him into containing Cade's magic so that it didn't run riot through the rest of the house. "Might have blown out every other window in the place, and in the bakery besides," Mistress Threadchaser always said to finish the tale. "Cayden is that powerful—but *my* boy, he's that strong!"

Once Jeska announced himself prepared, and Mieka had agreed with Cade on the exact sequence and nature of the magic, and Cade had done the minor shifts in the spells already within the withies, Rafe sank back into his chair with a long sigh of weariness.

"We go on at eight? Fine. Wake me five minutes before the show."

"What you want is your tea, mate." Mieka sprang to his feet and bounded lightly for the kitchen door.

Cade leaned towards his fettler, frowning. "Are you sure you'll be ready for this tonight? Or maybe I ought to be asking if you can *cope* with him?"

Rafe shrugged. "It's a different sort of tired, y'know."

Nodding, Cade settled back again. He knew what Rafe meant. There was a look his friend wore sometimes after a performance that meant he'd spent the evening fighting to discipline an erratic or inexperienced glisker. This was not the same. Rafe had been modulating and adjusting, not struggling for control. The tired that came of satisfying work was entirely different from that of a long battle to a disappointing end.

Jeska packed up the scuffed leather portfolio where he kept his charts, saying, "I can't stop. Make my apologies to Mistress Threadchaser, if you would. And I'll have to meet you at the Downstreet—I've accounts to be totted before supper." As difficult as he found reading, arithmetic came as simply to him as breathing. Jeska supplemented his mother's always shaky finances by keeping the books for a dozen local businesses.

"Our duty to your mum," Rafe said. He had very pretty manners.

"Travel safe," Cade added, and when Jeska had left the sitting room turned again to his fettler. "You really do look worn out. Are you sure he fits?"

"Even boots made to measure start out a little stiff. But he knows what he's doing, and what's better, I know what he's doing. It'll come right, Cade, stop fretting."

Nodding once more, he pushed himself to his feet. "I'll bring in the tea."

He knocked politely on the kitchen door—Mistress Mirdley had more than once threatened to smack his bottom for startling her at her work. The day she'd carried through on the threat had given him the biggest surprise of his life. There had been a napkinful of sweets on his pillow that night by way of apology, but he had never again forgotten to knock.

No one answered from the other side of the kitchen door, and as he listened carefully he understood why. Mieka was talking. Did Mieka ever stop talking?

"—shoulda seen me fa's great-auntie, ears like big floppy bat wings—took all four brothers and a sister or two to hold her down in a spring breeze or she'd take flight! Mum was horrid scared I'd turn out the same, but it appears I got the best of all things Elfen," he finished without a trace of conceit. Only stating the facts.

"And there are eight of you? Mercy!" exclaimed Mistress Threadchaser.

"Eight," the Elf confirmed, "and no two sets like another. My older brothers, they're all Human, down to the last curly red hair. Six foot five, shoulders like cannon mounts, no more magic in them than can stir the soup—which neither of 'em can bring to a boil. Not that it's so unusual in our family—not much Fire Elf, we're none of us very good at that sort of thing. But the Air and Earth and Water, my younger sisters got those and those only. They look like the Greenseed line, mostly—or so Fa says. For a while they were hoping they'd top five feet, but that's not gonna happen, not in this lifetime. White hair at twelve years old, eyes almost black, and a set of teeth on each of them that'd gnaw through a tree trunk in a twitch of a wyvern's tail. Ears like the sails on a schooner, too," he added, and Cade could hear the smirk. "Mum found a chirurgeon—a good, careful one, mind—to refine them just a bit, and take care of the teeth. Me an' Jinsie, though, we got the best of the Elf and the best of the Human, with a bit of Wizard and a dash of Sprite for spice."

Blye asked, "She's your twin sister, and that much alike?"

"Mirror image, almost. She's not quite as pretty as me, though! Twins aren't usual with Elfenfolk, of course, but it's the clue we've some Piksey knockin' about somewhere, and makin' quite a racket with it, too. They whelp twins as an iron-bound rule. The new little mites, they're only two years old, a boy and a girl—and it looks as if the one's pretty much Water Elf from the Staindrop and Stormchill lines, and the other's anybody's guess, 'cept he's determined to grow up to be a dragon!"

As Mieka paused for breath and the ladies laughed, Cade knocked again. Invited to enter, he found the coziest imaginable domestic scene: Mistress Threadchaser in a big cushioned chair by the blazing hearth, Blye in the matching armchair opposite her, and Mieka hunched on a low wooden stool between, two pottery bowls at his feet and one in his lap as he shelled walnuts. He looked up as Cade entered, and his hair shifted around his pointed Elfen ears, and a wide smile revealed white, square, very Human teeth.

"Quill! There you are! Hunger finally got the best of you, then?"

"Oh, good Lady have mercy on us," Mistress Threadchaser cried with a quick glance at the clicking clock on the sideboard. "It's gone five and you poor things must be starved! Here, I'll take care of those later," she said to Mieka, who shook his head.

"I finish what I begin." He twirled a finger above the bowl on his knees, and a little whirlwind surged upwards, emitting a series of sharp cracks. Then the blur split in two and descended neatly to the bowl of nuts and the bowl of shells. Beaming, Mieka looked about for approval—just as a last walnut hurtled from the bowl in his lap and struck him right in the nose.

Cade laughed at him. Mistress Threadchaser asked anxiously if he was all right. Blye, however, sat back in her chair and frowned.

Cade asked her about that later, after they'd devoured the usual lavish and excellent tea and were carrying his crated glass baskets to the Downstreet.

"Bit of a jester, isn't he?" she murmured. "I mean, look at him."

Mieka was loping along beside Rafe, who had livened up considerably after his mother's cakes, fruit breads, and sausage salad. Usually he was quietly self-possessed before a performance; Cade had expected him to be completely silent, in fact, on their way to this oh-so-important booking. But Rafe was trading quips with Mieka, laughing, even snatching the cap off his head and holding it high out of the Elf's reach to tease him.

"Why didn't he crack the walnuts by magic in the first place?" Blye went on. "If he'd got finished faster, maybe Mistress Threadchaser had something else she wanted done."

Cade eyed her sidelong. "You don't like him, do you."

"I like him fine. He's funny, he's a charmer, and he's no chore to look at, that's for certain sure."

"P'rhaps a little *too* much the charmer?" he guessed. "Did he pay you a compliment you didn't believe? Not that you ever believe a compliment." Her blush told him all he needed to know. "Leave off, Blye, he's just a puppy, all excited and wriggly over joining us, wanting to show off a bit. It's the player in him."

"That remembers me, Cade—on the walk over, when he wasn't asking questions about you, he was trying to figure a name for the group. I'm hopeless, I've no imagination to speak of, but he wasn't doing much better."

"Something will occur to us," he replied. "What kind of questions?"

"Oh, just things," she evaded. "He's not very subtle. That last walnut, for instance—it was on purpose. Didn't you notice?"

"He did it to get a laugh? What's wrong with that?"

"As I said. Look at him—a clown."

"He was really good with 'Silver Mine,' y'know," Cade told her quietly. "There's thought in him, and honesty. He's more than a clown. You'll see that tonight."

"P'rhaps. But the 'Princess' isn't exactly grand tragedy, is it? And are you sure he won't make *that* into a farce, the way you say he does the 'Sailor'?"

"He wouldn't dare."

She arched her brows eloquently, but said nothing more.

"Cade!" Mieka had danced back towards them, his moss-green cap stowed in his pocket where Rafe couldn't get at it again. "We still need a name. There's a group over the North End goes by Wishcallers, and somebody else that thinks if they're lucky they'll get mistaken for the Shadowshapers by naming themselves the Smoke-catchers." His nose wrinkled with disdain. "We need a contrast, I think, don't you?"

"Good idea," Blye said. "So that nobody thinks you're trying to imitate anybody. Something solid. Rock, brick, stone—"

"Brickballs," Mieka offered, grinning.

"Brickbrains," she tossed back at him.

Rafe had paused to let them catch him up, and contributed dryly, "Pebblebrains, more like."

"What about 'stone' something, or something 'stone'?" Blye asked. "Keystones?"

"Not bad," Rafe allowed. "Nice imagery—a bit nervy, implying we're the ones holding everything together—"

"—when it's really only you, O Great Fettler?" Mieka scampered ahead, then turned and walked backwards so he could talk to them. "Lodestones. Nobody can resist us, we'll draw them in like magnets!"

Cade wanted to join in their banter, but a slither of a chill down his backbone caught him unawares.

"Lodestars? No," Blye decided at once. "You're none of you Fire Clan, and they're touchy about who thinks to associate with them."

Mieka was scowling. "Stone . . . Stonesmiths—I hate it. Stoneciphers? Hewstones? Whetstones? Even worse. Come on, Quill, you're the wordsmith!"

"Headstones—everybody needs one eventually," Rafe said.

Mieka began a mocking singsong. "Limestones, Sandstones, Gemstones, Cornerstones—"

"No!"

The protest burst out of his mouth before he could remember why it was the worst word in the lexicon. As they stared at him, he lost track of where he was and even who he was, and he was back in the dim, run-down tavern listening to someone called Tobalt say, *"When the Cornerstones lost their Elf, they lost their soul."*

"Quill?"

Soft voice, worried and even a little frightened. Gentle touch on his shoulder. He looked down into those eyes and if the glass baskets hadn't been cradled in his arms, he would have grasped Mieka with both hands, to keep him here and safe and alive—

"Cade, what is it?" Rafe's deep voice, raspy with concern.

"Back away," said Blye. "Let him breathe."

She knew. Of course she knew. But he couldn't look away from the Elf, the Elf he would one day lose, and with him his soul, and he would go cold inside and heartless and cruel, he knew it, he knew those things were inside him and if he wasn't careful, if he didn't do everything exactly right, if he made even one wrong choice—Sagemaster Emmot had told him that very first night, hadn't he, told him what a ruthless decision it was to leave home and friends to seek magic, a decision Cayden had made without a single qualm—

"Cade!" Blye had pushed Mieka aside and was gripping Cade's face between her hands. She snarled over her shoulder as Mieka protested, and swept the sweat-damp hair from Cade's face. "Are you back?" she asked in a low voice. "Have you come back?"

He nodded and caught his breath. "Yes," he muttered, looking into her dark eyes that were so wonderfully familiar—eyes that didn't compel feelings he couldn't put names to.

"What just happened?" Mieka demanded. "Quill, what does she mean, 'Are you back?' Back from where?"

"Leave it," Rafe said. "Come on, we've a show to do. Come *on*, Mieka!"

Blye asked him exactly nothing during the rest of the walk to the Downstreet. He could only imagine what must have been on his face, in his eyes, during the turn, as Master Emmot had always called such things. *"Turns your brain right round inside your skull, doesn't it? Not to be mistaken for the kind of 'turn' a lady succumbs to when the fit of her corset is too tight—although it's rather like the fit of your thoughts is too tight, isn't it?"*

Too many thoughts. Too many feelings. Too many memories that weren't, but might be—and all of it so huge that his mind couldn't sort it without reasoned reflection, which the Sagemaster had taught him to do and which he had unwisely neglected to do since the dreaming about that derelict tavern.

In the few minutes remaining to him before the most important performance of his life thus far, he tried to run through the basic exercise of organizing the separate elements of the vision.

Hopeless; all he could think about was Mieka.

As he paused for a deep breath before walking up a short flight of steps to the Downstreet's back door, he decided his instincts were correct. Mieka *was* the crucial element. From him—from losing him—all else would come. Cade didn't know how they had lost the Elf, or when, or why. But he could change things. He knew he was young, that he'd had scant experience adjusting the futures he'd seen in his dreamings. But he had made choices, conscious choices, to avoid futures he feared. He blinked at the darkness in the back hallway of the tavern, and Blye's hand on his elbow guided him towards the stage and the knee-high wooden riser where the glass baskets had to be arranged for the show. She helped him with the crates, still not questioning him. Good of her to choose not to pester him . . .

And then he realized that he had come to a point in his life where futures depended not just on his own choices, but on those made by others as well. He had to reckon on their desire to change things—or to change themselves. He would be at the mercy of their decisions.

This was no scene he was writing, no playlet where he could decide who did what. He could not control this. He knew that. He also knew himself well enough to know that however useless it might be, he would make the attempt.

Blye had disappeared, presumably to find a drink and a seat someplace where she wouldn't be noticed. It occurred to Cade to wonder if she was the wife Tobalt had mentioned. No. Impossible. Blye would never leave him.

"Cade, we're about ready."

Rafe was there, stacking the padded crates out of the way. He asked no questions, even though he had known Cade long enough to recognize a turn when he saw it. Jeska hopped up onto the glisker's little platform, unaware of what had happened on the walk over. He rubbed Cade's shoulder affectionately, smiled at Rafe, and jumped down again to take his place center stage, eager to begin. And then Mieka was there, pushing the glisker's bench forward, setting the baskets on it, swaying and reaching as if already at work, making adjustments until satisfied. He didn't look at Cade as he stepped back, and instead addressed Rafe.

"See what I mean about the roof timbers?"

"Play to the right, you said. But the bar's at an angle back there, and I don't want to bust any glasses before I get the feel of the bounce."

"Break as many as you like," Cade heard himself say. "Shatter them to splinters."

"Are you insane?" Mieka gasped.

"I won't have it get round that I'm a fettler who lost control of his glisker's magic," Rafe growled.

"That's the last thing anyone will say about you," Cade told him, meeting his eyes. He still couldn't quite bring himself to look at Mieka. "Because you're going to make it obvious that you did it deliberately. Word will get round, right enough—that we've a strength and a power no one can match."

"The tavern keeper will have our balls on a platter." But Mieka was beginning to look intrigued.

"Before or after his wife kills us?" Rafe inquired caustically.

"She won't be killing anybody, and our balls are perfectly safe." Cade forced himself to look into those eyes. "*You're* going to charm her out of any temper— and what's more, you're going to charm her into replacing her glassware at a price she can well afford. Once people start talking about what they'll see here tonight, she'll need more anyway, to serve all the new customers."

Mieka looked at him with frank admiration. "And here I thought *I* flew high and wide!"

"Try to keep up," Cade said, and laughed. *His* choice, this; *his* decision. Made a spectacular first appearance at Trials, had they? Why wait? *Spectacular* could just as easily start tonight.

Five

THERE SEEMED SCARCE ten minutes between the time Cayden fell into his bed and the vehement return of consciousness in the form of his little brother, Derien, bouncing on the mattress, making the supporting ropes whine and the bed frame creak.

"Wake up, wake up, wake *up*!"

"No!" he growled. "Get off and go away!"

"But you have to see, you have to read it! C'mon, Cade, wake up!"

He made a grab for the child, who giggled and leaped from the bed, waving a broadsheet so fresh-printed that the ink had left smudges on Dery's fingers. "Read what? Did somebody—?" Rolling out of bed, he lunged, and almost missed. The page tore. "Give it here!"

"Don't worry, I bought four of them—one for each of you," Dery said, handing over the rest of the sheet. "You're mentioned by name—well, *your* names, and not spelled right, because you don't have a real name yet, do you? But—"

He babbled on; Cade didn't hear him. Two long strides took him to the dormer window, and by the fragile sunlight of a wintry morning he scanned the broadsheet for names, any of their names, spelled right or not. There, in one of the thin columns printers used to fill a page when there wasn't enough real news or a shop notice couldn't be wedged in, were three sentences.

AT THE DOWNSTREET last night, a smashing good show by four local lads not yet knowing what to call themselves. Led by tregetour Cadan Silversun, with fettler Rafcadio Threadspinner, masquer Jeshika Bowbender, and energetic glisker Mekal Windthistle, it was a performance of

*the sort rarely seen in players not already on a Circuit.
Catch their show while it can still be seen for the price of
a tankard.*

"—have to think up *something,* Cade, people need to
know who you are so when the placards go up they
know who they're looking for—"

He wanted to yell and laugh and just explode. But he
restrained himself, and looked round from the window
with what he hoped was a casual shrug. "Not quite as
nice as if they'd got our names right, but it's a start."

With a howl of outrage, Dery bounced back onto the
bed, grabbed a pillow, and began pummeling him with it.
Cade laughed, picked up him, and tickled him. The pillow burst, the feathers flew, and all at once a chilly voice
addressed them from the doorway.

"If you're *quite* finished, I would appreciate a few moments of the famous tregetour's attention."

"Did you see, Mum? Cade was *wonderful,* and now
he's famous, and soon he'll be rich, and then—"

Cade experienced a sudden aching inside as his little
brother abruptly realized what would happen once there
was enough money. Excitement dropped from the child's
face like the magic from a masquer changing characters.
Cade reached out a hand to ruffle the thick brown hair,
and smiled reassurance. But he couldn't lie; he couldn't
say he wouldn't be out of this house as soon as may be,
no matter if the address was a disgrace and a scandal
compared to Redpebble Square.

Their mother ignored the change in mood. "Leave us,
Derien."

"Go on, then," Cade said gently to the child. "Tell
Mistress Mirdley I'll be down soon for breakfast, won't
you? And don't you yaffle down all the muffins, either—I
can smell them all the way up here. Beholden, Dery."

Derien slumped off, and Cade regarded Lady Jaspiela

through the last drifting fall of feathers. His name (misspelled or not) was in the newspaper. He had known it would happen eventually; he hadn't expected it quite this soon. Well, that was what a couple of shelves of broken glassware would do.

His instincts had been right. He'd have to heed them more often. That Her Ladyship would be raging at him for the next little while required no instinct at all. First would come a description of her mortification that his name had appeared in so disreputable a broadsheet as *The Nayword*. She would progress to a renewed demand that his name show up in the *Court Circular* instead, preferably in connection with a prestigious appointment. Then she would move on to the usual lecture about what a disappointment he was and that the very least he could do was cease to parade his inadequacies in front of his little brother, who deserved a much better example, and so on and so on.

Cade decided he didn't much want to hear any of it.

"Don't bother," he said as she was drawing breath. "I'll be gone from here as soon as I've the coin to manage it. Which won't be long if the papers keep mentioning us, so p'rhaps your time would be better spent beseeking the Lady to favor us, instead of repeating all the things I've heard a thousand times before."

Her brows arched in the expression that always meant *Remember who I am!* By which she didn't mean she was his mother, and therefore he owed her respect; she meant she was a Lady of the Highcollar Name of the Wolf Clan. That, and a se'en-penny piece, would get her through the palace gates for one of the weekly tours of the grounds.

"The sooner we're a grand success, the sooner you'll be rid of me," he added, just in case she had missed the point.

She did something unexpected then. She asked, "Who is this 'Windthistle' person? The one who is so . . . energetic," she finished, as if it were a particularly unpleasant disease.

He shrugged. "You read the broadsheet. He's my new glisker."

"I see."

She was a beautiful woman still, pure Wizard in looks: thick straight hair she wore in a swirl of golden silk at her nape, long bones, brown eyes, high rounded brow. Of the other races in her ancestry, none showed. She was said to resemble her mother, who had so disastrously aligned the Highcollar family with the Archduke. Cade had no way of judging, as the old lady died long before he was born and there were no extant imagings that depicted her. Rumor had it, though, that the Archduke's son, current holder of the title, had met Lady Jaspiela once, a chance encounter at High Chapel, and turned quite pale. Evidently he still had memories of a woman as haughty and as dangerous as she was beautiful. As little as Cade relished being Lady Jaspiela's son, he liked being Lady Kiritin's grandson even less. All at once he wondered if perhaps he might have a thing or two in common with the present Archduke.

Dark eyes swept Cade head to foot, and then inspected his face, as if trying to remember the reason why he inhabited her home. "An Elf," she said. "And with that name—Air, is he? Yes, of course he would be. I trust I won't be seeing him anywhere near here."

"No more than you ever see Rafe or Jeska. Now, if that's all, Mother, I should get to work on tonight's performance."

"If you must."

Did she *finally* understand? Not likely. "Yes," he replied. "I must."

She never simply exited a room. She swept, strode, stalked, glided, drifted, anything rather than just put one foot in front of the other. And there were always sound effects. The slurring of her skirts, the tap of her heels, the tinkle of her jewelry, the sharply meaningful click of a closing door—the imperious voice raised just that fraction that meant it was a lazy, neglectful servant's fault that she must raise her voice at all. Today she called down the stairs for the footman, which usually meant she had an appointment somewhere and required a hire-hack. Cade knew perfectly well that she would be making appearances at her friends' homes this morning to pretend total ignorance of last night's triumph. How they informed her of it, whether their attitudes were excited or patronizing or pitying, would dictate her response. Compliments—genuine compliments, not the kind soaked in acid—she would wave away with a shrug, a change of subject, and a mental note not to further cultivate the acquaintance, for no real lady would be thrilled by something so vulgar as a son's name in a broadsheet. Condescension she would greet with a sigh and a shake of the head, and expressions of gratitude for sympathy that hadn't been offered. Commiseration for the indignity of having a son who performed for anyone with the coin to buy a drink would in all probability bring the daintiest of quivers to her mouth, as if she bravely restrained tears.

Someday, he promised himself, he would write a piece incorporating all her arrogance and pretentiousness, and even though she would never see it, those who did would laugh about it to their wives, who would know instantly who had been his model. And Lady Jaspiela really would have reason to weep.

A childish ambition, he knew. Perhaps by the time his work was performed in the real theaters frequented by the husbands of her friends, he would have outgrown the need to pay back humiliation for humiliation. But she would make such a wonderful character study for Jeska . . . and that was as good an excuse as any to use her however he saw fit. He was an artist, writing for other artists to entertain an audience; no one was exempt from becoming fodder.

Mothers, he reflected as he got dressed, were always an interesting topic. Jeska did an excellent Mother Loosebuckle, a stock character in farces popular for their exceedingly low humor. They'd have to give one of them a try, now that Mieka had joined them. Jeska could have plenty of fun with any of the playlets—and Cade could just imagine the Elf, dancing behind the glass baskets, flinging magic far and wide as he chortled his way through the piece.

He was grinning as he magicked the strewn feathers into a tidy little white mountain on the bed—a simple Affinity spell, roughly the opposite of that Mieka had used to shell walnuts. He'd restuff the pillow later. Right now he was hungry, and eager to start the day's work, to see Mieka and Rafe and Jeska, to laugh over their "smashing" show at the Downstreet. Mieka had talked about possibly sneaking his twin sister in tonight, if Blye would come along to help. It really was rotten that women must hoodwink their way into any performance— Blye had almost been grassed last night by a drunk who collapsed against her and discovered unboyish curves beneath her clothes. He'd been so squiffed, no one paid him any attention when he stuttered about a girl being in the tavern (everybody thought he meant the Sweetheart), but it had been a near thing.

Still, what was the worst that could happen? Surely nothing more terrible than getting thrown back out on the street—

{ —out on the street, just beneath the vast awning that sheltered the theater doors, a bizarre little group coalesced. Three anxious boys who didn't move like boys at all, two outraged constables, and one gaudily clad woman who didn't move anything like a woman. She

didn't sound like one either as she—he—shouted that
they'd best leave their hands off or answer to someone
more important than they'd ever dreamed they'd meet in
their whole miserable, worthless lives—}

Cade clutched at the banister for support, dizzy, as the
scene came and went in the space of five heartbeats. He
didn't recognize the girls dressed as boys, or the man
dressed as a woman, and he'd no idea what they thought
they were doing. When his breathing had calmed, he re-
created what he'd just seen and became even more
confused—not just by the glimpse of that very odd possibility, but by what might have prompted it. Trace it
back, then. He'd been thinking about Blye, and how
she'd nearly been caught, and he had just barely started
wondering how she'd get Mieka's sister safely into and
out of the Downstreet tonight, and before that he'd speculated about the Mother Loosebuckle playlets, and—

{"Mother—oh, I want him, I want him so much!"

"He's full fair, I'll grant, with everything best about all
his bloodlines, but you know what you're in for."

"I don't care. I want him. I love him." She paced the
firelit darkness fretfully, slight and shadowy, flames
glinting off masses of long bronze-and-gold hair.

The other woman was older, worn and sour. "It's a stupid thing you've done, casting your glance on such as
him."

"Ah, but he wants me as well. Men have looked at me
since I was ten, you know they have—"

Smugly: "I made sure of it." Surprisingly beautiful
hands plucked up the rich dark folds of a gown that
spread across her knees, and a silver needle began darting in and out, in and out.

"I know, and I'm grateful. But how *he* looks at me—it's
all those looks and more besides, there in those eyes.
He's mine already, I know he is! All I have to do is
reach—" She laughed, flinging her arms wide and then

wrapping herself tight, grasping her own shoulders. Her hands were her mother's hands, slender and delicate.

"Now you're fooling yourself, girl. His kind, they never belong to anyone. All you can hope is to tame him for a while."

"Just because you couldn't keep my father doesn't mean *I* won't be able to keep *him*!"

The needle paused, a glare of firelight turning it crimson. "What you'll keep is a mannerly tongue in your head!"

"You know it's true. Your mistake was waiting too long. You left it too late. He's much younger than Father. He can't have found a bonding yet."

"You think he's untouched, do you?"

"I don't care how many girls he's bedded. If any of them meant anything, he'd be with her. But he's not. And that means he can be mine. I want him. And you're going to help me get him."

The pretense of sewing was abandoned, and the graceful fingers dug deep into velvet the purple-black of over-ripe plums. "It's a long time since I used that part of me."

"I've more of it than you. I've got it through Father. I can help. It'll be just that much stronger, don't you see? You'll have to teach me, but—with both of us doing the workings, and him so young—"

"Hear me, girl. Search inside yourself. Is he what you really want? Are you willing to go through the work to tame and bind him? Those days he was nearby, the letters he writes—that's but the start of it. When he sees you again—"

"Next week! Only next week, and I'll have him for my own—"

"Mind what I'm telling you! It will be long and difficult, and sieve your heart's blood. He'll not know what's happening to him, but he's Elfenblood, just like your father, and he'll sense *something*. Like as not, he'll fight without even knowing he's fighting. They don't conquer easy, and can rarely be broken."

"You left it too late with my father," she said again. "And you were never as beautiful as me, you know that, you've said it yourself. I'm not meaning to be cruel, but you know it's true. With him so young, and me the way I am, and your workings upon him and mine added to them—"

Her mother glanced up, and a look spread across her face, something sly and shrewd and predatory, a frightening parody of what had perhaps once been a smile winsome enough to snare a wayward, willful Elfen lover. "Dearling mine, he'll have no chance at all."

Cade struggled out of firelit darkness into the thin winter light of the stairwell, his empty stomach roiling and his head threatening to explode. Laughter echoed from the rafters overhead, rattled off the wrought iron stairs. He would know that laughter if he ever heard it for real. He was afraid he would hear it in his head, unreal, for the rest of his life.

The turn had taken him more viciously than any ever had before. His thoughts had splintered worse than usual, and the panic was something he hadn't felt this deeply in a long time. His knees hurt, his left shoulder felt bruised—he blinked, and was disgusted to find he'd fallen. A different fear assailed him then, for what if he'd been taken halfway down the stairs and tumbled the rest of the way down and broken his neck? There'd be no one to warn Mieka then, no one who knew to look for the bronze-gold hair and listen for the laughter—

Mieka? Was that whom she'd wanted so desperately?

Instinct told him *yes*.

He spent a weary while reassembling the bits of himself: reality fitting back with reality, dream joining into dream, unaccomplished pasts and possible futures tucked back into their places. At length he pushed himself to his feet and trudged down to the kitchen, needing the warmth of the big hearth and of Mistress Mirdley's grumpy affection.

Why the Elf? And why—as yet—no foreseeings that actually featured him? Two men in a run-down tavern, talking about him as if he were dead; two women in shadows, talking about him as if he were some wild thing they would catch and tame—and break. But nothing that showed Mieka as he would be—

No, as he *might* be. For there had been that one glimpse, just one, of silvering hair and lines beside those laughing eyes—

"Always, always keep it in your mind that what you see is what is possible. Not positive, and sometimes not even all that probable. You can change it. It's a dangerous and uncertain thing to attempt, but with care and wisdom, you can change it. Only you must be very, very certain that you're willing to accept the future you've made by that changing. Can you live with it? Perhaps more importantly, can you live with yourself for having dared to act as a God?"

The muffins smelled even better now that he was in the back hallway, but he felt he deserved a reward for surviving that dangerous and unsettling turn, something more bracing than tea and fresh-baked muffins. The stillroom door was slightly ajar; he shoved it open and looked around for any congenial bottles left about. Ah—there, on the worktable below the shelves of spice jars, a lovely squat brown bottle of ale, still corked.

Empty. Someone, probably the footman, had finished it off and plugged the cork back in. He shook the bottle once more to make sure, and then hurled it into the darkest corner of the stillroom.

How he was growing to love the sound of shattering glass.

"Cayden! Is that you?"

He should have pulled the door shut. Not that it would have helped much—Mistress Mirdley had hearing as sharp as if her ears were Elfen instead of Troll. "Sorry!" he called out. "I'll just sweep this up and be there in a moment!"

But she was in the doorway, short and stubby and brown as the bottle he'd just broken, arms folded, small sharp eyes flashing below a frown. "Wondering half the morning, I was, if you'd condescend to make a meal in the kitchen as usual, and not order me up the stairs with a tray. Famous tregetour now, are you? You'll have your breakfast where you always do, though, until you can afford a servant of your own to fetch and carry to your whims! Oh, leave that, I'll clean it up later. Come eat."

He did as he was told. Everyone did as Mistress Mirdley told them—even Lady Jaspiela. The Trollwife had served the Silversun family for generations, although she was forever threatening to abandon civilization entirely and find herself a nice, quiet, secluded bridge somewhere to guard for a lord whose agent came round once a year, if that, to collect the tolls. Grumbling at travelers was preferable, she avowed, to raising a pair of miscreants passing themselves off as Wizards, and half-noble ones at that.

"Don't you leave anything on this plate," she ordered as he sat before a small table bearing a large meal. "Skinny as a stick, no matter what I do. Eat!"

He grinned and stuffed half a butter-drenched muffin in his mouth before she could do it for him—which she had been known on occasion to do. He knew better than to talk with his mouth full, and so waited until he'd washed the muffin down with fragrant cinnamon tea before saying, "I'll bring my new glisker to dinner one night, shall I? Not a pingle in him, that Elf."

"It *would* be nice, having all my hard work appreciated for a change by a boy with an appetite instead of an attitude," she retorted. Quite without magic, although nearly as quick as, two more muffins appeared on his plate. "And talking of honest work, Herself left you a bit to do out front." When he looked a question at her, she added, "Snowed last night, didn't it?"

He hadn't noticed this morning—well, he hadn't noticed anything other than the broadsheet, even while standing at the window. But now he knew why his mother hadn't berated him as he'd expected: The weathering witches hadn't got round to Redpebble Square yet, and she'd want him to clear their front walk of snow. She enjoyed providing the neighbors with proof that powerful Wizardly blood resided at Number Eight. Melting snow might be the work of those with no other skills at all, a task for menials, but it was magic all the same.

Cade didn't mind doing the little things that would keep her quiet about the big things. It cost him nothing but time and a bit of magic. As he dug into scuffled eggs with cheese, and the chicken sausages that were Mistress Mirdley's specialty, he was more concerned with the fact that he honestly hadn't noticed the snow. Sagemaster Emmot had admonished him day after day to pay attention to the world around him, not just the worlds inside his own head, and not let his mind dart about like a dragon perched on a fence between a sheep pen and a pigsty, unable to decide what to chew on first. The parts of his mind that he couldn't control could get him into serious trouble. Another turn like the one on the stairs just now, and he might break something. Master Emmot had mentioned a few times that precautions might become necessary as he got older, if his foreseeings strengthened so that he had the longer sort of visions waking as well as sleeping. But in his almost five years of study, and the two years since, there'd been only a few waking turns and all of them very brief. Shock usually immobilized him for a minute or two, so he didn't fall or knock into anything. But if the seeings were going to be as lengthy as the one on the stairs this morning . . .

. . . life could become very awkward. There had to be a way to control what happened to him. Other Wizards with Fae blood who were taken the way he was must have discovered a means of keeping the visions confined to sleep, when they were safely in bed. There must be methods or techniques of control. Sagemaster Emmot hadn't mentioned any, but there must be.

Mieka's twin sister didn't risk attending the performance that night. Blye stayed home, too, her father having had one of his very worst days. The tavern keeper—and, more to the purpose, his wife—watched with contentment the swollen crowd in the Downstreet, and flinched only a little when first one row and then another of their cheaper glassware (carefully pointed out to Rafe before the show) splintered along the bar. The four empty beer pitchers didn't please them as much; the barman and one of the serving girls were picking shards from their clothing for an hour afterwards. Rafe made sure to apologize eloquently to the girl, but not so eloquently as to make Crisiant jealous if she heard of it. Bespoken to each other since the age of thirteen, Rafe and Crisiant would have good reason to like the sound of shattering glass, too, if it resulted in trimmings that piled up enough for them to get married.

On the walk back to the Threadchaser home for an after-show supper, Rafe took Cade's arm to hold him back from Jeska and Mieka.

"I didn't mean to do the pitchers," he confessed worriedly. "The glasses, yes—but it got away from me a bit, and that's never happened to me before."

"Ease up," Cade advised. "No harm done." A dollop of cold water hit him on the bridge of his nose, and he looked up. The icicle melting down from a shop sign was as clear as a perfectly made withie, sparkling in the

Elf-light from a corner streetlamp. He reached high and broke the icicle off, weighing it in his fingers. It was as cold and dead as the spent glass twigs bundled in the black velvet bag in his other hand; Mieka had released, Jeska had used, and Rafe had disciplined more magic than usual, shattering all that glassware. He'd have a long day tomorrow, respelling withies enough for the next show.

Not that he minded. Not at all. The sound was wonderfully satisfying, and the audience's reaction even more so. Better still was the jingle of coins at the bottom of the velvet bag, his share of the night's trimmings. But best of all was something the tavern owner's wife had said while reassuring him that his glass baskets would be perfectly safe upstairs in her very own chamber.

"I watched our customers tonight, until I couldn't just watch, if you see what I mean. You caught at me, especially that mad little glisker of yours, and I've seen them come and go these ten years and more. It's not the shock of the shattered glass that's the new standard to measure by. All that does is get you talked about. No, mark me well on this—it's the shock of how good you really are."

"No harm done at all," he reassured Rafe again. "You know what the mistress told me? That we're the new standard to measure by." Cade grinned. No, he didn't mind the poor spent little twigs in his bag one bit.

"So I'm to pretend I did everything on purpose, is that it?" Rafe didn't sound pleased.

"Nobody knew. Nobody even guessed."

"*I* knew."

"You fret too much." Cade nudged him with a shoulder, smiling, and they walked on.

The four of them were taking a shortcut back to the bakery, and had reached the section of Beekbacks known as Chaffer Stroll. The prostitutes who walked it were garrulously living up to the name. "Ooh, it's a lovely little Elfer-boy, innit?" and "Me, I'm for the big tall one with the beard!" and "Pretty enough that golden one is that I'd pay him!" This earned a snort from a girl across the street who yelled back, "An' that's the only way you'll ever put hands on 'im, Ferralise!"

"Damn it, Cade," Rafe suddenly growled, "you don't understand. It slipped out of my fingers. That doesn't happen to me, not ever!"

Jeschenar was feeling either very rich tonight or very happy with his performance, because he sauntered up to Ferralise, bowed, kissed the inside of her wrist as if she were Princess Iamina herself, and pressed a coin into her palm. "A drink on me, sweet." He grinned.

"Come join me and I'll drink you down, Sun-face!"

"Another time," he told her with an expression of regret that Cade might have believed if he hadn't known Jeska to be a consummate masquer.

"Cade, I'm not joking around," Rafe insisted. "It got away from me."

"This was only the second time we've done things that way." He tossed the icicle into a snowbank left behind by lazy weathering witches who had only moved the snow from the street and walkway, not melted it as they did in better neighborhoods. "You're not used to it yet, that's all."

"'Used to it'?" Rafe grabbed his shoulder and roared, "Will you fucking listen to me? I lost control!"

Cade was so startled that he lost his hold on the spent withies. He winced at the muffled splintering as the bag hit the paving stones. Not in the dozen and more years he'd known Rafe had he ever heard him raise his voice, and certainly not like this. Jeska swung round to stare.

"Oy, Sun-face," Ferralise was saying, trying to cajole his attention back to herself. "You can bring yer friends, and fer free, like. Always exceptin' that one," she added. "Lady witness it, the face on him!"

No question whom she meant. Cade crouched to pick up the velvet bag, head bent to hide that face until he could arrange it in the contemptuous glare he used as a reply to such insults. He was quite good at it, usually; he'd had enough practice. It was all in the attitude, a thing his mother had inadvertently taught him. But before he could rise to his full six-foot-two with sneer intact, he heard Mieka laugh.

"Oh, darlin'!" the Elf exclaimed. "First off, it's not the face on him that's his most impressive attribute, it's what's about three feet lower down." He approached the trull, who topped him by a good handspan and outweighed him by at least twenty pounds. "Second," he went on in a sweetly confiding tone, "the way we work is, all of us or none of us." He tapped her lightly on the chin with one finger. "Professional though you are, you'd never survive *him*, let alone us three others besides."

Ferralise treated her giggling coworkers to a snarl of outrage and raised a clenched fist. Mieka danced mockingly out of reach, stuck out his tongue at her, and leaped over a snowbank to the middle of the street.

"Last one home has to come back tomorrow night and fuck her!"

He scampered off, leaving only laughter behind him. When Rafe set out after him, Jeska close behind, Cade looked once more at the fuming and furious Ferralise. Her attention was on his crotch. Her rapt attention.

He couldn't help it; he started to laugh. "You better hope I can outrun them, *darlin'*," he told her, wedged the velvet bag under his elbow, and took off.

Long legs were an advantage. He caught up to his chortling, breathless friends by the end of the next block.

Jeska was holding his side, breathing hard. "I don't think I've seen Rafe move that fast since the time Crisiant got back from a whole month at her gran's!"

"You really *want* to be last in my front door, don't you?" Rafe shot back.

"Has to be, doesn't he?" Mieka taunted. "After all, he already paid the fair Ferralise for the privilege!"

Jeska lunged for him, and suddenly they were all running again, and laughing, and didn't stop until they piled up in the Threadchaser doorway, all four of them trying to push through at the same time. They ended up falling over each other into an ungainly sprawl on the vestibule rug, and it was a good five minutes before any of them had breath enough to get through half a sentence of explanation (carefully censored for Rafe's mother's ears) without collapsing into giggles again.

Mistress Threadchaser waited them out, fists on her hips, a vastly tolerant expression on her face. When at last they'd sorted out arms and legs and were arrayed about the sitting room grinning like idiots at each other, she picked up the bag Cade had dropped and frowned as a broken withie slid from a hole sliced in the velvet. "You'll be having some work to do tomorrow," she observed, handing him the bag.

He stared at it, stunned. He'd heard no clink of coins. Upending it onto a nearby table, he groaned as a single se'en-penny piece fell out with bits of broken glass.

"Here," Mieka said at once, digging into his pockets. "Have mine."

Mute with shock, he shook his head.

"You're the one as earns it, working as hard as you do. Besides, what'll you use to buy replacement withies? Mistress Blye can't afford to extend credit, not even to you, not until the Downstreet pays for their new glassware. *Take* it," he ordered, and dropped a double handful of coins on the table.

"A loan," Cade managed at last. "Just a loan, all right?"

Mieka smiled down at him. "Me old fa says a loan is just payment of a debt owed on a bet lost."

"Did you? Lose a bet, I mean?"

"Only with meself."

Before Cade could ask anything more, Jeska suddenly snapped, "Rafe, will you *please* sit down?"

The fettler turned sharply, and in doing so nearly knocked into his mother, returning to the sitting room with a laden tray. In the resulting juggle of plates, cups, and bowls, Cade took a long look at Rafe. Something he hadn't seen earlier, on the walk back, was all too obvious now: even in the mellow firelight, his pupils were pinpricks of black within the gray-blue irises. And above his beard his cheekbones were ruddy red, even though he'd long since caught his breath back.

Cade looked over at Mieka again. The same shrunken pupils, the same flush of color. The same restless exuberance, he realized.

But Rafe's sudden wilting into a chair, as if all the energy had bled out of him, was not repeated in the Elf. Supper was devoured, good nights were said, Rafe dragged himself up the stairs, and still Mieka was wide awake and lively as a puppy let off his lead.

Returning to Beekbacks, Jeska took the corner for home and Mieka walked along beside Cade, casting nervous sidelong glances that annoyed Cade into speaking more roughly than he'd intended to someone who'd just lent him quite a bit of money.

"I've never heard Rafe yell before. I've never seen him fidgety like that. He told me his control slipped tonight, and he didn't mean to break the pitchers. Was that you, playing the fool by glutting the magic?"

"No."

"I don't care how good the show was, don't ever put him or yourself or the audience in danger again."

"I didn't."

Cade stopped near a streetlamp and grasped Mieka's upper arm. For a long moment he looked down into those eyes—sullen, dark, and guilty—as Elf-light crackled softly within the heavy glass lamp close by.

"What was it, then?"

A shrug, but no attempt to break free of his hold. "He was tired. I fixed it."

He waited.

"He had enough whiskey to get to sleep tonight—you saw it, he could hardly keep his eyes open—"

"What does drink have to do with anything?"

"It's the offset, innit?"

"The offset to *what*?"

Another shrug of thin shoulders. "You take it when you need it, and when you don't need it, you don't take it."

"And you decided Rafe needed it, so you gave it to him. What was it?"

"Bluethorn. A bit in his tea yesterday, a bit in the ale he had before the show. He was tired, and then he wasn't."

"Bluethorn?"

"Nothing serious. He'll've slept it off by tomorrow."

"Will he need more?"

"If he does, I won't give it to him without telling him first, all right?"

"What happens when somebody starts to need it—really *need* it? That happens to some people with alcohol." Notoriously, sometimes; he flicked the thought of his father out of his head at once.

"So? You stop for a while. Ease up, Quill—it's all right."

"What other things do you know about?"

"What do you mean?"

He couldn't believe he was saying this. "Just for instance, if somebody wanted to . . . to dream."

"Waking dream or sleeping dream?" Mieka searched his eyes, then shook his head. "You Wizardly types call it going lost, Trolls call it blocked, and if somebody's got too much Gnomish blood they just call it dead, because they can't take anything at all. My folk have gathered up recipes since forever, and people like Auntie Brishen make a life's study of Thornlore."

"I thought she distilled whiskey."

"That, too. There's some things as make a Goblin sick for a week, and some that turn a Wizard wicked crazy until it wears off, and what dragon tears do to an Elf isn't anything you want to know. A lot depends on how much of what blood you've got in you. The Human in me lets me drink—something me old fa can't do, by the way, without he goes all grinagog and silly with it, and after that he's snarly for three days. The Elf and the Wizard and the Piksey are too strong in him, y'see. You're a bit of almost everything, so you can probably take anything you fancy." He paused, placing a hand over Cade's where it rested on his arm. "What're you hiding from, Quill, that you want to go lost?"

"Nothing." He was lying, of course, and Mieka knew it. "I just—if it's safe, I'd—I mean, I think it'd be interesting, y'know—to find out."

"Blockweed for a beginner like you, I think. Tomorrow night after the show?"

Cade nodded. They had a few days off before next week's three-night booking at the Downstreet. He'd use the time to rest, respell old withies and work new ones to replace those broken tonight—and see what sort of dreams blockweed could provide. What foreseeings he could go lost in. He should have been appalled by the whole notion. But he wasn't.

"How can you be your age, and live in Gallytown all your life, and not know about any of this?"

"From the time I was thirteen until I was almost eighteen, I lived—elsewhere," he finished awkwardly, not yet ready to admit certain things to someone he'd known less than a week.

"You'll tell me someday," Mieka said softly. "Just like

you'll tell me what happened last night, when Blye wanted to know if you'd come back. You can trust me, you know. I promise I won't disappoint you, Quill, or hurt you, or laugh at you."

He wondered if that was true. He wanted it to be true.

"We were good tonight," Mieka offered suddenly, kicking at a pile of snow. "We've some rough edges yet, but those will polish down. Another month, I think, and we'll be sharp as the shoulders on the King's Guard. There'll be none to touch us, Quill, none at all."

"The new standard," he heard himself say. "The standard everyone else is measured against. The touchstone."

Mieka caught his breath, a smile beginning on his face. "Is that what you want to call us, then?"

Startled, he could only stare down at those eyes. They were green and brown and gold, shining with barely repressed excitement.

"More than a bit nervy, that," the boy went on teasingly. "Setting ourselves up as the mark for everyone else to beat! Touchstones, all of us—"

"No." Gruffly, his voice a rasp he hardly recognized, he said, "What you told that trull tonight—about all of us or none? We're a knot of four ropes. Everyone else calls themselves a plural—Shadowshapers, Wishcallers, Shorelines—they're not *together,* do you see what I mean? There's no unity. They're still separate parts, even when they're performing. It's why Vered and Rauel could even *consider* doing a show with a different glisker—"

"I didn't suit them, I told you that. It was the worst possible fit—"

"I know. It's us three you fit with. But we're not a plural. We're separate people, but when we work together we make a whole, a single thing. Touchstone. Just that. Not a collection of things but one single thing, all of us together."

Mieka watched his eyes for a long time before saying,

"All of us together. I've never before belonged to anything worth belonging to."

It was only as he trudged wearily up the five flights to his room that he remembered the word's other definition. A touchstone wasn't just the metaphorical standard by which something was judged. It was a real thing that existed in the real world: the stone that was the test of truth.

Six

ONCE RAFCADION SLEPT off the bluethorn, and Cade figured he wouldn't be *too* dangerous when he got angry, he mentioned—in private—what Mieka had done.

Rafe didn't get angry.

"Right little cogger, innit he?" the fettler drawled. "Does he plan on doing it again?"

"Not without asking first."

Cade scrutinized his friend, puzzled by his attitude. They were seated in Mistress Threadchaser's kitchen, sampling various tarts judged not quite perfect enough to be offered for sale in the bakery shop. The crusts were slightly too brown, or the filling had settled slightly uneven, or something else was slightly amiss that Cade had never been able to see and didn't care about as long as it resulted in sinking his fork into the best pastries in Gallantrybanks. Having had his fill of pear-walnut, he dug into custard flavored with some kind of citrus, looking a question at Rafe, who grinned and shook his head.

"You'll be wondering why I'm not swearing a holy vow to rip his lungs out. I would, except for this. What he told me about the ceiling, it made all the difference. If

I hadn't known, the magic really would have got out of my hands and there'd be more than glassware broken."

"So the bluethorn he gave you that made you almost lose control is canceled out by the information he gave you that meant you didn't lose control?"

"One can always count on a wordsmith for a fine, concise summary," Rafe observed. "Whatever would we do without you to explain us to ourselves whether we want you to or not?"

"Let's stuff a gag in his mouth and find out."

Crisiant Bramblecotte let the door to the bakery swing shut behind her, and Rafe leaped up to take the heavy stack of trays from her hands. As he did so, he leaned down for a kiss. She was tall, sharp of feature and sharper of tongue, her perfect creamy complexion emphasized by thick black curls, straight black eyebrows, and long black eyelashes that proclaimed Dark Elf just as surely as her stature spoke of Wizard. Cade had known Crisiant as long as Rafe had. The local littleschool for Wizardly children shared a playground and some generalized classes (arithmetic, history, reading) with a school for those lacking magic, and he remembered the precise moment he'd turned to throw a ball to his friend and found Rafe staring slack-jawed at the laughing girl running towards the nearby swing sets. To hear Rafe tell it in afteryears, one glance from those amber-brown eyes had been enough to render him helpless for the rest of his life. Crisiant always retorted that having a ball knock him in the head half a second later might have had something to do with it. She tolerated but had never much liked Cade, for reasons he understood well enough: the life of traveling players, agreed upon when the two boys were barely fifteen, would take Rafe from her almost half of every year. They had never spoken about it, but Cade knew. He also knew Crisiant had never and would never ask Rafe to give up his work, his dream, this thing he was so good at, this thing he loved so much. Cade didn't mind that she resented him; better she should blame him than Rafe.

He smiled his sweetest and said, "One of what you just gave him would shut me up just fine, y'know."

She snorted. "Keep on with the hallucinations, Cade, and they'll chuck you into Culch Minster. Rafe, your mother says your da won't be back for another se'ennight. I'll stay to help her in the shop, shall I?"

Rafe laughed a singularly suggestive laugh and kissed her again, for staying to help in the shop meant staying overnight upstairs, a convenient floor down from Rafe's bedchamber. Cade hid his face behind his teacup, but not because he didn't want to watch them kissing. *Hallucinations*—Gods, if she only knew.

He'd had another turn this morning, fortunately a very brief one and while he was sitting on his bed, but the abrupt vision had lingered to taunt him all day. The girl again, the one with bronze-gold hair and beautiful hands, seated before a hearthfire, sewing just as her mother had been doing in the first foreseeing. He stood behind her, trying to get a look over her shoulder at the work in her lap. He knew it wasn't a skirt or a bodice she worked on, but something else, something she was be-spelling, because although he still couldn't catch a glimpse of her face, he could again hear her voice. She was murmuring, almost crooning a song, to the soft dark fabric in her hands, as if it were a living thing to be coaxed and cajoled and soothed. He recognized none of the words. That scared him.

Still, what was he supposed to do? Take Mieka aside and warn him? *"Listen, one day you'll meet a girl, probably the most beautiful girl you've ever seen in your life. But be careful. She and her mother want to 'tame' you. I heard them say it. They want to trap you and own you. So if you see a girl like that, run like all hells in the op-*

posite direction." Yes, it would be dead easy to present it to him just that way. Simple as peeling a turtle.

"Time you two were going, I think," Crisiant said once Rafe allowed her the use of her lips again. "You'll be coming back here as usual for some supper? Your mother's experimenting with that new spice Lord Piercehand ships home from—" She paused as if searching for the name, then shrugged. "—from wherever it is. I can't keep up with all these faraway findings."

"I'm glad I'm not in school anymore," Cade observed, "and having to learn them. Every ship as docks nowadays, a week later there's a broadsheet announcing five more new places with names nobody can pronounce."

"You keep up with it all, though, don't you?" Crisiant asked, frowning.

"I like the imagings," he admitted. "And Dery likes the maps."

"But how much of those imagings can be believed?"

He shrugged. It was a strange art, that of the imager. It wasn't like the magic of a painter or sculptor, ancient skills with hundreds of practitioners ranging from the brilliant to the hopelessly inept. There'd been a boy at Sagemaster Emmot's academy who'd had the knack for it, and if all the students there had been odd, Arley Breakbriar had been downright weird. His big blue eyes would go all hazy and dreamy as he stared at whatever had caught his attention, while his fingers twitched over a single withie for many long minutes. Finally he'd wake up again, and shake himself, and smile a shy, rueful smile. Later on he'd release the magic, and on paper or parchment, or sometimes the walls of his chamber, there would appear an exact rendering of whatever he'd seen. Just how the images went from his eyes to his head to his fingers to the withie to a finished picture was something Cade didn't understand and never would—he'd tried it a few times, under Arley's stammering guidance, and whereas he might have thought it similar to the process whereby he imbued a glass twig with magic for the stage, he'd never managed to transfer an image onto paper. It took a glisker to render Cade's magic.

The painters and the sculptors, they could guide and modify their visions—just as Cade could do. But an imager was limited to reproducing precisely what he saw. The technique had been developed over the last fifty years or so, and its practitioners were rare, and especially coveted on voyages across the Ocean Sea. The last Cade had heard, Arley had signed on for just such a journey. One reason he kept track of the broadsheets was in hopes of seeing his friend's name. But he hadn't, not yet.

"Anyway," Crisiant was saying, "Jeska has a good appetite for new things, and your mother would like his opinion."

Rafe had been listening to this with an indulgent twinkle. "Why don't you just say it?" he teased. "No need to excuse it with a new recipe." When she smacked him a good one on the arm, he laughed and told Cade, "She wants to meet the Elf. See if he's really as mad as I've made him out to be."

"I'm sure the description didn't do him justice," Cade said. "P'rhaps some night next week you and Blye can come to a show? Mieka's sister wants a look at what we're doing, as well. You could all sneak in together. You know how good Blye is at dressing up like a boy."

Crisiant shrugged. "I'll sit in on a rehearsal, if that suits. I waited too long to grow a figure to want to hide it."

"And it's a lovely one grew onto your scrawny bones," Rafe assured her with a grin. "See you later tonight, sweeting."

"Unless," Cade remarked with entirely specious innocence, "you *were* the last one through the door yesternight, in which case—"

"Your servant, lady," Rafe told Crisiant, kissed her

one last time, and hauled Cade out into the alley with flakes of pastry still on his chin.

They met up with the other half of Touchstone on Beekbacks, and didn't take the shortcut down the Stroll. Mieka teased Jeska about the crushing disappointment he was dealing the luscious Ferralise, until the masquer finally threatened to shove a withie up his nose. Cade exchanged grins with the Elf, and as Rafe and Jeska walked ahead, hung back a bit.

"He's not angry—about the bluethorn, I mean. Just don't ever try anything like that again."

"Promise. Did you decide about the blockweed?" Not waiting for an answer, he went on, "Me, I've just a little bit of a blue thornprick going tonight. You can try some if you like. I've extra."

Cade shrugged and shook his head. He wasn't scared, exactly; more like he wanted to be in private when he went lost for the first time. To lose himself someplace where the ugly or frightening dreams couldn't get at him . . . to lose awareness of the rest of the world for a while and dream as he pleased . . .

There was a capacity crowd at the Downstreet. Word had spread. Jeska responded as all masquers did to the audience's excitement, and was even better than usual. All three of them were. Jeska's nuanced performance, Mieka's wild energy, Rafe's stern and subtle control— but as Cade watched from stage right, he noted something apprehensive in the fettler's eyes. The control was *too* rigorous. Rafe was being cautious—which meant that what the people had come to see tonight wasn't going to happen.

So Cade did it himself. The other three actually flinched as glassware shattered along the bar. It was an interesting little exercise, Cade thought, unleashing just enough power to break a full pitcher of beer held aloft by a startled and horrified barmaid. To choose a target, to focus, to direct the magic as narrowly and precisely as he could, like a flying needle—this took skill, and he was delighted by the results. The drenched barmaid was the one who had sneered at him the other night after the show, and tried to serve him blashed whiskey.

Then he heard the splintering of glass onstage. Cade swung about and saw Mieka poised atop the glisker's bench, throwing spent withies into the air and deliberately bursting them as they fell. Tiny shards of glass rained down, just missing the infuriated Jeska. The audience gasped, cheered, shouted encouragement. He took a bow, then another, and tossed an intact glass twig into the crowd for a souvenir.

"It was only the flawed ones," he protested half an hour later as he and Cade and Rafe made their way back to the bakery. "Had to replace them anyway, right?" Laughter rang out and he danced a few steps down the icy cobblestones. "Why should Rafe and you have all the fun?"

The rage was as sudden as it was frightening. And it wasn't in his power to fight it off. Without conscious thought, Cade reached out and grabbed him by the front of his tunic. One look into those huge eyes told him he'd never be able to say this to Mieka's face; he spun him round and took him by the scruff of the neck and pushed him against a lamppost. "Shut up! Just shut the fuck up!"

Cheek to cold metal, tremors running through him, Mieka whimpered softly but stayed still, making no move to defend himself or to escape.

"I'd ask where you went to school, turning out this ignorant," Cade hissed, "but it's bloody obvious you never went to any school at all—and even if you did, you never paid attention. But you'll pay attention now, and remember every word. Those lovely glass sticks you throw about are strictly controlled by the law. Wizards aren't allowed to make them. Glasscrafters who do are inspected." As he felt muscles tense along Mieka's back, he shook him. "Did the one you threw to the audience have a hallmark? Did it? Or maybe there was magic still lingering inside—did you think of that? Did you? That's why Jeska stayed behind tonight. If we're lucky, he'll find whoever caught the one you threw and get it back. But whatever he has to pay for it, you'll pay him back double." Another flinch of protest; Cade pushed him harder against the post. "Be glad I don't make it triple."

Rafe caught his eye, frowning slightly. "Cade—"

"You shut up, too! This stupid little cullion needs lessoning." Leaning even closer, so that his lips were a breath away from the tip of one pointed ear, he whispered, "Do you know how withies were used in the war? Shall I educate you? Wizards on both sides stuffed magic into them, just the way I work them. Only what *they* put in was cursing magic that killed and maimed. Some were naught but dazzle-spells—but they could blind. Some, on the skin, were like slow acid. In the lungs—if you took a breath when one exploded nearby, you were dead if you were lucky. If not . . . Blye's father could tell you all about it."

Mieka whimpered again. "Cade—please—"

"Wizard glasscrafting is forbidden. Did you think it was just the Guild protecting its own? It's especially forbidden to me. Do you know what I had to swear before I could so much as hold a withie in my hands? Of course you don't. You're a rude little fuckwit who thinks he's the Gods' gift to the glisker's bench. My grandmother devised some of those spells. Her personal favorite, so I'm told, was a delightful variation on the one that lets people feel the warmth of the sun across their faces. Lady Kiritin ignited their skin and burned them alive."

The Elf-light in the lamp over their heads flared as he reacted. Cade smiled grimly as Mieka's whole body winced, and saw the boy's hands grip the post for support. There was a small, frightened word that sounded like *I*. Cade ignored it.

"You know what'll happen to me if I put a foot wrong? First they'll cut off my thumbs. Then they'll take as much of my magic as they can reach and lock it up inside my head during the five or ten years I'll spend in Culch Minster with the rest of the Kingdom's garbage."

"Enough, Cayden," Rafe murmured.

"You'll escape punishment for knowing me—you're only an Elf, you can use withies but not bespell them. And you Elfenkind, you stayed out of the war, didn't you? Hidden, nice and safe inside your ancestral forest hovels—"

"Cade!" Rafe gripped his arm. Cade shook him off.

"None of *you* ended up in prison after a battle, did you? They probably wouldn't do anything to Jeska, either. But Rafe, he's almost as much Wizard as I am, and he works with me, and they'd take him, too. So the next time you have an impulse to throw a pretty glass twig in the air and shatter it on its way down, ask yourself something, won't you? Ask yourself if you trust Lady Kiritin's grandson."

"Enough," Rafe said again.

Cade flung Mieka away from him. The boy stumbled, caught his balance, slipped on the ice, landed on his backside in a snowbank. Rafe held out a hand to pull him up, but he ignored it and sat there, staring up at Cade. There was a red welt on one side of his face where warm skin had been burned by icy metal, running diagonally from his temple to the corner of his mouth. But the fear that had shuddered in his body was nowhere visible in those eyes, and when he spoke his voice was steady and clear.

"I don't care who she was. It doesn't matter. You could never do anything wicked. It's not in you to be cruel."

Cade's turn to stare. Good Gods, hadn't he just proved the exact opposite?

"Cade? Cayden!"

He blinked, felt frantic hands touching his face.

"What it is, Quill? What's wrong?"

He was holding Mieka by the front of his tunic, fingers bunched in thick blue wool.

"Let go now, Cade." Rafe's voice, deep and calm. Rafe knew. Rafe understood.

Cade unclenched his fingers and watched them tremble. "What did I say?"

"Nothing." Rafe was reassuring, his strong arm around Cade's ribs keeping him upright. "It's fine. Nothing happened."

"Yes it did," Mieka whispered. "You both know what just happened. Why won't anyone tell me?"

Rafe growled a warning, and drew Cade gently over to a bench. But he let go too soon, and Cade stumbled against the metal pole. He squinted at the sign it supported, was informed that this was the queue for Central Gallantrybanks Coach Line Three, Law Courts and Adjudicators Chambers.

"Rafe—"

"Not now, Mieka. Leave him be."

"But—"

"Shut it!"

Cade heard them arguing but couldn't much care. Sliding onto the bench, he mused for an unfocused moment on how much simpler his life would have been had he taken his great-grandmother's advice and become a clerk in a law partnership. His only worry in that sort of life would be whether or not he'd be in time to catch Coach Line Three, Law Courts and Adjudicators Chambers . . . of course, Great-Granny Watersmith had been quite, quite mad . . . took dozens of teacups outside to gather up rain and poured the water into a washtub and complained when a new gown didn't show up . . . he did have rather unusual forebears, no denying it . . . his father always said Uncle Dennet had been damaged in the war, but perhaps it had been an inheritance from their grandmother . . . had Great-Granny foreseen things, too, and had it worn away at her sanity until her mind splintered like glass withies high in the air tonight on-stage . . . or had he dreamed that, too?

He wrapped his half-frozen fingers around the sign pole. Behind his eyes was an image of Mieka's hands—unusual hands, the ring fingers and little fingers nearly the same length—clenched around the lamppost. There had been fear in those hands, and in his voice. What was it he'd tried to say? Cade heard it again, over and over, finally hearing it for what it was.

Not *I. Light.*

And now it was another voice he heard in memory, cold, dispassionate, contemptuous as were all Wizards who had done battle when they talked of Elves who had not.

"The story is that Elves contributed willingly to the safety and convenience of Gallantrybanks and other important towns. Light glows up in the streetlamps whenever the city grows dark—whether it be nightfall, rain, fog, or snow—it happens so predictably, in fact, that it seems almost instinctive. That's because it is instinctive.

"Our King's predecessor punished the Wizards who had fought for the Archduke. But he punished the Elves as well for shirking their duty to him, for not fighting at all. Every adult Elf in Gallantrybanks was placed, one by one, into a lightless chamber. Elves are terrified of the dark. In their fear they instinctively conjure Elf-light. This light was collected by Wizards, again plunging the Elf into darkness, which created more light, and so on until the Elf was exhausted. Then the next one was brought in, and the process repeated.

"Ever since, when it begins to grow dark, the Elf-light

awakens because there lingers within each glass lamp a portion of an Elf's fear. With sunrise or the passing of a fog or storm, the Elf-light fades with that fear.

"An interesting corollary is that particularly sensitive individuals can on occasion sense the fear if they walk too close to a streetlamp. These persons are not always obviously Elfenblooded, and might not be instinctively afraid of the dark. But it's one of many possible clues to a disputed or denied ancestry, this ability to experience the terror lingering in an Elf-lit lamp."

Cade turned as someone called his name from up the street. Jeska, running as quickly as he dared on slick cobbles, waving a spent, dead, but still dangerous length of glass in his hand. "Cade! Got it!"

"Beholden, Jeska." He tried not to notice his masquer's confusion at the little scene presented to him: one angrily bewildered glisker, one adamantly stern fettler, and one absolutely exhausted tregetour, not one of whom would look at any of the others. Pushing himself to his feet, Cade held out a hand for the withie. "What did it cost you?"

"A kiss." Jeska was as blue-and-golden beautiful as an Angel in a chapel window, but at times he could produce the wickedest grin this side of the entry to any hell one cared to contemplate. "The man who caught it, he's trying to court the elder daughter. She and her sister hide on the stairs, y'know, to watch us. Gave it to her, didn't he, with bows and flourishes, I'd imagine. But we struck a bargain, she and I—while her mother and her suitor weren't looking, of course!"

"Of course." Yes, Jeska always found a way. Bless him. He experienced a moment of wickedness himself at the thought that he ought to carry through his threat, and make the Elf pay twice—no, he'd *seen* that, not *said* it—hadn't he?

"Time to get home, mate," Rafe said, and slung a

companionable arm around Cade's shoulders. "I'll see him to Redpebble, Jeska, don't worry."

The dismissal was conclusive. Jeska wished them a good morrow and jogged off home; Mieka had the sense to do likewise, though he was still scowling.

It seemed a long while later that Cade blinked in the sudden light of an opening doorway. Mistress Mirdley's startled exclamation made him wonder vaguely just how awful he must look. She settled him before the kitchen hearth, draped a blanket across his shoulders, and put a mug of hot tea into his hands.

"Turn took him, did it?"

He closed his eyes and sipped at the tea, and let them discuss him as if he weren't there.

"Right out in the street. That's the second time in the last few days. The ones someone witnessed, anyway."

How had Rafe known? Had he talked to Blye?

Mistress Mirdley clucked her tongue. "It's changes that set him off sometimes. Things becoming different than they were. That, and fretting himself instead of sleeping. The shows go well, don't they?"

"Better than we ever were before—and that's a difference. Another is the venue. It's not just a tavern, it's got an honest stage. And then there's the Elf."

"Hasn't brought him round here yet. What does Blye think of him?"

"I'm not sure."

"Hmph. I'll ask tomorrow. And I'll make sure he rests, will he or won't he!"

"We've four days until the next booking—the Downstreet again. He haggled it out with the owner tonight after the show. I think he's angling for more pay as well as the trimmings."

"And Blye's contract," Cade said, not opening his eyes.

"Master Silversun speaks!" exclaimed Mistress Mirdley. "Finish that and haul yourself up to bed, child. And you, Rafe, mind how you go and give my good wishes to your mother."

The Trollwife chivvied him up the wrought iron stairs all the way to the fifth floor. She turned back his bed, plumped his pillows, and would have yanked his tunic and shirt off over his head as if he were still a little boy if he hadn't roused himself enough to assure her he was perfectly fine and really did remember how to undress himself. At last she closed the door and he was alone.

When the small, square leather wallet fell out of his tunic pocket, he simply stared at it where it lay on the floor. In the light of a single candle—he was too weary to work any magic—there glinted at one corner of the green leather the stamped image of a thistle. The gilt had mostly worn off it, and also from the irregular pattern tooled around the edges. Cade held it close to the candle and squinted, thinking that a clumsy hand had spoiled the design of one shape repeated over and over. But it proved to be three different images: raindrop, seed, flame. Water, Earth, Fire. Though he wasn't sure exactly which Elfen lines Mieka could claim—had he said something about Greenseed, Staindrop, and Stormchill in Mistress Threadchaser's kitchen?—the symbolism was obvious enough.

When he saw what lay within the wallet, Cade knew the leather was wyvern hide, the kind favored by Elves in their spellcasting, this one imbued with a cushioning bind to protect fragile items. It was a magic he wished he knew, in fact, to keep safe his glass baskets and withies.

This wallet kept safe three things: a little paper twist of crushed greenish powder, a note giving directions on preparation for use, and a single delicate glass thorn about an inch long, its sharp tip sealed with a bit of green wax.

Mieka's handwriting was rounded and childish. He couldn't spell. The instructions were straightforward, and so was the sentence at the end of the note.

Don't worry about going too lost, Quill, I'll always come find you.

Seven

"WHAT IN THE world are those?" Blye snatched the new gloves from his hands, darting around her workbench, laughing as she waved them at him. "Cheveril, are they? Mmm—*finest* kid leather, softer than soft ever could be. And such an elegant shade of gray—almost dark enough to be mistook for black, innit?"

"Blye, give 'em back!"

"I *was* right, the Elf's got you peacocking! Five weeks you've known him, and see what he's accomplished! What's next, lace ruffles at your throat?"

"What's next is my fingers laced around *your* throat if you don't give those back!" But Cade was laughing, too, and when she finally gave a low, flourishing bow and presented him with the gloves, he bowed in return. "These aren't all I brought to show you, though."

Her nimble fingers returned to the task of stacking a series of nesting bowls, five to a set, green-yellow-blue-red-orange. They were her own design, he knew, but executed by her father all this spring for they must bear his hallmark to be legally sold at prevailing prices. The Guild's rule was such that anything hollow and hallmarked must be fashioned by a registered Master. Apprentices and assistants could make the handles of various items, the glass coils of stemmed and footed goblets or vases, or diverse implements, but the hollow part of any article had to be the

Master's work if it was presented for public sale. This of course included withies. Blye's father had joked once that essentially the Guild gave him the authority to fashion emptiness, to make a nothingness for other people to fill.

"Don't pretend," Cade scolded as Blye elaborately ignored him. "You're not interested in getting those ready to be shipped. You want to know about my other surprise."

"Hmm?" She glanced up as if distracted from concentration on her work, and pushed silvery blond hair out of her eyes. "Oh, are you still here?"

"Leave over," he advised, "you're no good at it. This is what I really came to show you."

He'd shown it to Rafe first, when he arrived early to rehearse in Redpebble Square's undercroft. Then Jeska arrived, and finally Mieka. It was a good thing Lady Jaspiela was out for the afternoon paying calls, or she would surely have collapsed in shock at the whoop that echoed from the kitchen all the way upstairs to where Derien was supposed to be doing his lessons. Then again, considering that it was Mieka doing the yelling, she might simply have smiled.

"So what is it?" Blye demanded, abandoning the glass bowls and the pretense that she wasn't interested. "Something better than those gorgeous gloves?"

Cade handed over the invitation with its many ribbons and heavy wax seals. Blye stared at it, almost as if she were afraid to touch it in case it might not be real, then grabbed.

"'The Office of the Lord High Master of the King's Revelries,'" she read out, "'desiring that the players terming themselves Touchstone present themselves to perform for His Gracious Majesty's pleasure certain of their several works on a day to be determined at the Castle of Seekhaven, do hereby request said Touchstone to so attend upon His Gracious Majesty.'" She whistled between her teeth. "Do they really talk like that at Court?"

"Don't know," he grinned. "Don't care. It's Trials, Blye, even though they never call it that."

"Trials!" She seemed stunned. "Which of your 'several works' will you be doing, then?"

"None of them."

"But it says—"

"That's just a polite fiction. All Trials are done with one of the Thirteen. Lady and Lord, I hope we get a good one!"

"I think you all deserve a present," she decided, "to celebrate."

Looking wide-eyed around the room: "Haven't you enough to do? The Downstreet—"

Blye laughed. "That's *work*. This will be *fun*." Then she chewed her lip for a moment, a frown knitting her brows. "Cade . . . have you thought about it? I mean, it was going to come up sooner or later, now you're leaving inns and taverns behind for real theaters."

"Thought about what?"

"Well . . . what're you going to break now?"

He'd had no answer for her that day, and two weeks later, when it was almost time to leave for Seekhaven Castle, he still hadn't come up with anything. Neither had anyone else.

Touchstone's original contract had stipulated only three nights at the Downstreet. But the day after that third show, instead of three sentences filling an empty spot in a local broadsheet, the theater column of the *Blazon* gave them three words in the "recommended" section: *Touchstone at Downstreet*.

On that memorable afternoon, Jeska had arrived breathless at the Criddow Close door to the Silversun home with news that couldn't wait. Walking along Beekbacks, he'd overheard a cluster of young men arguing about Touchstone as they waited for the public coach. One of them had seen the Shadowshapers at the Kiral

Kellari, and said Touchstone was just as good. Another said it was shocking, a group so wild as to actually shatter glass—but he couldn't wait to get to the Downstreet the next time Touchstone played.

Hearing this with satisfaction, Cayden winked at Mistress Mirdley. "Bring out the best cups, then, won't you?"

"And the priciest tea," she agreed, chuckling with a sound like a rock wheel grinding across cobblestones.

Confronted with Jeska's bewilderment, Cade explained, "He's here. The Downstreet's owner. We're about to start negotiating." He laughed at the grin that spread across the golden face. "He's in there right now, Jeska, melting snow onto my mother's best rug!"

As Lady Jaspiela came in from making calls that wintry evening, the unexpected guest was on his way out, having conceded rather more than he'd hoped but having gained what he needed: Touchstone. The tavern keeper and the titled lady stared at each other in the vestibule, and after resisting for a moment the haughty arch of her brows, he helped her off with her cloak. She gave him a curt nod, swept into the drawing room, and stopped with a tiny, inelegant blurt of surprise at the scene greeting her.

Her elder son, his childhood friend, that blond boy whose name she never bothered to remember, an Elf, the Trollwife, and the glasscrafter's graceless daughter were all taking tea together from her finest porcelain cups. When her younger son danced out from behind a chair, waving what looked like a pair of child-sized withies, her hand went to her throat as if to strangle a shriek of outrage.

Cade had been watching for all of it. He knew exactly what was going through her mind. He smiled at her, lifting his cup in salute. "Mother! You're just in time to help us celebrate!"

The smugness of his voice snapped Mieka's head

around from teaching Derien how to juggle. In the abrupt silence, those eyes went from Cade to Lady Jaspiela and back again. A look of fiendish cunning crossed his features, swiftly replaced by his most ravishing smile.

"Your Ladyship! I am permitted the privilege at last!" There was a bow (with wrist flourishes), then an accusing glare over his shoulder. "Manners, Cayden!" The switch back to warm admiration was as dizzying as if he'd used the magic of a withie to spell his own face. "Though to see Your Ladyship, I'd thought he'd be introducing me to a sister or cousin. Your most humble servant, Lady!"

It lacked only another bow and appreciative smile to complete the conquest. The real privilege, as Rafe later told Crisiant, was the opportunity to watch it happen.

It wasn't so much what Mieka had said that afternoon— the compliments were only slightly above the standard obsequious nonsense expected at Court—as the way he used those eyes when he said it. In the process of bespelling Lady Jaspiela into submission without use of magic, Mieka deftly persuaded her to repair to her own chambers where their noise and commotion could not disturb her after what must have been a long day—and just between us, Lady (in a low, confiding voice), is Princess Iamina's husband really as free with his hands around lovely women as rumor has it? This with a quick glance down her figure, giving the impression that he just couldn't help himself and undoubtedly the Princess's husband couldn't, either. Cade felt his face ache with the effort of compressing a smirk as he watched a second implication sink in: that he believed her to be of a rank to associate with Princess Iamina and Lord Tawnymoor, and, further, to know their circle intimately enough to share such choice gossip.

He found Dery's reaction almost as entertaining as their mother's helpless surrender. The boy positively gawked, mouth hanging open and brown eyes as wide as the porcelain teacups. Mistress Mirdley had turned her back on the scene, prodding an iron poker into the fire with rather more vehemence than strictly required, her shoulders shaking suspiciously. Rafe sat back to enjoy himself; Blye hid her grin behind her cup; Jeska watched so intently that Cade was in no doubt he was taking mental notes on the performance.

At length, Mieka returned from escorting Lady Jaspiela to the staircase and plopped down on a cushioned footstool. "If there's anything stronger than tea in this house," he whined, "now would be a perfectly splendid time to drink it!"

"How did you *do* that?" Dery asked, still awestruck.

"Do what?"

Cade snickered at the exaggerated innocence. "Send Her Ladyship up to her room without any supper."

Mieka looked shocked, then spread his hands in an all-encompassing shrug. "The trick," he explained to Dery, "is to deduce what people want to be talked into doing anyway, and then do all the talking that talks them into it so that they don't have to talk at all." He tilted his head at Cade. "Just what you did this afternoon, whether you know it or not. He *wants* us to play at the Downstreet. He *wants* to be able to boast that we're breaking so much glassware with the power of our performances that he had to secure a whole new contract to resupply the bar." He winked at Blye. "Can't have patrons slurping out of an open barrel in the middle of the room, can we?"

"Of course not," she replied gravely, dark eyes dancing, and Cade ventured to guess that she was growing to like the Elf. Gulping down the last of her tea, she rose and said, "I should be getting back to Da now. Beholden, Mistress Mirdley—and you, Mieka, for a show I didn't have to sneak in to see!"

The contract Touchstone signed that afternoon was

for five weeks, thrice a week on sequential nights, nonexclusive, so they could travel to other towns betweentimes to perform. The contract Blye took home for her father to sign was to provide replacement glassware to be kept on the shelves behind the bar—that way no hallmark was necessary because they would never be used to serve drinks: every night Touchstone would be shattering them, and every morning they would be replaced. Cade had expected her to grump a little about compromising her skills, but she only shrugged, saying that the work didn't have to be good, just loud.

And so the weeks had hastened by. They gained more confidence in the playlets they already knew, added more to their folio, and the Downstreet was packed every time they took the stage. They had other bookings in Gallantrybanks and at least one outside the city each week, for money as well as food and beds and trimmings. There were coins in their pockets, and new clothes on their backs, and it had suited Crisiant to tell her skeptical parents that if things kept on like this, she'd be married to Rafe by Wintering.

Then the royal command arrived in late spring, cloaked as an invitation. They had two weeks to prepare for Trials, and although at every rehearsal Blye's question came up again—absent bar glassware, what were they going to break?—none of them had an answer. They merely shrugged at one another and went back to sorting the traditional, basic versions of the Thirteen Perils.

These playlets described the deeds through which the ruling royal family had first got and then held the throne. No one king had accomplished them all; the actual incidents had been spread out over several centuries, conveniently long ago. There were cataclysmic battles (with and without magic), clever solutions to diplomatic difficulties that humiliated other kings, daring rescues, tournament victories, wise judgments of law—the whole panoply of kingly endeavors. Some of them were more exciting than others—the Eighth, for instance, was the tragedy of an heir's death by treachery. But all the Thirteen were always treated with proper reverence, attributing to the royals all the virtues and making the villains utterly heinous.

Through the years the tales had been ... *embroidered* was a polite word for it. For example, a knight defeated in a tournament had somehow been transformed into a Giant; rather than an insurrection of his own seditious nobles, the king in question had done battle against demons, and so on. But even taking away all obviously overstated aspects, the list of the royal family's accomplishments was impressive.

"What must it be like," Jeska mused one afternoon during rehearsal, "to be the right-now king, or the heir, and have to sit watching while your ancestors are shown doing all these impossible things?"

They were in Mistress Bowbender's cellar—dry now that the rains had finally eased—where they could unleash more magic with less risk of damage than in Rafe's mother's sitting room. The disadvantage of the setting was the same as in the undercroft of the Silversun home: a chilly spring that had all of them in heavy tunics and coats despite the little firepocket Mieka had brought and Cade had stoked. Cade alone wasn't wearing gloves, because he was the one who had to do the writing. His new cheveril gloves were thin and supple enough, but he didn't want to spoil them with inkstains.

The horror of Trials was that they had to be conversant with every single one of the Thirteen Perils. After arriving at Seekhaven Castle, they would draw the token that indicated which they must perform, with two days to perfect their interpretation. These versions must be suitably respectful, but different enough from every other to set a group apart and earn a place on one of the three Circuits: Royal, Ducal, Winterly. Everyone started out on Winterly, which was a test of professionalism and endurance. The other two tours were scheduled for spring and summer, but Winterly was just what the name said it was. The ambitions of more than one group of players had frozen solid, never to be thawed, after a single Winterly Circuit. They either went back to playing taverns or gave up altogether.

That would not happen to Touchstone, Cade promised himself. And as they worked on each of the Thirteen, he found that collective effort actually provided him with new ideas. And he'd need them, he thought miserably, to spark some life into these tired old stories.

Jeska's speculation had caught Mieka's fancy. "Now, there's a slant," he said. "How *would* it be, all that pressure to live up to what your great-great-great-grandsir did, even if everybody knows half of it's lies—Quill, could you work that in?"

He thought about it for a moment, then began filling the margins of his notes. "He can be wondering what his grandsir or whomever would have done, and whether he can live up to it. And then he gets the chance to find out, doesn't he? At the ending I'll give him some lines about how he hopes his own descendants will live in peaceful times, where they won't have to rush about fighting Giants or dragons—"

"Doesn't every king hope to distinguish himself?" Rafe asked. "Write his name in the histories, all that? Wars and suchlike, that's how a king gets remembered."

Cade scribbled on, listening as Mieka countered, "But how much better it would be to be known as—I don't know, Bentifian the Beloved, or Pardrig Peacemaker. Someone more interested in helping people live good lives than getting them killed in wars."

"How many of the quiet kings get remembered?" Jeska pointed out. "You had to make *those* names up!"

"My favorite was always Raquian the Rapacious," Rafe said. "Remember, Cade, in school when we learned about him, and how glad we were to've missed that particular century?"

Mieka said stubbornly, "I'd think a king with any care for his country at all would *want* to have people wishing they'd known him and lived during his reign."

"Not all that exciting, though, is it?" Jeska asked. "Norbilan the Nice hasn't quite the punch of Seyen Warseeker."

Mieka gave a crow of triumphant laughter. "Ah, but who's the one who built the castle we're headed for, to *seek* a *haven* in his old age when he'd got tired of battles? None other than!"

Cade looked up from his notes in time to see Jeschenar bow his head over hands clasped in surrender. "I can work that idea in, too," Cade offered. "I can put something like it into all of them, so that no matter which one we draw, that will be our perspective. We'll make them think about something they might not have thought about before."

"You're assuming Prince Ashgar *can* think," Rafe mentioned dryly, "which is a fairly bold assumption."

Cade dipped fresh ink onto his pen. "My father has intimated on occasion that something goes on between his ears besides keeping track of how many boar he's skewered and how many women he's screwed."

"So what exactly does your father do at Court?" Mieka asked.

He didn't look up. "First Gentleman of the Bedchamber. Which is why he knows how many women there've been."

Mieka made the obvious mental jump; Cade had expected nothing less. But there was no shock or disgust in his voice as he said, and quite offhandedly, too: "You mean he's the royal pimp."

In the silence that followed, Cade couldn't help but glance over at the Elf. Neither Rafe nor Jeska would look at him now, pretending to be involved in their folios, but Mieka seemed to have been waiting for Cade's full attention. His expression was both puzzled and sad.

"Your parents don't understand the first thing about you, do they? Nor about Derien. To think that either of you would tread in those footprints."

"*That's* different," Rafe remarked. "Usually people ask why Zekien Silversun isn't richer, considering what he does for Prince Ashgar."

"Pimping doesn't pay what it used to, evidently," Cade replied. "Can we get back to work, please? I want to incorporate these ideas into all the Thirteen, so let's go through them in order."

Rehearsal broke at tea, and they all trooped upstairs. As was her habit when they weren't using her sitting room, Rafe's mother had sent along a selection of baked goods for them—and for Mistress Bowbender, who had neither the time to spare from her work as a supervising charlady to bake treats, nor money enough from that job to afford to buy them. Rafe, Cade, and Mieka always professed themselves still too full from lunching to eat much, which fooled Jeska and his mother not at all but which spared their pride.

Mieka offered to walk with Cade back to Redpebble Square, taking the new green velvet bag of withies. He had long since becast it, and the crates holding the glass baskets, with the same sort of cushioning spell used in the wallet he'd given Cade weeks ago, reasoning that they broke enough glass on purpose. The wallet had passed back and forth between them several times, even though blockweed hadn't done for Cade what Mieka had expected it to. That evening, walking towards Criddow Close, where Blye was waiting to join them for supper, Mieka took back the empty wallet and stuffed it in a pocket, shaking his head.

"I still don't understand why you want to keep on with this. You must have the oddest combination of bloodlines in Gallantrybanks, for it not to work on you. Auntie Brishen would love to find out why."

"It works fine."

"But you don't dream. That's no fun. All it does is send you to sleep."

Even though blockweed hadn't worked the way it was supposed to, Cade didn't mind. For the first time in years, he didn't have to be afraid of sleeping, because there were no dreams to haunt him when he woke up. But he couldn't explain that to Mieka. Not just yet. He didn't know why he was so reluctant to share what Rafe and Jeska already knew. Surely there wouldn't be dozens of dreaded questions—look how Mieka had reacted to learning what Zekien Silversun did at Court. If he could accept that revelation without blinking, then perhaps . . .

Slanting a sidewise glance at the Elf, he smiled. "Before it does put me to sleep, though, there's a few minutes when my imagination goes free. It's incredible. I don't have the sort of dreams most people have. Never did. But these—I've seen so much, Mieka, things I want to write up not just as playlets but as sequences to perform one after the other, all on the same night. Original things. Not reworkings or revisions of the usual stuff, but *mine*."

"Tell me one."

"Not yet." But he softened the refusal with a smile.

For a moment it seemed as if Mieka might argue, but then he shrugged. "As you please."

They walked on, the city twilight not yet deep enough to rouse Elf-light in the streetlamps. Cade thought about what he might have done, all those weeks ago, slamming Mieka up against one of the lampposts. Was it true, what that extremely odd turn had shown him? Did Mieka really feel the captured fear so acutely? He hadn't asked.

Contemplation of the incident that had never happened had provoked other questions, too. Had it been instinct working to warn him what would happen if he lost his temper? Something had prevented him from hurting Mieka, something inside him that knew what would happen if he spoke even one more word—something that had stopped him before he could get started.

But why had instinct also given him Mieka's voice telling him he could never be evil or cruel? Was it because Cade knew those things to be inside him, and wished so much that they were not? *"His mind's cold, but his heart's colder."* He didn't want to become that. He knew it was possible. Perhaps he'd been warning himself, in a way, that Mieka believed there was nothing vicious inside Cade—and was a fool for thus believing.

Don't worry about going too lost, Quill, I'll always come find you.

Perhaps that was it, he thought suddenly, pacing off the cobblestone streets beside the uncharacteristically quiet Elf. Perhaps he'd never before seen Mieka in any dreams or visions because Mieka had to be the one to find *him*.

But the thing that startled him most had been the immediacy of the vision: not weeks or months or years from the moment he was in, but the very next heartbeat. That had never happened to him before.

It had never happened to him, before Mieka had found him.

All at once a hand grasped his elbow. "You have to dream, y'know. You can't live without dreaming, Quill."

He wondered wildly if Mieka had somehow guessed.

"People like you—they have to teach everyone else how to dream."

"What? What d'you mean?"

"Don't you ever look at the faces? Eager, anxious, hoping we're going to take them someplace wonderful, somewhere other than the miserable village or district they live in. Maybe they've been told by people who've seen us that they can count on us, we'll do that for them. And by the time they leave—"

He pulled a face. "By the time they leave, they're drunk."

"Stop that! Don't you understand what you do for them? *You dream.* Whatever it is inside you that got you through your childhood—"

Cade tried to pull his arm out of Mieka's grasp. But those thin little fingers were surprisingly strong. "What do you know about that?"

"Not as much as I'd like, but I can guess quite a bit. Forgive me for saying it, but I have only to look at you to know you were bullied and mocked when you were little. Jeska told me once that on almost the first day you knew him, you asked him to teach you how to fight with your fists instead of your magic, because that'd got you in trouble. I don't know the details, but I can guess. Still, whatever happened, there's something in you that got beyond it. Or maybe you escaped by going inside yourself. A lot of people do. What's different about you is that you found things other people never find. Maybe they never went looking ruthless or desperate enough, or maybe it's just not there for them, but *you* saw things, dreamed things. Most people don't, or don't dare. Or their dreams are little ones, just wishes, really, not the big grand daring stuff that scares most people witless."

He had never heard Mieka talk so seriously for so long. "You mean I have to do it for them? Teach them how?"

A nod of the dark head. "Did you ever notice that you don't make eye contact much? I mean, we'll be walking somewhere, just taking the air or heading over to chapel or off to see whatever sights there might be in some piddly little market town, and you don't look at people. I know why. You think that if you do, you'll see how they react to your face, the reaction you always saw as a child but never got used to, and the whole thing just makes you miserable, so you don't make eye contact. You miss a lot, that way. For one thing, you miss that they don't look at you like you think they do. They see your face, yes, and nobody could ever miss that nose—but they also see from your collar to your boots that you're a success, that the world has recognized you in the only way most people understand: money. What they see is someone they envy."

"Me!"

"You."

They stopped in the middle of a block of shops closed for the night. No one was about. Elf-light was beginning to glow in defense against darkness, and Cade could just make out the pensive face, the solemn line of the mouth.

"It's daft, y'know, this notion you have that pretty people don't have problems, that they don't get hurt or lonely or scared—"

"Ah, but they suffer so much more attractively!" Cade quipped.

"Stop it!" Mieka ordered again. "Everybody has a face like yours. If it's not the face, it's education, or birth, or accent, or not bein' smart enough or good-lookin' enough—that last, that's especially with women. Haven't you ever heard somebody say it? 'Such a beauty she is, she could have any man she wanted!' "

"Or the other thing they say," he mused. " 'Such a sweet girl, pity she's so plain.' "

"Exactly! A man who marries the girl who could have any man she wanted, he wears her like a medal he won in the war." He grimaced, with nothing comical about it.

"Once she opens her mouth, it's usually another story, but—"

"That's not very kind of you," Cade chided gently.

"But so often true! I can't help it that I find girls fun but ultimately boring. Your Blye, now, she's a shining exception."

"She's not 'my' anything."

"Well, we'll talk about that another time. We're talking right now about you not seeing what it is you really do. Some of the men watching, they just take, and that's fine—they pay for an evening's entertainment, and that's a nice, tidy little transaction. There's not one of them could ever complain he didn't get his money's worth. There's some who end the evening actually *thinking* about what they've seen. Those are the most satisfying, in a way. We've got to them somehow, reached something, y'know?"

"Sometimes," Cade said, "just as Rafe is letting everything fade, I get traces of . . . I'm not sure what it is. Echoes, maybe, of what they've just seen, things that linger not just because you and Rafe and Jeska are good at what you do, but because they *want* them to linger."

"Do you ever sense the ones who are so surprised they can't hardly think at all? They've just seen something they've never seen before, and it's shook them so hard they're just staggering inside. That's gratifying, only it's a bit worrying as well, because the next time they come to a show they're going to expect the same thing, and that's just not possible." A little smile graced his lips. "You can't get drunk for the first time twice. I know—I've tried!"

"What else happens that I never notice?"

Mieka was abruptly serious again. "The ones who come out of it wanting to dream their own dreams. Whether they can, or end up sharing, those are things we'll never know. But there's a spark, and we lit it, and that's one of the best feelings of all."

"I think I understand," Cade said slowly. "It's something else I sense every so often."

"But the ones as break my heart—those are the ones who come to see *your* dreams because they used to have dreams of their own and haven't anymore. They want to remember what it was like before it all burned out."

After a few moments, Cade said, "You're telling me I shouldn't use the blockweed anymore." Which would leave him open not just to the dreams while sleeping but the frightening turns that happened while he was awake. He hadn't had a single one since that first experience with the little glass thorn.

Mieka nodded gravely. "Your dreams are too important, Quill."

Of all the things he'd ever thought or felt about his dreamings, that had never occurred to him. "Important," he echoed.

"Yes. It's—it's the people we perform for, and it's me, and Rafe, and Jeska—but mainly it's you. Like I said, you *need* to dream."

Staring down at the boy who had spoken with the insights of a man twice his age, he promised himself never to underestimate Mieka again.

Eight

NOT SURPRISINGLY, EACH time Cayden tried to settle on a final version of any of the Thirteen Perils, he came up empty. This was not a promising omen.

All else seemed to be going splendidly. They would leave on the special coach for Seekhaven in two days. Everyone was packed. The glass baskets were carefully crated. Mistress Mirdley had consulted Mistress Threadchaser and together they'd decided what their boys would be taking along by way of food (in a gigantic hamper, enough to last a month). Auntie Brishen had sent a half-barrel of whiskey with Mieka's name on it. Cade had done the preliminary work on priming the withies, but couldn't finish until he knew which of the Thirteen they would draw. Not that he had enough withies to work from; Mieka's ruthless culling of those he considered substandard had depleted the collection. Blye had promised new ones before they left, but Master Cindercliff had been worse lately and she'd been tending him while trying to run the shop and get some work done at the kiln besides. At any other time, Cade would have helped her out, but this was *Trials* coming up.

He vacillated between calm confidence and a nauseating anxiety that blockweed soothed by letting him get some sleep. But what Mieka had said nagged at him—about the importance of dreams, and of *his* dreams in particular, a concept that still stunned him. He did want the dreams, but the ones that came before dreamless sleeping, the ones he could control, not the ones that invaded his mind with visions that might or might not come true. For the purpose of seeing what he chose to see, he'd become adept at judging how much of the prepared, liquefied mixture to siphon into the little glass thorn. Still, he was so edgy these days that less and less seemed to send him collapsing onto his pillows, rousing only when Derien or Mistress Mirdley pounded on his door in the morning.

Staring at the page on his desk, where the numbers *1* through *13* were all he'd written in the hour since dinner, he was within moments of giving it all up as a bad lot and reaching for the green wyvern wallet when Derien burst into his bedchamber.

"Aren't you ready?" the boy demanded, breathless from running up all five flights of stairs. "Why aren't you ready? Get dressed! Mieka's here!"

He was indeed, and dressed to the ears—literally. Cade frankly stared at the display of honey-colored silk shirt, turquoise velvet jacket with black lace overlay on cuffs that reached nearly to his elbows, black trousers, and black boots polished to a mirror-gleam, with a little golden topaz charm dangling from the tip of his left ear. Glad that Dery had bullied him into his best, Cade stood at the bottom of the stairs, just outside the drawing room door, and watched as Mieka once again beguiled Lady Jaspiela into purring contentment.

"—isn't *true*?" he exclaimed. "My mother will be crushed!"

"Well, it's not for lack of trying," said Her Ladyship with a refined sniff. "His reputation has become such that now he'll have to look farther afield for a bride."

"I've heard whispers about princesses and grand duchesses on the Continent."

"You're well-informed!"

"With these ears, Lady, it's difficult not to listen!"

Cade heard his mother's laugh ring out—a real laugh, not the delicate tinkle she had spent a lifetime perfecting—and shook his head in amazement. The Elf was capable of anything, it seemed.

"Good, isn't he?" Derien whispered beside him. "D'you think he'd give me lessons?"

"You do all right on your own. Besides, I think it has a lot to do with those eyes."

With a resigned sigh: "I s'pose. You'll be wanting this," he added, and pressed something small and cool into Cade's palm.

It was a collar-pin, beautifully worked in silver, depicting a falcon in flight. "Where did you get this? Did you buy it? Dery, you've better things to spend your money on—"

"Better than my brother's nineteenth Namingday present?" He chortled softly. "Forgot, didn't you? Mieka told

Mistress Mirdley and me not to say anything, and not even make a special supper, so it'd all be a surprise."

"It is that," Cade admitted. He did have a habit—a deliberate habit—of forgetting his Namingday. His parents were just as glad not to have to make an expensive fuss. Mistress Mirdley customarily marked the occasion with his favorite foods or a pie, Dery usually drew a picture with his best colored pencils, and once—just once—Blye had given him a kiss. His first, as it happened. They'd been twelve. This gift from Derien and whatever Mieka planned for tonight were unprecedented. He didn't know how to react.

"Here," Dery said, taking the pin, hopping up two steps so he could reach. "You needed something new for Trials besides that gray coat Father sent from the Palace. He says it's more fashionable these days to put this in a neckband, especially the sort with ruffles—raise your chin!—but Mieka's right, you shouldn't ever try to style yourself a fribbler. Simple and elegant, and no fuss. There," he concluded, critically surveying his work. "The falcon looks like he's flying!"

"It's beautiful. Beholden, Dery," Cade managed, and gave in to his affection for the boy, and hugged him tight.

"Have a wonderful time, and come tell me all about it when you get back! I swear I won't be asleep," he added as a protest formed on Cade's lips. "And even if I am, promise to wake me up!"

"And what exactly is it that you won't be able to wait for tomorrow to hear?"

"I'm not telling! It's Mieka's surprise, just like this was mine." He touched the collar-pin. "You look good, Cade. You really do."

He rolled his eyes. "Flattery just *might* get you a waking-up when I come home."

"Oh, I'm positive you'll come tell me—you won't be able not to!"

"That special, is it?"

Dery folded his arms and tried to look stern. "I'm *not* telling!"

"That's the way! Keep to the oath!" exclaimed Mieka from behind Cade. "And you needn't try to winkle it out of *me,* either," he warned. "Tease us or taunt us, threaten us or torture us—"

"—we'll never tell!" finished Dery. "Now, hurry up, it's just struck seven!"

Adding to the astonishments, Lady Jaspiela wished them a pleasant evening as Mieka took his extravagant leave of her before tugging Cade into the vestibule. As they donned their coats, for one of the few times in his life Cade voluntarily examined himself in a mirror. Same long-jawed, beak-nosed, wide-browed, sharp-boned, undeniably plain face, but there was something different in the way he held himself, perhaps because of that touch of elegance given by the falcon pin; something different about his eyes.

Mieka bumped him with a shoulder, laughing at him in the mirror. Cade blushed at being caught staring at himself.

"Oh, you're a right eye-catcher tonight, you are, and that's a fact," the Elf murmured. He stood back a step and looked Cade over. Black trousers, pewter-gray shirt, charcoal silk tunic with dark red stitching at neck and hem—he'd taken the Elf's advice about clothes, and the smirk on Mieka's face meant that he knew it. "It's good there'll be no girls about at the place we're going, or you'd never make it home tonight at all. And you just can't disappoint the bantling, Quill, nor make him wait for tomorrow—he's been so good at keeping the secret."

"What secret?"

A grin was the only reply.

A hire-hack took them from Redpebble Square past the city mansions of middling-rich lords and very rich merchants, all the way to Amberwall Closure. This was another of the tincted districts of houses, long forsaken as a residential area and instead occupied by various businesses. The first two floors of each building were taken up by stores, snack shops where office clerks went for lunching, three rival tearooms, and, on the second floor of what had once been the home of the long-forgotten nobleman whose quarries all that dark gold rock had come from, a tavern.

The streetlamps were blazing bright when their hack stopped at the edge of the square. There were too many other vehicles, from pony carts to grand carriages, all woven together in an intricate knot, to permit a closer approach. But Cade suddenly knew where they were going, and sat back against the worn leather seat, stunned. Mieka paid the driver, hopped to the cobbles, and glared his impatience. Cade shook himself out of his shock and climbed down.

"Kiral Kellari?" Cade breathed. "Are you joking?"

"Happy Namingday, Quill!"

They started across the square, dodging others intent on hurrying to the tavern made famous in the last two years by the quality of its stage shows, and by one group of players in particular. Cade, taller by half a head than most of the throng, glimpsed the scrum at the entrance and frowned in dismay. "We'll never get in, never."

Mieka grabbed his elbow and pulled him away from the untidy horde, saying, "Haven't you learned *yet?*"

Halfway down the block was perhaps the narrowest ginnel Cade had ever seen, scarcely wide enough for a drainage trench to the gutter. Gallantrybanks was webbed with these constricted little passages between buildings, shortcuts that allowed foot traffic from one street to another. Sometimes secondary passages would branch from a ginnel—there were several of them in Redpebble Square, a lovely maze to play in—leading to very private doors into houses or shops, or all the way through a building to the next alley. Unlit ginnels like this one made admirable hiding places for footpads who preyed on the unwary, and Cade held his breath as Mieka tugged him down a tributary passage.

Now it was seriously dark. Cade conjured a tiny flicker of bluish light over their heads before he was entirely aware of it, or realized why: Mieka was almost all Elf, and all Elves were afraid of the dark.

"No need for that, Cade. We're here."

Here was a solid brick wall. But as he doused the light, he caught the gleam of a flat brass plate with a spigot projecting from it. Mieka flattened his right palm to the plate, fingers on one side of the spigot and thumb on the other, and a portion of the wall glowed for a moment before vanishing. Cade was pushed through the doorway, and Mieka skipped after him before it solidified again.

A steep flight of wooden stairs was lit irregularly by torches that reeked of pitch. The Kiral Kellari had always been a strutty place, proud of the exotic interior that went with its exotic name, but there was no advantage in spending money on the back halls. Halfway up was a landing and a closed door through which seeped the commotion of several hundred men drinking, talking, laughing, impatient for the show. Mieka ignored this door and led Cade to the top of the stairs, where a sign above another door proclaimed ARTISTS ONLY.

For some reason, Cade balked. Mieka looked up at him, smiling in the flickering torchlight. "First time? Wrap your brain around it, Quill. This is where Touchstone enters from now on."

The door opened onto a small, overheated, underventilated tiring-room, with a round table in the middle covered in faded sky-blue velvet and wine bottles. The same velvet swagged the walls, upholstered the one-armed sofas along the perimeter, and curtained another doorway: STAGE. The room was empty; the only sign that anyone had ever been in here was a collection of hammered-silver goblets left lying about.

"Where is everybody?" Mieka wondered as he shrugged out of his coat. "I thought we'd have time for introductions beforehand. They must be setting up. We're later than I thought." He slung their coats behind one of the sofas and pointed up at the sign. "And you can get used to walking through *this* sort of door, too!"

Cade did walk through it, with a little tremor of nervousness—and impatience, because this wasn't yet Touchstone's night to play the Kiral Kellari. In one direction was the stage, but they went instead down a short flight of stairs into the familiar rowdy environment of a tavern packed with men of all ages who were already half-drunk and intended to get drunker—but not before they enjoyed the show.

Mieka elbowed a path for them to the bar. Whatever he said to the woman at the taps ensured that their ale was poured into the same kind of silver goblets Cade had seen earlier, not the cheaper pewter versions. Nodding his appreciation, he took a swallow and looked around.

The velvet draperies behind the bar were a darker shade of blue than the faded ones in the back room. The curtains across the stage were dyed a dizzying swirl of all the blues and greens of the sea. Cade thought it vulgar and distracting. The matching glass-shaded lamps on the tables were effective, though, their fragrant oils a distinct improvement over the torches in the back hall—though he wondered how much magic it would take to overcome those scents during a performance. "Silver Mine," for instance, would be a right laugh if the air reeked of roses.

Someone's magic had patterned the midnight-blue ceiling with twinkling stars that trickled golden Piksey dust—illusion, but very pretty all the same. The whole vast room sparkled with the gleam of silver and pewter and lamplight, reflected in the hundreds of palm-sized mirrors affixed to the dark blue draperies all over the side wall, framed in hammered tin. The Kiral Kellari's theme statement, however, was the wall that those mirrors reflected in fragments. It was a huge mural that stretched from the main doors to the side of the stage and all the way to the starry ceiling, an aquatic scene featuring a Mer King and two dozen or so of his ladies drifting about his cellar choosing wine. Never mind that pouring liquids was plainly impractical underwater; logic, after all, had very little to do with magic.

The painting echoed the Kiral Kellari's projecting triangular bar and the array of goblets and bottles behind it, but instead of blue curtains and lamplit tables, the underwater scene featured chairs made of huge, bright, unlikely flowers and rippling green seaweed, illuminated by darting clusters of tiny golden fish. If the monarch's square jaw and slightly receding hairline were reminiscent of Prince Ashgar, the ladies were rumored to be modeled on his various mistresses. For a man of only twenty-six, he'd notched up quite a few. Cade knew for a fact that if anything this collection was lacking another two dozen or so women. But the moving, living mural was a lovely piece of magic, and he wondered who had worked it.

He also found himself wondering how much that magic would interfere with what happened onstage, and how much the owners of the Kiral Kellari would mind when Touchstone shattered all those lovely little mirrors. . . .

There being quite a few naked breasts on the wall—he hadn't yet seen all that many in real life, and hoped he'd never grow indifferent to the sight of them—it took him a while to notice a slightly stuttering change of color on the third tier of bottles behind the bar and again on the ranks of barrels. He stifled a snigger, for he knew now who had paid for the painting: Franion's Finest Bottled Ale, Bellchime Keggery, and, of all people, Master Remey Honeycoil.

A stout, bespectacled man in a dreadful purple-spangled jacket clambered up onto the stage. So swiftly that it might have been a spell, the room was silent.

"My lords, gentlemen—the Shadowshapers."

Cade had seen them early on in their career, and he knew Rauel from talking with him at various neighborhood taverns. Now that he was working regularly and could afford visits to places like this, the Shadowshapers were no longer booked into places like this. They played at the real theaters now, places where one had to buy an actual ticket. He had no idea what they were doing here tonight, but he wasn't disposed to complain.

The curtains parted, revealing the group. At the tregetour's lectern stood Rauel Kevelock, his coloring proclaiming more Dark Elf than was usually seen except in the North Province where he'd been born. He was almost as innocently beautiful as Mieka, but the long bones spoke of Wizard and the round face more than hinted at Piksey. In front was tall, sinewy Vered Goldbraider, Wizard-blood competing with Dark Elf and Light and even Goblin to striking effect, long white-blond hair contrasting with nut-brown skin. On the left, at his own lectern, was Sakary Grainer, whose mother was almost entirely Human and whose father was almost entirely Wizard; he looked the former, with his red curling hair and blue eyes, but magic strong enough to make a fettler proved him the latter. And at the glisker's bench, behind an array of glass baskets full of withies, sat Chattim Czillag, whose bloodlines were anybody's guess, except for the Elf that was essential to his art. He was short, skinny, dark-haired, and blue-eyed, with a whimsically irregular face that attracted even though it wasn't at all handsome. No one knew where he came from, but no one really cared, because he was brilliant. Odd, Cade thought suddenly, how a glisker had been the catalyst for the Shadowshapers, too; one clever, talented little Elf, making all the difference.

He glanced down at his own glisker and whispered, "Beholden, Mieka. Best Namingday ever."

Mieka grinned from ear to pointed ear, then took both their silver cups and set them onto the bar just as soft tendrils of magic began to drift through the room, and all else was forgotten as the audience was gathered slowly, subtly into the hands of experts. Darkness like smoke swirled out from where the glisker sat, enwrapping each table lamp, cloaking in shadow first the mural and then the opposite wall of mirrors. In the dimness onstage a light tiny and bright as a candleflame glistened, drawing all eyes. And from it the play emerged.

Their first offering was "Dancing Ground." It told the story of a brave and fine-looking knight who, spied one afternoon by the Elf Queen, was invited by her to join the evening's dance. Wisely, he declined. Even to watch the dancing of the Elves was to lose all perception of time; it might seem that only hours passed, but in truth it could be many long years. And if watching was dangerous, what would happen to the mere Human who actually danced with them?

The Elf Queen hid her annoyance and offered gifts—which he was tempted to accept, for he was in fact riding to his own wedding. What marvels could the Elf Queen give him that he could bestow upon his lady for her delight? Riches were offered, and jewels, a never-empty golden wine goblet, and a magical bow and quiverful of enchanted arrows. But wisdom was yet with him, for he declined all gifts no matter how tempting. Being a mannerly young knight, he apologized for the necessity, and gave his explanation why he must ride on.

Now the Elf Queen was both angry and jealous. But

again she disguised her feelings, and walked down to where the forest met the lake, to the place where her kind danced the night into morning: a large round dancing ground, marked at the edges by pebbles of silver and gold, and great shining diamonds. She bent down and plucked up a particularly fine gem, and a chunk of gold to go with it, and told the knight she wished to offer his bespoken lady a gift for the wedding. He saw no reason to refuse such generosity, and when she tossed the diamond and then the gold towards him, he caught the one in his right hand and the other in his left. And thus he had no hand to reach for his sword when the Elf Queen—

But that wasn't how the Shadowshapers played it.

She had picked up the diamond and the gold and was about to fling them when the knight suddenly said she had not yet offered the only thing he really wanted, the only thing that meant anything to him. The Elf Queen demanded to know what that might be. The knight smiled, and said, "Give me your promise that after I've danced with you, the gift you'll give me is that which I most desire."

Intrigued, she agreed. And so they danced.

What Chattim did then was nothing short of amazing. Into the crowd, seemingly created from the chunks of gold and silver and diamonds, he flung separate bits of longing for those things men most desired: money, success, love, a beautiful wife, plenty of children, a fine home, an imaginative mistress, a bottomless barrel of beer. And as each man present grasped instinctively at what he wanted most, the magic expanded under Sakary's skilled direction, permutations multiplying into vague and then specific visions, feelings, thoughts. Cayden held himself separate to observe what was happening: that every man's most cherished desire was, for the length of this shimmering magic, granted.

Perhaps even more remarkably, as the enchantment

slowly ebbed, not one man sighed with disappointment, nor frowned his frustration, nor surreptitiously wiped moisture from his eyes when that thing he most longed for faded from him. So gentle, so careful was Sakary that it was only pleasure that remained, and deep contentment.

Cade held himself back from this, too. The thing he most desired . . . He didn't want to know. He didn't want his mind or his heart to reach for the magic that would let him feel it for certain. Instinct told him that to know would be fatal to his work; experiencing such fulfillment would destroy the hungry striving that goaded him. Part of him wished he could share just a little of the audience's satisfaction, and that part reached out a tentative fingertip, like a child trying to touch a raindrop on the other side of a window. Most of him backed away from it, and as the power seeped from the room in a slow swirl of shadows, he was unsurprised to find that both his hands were clenched into fists.

Why didn't he want to know? All these men—for a few moments they had possessed what they most desired. Or at least they thought they had. They now knew what it felt like. Whatever they saw or felt or discovered about themselves—why didn't Cade want the same? Why did it feel so dangerous even to speculate?

What was it, he asked himself, that he wanted more than anything?

And what would he do to get it?

And then, without warning, another question: What about the Elf? What was it that *he* was feeling right now? Had he touched what he most wanted, taking it into himself, satisfying whatever dream or need was hidden deepest in his soul?

The applause began, startling Cayden out of his thoughts. Though it was boorish to throw trimmings onto a real stage in a real theater, there was no such rule

TOUCHSTONE

129

here. The chink and chime of coins was almost as loud as the clapping of hands. Vered, whose interpretation of "Dancing Ground" this had been and who'd acted as masquer, ignored the coins bombarding the stage, leaving it to Rauel to come out from behind the tregetour's lectern and do the smiling and the bowing and the collecting. Vered strode to the abandoned lectern and gripped it with both powerful hands, looking grim.

"Ooh, *that's* trouble," Mieka said under his breath, and Cade leaned down to hear. "I thought something was going on." Cade's nudging elbow encouraged him to elaborate. "Didn't you feel the tweaks Rauel kept giving the backdrop while Vered was playing the knight?"

"All I noticed was he made more switches back and forth than I could count, and faster than I've ever seen it done," Cade admitted. "Impressive."

"Well, while he was doing that, and Chat was giving him what he needed to do it with, and Sakary was keeping it all reined in, Rauel was fooling with the dancing circle. And did you notice when Chat sent the wishes out, the change in the taste of it? Rauel focused in on what each man wanted, and gave it to him." He shook his head. "I'm not sure if he wanted to put his own hallmark on it so Vered doesn't get all the credit, or if he was doing it to provoke."

"Maybe he just couldn't help himself," Cade mused, turning back to the bar to order another drink. "There's times when I—" He broke off abruptly, realizing what he was about to reveal.

Mieka guessed anyway. "You think I never sense it?" he demanded. "Is it that even after two months you don't yet trust me, or you 'just can't help yourself'?"

"I do trust you. But I'm not used to that yet."

Mollified, the Elf signaled the barmaid for a second round. "Think a moment on what you'd feel if some other tregetour messed about with *your* work." With a shrewd upward glance, he answered the question. "You'd string him up by his balls and shove a few dozen withies up his nose, that's what you'd do." Handing Cade a fresh drink, he said, "Do you want to find a table this time?"

"I'm fine here." He nodded off to their left. "Who's that, do you know? The one in the emerald neckband that somebody really ought to teach him how to tie."

Mieka sniggered into his silver cup. "That's Pirro Spangler. Him and me, we took lessons from the same Master. He'd *like* to work the way I do, but he's built too Human."

Giving the glisker a once-over, Cayden was compelled to agree. The young man was not quite as tall but fashioned twice as solidly as Mieka, bull-shouldered and deep-chested, with powerful arms. He'd do fine working traditional, but Mieka's style—no, not near light or quick enough.

"All Elf in the ears, though," Cade remarked. Peeking shyly out from a tangle of dark brown curls, they were rather large but gracefully shaped, the tip of the left one decorated by three tiny silver hoops.

"More than can be said for that one over there." He hooked a thumb, very rudely, towards the apex of the bar.

Cade knew instantly whom he meant. Lank brown-blond hair, wide-set blue eyes, and the unmistakable signs of surgery on his ears. Where there ought to have been a gentle inward furl rounding a Human ear, there were only hard edges. The young man looked their way, caught them examining him, blew them a mocking kiss, and turned his back.

"Fraud," Mieka muttered. "He's no more Elf than Yazz. Look at his ears. He was never kagged."

"What?" He squinted but remained unenlightened.

"Like a tooth stump left in somebody's jaw—"

"I know what it means." He'd learned the term from Jeska, to whom it had been done. "You're saying a chirurgeon never touched him?"

"Only to make it look as if another one had."

"Why would somebody do that?"

"To pretend he's Elf when he's not—or more Elf than shows on the outside, anyway." He drained his ale and turned the goblet upside down on the bar to indicate he was finished for the night. "They're about ready again. This should be interesting. Rauel's piece this time—I wonder if Vered will muck about with it."

Vered didn't game Rauel the way Rauel had gamed him. He stood at the tregetour's lectern, straight-spined and solemn, giving every evidence of rapt attention. But Cade detected something coldly resentful in his eyes at Rauel's hilarious rendering of "Piksey Ride." Chattim could be seen laughing to himself as he created the weary and worn-out nag ridden nightly into exhaustion by Pikseys. Rauel's befuddled farmer had everyone howling, and Cade appreciated the spry delineation of the Pikseys as dancing outlines all over the tavern. Still, he had the feeling that Vered considered such light entertainment beneath them.

Shadows again swept the tavern, and slowly vanished. Show over, Mieka took Cade backstage to the tiring-room, where the Shadowshapers were holding court, one on each of the four blue couches. The youth with the fake kagged ears was talking earnestly to Rauel. Beside him was a tall, lean, intense Wizard, his face all angles, his black eyes scouring the crowd as if looking for, and knowing he wouldn't find, a reason to linger. He appeared, in fact, to have taken lessons in Haughty from Cade's mother.

"Mieka!" Chattim waved, and Mieka dragged Cade over. The glisker's face was even more comically asymmetrical up close—one cheekbone wider than the other, the mouth lopsided especially when he smiled, the nose taking a sharp right turn below the bridge. Even the cleft in his chin was off-center. But there was so merry a nature clear in his blue eyes that he really did seem rather good-looking.

Introductions were performed, and Mieka settled on the sofa beside Chattim. Cade listened as Blye's withies were praised even though Blye's name never was mentioned, and hid a grin. Someone drifted by with a tray of drinks, and Cade snagged one before wandering about the room, hearing snatches of conversations that didn't much interest him, but enjoying the atmosphere of sleek success . . . even if that success wasn't his own. Yet.

"—fuckin' snarge, that's what he is," snarled someone behind Cade, and he turned to find Vered Goldbraider grabbing two silver cups of wine, which he poured down his throat one right after the other. He came up for air to find Cade looking at him, and his black eyes narrowed dangerously. "Liked the ending, did you? All sweet and delightful, sunshine and smiles—"

"It's kind of supposed to end that way, isn't it?" Cade ventured.

"Not in *my* version it fucking doesn't!"

Oh; wrong playlet. Cade tried to make amends for his mistake. "Unusual, though, wasn't it—having the knight outsmart the Elf Queen like that—"

"And there it should've ended." Vered wasn't quite as tall as Cade, and as his head tilted back so he could look Cade in the eyes he swayed a bit on his heels, already quite drunk. "He tricks her. They dance. The end."

All at once Cade understood. "Which makes every man in the place wonder what *he* would've asked for, what's more important to him than anything else in the world."

"Exactly! Make 'em *think*, wouldn't it? That's the way I'd end it. But not him. No, not him! *Feeling's* the thing— Lord and Lady preserve him from ever having a single *thinking* moment in his life!" He turned a glare on Rauel, who was laughing with the burly little glisker Mieka knew. Another young man had joined them, delicate and compellingly beautiful, with dark curling hair and a graceful body. But he was somehow sinister, too, somehow dangerous—especially when seen next to Rauel's boyish, wide-eyed charm.

"It didn't *not* work, though, did it?" Cade was astounded by his own temerity in discussing the work as if they were equals. "I mean, not the way you intended, but it was effective all the same." The audience had been washed with emotions and images, and that was what all good theater was supposed to do. Even if they hadn't been forced to think during the performance they'd certainly think for days afterwards, just as Vered said he wanted. What the Shadowshapers had done tonight what not just good theater but *great* theater. Through their art, every man in the audience had learned something about himself, something true.

Almost every man in the audience, Cade suddenly corrected himself. And again he wondered what it was that Mieka most desired.

Vered was frowning. "I know you, don't I?"

"You know my glisker. Worked with him, once. Mieka Windthistle."

"*Your* glisker now, is he?" He laughed, so heartily that Cade was within a moment of being annoyed when he went on, "No stopping that little Elf, is there? I think I heard something of it—you'd be Silversun?"

"Yes. Cayden Silversun."

"Got it! Touchstone!" With a cynicism that was almost a challenge: "They say you're the next us."

Cade ought to have known that even his blandest smile wouldn't fool someone like this. A gaze both wily and wise bored into him.

"But you'd rather be the first *you*. Grab that by the throat, Cayden, and hang on tight. And if you value your sanity, don't ever let another tregetour work with you."

"Not in a million years," Cade said fervently.

Vered laughed once more. "And here's your Elf. So you're with players worthy of you now, eh, Mieka?"

He gave Vered a grin and an elaborate shrug. "We fit, the four of us. And I s'pose all is forgiven—Sakary's speaking to me again, anyway. Why'd you do this show tonight? I thought you were done and dusted for Seekhaven."

"Had to try out the new pieces. We'd thought to make this a surprise appearance, but I s'pose word gets out fast."

"It does," Mieka acknowledged, "if you know where to listen."

Vered took the winecup right out of Mieka's hand and drained it in two long swallows. "Did the wall remember you?"

"It did. Beholden."

"It was Chat, not me. But you gliskers all stick together like scales on a wyvern's wings. Talked to Pirro lately?"

"Not much. Has he settled yet?"

"He's like you—can't find players who suit him. Sakary's got a notion he'd work well with Thierin over there, but Rauel and me, we think alike on that if on bloody little else. Thierin gives us the eeries."

Glancing in the direction Vered indicated, Cade saw the disturbingly beautiful youth he'd noticed earlier.

"So you're for the Royal Circuit after Trials, are you?" Mieka asked, adding blithely, "We might see you there."

Cade choked on a gulp of wine. Vered laughed again, lighter, genuinely amused at the notion that anyone could do so well at Trials as to bypass the Winterly and Ducal Circuits entirely, right straight to Royal.

"You're frustled for it, no mistake." Taking an unsteady step back, he made a show of eyeing Mieka's clothing. "I never saw you half so fine when you were hangin' round last year." He winked at Cade. "Such a forlorn little Elf, it was, alone and alack, and just aching to show us all how it ought to be done!"

Cade arched an eloquent, teasing brow at Mieka, who blushed and said quickly, "Only until Rauel mentioned that he'd seen some players over on Beekbacks, and knew the tregetour, and they could use a glisker who knew what he was about."

"I'm beholden to him, then," Cade said, smiling.

"Go and be properly grateful, then," Vered advised, "before I wring his neck for him." But by now anger had been drowned in wine, and he was humming dreamily under his breath as he moved away in search of another goblet.

Cade was quiet for a few moments, watching the crowd, feeling both out of place and completely comfortable. These young men spoke in words he knew and used and understood, but he wasn't entirely sure *they* would understand *him*. The vocabulary of the theater, of tregetour and glisker, masquer and fettler, scenes and playlets and the pestilential Thirteen—he had all these things in common with all these people. But he also knew himself to be different.

"Have you been dreaming?"

He nearly dropped his wine. "What? No. I mean—what d'you mean?"

"I wrote to Auntie Brishen," Mieka told him, looking grim. "She says that sometimes blockweed will take someone the way it has you, without dreams when you sleep. And that's not good, Cade. I told you. It's important for you to dream."

And that, he realized all at once, was what differenced him from all these people who ought to have been his peers. Who ought to understand him, and never would. It wasn't the kind of dreaming Mieka meant; it was that other thing that happened to him. Dreamless sleep was wonderful. But he didn't see anything, did he? He hadn't in weeks. And he needed to look. He wanted to find out if the man Tobalt still sat in a tavern somewhere and said that when they lost their Elf, they lost their soul.

What prevented prescience took away his ability to choose. It eliminated this thing that made him unique in this room and perhaps in all his profession. Control it, yes, if he could; use it, for certes, as he'd learned to. But give it up? Obstruct its lessons and its warnings? He'd always told himself this seeing of his was a burden, a chore, a curse. Humbling to know that he'd secretly treasured it all along, that he valued it, even needed it.

"All right," he told Mieka. "I'll take the dreaming, not the thorn."

They stayed a while longer, ignoring the time even when everyone knew it was past curfew bell. Mieka seemed to know most of the players here, and steered Cayden expertly through the room so he met them all. He found himself liking Pirro Spangler, who was Mieka's opposite in more than looks: quiet, calm, he smiled rather than laughed at his fellow glisker's teasing and expressed no opinions of his own at all. If he had the depths to be a glisker, he obviously saved it for the stage. But he did keep glancing over at the dark young Wizard with the curling hair, and Cade wondered if Pirro would agree with Sakary or with Vered and Rauel—and Cade himself—that Thierin was downright weird.

The close atmosphere began to give Cade a headache. Mieka seemed nowhere near ready to leave—and as the parish minster clock chimed midnight, Cade learned why. The stairwell door opened and into the room came a succession of very pretty, very unclothed girls, carrying silver trays heaping with little colored glass thorns.

He stared, trying not to. But it was a revelation, how callow he was, how unsophisticated in the ways of the capital city where, after all, he'd grown up. Evidently the years he'd spent at Sagemaster Emmot's remote seaside

academy had been the crucial ones, when it came to experimentation. Everyone here seemed experienced; they
plucked up red or blue or green or purple without hesitation.

As one of the girls paused nearby, he recognized a pair
of hands that seemed unable to decide between the purple and the blue. Small hands, with the little fingers almost as long as the ring fingers. Unmistakable hands.

Mieka felt his gaze and glanced up. Someone nudged
Mieka out of the way to snatch up half a dozen thorns.
In the jostle, Cade lost track of him. Then there was a
touch on his shoulder, and his gray coat was thrust into
his arms.

"Dery's waited long enough, don't you think?"

He nodded, and by the time they were back out on
Amberwall Closure he was buttoning the coat to his
chin. It was freezing cold, and there wasn't a hire-hack in
sight. He found his gloves in his coat pockets, and something else besides. He went over to the nearest streetlamp
to read the little card, thinking that perhaps along with the
coat his father had sent him a message of congratulations.
But the card was much smaller than the palm-sized social
notes his parents used, and advertised a business.

THE FINCHERY
17-19 OLD WEST PARAPET
Refined Diversions for the Discerning Gentleman

In his father's handwriting were the names of six women,
two of them crossed out, with one, two, or three little five-
pointed stars drawn next to the others.

"What's that?"

He tossed the card to the pavement and turned away.
"I think I see a hack lantern down that street."

A muffled snicker told him Mieka had picked up and
read the card. "Ooh, a *discerning* gentleman, are we?"

Cade ignored him.

"What's Kessa do, that she gets three stars?"

He began walking towards the hack, waving an arm.

"What d'you think—is she more 'refined' or 'diverting'?"

He heard rapid footsteps as Mieka hurried to catch him up.

"C'mon, Quill—what sort of pretty little birds do they keep at a place called the Finchery?"

He swung round, and one look at his face by lamplight sent the boy skidding backwards, out of reach.

"Ask my father," he snarled. "I'll introduce you, shall I, at Seekhaven? He'll be there with Prince Ashgar. You can compare notes on what makes a 'refined' fuck. And p'rhaps I'll take the opportunity to give him his Godsdamned coat back. It doesn't fit, anyway."

"Quill—I'm sorry, I didn't mean—"

"You never do 'mean' anything, do you? In fact," he finished viciously, "off the stage, you're about the most meaningless person I know."

Whatever he had hoped to provoke of anger or insult or hurt didn't appear on Mieka's face. Subdued and solemn, he looked up at Cade and said nothing.

The jingle of harness turned their heads, and they got into the hack. The silence lasted all the way to Redpebble Square. By the time he stepped down, Cade was regretting the ruin of one of the best nights of his life—knowing that he had only himself to blame. Pausing as he shut the half-door behind him, he found Mieka's face in the gloom and began stammering an apology.

"It's all right," the boy interrupted. "I understand."

"No, you don't," he snapped, frustrated, thus adding another personally distilled measure of guilt and regret to the mix. Why was he blaming Mieka for things that weren't his fault?

"Oh, but I do understand, y'know," Mieka replied

quietly. "There's some as are born knowin' how to say the wrong thing. You and me, we're two of them, we are. With each other, anyway." Then he glanced up at the house. "That's Dery's window, innit? With the light still lit? Go on up, Quill, he's probably fretted himself to a fever by now."

"Beholden for tonight, Mieka. Really."

"I know." He smiled, then settled back into the seat and called to the driver, "Waterknot Circle, please—just to the edge of the Plume. Dream sweet, Quill!"

Thus it was that, after months of knowing him, Cade finally learned that Mieka lived in the most exclusive riverside district in Gallantrybanks, within half a mile of the Palace itself.

Nine

SKETCHY THOUGH HIS retail skills were, in the usual way of things Cayden would have tended the glass shop several hours a day so Blye could keep up with work while her father was sleeping off the latest "guaranteed" cure. There was always something new, something that gave hope . . . for a few weeks, anyhow. Master Cinder-cliff would be better, sometimes for months. But the cursing magic was slowly rotting his lungs, and nothing could stop it.

This spring was different. This spring, Touchstone was preparing for Trials. The first time Cade showed up just after lunching to help in the shop, Blye sent him right back home.

"I can work in here just as well as—"

"No, you can't," she told him flatly. "You need quiet, not interruptions. Go on, get out."

He protested a while longer, but he knew she was right. So he trudged back up the wrought iron stairs and huddled in his bedchamber, writing, planning, making notes for Jeska and Rafe and Mieka, wishing he could call a rehearsal every single day. He couldn't, of course. Jeska in particular had other work that supported his mother; Rafe helped out in the bakery; even Mieka, whose parents were moneyed (that Waterknot Circle address proved it), had family responsibilities. Besides, too much rehearsal was as bad as too little. There was always the risk that they'd leave the performance in Mistress Threadchaser's sitting room.

About teatime the day after Mieka took him to see the Shadowshapers, Cade was in the kitchen with Mistress Mirdley, telling her and Derien all about it (again) while she prepared a food basket for him to take to Blye. He'd got to the part about how Mieka had sensed Rauel's tinkering with Vered's work when a sound like the screech of an infuriated falcon assaulted their ears.

It was the sort of alarm common along streets where potentially dangerous professions were practiced, especially anything to do with fire. Spelled long ago by Master Fettler Cadriel Silversun to alert him to trouble on his glasscrafter's premises, Cade had heard it several times when thieves attempted to enter the shop, and once when Blye's father lost his balance during a coughing fit and staggered hard against the kiln. For all that he recognized what it was, for a few shocked moments he simply sat there with a word half-spoken on his lips. But Mistress Mirdley instantly threw down her carving knife, and was shouting orders before the second shriek even began.

"Derien! Run fetch my cures bag from the stillroom, and be quick! Cayden, you come with me. Now!" She didn't wait for him to uncoil himself from the armchair by the fire. She hauled him up by an elbow and pushed

him through the back door. A few running steps—
staggering as she kept him off-balance—and they were at
the glassworks, just as other neighbors began spilling
into the street, frightened that there might be a fire.

The opening of the glassworks door seemed to be the
charm that silenced the screaming falcon: help had arrived. Ears still ringing, Cade now heard Blye's voice from
somewhere beyond the central workbench, swearing im-
pressively. Mistress Mirdley moved quickly, if clumsily.
By the time Cade had registered the rope of molten glass
cooling on the floor and the shattered bowl beside it, the
Trollwife had found Blye—sitting on the floor with her
hands in a bucket—and was yelling for more cold water.

Twenty minutes later, Mistress Mirdley had salved the
burns. Gawkers had been sent away with reassurances
that neither the glassworks nor their own houses were
in any danger. And Blye was still cussing—though at a
slower pace, and with fury, not pain.

"I *knew* I should've mended those gloves," she fumed
as clean bandages were wrapped around her hands.

Derien had retrieved the dragon-gut gloves from the
floor. "I don't think mending would've done any good,"
he said, poking a finger through a hole where the stitching had come loose.

"Five days, and not an instant less," Mistress Mirdley
said as she tied off bandages. "And don't you be rolling
your eyes at me, girl. You're lucky it's not five weeks.
Think about that, next time you try to work too fast to
get things done for those as scantly appreciates it." This,
with an accusing glare at Cayden.

Blye shook her head, silvery blond hair lank around
her cheeks and neck. "But I have to—they need—"

"Shoosh!" the Trollwife exclaimed. "I won't hear a
word!"

They glowered at each other. Cade knew who would
win. So did Blye; she relented with a sigh much sooner

than she would have with anyone else. But as Mistress Mirdley bustled out with Derien in tow and her bag of household remedies clutched in her arms, Blye suddenly turned pleading eyes on him. He actually backed up a pace, unnerved. He'd known her his whole life, and he'd never seen this anguish in her face.

"I'm so sorry," she whispered. "I haven't made your withies. I meant to do them a few days ago, but Da was so bad, and—"

"Don't worry about it."

"But you need them! It's *Trials*, Cade!"

"I can buy what I need."

"Mieka won't like that," she predicted—accurately, he was well aware. "He's got used to my work. I know both of you now, and I can fashion them to suit his magic as well as yours, and—"

"That's us humiliated, then," he said, striving for the laugh he knew Mieka could have got without effort. "So spoiled we've lost the knack of priming or using anyone else's withies—total incompetents, the pair of us—"

"Stop it, Cade! You *need* them for Seekhaven, you leave tomorrow, and—"

"—and you're going to be wearing those bandages for the next five days," he warned, "or what Mistress Mirdley will do to you, I don't like to think."

"You're not thinking at all, that's your problem," she snapped, sounding much more like herself. "I should've had them done by now—"

A lightly scolding voice from the glassworks doorway called out, "Don't you dare even consider it!" Mieka strolled in, a basket of food in his right hand and a bottle of brandy in his left. "I see I arrived at exactly the right time. You're both about to be very silly, I can tell." Setting down the basket, he plucked from it a nosegay of flowers and presented them to Blye. "These are for you," he told her, then sloshed the bottle. "And this is for all of us. Mistress Mirdley told me everything—and what she didn't, Dery did. Make yourself useful instead of just ornamental, Quill, and get us a vase and some glasses. A very small one for yourself, though. Glass, not vase," he added, grinning, as if Cade were too stupid to tell the difference.

Not that the only word to come out of Cade's mouth proved his intelligence. Not at all. "Why?"

"I'll tell you when we've had a drink."

Mieka had turned up at the Silversun kitchen to collect Cade so they could examine the new withies, and had been sent next door to the glassworks. That there were no withies to examine brought a passing furrow to his brow, but of speculation rather than annoyance. He helped Blye cradle her snifter between her bandaged hands, toasted everyone with a brilliant smile, and kindly waited for Cade to swallow before he said, "I bet you've watched a million times. And I bet she's an excellent teacher. So why not stop anguishin' ourselves about it, and *you* make them?"

The sudden jolt of dislocation was like having an arm wrenched from its socket, only more frightening than painful, the thoughts and memories and seeming memories jostling each other for precedence, for attention—

"He can't," Blye was saying from a very great distance, or perhaps another place and time entirely, Cade wasn't sure. "He's not allowed."

"I know," Mieka said, sounding supremely unconcerned. "Quill's a Wizard, forbidden to do aught to a withie except prime it for a play. So what?"

"Mieka," Blye warned.

With a long-suffering sigh: "Oh, you mean that business about his grandmother?"

The world shifted again. He knew. How could he possibly know?

Cade's brain settled back into its rightful position—no,

a new one, a place that took into account and adjusted for things he hadn't thought the Elf knew. And how had he found out, anyway? He set his glass down and turned a narrowed gaze on Blye, who was still staring at Mieka, horrified.

"You don't understand!"

"Oh, I understand just fine. Happily, I'm not quite the fool I look. You told me yourself that your da gave Cade lessons a long time ago so he'd understand exactly how withies are made and how to prime them. He wasn't s'posed to, but he did. 'Every player should know substance and subtleties,' isn't that what you told me he said? If your da, one of the woman's victims, can overlook whose grandson he is—"

"We've never held that against Cade!"

"You see? And besides, who's to know except the three of us?"

Cayden didn't listen as they went on arguing. He was too occupied with trying to organize this new information, make it fit as Sagemaster Emmot had taught him to do. How had Mieka found out? Had he asked Blye to explain Cade's reaction to the first shattered withies this winter at the Downstreet? Had Blye told him about Lady Kiritin then?

Did it matter?

Well, yes. It did. That turn of his, when he'd shoved Mieka up against a lamppost and snarled at him—yes, he had to have found out after that, or the turn would never have happened. That meant it could now be relegated to the part of his mind labeled *Never-were,* and gratefully forgotten.

"I'm telling you he can't," Blye was insisting. "It's illegal!"

"Fuck that!" Mieka exclaimed, patience gone. "*You* making them isn't legal either, yet you do! I need six new withies, and I need them by tomorrow, so let's bloody well get started!"

Afterwards, Cayden understood that he'd been wanting to do this for years. Just to see if he could. Or perhaps to prove that he could without his grandmother's taint suffusing his work. He had indeed watched first Blye's father and then Blye herself fashion withies ever since he could remember. And she was a very good teacher. A few false starts, and three finished pieces that didn't meet Mieka's standards, and it seemed that no time at all had passed before he was looking at the workbench, where six new withies—one of them faintly green, two tinted red-orange, three a very pale blue—were laid out for polishing.

Except to inspect each, and reject three, Mieka had sat in a corner, silent and motionless, completely unlike him. Even as Cade thought this, while taking a much-deserved swallow of brandy, he realized he was wrong. At the glisker's bench, Mieka was a constant blur of motion. But away from it, in private, he chose a chair and a position— legs crossed or folded to one side, knees drawn up or splayed, hands on the arms of a chair or resting loosely in his lap—and stayed there.

He didn't move now as he said softly, "That's done, then."

"Done," Blye agreed. "I'll polish them up tonight and leave them with Mistress Mirdley for you in the morning."

"I'll take them," Cade said. "I can polish them when we get to Seekhaven."

She shrugged her shoulders. "As you wish. You know where the buff papers and glossing cloths are. Be sure to take enough." Rising, she reached for the brandy glasses with her bandaged hands and cussed under her breath.

"Let me," Mieka offered, rising from his chair. "Time

everyone got some sleep, I think," he went on as he took the snifters to the back room and rinsed them in the sink. "Takes more magic out of you than you thought, eh, Quill?" he called through the open door, and Cade glanced up from where he slumped at the workbench. Before he could organize his wits for an answer, the boy was back. "We'll say sweet night, now, Blye—I'm much beholden, and please forgive me for swearing at you."

Cade wasn't sure how Mieka managed it, and he was too tired to puzzle it out, but it wasn't long before all those wrought iron steps were below him, and he and the Elf and the six withies wrapped in a scrap of black velvet were up on the fifth floor. A little while after that he found himself tucked up in bed, clad in a soft night-shirt, with no idea at all how he'd got there.

"You really needn't worry, y'know," said Mieka. "About your ancestors, I mean. Your father does what he does, it's nothing to do with you. Lady Jaspiela, she's a bit of a wart, but she's learning to respect you whether she knows it or not. And Lady Kiritin . . ."

Cade flinched and turned his head away.

"Lady Kiritin," he repeated softly, "doesn't matter at all. It's not in you to be wicked, Cade, nor cruel. I'll see you tomorrow daybreak. Dream sweet."

If he dreamed, when he woke the next dawn he didn't remember. The first thing he saw was the black velvet wrapping the six new withies . . . that *he* had fashioned, flouting laws made necessary by his own grandmother. He felt reckless and triumphant and uneasy, and re-minded himself to tell Mieka that all six withies would have to be "accidentally" broken right after Trials.

He lingered in bed for a time, knowing he ought to get moving, get dressed, get over to the palace grounds, where the special coaches taking players to Trials would soon be loading up. Something kept him motionless, staring at the velvet on his bedside table. He could always sense the withies when he held them in his hands, after he'd filled them with magic. These, however, though not yet primed, seemed almost to call to him, fragments of feeling and sensation urging him to settle them, complete them, ready them for Mieka's use. Surely it was illusion, that they trembled within their wrapping.

Everyone bound for Trials departed Gallantrybanks for Seekhaven Castle on the same day and at roughly the same time—including the Shadowshapers in their own luxurious wagon. They would use post horses along the way, just as the other coaches would, and competition for the best animals would be uncompromising. The Master of His Majesty's Revelries provided the conveyances, but royal generosity did not extend to paying extra to the ostlers to save the best horses for those commanded to His Majesty's presence. It was obvious, therefore, that one of the most modern and well-sprung vehicles in the Kingdom would soon outstrip the other coaches. The Shadowshapers had only themselves and their equipment to transport; the king's three enormous coaches were loaded down with three groups of four young men each, with all the effluvia of their profession, their personal belongings, and, in one case, a very large hamper of food and a half-barrel of Elf-brewed whiskey.

The last two items won Touchstone a ride in comfort. At the first stop, their coach arrived before the others and the driver laid claim to the strongest horses while the restless young players who'd just spent six hours in a physically confined and professionally hostile environment piled out to stretch their legs as far as the taproom.

When the Shadowshapers came along less than ten minutes later, a pleasant rustic scene was unfolding beneath a crooked oak tree near the stables. Touchstone had decided to lunch outdoors. Cade, who'd spent the ride thus far with his feet firmly on the hamper, even when he was pretending to be asleep, was portioning out cold meats and cheese onto glass plates padded for transport with Mieka's exceedingly useful spell. Rafe was distributing glass forks and spoons. Jeska was slicing bread with a steel knife. And Mieka, who'd spent the ride perched on his aunt's whiskey barrel where it rested on the coach floor, was pouring generously into four glass beakers. The set of serving ware for traveling had been Blye's gift, created during the spring before her father had taken so ill.

They had not invited their competition to share.

They did invite the Shadowshapers, who returned the favor—and ensured their own continuing access to excellent whiskey—by inviting them to share their big, comfy wagon for the rest of the trip.

Accordingly, after the meal was finished, Touchstone's baggage and crates were transferred to the wagon's roof rack. The hamper and the half-barrel were loaded inside. Soon the eight young men had settled into the sort of extravagance that only the most successful players on a Circuit could afford. Mieka took a long, pondering look at the bunk beds, firepocket, screened windows, folding table, two cushioned chairs, and tidy little washstand with mirror, and announced, "I want one!"

Eight of them in a coach designed for four wasn't too much of a strain, especially after Mieka started pouring the whiskey again. As had become usual when Touchstone traveled, a singing competition followed the third beaker. Or perhaps it was the fourth. It turned out that Sakary Grainer, with a skinful of alcohol in him, was disposed to divulge the most singularly obscene drinking songs any of them—even Jeska—had ever heard, and in the most angelic voice imaginable. Awestruck, Jeska ceded the victory to the fettler with a little bow from the waist—and fell off the lower bunk onto the carpeted floor, where he spent the rest of the night delicately snoring.

Despite the doubled load, the Shadowshapers' vehicle made better time than the king's coaches, and thus obtained better horses. By noon of the next day, when Touchstone had expected to be enduring another six or seven hours of travel, they were instead waving a grateful farewell to the Shadowshapers before dragging their baggage up three flights of stairs to their assigned quarters.

The taverns in Seekhaven Town competed zealously to host players during Trials. Ten days of providing for the needs of hungry, thirsty, rambunctious men—especially the young ones at their first Trials—could on occasion damage the premises, but the Master of Revelries could be counted on to pay for repairs. Though it was avowed that allocation of rooms was strictly random, everyone knew that those players reported to be particularly promising received finer quarters.

Touchstone, it appeared, rated middlingly. Their room assignment was the top floor of a pleasant three-story inn with a view of Spoonshiner River through the elm trees. There were two bedchambers with a garderobe in between. Though the plumbing didn't extend above the first floor, and they would have to carry up their own bathwater, at least they wouldn't have to haul a tub up the stairs. A little room next to the garderobe featured a high-backed cast-iron monster with dragon-claw feet, its porcelain innards painted bright blue.

"Can you imagine having to drag this thing up here?" Mieka's attention was divided between admiring the tub and going through his pockets for enough spare change to pay someone to bring up water to fill it. "The sign says nine and a half—anybody got another fourpence?"

"If I say yes, do I get first wash?" Rafe asked.

"No."

"Fine." He disappeared back into the room he and Jeska would share.

"Rafe!" Mieka whined. "It's just fourpence!"

"First wash for me or no wash for you at all!"

Cade turned from splashing water onto his face from the bowl at the washstand, and sniffed the air elaborately, wrinkling his nose. "I'll contribute to the cause." He dug into a pocket and pulled out a se'en-penny piece. Mieka grabbed for it; Cade held it high over the boy's head, grinning. "That'll be thruppence back, or I get first bath."

"Cullion!" He made a face of dire menace, an expression he was at least twenty years too young even to attempt, and paid up.

By late afternoon they were all bathed, shaved, and dressed to attend High Chapel. Their competition might or might not arrive in time to make an appearance, but even if they did, the appearance they made wouldn't be anywhere near their best. And at Court, appearances were very nearly everything.

Not counting new players vying for the three places on the Winterly Circuit, the town and castle of Seekhaven played host to all the best in the kingdom: Trials, once passed, did not mean Trials never again looming. Each year the players on the Royal, Ducal, and Winterly were invited to perform before the assembled Summer Court. These invitations were understood to be exactly the sort received by Touchstone: *Prove yourselves*. A group could stay on the circuit they'd already earned, move up or down, or lose their place either because they weren't as good as they'd been or because someone else was better. It was, to say the least of it, a fraught ten days for all concerned.

Unless, of course, you were the Shadowshapers, acknowledged the best in the Kingdom, confidently expected to move up from Winterly to First Flight on the Royal, bypassing Ducal Circuit entirely. It had never been done before. Cade was proud that he knew, and after the journey to Seekhaven could claim as his friends, all four of the young men who would do it. If he was envious as well, he kept it to himself.

Along with the vouchers for their lodgings, food, various Court functions, directions to all the major landmarks in and around the castle, and their assigned rehearsal times, waiting at the town gates for Touchstone had been the official list of performances. As they strolled the clean-swept cobblestones towards the High Chapel where royalty sometimes attended services, Mieka ran through the list.

"Spintales—good enough, I s'pose, but on their way down, it's rumored. I shouldn't be at all surprised to find it true. Cobbald Close Players, they're naught but a huddle of tired old men. I don't know why they're still on any Circuit at all, let alone the Royal, but look for that to change. Hmm . . . if we can manage it, I'd like to go see the Shorelines."

Jeska looked over Mieka's shoulder at the schedule. "They're on an hour after we finish rehearsal. If we hurry, we could make their show. But why d'you want to see them? I mean, they were good in their day, but they're past it now."

"Just to see them one last time," Mieka said wistfully. "They were the first I ever saw. The minute they started their show, I knew what I wanted to be when I grew up." He paused, flinging a smile at Cade. "I was seven."

Jeska looked impressed. "Really? I was fourteen, and it was my Namingday treat from me uncle. The Golden-harts." He gave a soft, reminiscent chuckle. "I thought Mum would have a seizure when he brought me home that night and I said I wanted to be a masquer."

"She ought to've known, though, shouldn't she?" Rafe asked. "You'd been memorizing poetry and such forever." He winked at Mieka. "Still knows all the singsongs they taught him at littleschool. It's where he gets the tunes for those disgusting ballads. Just changes up the words a bit—kind of makes you wonder about the quality of education in this Kingdom. Now, *my* first sight of a players' show—"

Cade sniggered. "Which version are you going to tell this time?"

"The real one, of course," the fettler replied with injured innocence. "How could anybody lie to this face?" He pinched Mieka's chin and got his hand knocked away. "You want to hear it or not?"

"Should I believe it?" Mieka asked Cade, who shrugged.

"It was fated," Rafe intoned. "Me poor ol' grandda mistook the address of a warehouse for the address of a whorehouse, and in we went, and there they were: a half-drunken fettler, an entirely drunken glisker, and absolutely the ugliest masquer who ever took what passed for a stage, doing the naughty version of 'Feather Beds' while their tregetour sat in a corner with a naked girl on his lap."

Mieka's jaw dropped. Cade laughed and said, "He made his grandda stay till the end of the show—the one onstage, not the one in the corner! The only reason his mum didn't wallop him is because he couldn't talk about anything else but the play—"

"—such as it was," Rafe finished, adding virtuously, "I never noticed the girls at all. I'd already decided on Crisiant, so no other girls existed for me in the whole world."

"Or so he wants her to believe," Cade added.

"She's much too smart for that," Mieka scoffed. "How about you, then? What was your first?"

"First girl or first play? I was fifteen." He grinned. "For both."

"Good Gods! That old?"

Cade made a lunge for him, and he danced out of reach, laughing. Rafe snagged him by the scruff of the neck and shook him like a puppy. "Settle down," he advised. "Or all that bathwater and a fresh shave will be for naught because I'll throw you in the river."

"No, you won't," the boy retorted. "I'd tell your mum on you. She *likes* me."

"Settle down anyway. There's people will be looking at us, and it won't do to have them realize what we really are, now, would it?"

"And what are we, *really*?" Mieka demanded.

"Better-looking than the Nightrunners, anyway," Jeska said, pointing to a placard in a shop window. A very bad line drawing showed four sullen young men, pale against a black backdrop spattered with white dots that Cade assumed were meant to be stars.

"I saw them last year," Mieka said. "Down the South End. Dead awful, they were."

Cade paused to examine the advertisement, making mental notes on what not to do when it came their turn to commission placards. "They look as if they know it," he said at last.

"Not worth a splintered withie," Mieka agreed.

"How do you know all these people?" Rafe asked as they walked on.

"Somebody has to look over the competition. None of you lot ever bother."

"So what about the rest of these, eh?"

Mieka returned to scrutiny of the list. "Well, it'll be the Goldenharts' last year, they're retiring. Still good, or so it's said. Wishcallers—silly name—they're derivative at best. And their best isn't very good. They were in the coach with us yesterday."

Jeska gave a snort through his thin, elegant nose. "The ones who mumbled their names and then pretended to be asleep?"

Mieka nodded. "Hoping we'd blither away and give up all our secrets."

"I thought they were just hung over," Cade mused. "They certainly *looked* hung over."

"As for the rest of the players . . . surely you've heard of Redprong and Trinder."

Rafe pulled at Mieka's hand so he could see the page. "Are *they* still at it? It's—what, fifteen years since they first made Trials?"

Macielin Redprong and Laith Trinder hired their fettler and masquer on a seasonal basis, making a well-advertised virtue of each year's novelty, exploiting the well-known fact that nobody could stand to work with them longer than one Circuit. On one famous occasion they'd returned to Gallantrybanks halfway through the Ducal because their masquer had actually tried to knife Redprong. More than one of their temporary hires had quit the theater completely after a season with them.

"The Enticements, they've got to be nearing thirty-five by now, old men on their last legs," Mieka said dismissively. "They'll be gone by next year." Then he sniggered. "Oh, here's a rarity. Kelife and the Candlelights! The cheek of it, putting your own name on your players!"

"Speaking of elderly," Jeska said, "me mum's sister has the dyeing of his hair every four weeks or so when they're in town, and makes up packets for him while he's on the Circuit."

"Why does he bother?" Rafe wanted to know. "I mean, he's a bit of a swoophead anyway, isn't he?"

"She'll be painting the color directly onto his scalp soon. But he's married to Lord Coldkettle's wife's cousin, so it doesn't matter how old and worthless they are. Powerful friends at Court are worth at least a hundred fifty points in the judging."

"Mieka, who's this?" Cade pointed to a name he didn't recognize at all.

"You've met them—well, a couple of them. The other night at Kiral Kellari. The one pretending to be kagged, he's Lederris Daggering, and his dark glowering Wizard friend, his name is Mirko Challender. They were talking to Rauel."

"They were in the other coach, weren't they? I thought I recognized them."

"Pretending to be kagged?" Jeska's lip curled.

"Repulsive, I know," Mieka agreed. "I've never seen the Crystal Sparks—another asinine name, don't you think?—but it's said they're not bad. They might even be competition."

"Competition?" Cade laughed. "For *us*?"

"That's why we love you, Cayden," Rafe commented. "So modest and unpretentious. So humble."

Pressing his palms together in the conventional pose of worshipful stained-glass Angels, Cade batted his lashes and smirked. Mieka crumpled up the performance schedule and threw it at him. Jeska, with the reflexes of a street-brawler, snatched it midair and stuffed it in a pocket of his second-best tunic.

"And *that* will be sufficient mucking about," Rafe warned. "We're almost at Chapel. Some decorum, please."

The last corner had taken them onto a major street, wide and gracious, paved in red brick with quartets of pleached blue-leaf elms at stately intervals down the middle. The shops were expensive, the sidewalks scrupulously clean. Scores of people were all heading in the same direction, converging on the High Chapel, its twin spires and massive central tower gleaming white in the late afternoon sunshine.

"At least pretend you're civilized," Rafe went on.

"I know how to behave," Mieka protested. "I've had lessons."

Cade rolled his eyes. "I s'pose it wouldn't hurt to ask if you were awake during any of them?"

"Oh, it never hurts to ask, Quill. It just hurts to find out."

Ten

HIGH CHAPEL WAS required at Trials, not so much because the players would want to beseek any deity they could think of for help, but because one of the highlights of the town's year was getting a good look at the hopefuls and the established groups. The players who called themselves Crystal Sparks were at High Chapel along with everyone else connected to Trials. Now that Cayden knew them for Touchstone's competition—no matter how arrogantly he'd dismissed them earlier—he decided that if he could manage it, he'd try to see them perform. There was about their tregetour a sort of brooding disgruntlement that might make for an interesting interpretation of whichever of the Thirteen Perils they drew.

The High Chapel rite that evening was entirely typical, if celebrated with rather more pretentiousness—and much more expensive implements—than Cade was used to. A thurible made of solid silver encrusted with gems was wielded by a Good Brother in crimson silk vestments; a Good Sister even more splendidly attired in blue spurged the four corners with scented water from a golden bowl rimmed with pearls, using a glass withie swirled with green and tipped with a pearl the size of a baby's fist. Ritually purified, the congregation made the required bows to the images of the Lord, the Lady, their children who had become Angels, and the ancient unknowable Gods. Facing front again, towards the two stone plinths, one garnished with a small fountain and the other with a feathery blue flame, everyone sat down and prepared for the recitations.

Rafe's strictures on proper behavior had made some impression on Mieka. He was solemn enough when it came time to honor the Old Gods with a deep bending of his knees, but like most Elves he merely nodded to the Lord, the Lady, and the Angels. As the Good Brother took up his place behind the fire plinth and began talking, Mieka looked round at the windows, the statuary, the paintings, the carved wooden pews, the faces and fashions of his fellow congregants—anything, in short, was more interesting than the droning precepts of faith.

Cade silently agreed with him, but kept his gaze more or less on the Good Brother. He'd been trained long ago by his mother to present a pious face, no matter what his thoughts. That it was essentially a Wizardly faith being celebrated afforded him a cynical smile that never even got close to his lips. In theory, all peoples were equal. In theory, too, a citizen was a citizen was a citizen. But just as there were royals and nobles and common folk, so there was a hierarchy in heaven. The Lord and the Lady were tacitly understood to have been Wizards; the Angels were Human; everybody else came under the jurisdiction of the Old Gods, who remained conveniently nameless, faceless, and enigmatic.

He was as aware of Mieka's disinterest in the proceedings as he was of Jeschenar's authentic devotion: golden head bent, battle-scarred hands folded tightly together on his knees. There had been times in his life when Cade almost wished for Jeska's type of unquestioning faith. Almost, but not quite.

Despite himself, Cade found his gaze straying as the Good Sister took over the lecture. There was indeed much to distract the eye and mind. As expected in a High Chapel graced occasionally by royalty, the artwork was of the first quality. The statues of the Lord on the east wall and the Lady on the west were especially fine, bespelled to nod and smile as parishioners entered, to listen with grave approval to the recitations, and—as Flame and Fountain were conjured halfway to the gilded rafters—to spread their white marble hands in gracious benediction. Likewise the paintings of various Angels folded their feathered wings and smoothed their robes as they settled to listen to their Parents' praises, then bowed in reverence as the blessing was spoken. There was, Cade felt, a good reason why there were no representations of the Old Gods. He could just imagine the favorite deity of, say, the Goblins bending his, her, or its head in veneration of Wizards. If any Chapel—High or Low—ever displayed such an image, there would be riots.

Below each statue and painting, and somewhere in the brilliant colors of the stained glass windows depicting the scenic wonders of the Kingdom, were the names of the donors. At each parish chapel in Gallantrybanks, and in the other cities and major towns, a few local families and guilds would be credited. Here, there were as many donors as there were works of art. Anyone who was someone—or wanted to be—was anxious that their generosity be noticed by the royals. Cayden thought of the little seaside chapel he'd attended while at Sagemaster Emmot's academy: six short benches crammed beneath a low barrel-vaulted ceiling, no art at all. Only the two plinths, with tiny brass labels at their bases signifying that they had been the gifts of some long-ago lord and his lady. He wasn't sure if it made services more impressive, all this expensive art, or if it wasn't perhaps better to forego all the distractions to concentrate on what faith really meant.

What he knew for certain sure, though, was that the stained glass on the western side of the building was in the most ostentatious bad taste: the symbols of all the most prominent Wizardly clans, jumbled together in a broad landscape. There was enough of hills, forest, and sky to accommodate everything from his own clan's soaring white Falcon to a Squirrel clutching acorns, an Elk pacing a meadow, a Fox skulking through the undergrowth, and a Salmon leaping from a river. In the presence of this huge window, who would choose to listen to the service rather than search for the emblem of his clan?

At length the rite was over, and Cade slipped out a side door with his friends and made for the courtyard. They stood to one side as nobility, wealthy merchants and proud guildsmen with their complacently overdressed ladies on their arms, and other groups of players (some looking decidedly travel-worn) filed out of High Chapel. Cade had never seen so many of his own profession together in one place, and some of them famous, too. Rauel Kevelock smiled at him on his way past, and Chattim Czillag stopped to talk to Mieka for a moment or two. Cade didn't hear what they said, his attention caught by the high-pitched laughter of a group of young girls. Nominatives for the Good Sisterhood, they hid blushes behind gloved hands as the Sister Superior scolded them, urging them along towards the Minster. But their gazes darted from one player to another, and Cade realized they would rarely have been within sight of so many young men in their restricted virginal lives.

"That one's rather lovely, don't you think?"

Cade was appalled that Mieka had said such a thing about a Nominative—without lowering his voice, too. And he was even pointing at her.

"Chankings," Jeska sniffed, "compared to the tall blonde."

The Elf considered. "One wouldn't so much make love to her as climb her. I prefer them short, sweet, and shy."

"Shall we go for a scrape, then?"

Rafe growled at them. "Did I or did I not tell you to behave yourselves?"

"That was in Chapel." Mieka grinned; the girl he'd been watching giggled. "See? She fancies me."

"The way they live," Cade reminded him, "locked up most of the year, they fancy anything in trousers. Come on, we'll be late for supper."

"Oh, I'm hungry, right enough." He nudged Jeska with an elbow. "Let's see if we can split them from the flock, shall we?"

Exchanging a grim look with Rafe, Cade dug his fingers into Mieka's shoulder and hauled him towards the street. Rafe had hold of Jeska, marching him right along.

"But I wasn't going to, not really!" Jeska protested.

"*He* was," Rafe snarled.

Mieka laughed, and didn't deny it.

The twilight was deepening by the time they got back to their lodgings. Supper was provided, once they'd handed over vouchers that would allow the proprietor reimbursement from the Master of Revelries' treasury. They ate on the broad back porch, which Cade and Rafe obligingly lit with rows of little flames to spare their host a few candles. The family's Trollwife repaid them with the leftovers of the apple scrumping made for her employers' dinner, and Rafe graciously avowed it was as good as his mother's—not mentioning, of course, that his parents owned and operated one of the best bakeries in Gallantrybanks.

But when they finished eating it was barely nine in the evening, and there was nothing to do. Cade had just finished his second half pint of ale and was about to comment on impending boredom when he noted that his glisker had vanished.

"Where—?" he began, just as his masquer stood, stretched, and ambled down the porch steps towards the little garden's back gate.

"Prowling," Rafe said, flicking a finger to douse his contribution to the lighting. "I'm for bed, and some real sleep. That wagon bunk was too short last night."

Left alone with the echoes of the clanging gate and his own flickers of light, Cade shrugged and settled back in his chair, listening to the darkness. After a while he pushed himself to his feet and wandered up to bed, still listening. So much quieter here than at home, for all that Redpebble Square was far from the rowdier sections of the city. He could even hear the river a couple of blocks away, and closed his eyes to imagine it the way he'd seen it earlier in the evening, crumpled silk in some places and near-perfect glass in others, reflecting trees and buildings and little stone footbridges. But it was nighttime now, and across the water would glimmer Elf-light from the streetlamps, and the silver of the rising moon . . . there was a word for that, a lovely word . . . *moonglade* . . . the river was talking to the moon, the water conversing with the light, dancing and flirting in the preliminaries of love . . . the words were dancing in his mind now, words for the sounds and the feelings, the clean scent of the water and the silver moonglade . . . he knew precisely what sort of magic he would leave inside the withies, all the laughter and longing . . . Mieka would love this one, dancing behind the glisker's bench, colored glass twigs shimmering in his quick little hands . . .

[He sat beside the dark river, hugging his knees, breathing slowly the scents of water and crushed green grass and woodsmoke, listening to windrustle and distant chirring birds, feeling the languid warmth of the night—for once not trying to remember, interpret, catalog. What he sensed, and especially what he saw, these things were to be savored, not used. Silvery light glowed over the nearby hills, tempting, promising, and he held his breath. As the moon arced over the rise, and the river sparkled like a pathway of suddenly flung diamonds, he felt hands settle lightly on his shoulders. He didn't turn his head; he knew this touch, gentle and strong.

After a few moments Mieka whispered, "I knew you'd be here," and knelt behind him in the damp grass.

Moonglade shimmered the length of the river. Lingering drops of afternoon rain dazzled trees and pasture, and the whole world seemed suddenly slurry with stars.

"Did I get it right, then, Quill?"

He laughed softly, because Mieka already knew the answer. He gave it again anyway. "You always do. Whatever I give you, you give back to me better than I could ever imagine it. You always do."

In his sleep, Cayden smiled.

* * *

HE WOKE WITH a single blink. There were moon-thrown shadows in the darkness of the bedchamber. One of these shadows wandered about the room, seeming to shed pieces of itself onto the floor.

"Pick it up. All of it."

Mieka grasped dramatically at his chest. "Gods, Quill! Give me a seizure, whyn't you?"

He didn't have to ask what the boy had been doing. He reeked of sexual satiation like a noblewoman's gowns reeked of pricey perfume. "Just tell me you didn't break into the Minster."

"Mad I may be, but stupid? Never."

"I'd argue with that. We've the draw in the morning, and first rehearsal right after." He kept his voice steady and calm. "I need you rested."

The uncaring shrug was in his voice as he replied, "Then let me sleep in tomorrow." He fell onto the bed with a grunt of satisfaction, wriggling amid the pillows to burrow a comfortable nest. "Shoulda brought you along. She had an adorable little friend—"

"I don't want to hear about it."

"No? All right, then. Sweet dreaming, Quill."

Cade unclenched his fists and told himself he wasn't angry because he was envious. He was angry because tomorrow was vitally important. Their career—hells, their *lives* from now on—depended on what happened tomorrow. And that worthless little Elf had to go out prowling—

—and come to think of it, had Jeska made it back tonight?

"I'll cripple the both of 'em," he muttered, pulling his pillow over his head to muffle the snuffling snores coming from the other bed. "*After* Trials."

The next morning Cade was too nervous to eat. By the time he got downstairs Rafe was already up and fed—and quite abundantly, too, judging by the huge plate at his elbow—seated at the kitchen table writing a letter to Crisiant. Cade's arrival elicited a nod and a question: "Where's the Elf?"

He replied with a smirk. Far from allowing Mieka to sleep in, Cade had left him thoroughly awake: pillowless, coverless, and howling with outrage at the crisp breeze through windows Cade had flung wide open. Cade nodded his gratitude to the Trollwife as she gave him a huge cup of soothing tea. Her eyes were a soft lavender, unusual in her people, and the sympathy in them was an unexpected annoyance. How many tregetours had passed through her kitchen on just such a morning as this? He wasn't like any of them—Touchstone was different, unique—oh Gods, which of the Thirteen would they have to perform? Please don't let it be "The Dragon," or "The Prince's Plague," or "The Treasure"— He gulped tea but his stomach kept gnawing on itself.

A plate of eggs and fried bread was set before him. He simply couldn't face it. Turning to Rafe, he asked, "Where's Jeska?"

"Jeska," Rafe echoed musingly. "That's something we need to discuss."

Before he could ask, a voice from the taproom rose in a squeak of shocked dismay: "Holy Gods! What *happened* to you?"

"Oh," Rafe commented, returning to his letter. "The Elf's found him."

They came in together, the one torn between horror and giggles, the other defiant and guilty.

"I didn't know she was bespoken, all right?" Jeska snarled, then winced and groaned as his cut lip, black eye, and swollen jaw moved in directions no longer compatible with comfort.

"P'rhaps we should've attempted the Minster girls," Mieka offered. "Might've been safer. No great hulking boyfriends lurking about."

"You—you—" Cade's considerable vocabulary deserted him. Or else so many words came to mind that they all got tangled on his tongue so none of them could make it out of his mouth.

"Was she worth it?" Mieka wanted to know.

Another incautious use of facial muscles—this time for a smug grin—brought another moan.

"No teeth for your collection?" Rafe taunted.

"Part Giant, he musta been," came the reply, stiff-lipped. He looked down mournfully at bruised, scraped knuckles. "Bones like bricks."

"And you're still *alive*?" Mieka snagged a slice of bread and began tearing it into small pieces, handing each to Jeska with a mocking grin. "Chew gently."

They went on teasing the masquer while Cade fought real nausea. Jeschenar's physical beauty, especially that exceptional face, was something Cade counted on even though he never admitted it. Today—in less than three hours, in fact—they'd be presenting themselves, and that face, at Seekhaven Castle, intent not just on the draw but also on impressing the judges right from the start.

"Oh, don't look so tragic, Quill," Mieka chided.

"Nothing's broken." He paused, then squinted at Jeska. "Nothing's broken, is it?"

He shook his head and sipped warily at the tea handed him by the Trollwife.

"There must be a leech or physicker somewhere in town who can set him right," Rafe said. "We don't perform for another three days, after all—"

"I've a better plan," said the Elf, grinning as if the whole situation had been crafted exclusively for his entertainment. Or, Cade thought suddenly, for him to use in entertaining others. Whichever, Cade wasn't disposed to argue with anyone who had a practical solution to the cuts and bruises on Jeska's face.

He really ought to have known. *Practical* and *Mieka Windthistle* were not acquainted with each other. Indeed, they had never even been introduced.

Two hours later, the Elf was perched on an overstuffed footstool upholstered in garish green silk, fascinated by a process most men never saw. Cade had effaced himself into a corner, wishing he could hide behind the nearby draperies. Rafe lounged on a velvet couch, sipping from a dainty teacup of what their hostesses called *mocah water,* the latest importation from a land so new and remote it didn't yet have a name anyone recognized. Jeska sat rigidly before some of the most expensive looking-glass in the Kingdom as the queen's ladies-in-waiting made him beautiful again.

For Mieka, *practical* had meant marching right up to the castle gates, a thing that in anyone else would have been sheerest folly. But he shamelessly traded on Cade's father's position at Court, somehow got Touchstone through to the inner precincts of Seekhaven Castle, bluffed them past a succession of guards and footmen, and through a combination of cheek, charm, and chatter enlisted one of Her Majesty's younger ladies in the cause. This girl whisked the four players into private hallways, up and down several stone staircases, and at last into the royal apartments. Because the Court had yet to arrive from Gallantrybanks, they used the queen's own dressing room and the queen's own cosmetics to repair the damage to Jeska's face.

Cade watched mindlessly, not really paying attention. Every step he had taken inside this vast castle had been silently dogged by his father's name and function. He'd expected raised brows and curious glances once his name was announced at Trials, but he would have been in familiar surroundings—*his* familiar surroundings, the honest stage, where fiction was labeled as such, rather than the play-acting that everyone pretended was reality at Court.

One of the ladies—a delicate redhead with the most elegant way of moving he'd ever seen—approached him and smiled. "None of us can wait to see you play, Master Silversun. We don't have chances like this very often!"

The price of the ladies' artistry was a private performance. In secret. It happened all the time, but rarely did ladies have the opportunity to make the arrangements for themselves. Or, in this case, to have a quick-talking glisker arrange it for them.

"And I promise none of us will get caught," she added. "Or, if we do, all of us have enough credit with Her Majesty so that no one will be punished."

Punishment there was—specified in the law books, at any rate. It was hardly ever meted out. Ordinarily Cade would have relished the risk of flouting tradition, but this was different. If Touchstone were caught, even after they'd won a place on the Winterly, that place might be taken away as an example to others. And it would be the Downstreet, and cold wagon rides to distant taverns, and living at his parents' house for the next year until Trials came up again.

"The pavilion is lovely," she went on. "We've seen

other players there, when His Majesty wants to surprise the queen with a treat." She gave him a smile through long lashes that owed nothing to cosmetics. "It's rather exciting, sneaking about late at night, even if everyone knows where we're going and why."

Well, that was Court, wasn't it? Behaving as if subterfuge were necessary even when it wasn't. It must make a nice change from the *real* artificialities. Aware that he was confusing himself, he nodded again and managed a smile.

"Your glisker told us where you're lodging, so I'll send a note with the day and time—oh, and an official pass, so no one will question you in town or within the castle."

"Beholden, Lady," he said.

"He's a bit of a lad, isn't he? Your glisker."

He flinched as a pretty little silver clock on the wood-paneled wall chimed the quarter-hour. "I-I don't mean to hurry the ladies, but—"

"I quite understand." Turning to the work in progress: "Bodgerie! Aren't you finished yet?"

Cade hardened his face against a wince. *Bodger* meant "to fix something very badly." Not a reassuring nickname. The redheaded lady saw it in his eyes, though—one had to be clever about reading people's faces at Court—and smiled again.

"It's to keep her humble. She's quite brilliant, really." Tiptoeing, she whispered, "Why do you think Her Majesty always looks ten years younger than her age? And the last time Princess Iamina—" She smirked. "Let's just say she trips on cracks in the tiles and bruises her cheek or her chin, usually after she's caught her husband with someone he oughtn't to be with. But you'd never know it, after Bodgerie's been to her."

"Does Lady Bodgerie mend Lord Tawnymoor's accidental falls, too?"

Her green eyes gleamed appreciation of the oblique

inquiry. "No. He just tends to disappear for a few days after one of his and the Princess's—"

"—mutual clumsinesses?" he suggested, and a grin broke across her exquisite face.

"All done!" Bodgerie sang out, and Jeska stood and turned for inspection. "What do you think?"

"Gorgeous," one of the ladies sighed, without a hint of a blush for such frank enjoyment of a young man's looks.

Mieka pouted a little before bouncing to his feet. He gave the ladies a low bow. "We are more beholden than we can possibly convey—but we'll give it our best try any night you name! Your ardent servants, ladies, and do excuse us for running out on you like this, but we've an appointment."

"Go, hurry!" said the little redhead, and they went.

Along the way, following directions given to Mieka, Cade scrutinized his masquer's new mask. "A bit swollen still, but nobody will notice," he decided.

"Don't talk," Rafe advised Jeska. "You'll crack your face."

Jeska raised a hand in an especially rude gesture. As they rounded a corner into a marble-floored atrium— and the full view of all the other groups of players waiting for the draw—Cade grabbed Jeska's arm and yanked it down before anyone could see.

It appeared, however, that the moody tregetour of Crystal Sparks had noticed. Mirko Challender looked down his long, thin nose for a moment, then grinned and returned the salute with both hands.

An underling in the royal livery of sea-green and brown rapped a gold-topped staff on the floor, and into the abrupt silence announced the Master of His Majesty's Revelries. This proved to be a tall, skeletal personage carrying a brown velvet drawstring purse. He started talking, but Cade didn't hear him; his attention had fixed on the bag of tokens to the exclusion of everything else.

It took Rafe's elbow in his ribs to make him realize that Touchstone's turn had come.

Side by side the four of them walked to what Cade devoutly hoped wouldn't be disaster. A group of men stood just behind the Master, chains of office draping their shoulders in rivulets of silver. The judges. They looked directly at him when the velvet purse was held out and he reached in his hand and pulled out a small round token. Lord and Lady and Gods and Angels, why hadn't he offered a prayer or a pence at High Chapel yesterday—they needed all the help they could get—

It would have been hideous manners to look at the token. Besides, he didn't want to betray which of the Thirteen he'd drawn by an involuntary smile—or wince. He bowed, backed up the required two steps, and Touchstone returned to their places. Mieka was quivering with excitement at his side, Jeska stood as if his bones had suddenly turned to cast iron, and Rafe tried unsuccessfully to stifle a sigh of relief that the ceremonial part was over. Cade gripped the token in his fist and stared right back at the judges. It was so damnably unfair that his future would be decided by six fusty middle-aged men who had never stepped onto a stage in their lives, who didn't know the first thing about creating and performing so much as a blank-verse poem, who had no magic and probably even less taste—

"Cade."

He felt Rafe's strong hand at the small of his back and obeyed it unthinkingly, walking outside into the forecourt and then through the tall gates with absurd little towers on either side, across an equally ridiculous moat complete with lily pads, and eventually to the street.

"Not yet," Rafe said suddenly. "Wait till we're private, Mieka."

"But I want to *know*!"

"So do I. But not here, not out in the open."

At length Cade felt grass rather than pavement beneath his feet. They were walking along the riverbank towards a little grove of willows. Excellent trees, willows, he thought; lovely leafy curtains to hide whatever reactions would come once he revealed the token in his hand.

He rubbed his index finger over it, trying to discern the image stamped thereon. Oh Gods—wings—no, *no*, not that one—

"Quill?" Mieka asked, hush-voiced. "Which did we draw?"

Cayden tossed over the token. Jeska glanced at it and moaned. Rafe closed his eyes for a moment, then shrugged. He wasn't particularly fond of it either, but at least the magic he would be called on to control would be primarily visual, not emotional. Mieka's eyes widened, but he said nothing.

They'd drawn the Ninth and flashiest of the Thirteen Perils, nothing subtle about it; lots of dazzle and very little artistry, as far as Cade was concerned. Even if they did it brilliantly, they hadn't a hope of First Flight on the Winterly. Nothing in this piece could possibly gain them the necessary points.

They all knew it. Rafe didn't bother stating the obvious. Fatalistically, he said, "At least we'll be working regular this winter."

Mieka eyed him sidewise. "Yes, we will. And you'll be marrying the lovely Mistress Crisiant—"

"Using what, exactly, for money?"

"—at High Chapel, not Low," Mieka went on stubbornly, "because the players of the First Flight make the most in trimmings."

Rafe hooted with laughter. "And how do we get First Flight? Because of our charm?"

"No. Because of how Gods-damned fucking great we are!" Pulling aside the willow-leaf curtain they were all hiding behind, he went on crisply, "Did you bring the directions to the rehearsal hall? Good. Let's go."

They had drawn "The Dragon." Two characters: a Fair Lady held captive and the Prince who rescued her. The Dragon itself was nothing more than a threatening shape and some sound effects. The judges' thinking was rumored to be that the better the Dragon, the more impressed the common folk would be, and points were awarded accordingly. The playlet started with the Lady, who for a page or so whined about her dreadful fate. Then the Prince rode to the rescue: noble, unselfish, dedicated, courageous, and so forth. A switch was made back to the Fair Lady, who did a lot of hand-wringing as she commented on the battle that occurred outside the cavern she was trapped in. The environment around her won points as well. The Prince victorious, the finish was her reaction as he strode in to free and claim her, and of course she fell deeply in love at first sight. The End.

Cayden reviewed all this in his head on the walk to the rehearsal hall. This was akin to a cavern itself, a great drafty emptiness of a place with no seating. It was, however, the precise dimensions of the theater they would be allowed inside on the morrow. Thus it served as a preliminary venue, just to work the rough edges off a performance before refining it in the castle theater itself.

Touchstone arrived just as Macielin Redprong was concluding auditions for this year's masquer and fettler. Things did not seem to have gone well. A shudder of distaste, quickly repressed, jolted Cayden out of his anxiety over their draw; one look at the dozen or so rejected applicants provoked a rush of sheer gratitude that he was, as Mieka had put it, part of something worth being part of. To subject himself to Redprong, a man would have to be desperate indeed to become a player.

Redprong himself—a tregetour, though short and stocky and without a hint of Wizard about his

Gnome-and-Goblin looks—eyed the new arrivals haughtily from his place at stage right. "Come back tomorrow," he grunted.

Jeska stiffened with insult. So did Cade. Rafe caught his breath. Mieka began to laugh.

"As much hope of that as of me gettin' me ears kagged!" he jeered. "Get off the stage and leave it to those as knows what they're about, won't you? There's a good lad!"

When the celebrated tregetour had betaken himself off with a Gnomish hiss of fury, Touchstone claimed the stage.

And stood there, staring at one another in an abrupt and empty silence that somehow they would have to fill.

Mieka flipped the token into the air and caught it, over and over, frowning more deeply each time. At last, just as Cade was about to shout at him to for the love of all the Gods *stop* it, he snatched it from the air, tucked it in a pocket, and said, "So which of us has the scathingly brilliant idea?"

There were a dozen or so chairs on the stage. Jeska dragged four of them into a square and sat, waiting for the creative portion of the team to come up with something. His expression of calm confidence—visible even under all the makeup—settled Cade somehow.

"I wish we could show what really happened," he mused. "The dragon was real, but it wasn't a lady who was rescued from a cave, it was a treasure from a castle dungeon someplace up north, and the poor beast was chained inside to guard it."

"More noble, though," Rafe said, "rescuing a pretty girl from a hideous great fire-breather."

"Be a shocker, wouldn't it?" He smiled and shook his head. "Hauling up the money in a sling made of your second-best cloak after you've stuck your sword into a dragon that can't even see to bite you."

"We can tweak it, can't we?" Mieka pleaded. "As it

stands, in the version everybody does, there's nothing that will get us noticed—"

"And nothing that will get us tossed in quod for insulting the royal family," Jeska cautioned, speaking slowly and carefully.

"But it's *boring*!"

"It's the one we've drawn," Rafe said. "We'll just do it better than anybody ever did it, that's all."

"But—"

"Make an end to it!" Rafe snapped, and Mieka subsided with a scowl. "Fair warning—you try anything silly, and I'll shut you down."

Cade saw Mieka give the fettler a look that plainly said, *You can try!* He shrugged. They were stuck; they had to perform this; they had no choice.

But Mieka wasn't giving up. "You say it was a real dragon, Quill?"

"I did some research on all the Thirteen. My grandfather's tregetour left him his library, and the true stories are there if you know where to look." But the one book that was missing—the volume that told the truth about all the Thirteen and the history of the theater in unflinching detail—that book was the one book his grandfather's tregetour had never owned. *Lost Withies* . . . so ancient and obscure that few tregetours even knew of it . . . there were rumored to be five or six copies still extant. . . . He dragged his mind back from hopeless book-lust. "Remember what we were saying about putting in some lines wondering what his famous great-grandfather would've done? Whether he can live up to it? I think that'll work well here. And that would be different enough—"

"But the dragon was real," Mieka interrupted, scowling. He dug the token out of his pocket, looked at it, and suddenly flung it high in the air again, laughing. "So what we'll do is give them a Dragon that'll scare the piss out of 'em!"

Even on the Royal Circuit, audiences were used to threatening shadows only. Once Mieka explained what he wanted to do, Cade gaped at him, then joined in his laughter. A real fire-breather? Ideas for accomplishing it swarmed in his head—yes, it was possible, and more besides.

"If we do it, then let's *do* it. You and me, we'll make us a Dragon, right enough—and forget the Fair Lady, just stay with the Prince."

They could linger, he explained, with the Prince long after the usual switch was supposed to have been made. The Fair Lady's voice would provide commentary on the battle, just as the piece was always done, but the scene onstage would stay with the Prince and the Dragon. Mieka would have to provide Jeska with an enswathing illusion that would allow him to speak the Fair Lady's lines without the audience being able to see his lips move—all of this while he was wielding a phantom sword against a Dragon more real than anything anyone had ever seen.

"I'll work a cavern mouth into it," Cade said, "and the echo we use for 'Deep Dark Well.' The contrast between the battle and all her whining will be—"

"—will get us shouted off the stage!" Rafe interrupted. "This is one of the Thirteen, in case you forgot! We have to treat it with at least *some* respect!"

"Why?" Mieka asked, wide-eyed.

Cade threw him a grateful smile. "They'll be so busy being scared of the Dragon and amazed by the battle that they won't even notice how we've messed with it. And we'll be using the standard script. Most of it, anyway. We'll just be shifting the focus."

"But how do I act it?" Jeska wailed.

"Like you always do," Mieka replied. "Like you'd been birthed to perform this piece and this piece only."

"Heroic," Cade told his masquer. "Give 'em every move you've got. And at the end, you're exhausted. You've just defeated a Dragon, for fuck's sake! The girl's blithering on and on about how brave and noble you are, and how much she adores you, while you're practically dead on your feet."

"Seeing what she wishes to see?" Rafe suggested.

"Exactly." Cade grimaced. "Just like everyone else in the world."

"You're too young to be so cynical," Mieka observed, "or so me old fa would say. Will we be showing the Fair Lady at all?"

"We have to." But Rafe suddenly didn't sound very certain.

"And there's another thing that's never been done," Cade said. "We give them a real Dragon, a real battle scene, all the while with her voice giving the descriptions, and finally—"

"What?" Jeska asked. "Finally *what*?"

"We don't show her at all! *She* can be the shadow. Not the Dragon, like everybody else does it. You stay the Prince—"

Rafe was shaking his head. "And have everybody think we're not good enough to do multiple characters?"

"Who else is good enough to do a real Dragon?" Mieka countered, and tossed the token back to Cade. "This is brilliant!"

Jeska was nodding, his blue eyes alight with plans, his lips already framing the customary lines. But Rafe was still balking, skeptical.

"Look," Cade said, leaning forward with his elbows on his knees. "We're there to give 'em a show. They don't really care what sort, as long as it's something they've never seen before. If we weren't capable of multiple characters, we wouldn't be here in the first place."

"And first place on the Winterly is where we'll be," Mieka stated. "Is that High Chapel wedding a little more real to you now?"

Rafe's broad shoulders relaxed, and he gave a slow nod. "If this works, I'll let you hold the loving cups." He paused. "Mind, I'll skin you alive if you drop them."

Over the next hour, they paced the stage, planning, arguing, sparking ideas off one another like—like true silver and true gold sparked off a touchstone, Cade told himself. *This* was how it was supposed to be: the exchanging and enhancing of techniques, the almost instantaneous comprehension of a new ploy, the eagerness, the *joy* of it.

And though he didn't mention it, he was thinking all the while that there would be no opportunity for their usual attention-grabber. There would be no shattering of glass. If they tried it, the stewards would be on them like wolves on unguarded sheep. Everybody knew what Touchstone did at the end of a show. The fettlers who stood watch to protect the audience from everything from deliberate violations to nervous mistakes would be aware of every move Touchstone had ever made.

They would have to do this on sheer talent alone. And something within Cade was glad that this was so. There would be no flash, no gimmicks, no tricks. Just the work.

He wondered why he felt not the slightest misgiving. After all, Touchstone had first drawn attention with the glass-shattering stunts. Part of the reason the four of them were thrashing out the performance of the Ninth instead of getting ready for another show at the Downstreet was that the maids at the Downstreet swept up more broken glass in one night than most taverns did in a year.

But he knew he wouldn't mention his certainty that they would be great even without their hallmark move. He wanted his partners a bit edgy; they did their best work when they were just a touch anxious. Himself, he functioned most effectively *after* he had worn himself out with worrying. In fact, he mused, he had so little in common with these three it was ludicrous. Offstage, Jeska rarely if ever stopped thinking about girls and how best to bed whichever beauty had taken his eye. If Mieka had seen an open book since he left littleschool, it was only because one had fallen off a shelf in front of him. As for Rafe—despite his love for the theater and his determination to travel the Circuit, he was essentially a homebody, a confirmed nestcock eagerly anticipating marriage to Crisiant and a settled home with a dozen rambunctious children.

But the four of them understood each other on more basic and more important levels: they knew the work. Jeska was poised to become one of the legendary masquers. Rafe was only growing in power and confidence. Mieka was the most talented, if the most maddening, glisker Cade had ever seen.

And they're mine, he told himself. *Together we make this singular thing: Touchstone. The standard to measure against, the proof of worth. Let the rest of them strike their work against ours. They won't prove gold or even silver. Compared to us, they're wood shavings.*

"I think he approves," Rafe said suddenly, and Cade looked over at the three of them. They were watching him with varying degrees of speculation on their faces.

"How can you tell?" Mieka asked, frowning.

"He's got that look in his eye."

Cade let his smile widen. "Which one?"

Rafe snorted. "Which look, or which eye?"

He tossed the dragon token high in the air, caught it, and laughed, and wouldn't tell them what he was laughing about.

Eleven

EASING HIS ARMS into the close-fitting sleeves of his new jacket, Cayden resisted the urge to shrug and squirm until the garment was comfortable. It wasn't comfortable and it never would be; that was the whole point of fashion, or so Mieka had assured him.

"For everyone else but you," Cade had retorted. "I'd like to see you work the glisker's bench in something this tight!"

The boy had grinned and told the tailor to lengthen the jacket's cuffs. "Oh, and make sure the pleating at the waist doesn't make it look like half a lady's skirt," he added. "Fit it nice and snug down the hips, right?" Then, turning to his sister for advice: "Well? Will he do?"

"Compared to what?" asked Jinsie Windthistle.

Her twin made a face at her. "A kelpie in a red silk gown, what d'you think?"

"Oh, he'll do just fine, in that case." She smiled at Cade and gave him a wink. Her eyes, he noted again with a slight shock, were exceptionally blue. Her coloring was, in fact, the opposite of her brother's: pale eyes, white-gold hair, and a dusky cast to her skin that made those eyes even more startling. Jinsie was shorter that Mieka, with even slighter bones and even more delicate ears, but in character they were as alike as berries on a bush. Cade had liked her on sight; better still, she and Blye got on like a spring-spate river. By the time Mieka had dragged him to the trendy but not yet wildly popular tailor over on Narbacy Street, where one could get elegant clothing at still-reasonable prices, Jinsie and Blye had been to several of the Downstreet shows dressed as boys. And right fashionable boys, at that. This tailor was where Jinsie had got the appropriate attire for their impostures at secondhand.

Cade thought with gratitude of Jinsie as he dressed for Trials—despite the tedium of doing up the two dozen silver buttons she'd decreed must fasten his jacket, waist to throat. Even though they'd be performing in less than two hours, he wasn't at all nervous. This was partly due to how great they were going to look. Jinsie had chosen Touchstone's attire. She'd decided everything from the cut of his jacket to the material, a light blue-gray that lent some color to his face and gave his eyes a slightly blue cast. The silk was woven through with a tiny pattern of strawberry leaves—for luck, Jinsie had told him, after she'd bargained the half-bolt down to a price she deemed acceptable. Tonight, for Trials, each member of Touchstone would be wearing something made of this silk. Cade's jacket, Rafe's neckband (knotted to Jinsie's specifications and fixed with a silver-and-onyx pin in the shape of his clan's Spider, lent by his father), Jeska's collar and cuffs, and the front plackets of Mieka's shirt. Jinsie had decreed that they must have some sort of visual correlation.

"But we'll make it subtle," she'd said, pacing slowly around Cade where he stood on a little raised platform while the tailor worked. "Not like the Shorelines, with their silly matching tunics that don't fit."

"Or the Goldenharts," Mieka contributed, "with those yellow deer antlers on their chests. Always looks as if they're about to get stabbed."

"Or," said the tailor, most unexpectedly, "what I just made for the Shadowshapers."

"You did?" Cade craned his neck to look at the man where he knelt, fussing with the jacket's hem.

"Oh, yes. Very smart, though I say it meself—collarless black shirts, gray velvet jackets, black piping on everything. Though, as the young mistress says, not subtle. Master Kevelock, he's got himself a passion for embroidery." He stood, made his stately, critical way round Cade once more, and nodded. "Not like this at all. The Windthistles," he observed to Cade, "have always had taste."

Jinsie sniffed delicately. "Always excepting our brother Jedris, of course. Miek, you remember the time he showed up at Wintering in one of Mum's old skirts?"

As Cade choked on laughter, Mieka explained, "He'd had it cut up and sewn into a cloak—but vermilion just isn't his color, not with that red hair."

It appeared that *any* color was Mieka's color. It was those eyes, of course: they picked up the shade of whatever he wore, or its opposite, or a complementary color—it was impossible to guess which would result. Cade had given up trying.

As they stood facing each other in the upstairs bedchamber overlooking Spoonshiner River, Cade suspected that Mieka's assessment of him was likely to be more thorough and less satisfactory than his inspection of Mieka, so he had to smile when, reaching up to adjust the Falcon pin at Cade's throat, the Elf gave a deep nod of approval.

"Excellent. Really excellent, Quill. No, I mean it!" he exclaimed when Cade laughed aloud. "Jinsie was absolutely right about that silk. She usually is."

"You don't look half ugly, either," he teased. In truth, the touch of gray-blue suited Mieka admirably, especially paired with the black of the rest of his outfit. In public Mieka frustled as fine as any titled lord; onstage he was sartorially subdued.

"What I don't understand," Mieka said as they started downstairs, "is why you're not chewing your fingernails up to your elbows."

"We've got it done and dusted, Mieka. We're for First Flight on the Winterly Circuit." Feeling the boy's puzzled gaze, he turned and smiled. "Unless you'd *rather* I fretted."

"No, havin' me Quill anguishin' himself would distract me. I'm only hoping the bruises aren't still distracting Jeska."

"He seemed fine this morning."

"He's a very good masquer," Mieka retorted. "Nothing to worry about, though. I came prepared."

Reaching into his jacket pocket, he brought out a green leather implement roll like that used by Mistress Mirdley to store her best kitchen knives. Braided silk cords tied it together, gold to match the stamped design along the edges. Wyvern hide, Cade realized, and the seed-raindrop-flame pattern. Just like the wallet of blockweed.

"He won't take anything."

"He will if it lets him forget how much his jaw still hurts."

Cade shook his head. "He won't."

"If you and Rafe tell him to, he will."

After a moment's interior struggle, he asked, "Will it leave his head clear?"

"Perfectly. It just dulls pain for a few hours, nothing else."

To his surprise, he felt an abrupt longing as he looked at the familiar green-and-gold. It had been wonderful to sleep without dreaming, without even being afraid that he might dream. It had been even better to use just enough blockweed to give him half-waking dreams he could control and direct. Was there something in that very well-appointed roll that would work even more interesting effects?

"I won't get them muddled, if that's what you're thinking," Mieka went on. "Auntie Brishen gave me strict instructions how to use her emergency kit." Then, peering up at Cade's face, he arched his brows. "Oh! Is *that* what's in your mind? Let's get through tonight, and talk about it tomorrow, right?" With a laugh, as he leaped the last few stairs: "If we can think round our hangovers, that is!"

Cade nodded helplessly. He would never understand how Mieka read him so accurately. He wasn't sure he wanted to. "Didn't Auntie Brishen send anything useful for that?"

"A hangover's like the common cold, y'know— impossible to cure, no matter how hard anybody tries. Humans," he observed with a sad shake of his head, "have much to answer for."

"Then again," Cade countered, "if *you* weren't partly Human, you wouldn't be able to drink without hangovers that last a week."

"Doesn't spare me gettin' sniffles and a sore throat, though, does it? Rafe!" he bellowed suddenly. "Where are you?"

They both jumped as Rafe stepped into the stairwell from the back hallway. "Here, Your Lordship." He swept them a Court bow. "Move your ass, Your Lordship, or I'll kick it all the way to the castle. Or the river. Which-ever's closer."

The sharpness of his voice aroused Cade's suspicions. No doubt of it: Rafe was nervous. So was Jeska. The masquer's bruises hadn't faded, and at final rehearsal yesterday he'd held back in his gestures and his vocal modulations. His face would be carefully transformed by Mieka so that during the Fair Lady's speeches no one would see his lips move, but Cade needed all the elo-quence of movement and intonation Jeska could give him. He caught Mieka's gaze, glanced at the green leather roll still in his hand, and nodded.

That Jeska put up no fight should have given Cade a bad case of nerves. But he'd dreamed last night.

{The tavern had become a landmark, with blue enamel plaques on the wall to prove it. TOUCHSTONE, CRYSTAL

SPARKS, BLACK LIGHTNING, HAWK'S CLAW. All of them had started here. The Downstreet: origin of legends.

A long-boned man with graying reddish-brown curls and almost golden skin sat on the stage playing an eight-stringed lute. His music had an almost casual beauty, as if hinting that if he really exerted himself, his listeners would scarce be able to bear the magic of it. The sound threaded like drifting smoke through the empty tavern, gliding around the pretty barmaids polishing the tables, swirling about the uneven roof timbers. Over in the back corner two men sat opposite each other, glass goblets gleaming on the wooden table. One of the men was dressed richly, elegantly; the other had inkstains on his thick fingers and shirt cuffs.

"I must've written a dozen or more pieces about them through the years. They always were the best." Tobalt paused for a sip of wine, licked his lips delicately, and regarded the goblet for a moment. "These are exact copies, you know. No matter how many years it's been, they keep the same design."

"You said you met them after their rather sensational appearance at Trials."

"I didn't see the performance, but I knew somebody who did, and he tipped me that they were something special."

The younger man scribbled notes on a long sheet of paper. "There've been rumors about that ever since."

"Most of them started by Mieka Windthistle!" Tobalt grinned. "He admitted last year that he's never bothered to keep track of any of the stories he makes up to keep people guessing. And they say *Cayden's* the one with the imagination—!"

"They did what no one had ever done, that year at Trials."

"The first of many innovations. The Shadowshapers,

they always pushed the limits of what could and couldn't be done. And nobody's better at giving solid versions of the old standards than the Sparks. Hawk's Claw is doing some interesting stuff these days, too. But the way Touchstone works—they glint off each other, you can see it when they're onstage, when they've just walked on and they all glance at each other. And again, when they've finished, and Jeska will collect all of them with a look. There's a silent laugh amongst them when they know they've been spectacular."

"They've had their problems through the years, though," the second man suggested.

"On and off the stage," Tobalt agreed easily. "Coming from within and without. But Touchstone is still together after twenty-five years."

Tobalt, talking to a reporter in the Downstreet (and Cade kicked himself mentally for not having recognized it before). But different, so different. Nothing about losing the Elf who was their soul. Whatever had happened, whoever had made the crucial choices, that cold and heartless future was gone.

He smiled at his friends, his partners, as they waited to take the stage. And in their eyes he saw the glint Tobalt had spoken of—*would* speak of. That *everyone* would speak of. He tried to imagine all of them twenty-five years into the future . . . lines on their faces, gray hair, less hair, more waistline . . . he couldn't do it. To him, they would always be as they were right now: young and eager, their faces bright with excitement and confidence, their eyes looking to him as the source of that confidence. And all at once he laughed, and took Mieka aside, and whispered a few words that made the Elf chortle quietly and nod agreement.

And then they were onstage.

Fliting Hall seated six hundred—three times the biggest audience Touchstone had ever known. The name had come from its original purpose as a sort of interior tilting yard. Three hundred years ago, more or less, the king at the time had grown weary of losing his best warrior knights to peacetime duels, and thus had decreed a change in the manner of their brawls. A formal challenge was issued, the parties agreed on a time, and the least lethal of swords—thin, flexible foils—were handed out from the monarch's own armory to make sure no one cheated by strengthening, stiffening, or poisoning a blade. Padded gambesons protected the combatants' bodies from throat to groin. Those of the court with an interest in the proceedings, or merely an interest in minor bloodshed, lined the four walls. Chairs were set for official arbiters. Hostilities were thereby civilized.

At some point, however, the battles became verbal as well as physical, and eventually swordskill yielded to wordplay. The exchanges of invective and mockery were formalized, sometimes into poetry, and the arbiters became judges. Their verdict about which challenger had delivered the final sizzling retort decided the contest. From fighting to fliting, from duels of swords to duels of words—but the age of spontaneous wit had given way to predetermined scripts. And now Trials were held in Fliting Hall every summer, with judges deciding the outcome not of combat but of competition—though a nod to the place's original purpose was preserved in the levels of each Circuit: First, Second, and Third Flights.

The hall had been turned into a genuine theater, with a wide stage concealed by two swagged sets of velvet curtains, sea-green and silver. Rather than crowd spectators around the edges, there were permanent seats, more rows of them than Cayden had ever seen, rising gradually towards the back so that everyone had a good view of the stage. The rough-faced stone of the original had been paneled in more acoustically appropriate wood, carved at regular intervals with scenes representing The

Thirteen. Fist-sized glass globes using blue Wizardfire, not the more subtle golden Elf-light, glowed over each of six doors and all the way around the carved juncture where walls met ceiling. Cade had given a wordless glare of warning as they entered, pointing to the globes, then to Rafe and Mieka. The fettler nodded wry agreement; the glisker looked rebellious for a moment, then shrugged and smiled.

As "The Dragon" progressed, Cade kept careful watch on the audience. Not on the judges, seated in their own special box in the middle of the theater; they would decide what they'd decide, and Touchstone would have to accept it. Besides, he already knew their decision; he'd dreamed its aftermath, hadn't he? No, he watched the audience because they were the ones who would talk later on to their friends. And by the expressions on their faces as the Dragon appeared—taking up half the stage, a real tail-lashing fire-breather—they would be talking about this for months.

Simultaneously, of course, Cade was doing his usual monitoring. It was extremely odd to sense the presence of the stewards, guarding against any dangerous foolishness brought on by nerves. He wasn't accustomed to other people's magic being in use during a Touchstone show. But what really struck him—and Rafe, too, by the slight, startled movement of his shoulders—was that after the Fair Lady started bewailing her plight, the stewards relaxed their grip. They had decided that Rafcadion Threadchaser was a fettler who knew what he was doing. Sneaking a glance at the faces half-hidden in the back of the hall, Cade wanted to laugh when he saw that the four men weren't attending to their usual duties. They were watching the show.

Cade couldn't blame them.

From his one night glisking for the Shadowshapers, Mieka had learned—barely, which was why Sakary

Grainer had had such trouble with him—how to create a swirling gloom from which the play coalesced. Now he used the same technique to create the Dragon. The dread that crept down the spine, the fear that hollowed the chest, the grim determination to gut it all out even though tremors shook the muscles—he played lightly, delicately with all these things, before he made the Dragon. And when he did, and the fire erupted from its gaping mouth that reeked of congealed blood and rotting flesh, every man in the hall twitched and gasped, and some of them even shielded their faces with their arms.

Spectacular? Sensational? Oh, yeh, Cade told himself with an interior grin. Mieka was so good at subtle quivers of sensation, and Rafe was so good at ensuring that they stayed subtle—even for the most susceptible in the crowd—that most of the audience, sophisticated theater patrons that they were, not gullible provincials, actually took an instant or two to examine their hands for blisters and blackened skin that magic had persuaded them must be there.

The phantom burning was forgotten when Mieka did as Cade had suggested earlier, and tossed Jeska a withie to use as the core of his illusory sword. As the glass twig spun end-over-end in the air, the audience saw it transformed by Cade's magic in Mieka's clever hands to a long, broad blade of shining silver. Jeska snatched it by the hilt and began the Prince's battle with the Dragon—all the while using the Fair Lady's voice to describe the frantic action.

Blood darkened the sword, dripping to the rocky ground. The Prince's parries began to falter. The Dragon roared and threw its head back almost to the ceiling, fire gushing from its jaws. The Fair Lady screamed—just as the sword plunged into the Dragon's heart. The thud of the massive body hitting the stage was like a thunderclap shuddering through the theater.

Exhausted, the Prince sank to his knees as the girl's voice trilled passionately of her love for him. He looked up as she ended her speech, dark eyes glazed, uncaring, even rather cynical, as if to say, *I just killed a dragon for you—you're supposed to be in love with me, you silly girl.* Then he reached a hand to the Dragon's outspread wing, almost touching it, fingers trembling with weariness.

"Enough?" he rasped. "Good enough? Brave enough? Will my son's sons sing of it—wondering all the while if they'll face down dragons of their own?" Using the sword to push himself to his feet, swaying, he shook his head. "They'll know their own dragons, in their time. Let them sing not that I was mindlessly brave, but that I was frightened and overcame my fear. *That* is the legacy I leave them, the same, I see now, that my fathers left to me. The overcoming is what fashions a man into a prince, and a prince into a king."

The shades and sensations faded quietly, drawn from the far corners of the theater, returning to the stage. It was a long, tense wait, but the applause when it finally came stunned Cade's ears and pounded inside his chest along with his heart.

He met Rafe's gleeful gaze; they both knew Touchstone would be First Flight, and making money enough to give Crisiant a High Chapel wedding as grand as any titled lady's. Jeska rose lithely to his feet, grinning as he tossed the withie back to Mieka—who laughed aloud, standing on his glisker's bench amid the glass baskets, arms outspread as if to catch all the cheers and applause. But he didn't catch the withie. He shattered it in midair.

A million tiny slivers of glass tinkled to the stage between the glisker's bench and Jeska. Cade heard every single one in the sudden hollow silence. And his certainty of triumph and the future splintered with them.

* * *

"MASTER SILVERSUN?"

His head seemed to weigh quite a bit more than it had a few hours ago. Or perhaps he'd somehow lost or misplaced the muscles of his neck. Perfectly reasonable to prop his jaw in his palm as he scowled up at the cullion who'd interrupted . . . um . . . whatever it was he'd interrupted. Cade wasn't entirely sure, except that it had involved a very large glass filled with very excellent brandy. Filled many, many times, in fact. And emptied.

"Master Silversun."

"Unh?"

"Court courier, sir."

A roll of parchment was placed on the table before him, right next to his glass. His tragically empty glass. He mourned it for a moment, then picked up the letter. Ribbons and wax seal all present and correct. *Touchstone* written on the outside in the elegant scrawl affected by the nobility.

"I'm to wait for a reply, sir."

"Havva sit-down." He waved vaguely to the place where there ought to have been more chairs. Or a bench. Or something.

"Beholden, sir, but no." And the boy assumed the parade stance of a Royal Guardsman, hands clasped behind his back, chin high.

"Whassat?"

At the sound of his glisker's voice, Cade let his hand rotate his head a little in the Elf's general direction. Arms braced and palms flat, Mieka was leaning on the table as if the table was the only thing holding him up.

"Court," Cade answered.

It seemed to be explanation enough. Mieka nodded wisely once, twice—and on the third nod began a slow descent towards the tabletop. A strong arm circled his chest from behind and lowered him more or less gently to a bench shoved into range by a booted foot. Cade recognized the arm (Rafe's) and the boot (Jeska's). Thus identified to his satisfaction, it really was too much effort to focus on the rest of either of them. So he looked at the parchment roll instead.

After a time, he decided that something wasn't quite right. The invitation to Trials had been decorated with wide sea-green and silver ribbons, and a big brown wax seal, much more impressive than this pair of thin pink ribbons and smear of blue wax. He looked at it some more—and flinched when the boy coughed politely beside him.

Oh. He was supposed to send back an answer.

"Will you *open* it, for fuck's sake?"

He lifted his head—still very much heavier than it ought to be; perhaps it was the weight of the gigantic drum pounding inside his skull—and met Rafe's narrow glare.

"Izzint the Reveleries—Revulseries—" Whatever he was trying to say, it wasn't coming out right. It didn't matter; they'd got their First Flight on the Winterly, and he hadn't had to murder the Elf after all.

Mieka gave a whining sort of mumble and curled onto his side atop the bench, cheek pillowed in the crook of his arm. Cade thought idly how awkward it must be, finding the right position so the tip of his ear didn't go numb. . . .

"Jus' opinnit, eh?" Jeska was sitting beside him—how had he got there? As the masquer reached for the parchment, he overbalanced and slid half across Cade's lap.

Pushing him more or less upright, Cade finally picked up the message—it took both hands to do it—and picked at the little blot of blue wax. He'd scraped a gouge in the parchment without actually breaking the seal when Rafe growled and snatched it out of his hands.

"Invitation," Rafe finally said.

"Got that already, dinnit we?" Jeska frowned, befuddled.

"No, to the castle. Tomorrow night after cur—" A mighty belch interrupted the word. "—few."

"But what about First?" Jeska asked, almost in tears. "Dinnit we get First?" He turned drowning blue eyes on Cade, and wiped his nose. "I was *good*. Wassunt I good, Cade?"

"The best," Cade assured him. "We got First, Jeska."

Rafe carefully smoothed the parchment onto the table. "The castle," he repeated, then looked at the liveried servant boy. "Honored. Charmed. Delighted. Can't fuckin' wait—"

All at once Mieka scrambled himself upright, wreathed in smiles, rocking lightly back and forth as if warming up for a show. "The ladies!" he announced happily.

This made no sense whatsoever. But then, so little of what the Elf said and did made the kind of sense that made sense to Cade. All the same, he gave a nod and a smile, because they seemed to be the order of the evening, and said, "Brilliant!" And never felt his face hit the table.

* * *

BY THE NEXT noon, Cade had more or less convinced himself that rising from his bed wouldn't shred every muscle currently (barely) holding him together and dislocate every bone in his body.

He turned out to be correct, but it was a very near thing.

He had never been so repulsively drunk in his life. He was paying for it now in a hangover so vile that even his eyelashes ached.

The sight of Mieka's empty bed brought a resurgent longing to get his hands around his glisker's throat and strangle him, but it took a moment to figure out why.

Oh. The shattered glass withie.

He'd thought his heart would freeze in his chest,

become a lump of solid ice that anyone could reach between his ribs and yank out of his body. Here was proof positive that his own choices counted for almost nothing. So he'd seen Tobalt in the Downstreet twenty-five years from now. So what? With a single flash of rebellious magic, Mieka had shattered not just the spent withie but potentially Touchstone's whole future. The startled eyes, the shocked faces, the gasps of outrage—hundreds upon hundreds of them—he moaned softly, leaning forward with his hands gripping his skull. It could have been absolute disaster.

That it hadn't been was hardly the Elf's doing. The grim expressions of the judges and the agonizing wait for their decision had clawed into Cayden's guts. In the end, that they had accepted Touchstone for the Winterly Circuit, and moreover assigned them First Flight, was in spite of and not because of what Mieka had done. Cade had been told so in unambiguous language when the scores were read out and the coveted brass medals signifying their new status were handed to them.

"Keep him under control, boy," one of the old men had growled. "You're lucky we don't send you back to Gallantrybanks with citations instead of medals."

"Yes, m'lord," he'd breathed, shaking, the token of triumph cold in his palm.

Two other judges said nothing, merely glared. The fourth told Cade, "You nearly lost First. Had it right in your hands, right up until that stunt at the end. I had to argue them into it."

A fifth judge sniffed and turned away, but the sixth had some advice. "Silversun? Find yourself another glisker."

Pride had forbidden him to react. Furious as he was with Mieka, he also knew there wasn't a glisker anywhere to touch him. *Mine he is, and mine he stays,* Cade had told himself. *Even when I want to kill him.*

The urge to slap the insolent grin from Mieka's face had not abated until they'd toasted victory with many, many bottles of fine Frannitch brandy (contributed by their hosts, thrilled that *their* boys had won First Flight on the Winterly and given their inn bragging rights for the next year). It was just as well that on the walk back into Seekhaven Town, Cade had been carrying his crated glass baskets; had his hands been free . . . As it was, he'd snarled at Rafe, "Keep him the fuck away from me," and stayed silent all the way back to the inn. Then he'd taken a seat at the table on the porch and got deliberately, disgustingly drunk.

A scratching noise abraded his aching ears. Before he could decide whether it was a mouse in the walls or a tree branch against a window, the bedchamber door opened.

"Cade? Are you—oh. You're awake."

He would have thrown Mieka out but for two things. First, he wasn't entirely sure his knees would last long enough to carry him to the door, and second, the boy held a very large teapot in one hand and a cup in the other. As the contents of the former filled the latter and the steam wafted towards him, smelling of cinnamon and some even more exotic spice he couldn't identify, he decided to let the boy live. He took the cup and downed half the scalding contents in three gulps.

"It's lovely outside," Mieka ventured apprehensively. "Clear and very warm, and—"

Cade lifted his gaze from the cup. Mieka managed a rather sickly smile and thereafter kept his mouth shut.

At length, revived sufficiently, Cade condescended to address the Elf. "Beholden for the tea. I ought to break every bone in every finger of both your hands." Then he looked more closely at Mieka's face. There was a patch of reddened, raw skin on one cheekbone, and a bruise blooming around it.

{He looked down at that arrogantly beautiful face, hating the drunken smirk, the smug certainty that he would be forgiven anything, everything. All at once he wanted nothing so much as to smash his fists into that face until it was a bleeding, broken ruin. But as his arm raised, he decided instead on another and perhaps deeper kind of hurting. And so he cracked his open palm across the Elf's cheek, a deliberate insult.

The cry of pain, the look of betrayal in those eyes—he stared down at Mieka where he'd stumbled to the floor and said very quietly, "Don't you ever show up this drunk again. Not ever."

"Fuck you!"

He reached down and his left hand fisted in the stained white shirt. He hauled the Elf vertical and didn't let him go as his right hand lifted once more—and descended again and again and again and again—}

Cade covered the few seconds of the turn by reaching for the teapot. He hoped the tremor in his fingers would be attributed to his hangover. He half-expected to see Mieka's blood on his hand.

"I see you noticed my face," Mieka said ruefully. "There were a few more stairs than I thought, on the way back up here last night. But I remember what the ladies did for Jeska and—oh Gods, I almost forgot! It's not just the ladies who want to see us perform! Prince Ashgar's man came round this morning, we've a command to the castle! Nobody gets two invitations at their first Trials, Quill, *nobody*!"

Cade stared at him, trying to drag his weary brain back from the frightening image of himself beating Mieka senseless, trying to understand what he was being told. Two shows? They were bidden to the castle twice?

Sharing the news had restored Mieka's spirits; he bounced onto his own bed, grinning. "You can break my fingers *after*," he teased. "And if you're feeling tolerably sane again, we ought to decide what we'll be doing for the ladies tonight. C'mon, Quill, finish your tea and let's get to work!"

Twelve

NOT A DOUBT of it: the waking turns were more frequent and more severe. Cade didn't want to believe that this coincided with Mieka's arrival in his life, but had to admit it was true. His only recourse was to intensify practice of the disciplines Sagemaster Emmot had taught him. That there was another alternative—getting rid of Mieka—didn't deserve an instant's thought.

Mine he is, and mine he stays.

No matter how many different kinds of trouble he caused.

A thornful of whatever painkiller Jeska had used was enough to dull his hangover, and enabled Cade to face the late performance for the ladies of the Court. It also allowed him to think clearly enough for long enough to decide that he'd have to let Mieka in on his secret soon. Perhaps if the boy understood how drastic the consequences of his actions could be, it would tame him a little, cause him to think about what he did before he did it—

Lord and Lady, what was he contemplating?

"And what would you tell someone like that? 'Live your life the way I need you to live it! Don't be yourself, make your choices according to what I want!' Oh, you could make that person feel guilty enough to get the results you want. You could make a free and independent soul into a slave, frightened of setting a foot outside the door in case it produces an unpleasant future. Or you

could keep your silly mouth shut and not burden other people with the foreseeings that burden you." Emmot smiled with mirthless irony. *"Your choice, Cayden. Always your choice."*

It was obvious to Cade that he didn't get angry at other people quite as often as he used to. This might have been attributable to growing up, realizing that success was at last within reach, learning that his work really was as good as he hoped it was. The truth, though, was that much of the annoyance provoked by others was now being directed at Mieka, who was capable of making him more angry than anyone else he'd ever known. He'd felt it that first night, hadn't he, when the tryout with a new glisker had resulted in astonishment after astonishment? He'd thought at first that it was only because he hadn't scripted the changes Mieka had made in "The Sailor's Sweetheart"; he knew himself to be that arrogant about the work, and that domineering. But once it had become clear that, as Rafe had said, Mieka *fit* with them, he'd begun to trust the Elf. For all his mad whimsies, Mieka cared deeply about the work. It was his life, just as much as it was Cade's and Rafe's and Jeska's.

No, it wasn't Mieka's unpredictability onstage that so infuriated Cayden—though the shattered withie at Trials had been a reminder that he was likely to do almost anything if the impulse struck him. Instead, Cade remembered the snow and the streetlamp, and the words he'd never said—and the uncanny echo of the foreseeing in real life: *"It's not in you to be wicked, Cade, nor cruel."*

And yet—hadn't he seen himself slap Mieka so brutally that it knocked him to the ground? Hadn't he beaten him bloody?

He would have to control his temper. That was the start and the finish of it. No matter how angry he became, and no matter how much the Elf deserved that anger, Cade could not give in to it. If he sometimes just had to succumb to the urge to hit something, the world was full of walls and doors, furniture and glass windows—and other people. But not Mieka. It was too dangerous for reasons he would never, could never, explain.

Thus settled in his mind, Cayden could relax and enjoy the torchlit walk to the castle that night—especially as the ladies had sent three liveried pages to carry the crates and withies and Rafe's new oakwood lectern that had been his parents' gift on making Trials. Trusting the security of Mieka's cushioning spell, Cade had no qualms about letting the boys take charge of the glass baskets. But Mieka was oddly reluctant to part with the black velvet bag of withies. Cade couldn't make out the expression on his face—it was there and gone even faster than usual—before he gave an awkward little laugh and told the lad to have a care.

"If the glass breaks, all the magic will escape," he confided, "and you might end up crying all night, or laughing into the middle of next week, or with a stiffcocking you won't be able to ease for a month—"

"Leave off," Rafe chided, adding to the saucer-eyed boy, "He's not serious, don't worry."

Looking none too reassured, the page gulped, nodded, and clasped the velvet bag to his chest with both arms. Had it been an infant, it would have suffocated.

The pavilion where Touchstone would perform unofficially for the ladies of the Court turned out to be a hammered copper roof balanced on thirteen pillars with seating beneath for approximately five hundred.

Torches lit the path through the castle precincts. Past little walled gardens they walked, glimpsing paved courtyards that featured potted specimen trees from distant lands, fountain pools, knot-gardens, and fish ponds. After a long walk across an expanse of close-clipped grass, the players were led to the pavilion by the little red-headed lady who still hadn't mentioned her name. When

Cade at last saw the circular copper roof half-embraced by a grove of beeches and poplars, he nearly tripped over his own feet. The thing was gigantic. Worse, it was outdoors. They'd never played an outdoor site—though there were several on the Ducal and Royal Circuits, and one reason for starting out on the Winterly was to provide groups a look at where they'd perform if they made it up a notch in the next Trials.

Lady Redhead, as Cade had no choice but to call her, stopped at the short steps leading to the stage. "Here's where I leave you—but not for the whole of the evening, I hope," she added with an eloquent glance up at Cade. "I'll look for you after." And she melted away into the chaotic crowd.

"*He* won't be comin' home tonight," Rafe advised Mieka.

"All the more privacy for me!"

Jeska shook his head. "Oh no, mate. The Trollwife was specific—no girls in our rooms. That means you'll have to find someplace else." Then he winked and whispered, "The hayloft will be free tonight."

Mieka sniggered. "Chose a sneezer, did you? Or does she just want something a bit less rustic?"

"Will you shut it?" Cade demanded. "Where do you want to set up? Stage forrards or stage back?"

They arranged themselves a bit farther to the front than usual, considering the size of the place and the lack of walls. Rafe paced back and forth across the stage, calculating the potential rebound off the support pillars and high, peaked copper roof. Mieka joined him on two of these surveys, then helped Cade set up the glass baskets. Cade looked out at the casual jumble of chairs, wondering helplessly how to signal that they would soon begin. But Lady Redhead had been watching, and came forward and lifted both dainty little hands.

It took a few moments, but the two hundred or so ladies found seats and quieted down. A tremor of expectation and excitement rippled through the crowd. And abruptly Cade realized that for the first time, they were standing in front of an audience composed entirely of women.

Should it make a difference? They hadn't really discussed it, not in direct terms. They'd chosen two standard pieces, both of them liberally rewritten by Cayden over the last months. The first was quite short, the second rather longer. Jeska had wanted to do two cloyingly romantic playlets; Rafe had snorted his opinion of this, Mieka had shrugged indifferently, and Cade had said, "The idea is to make them remember us, and talk about us—and anybody who thinks the ladies stay silent and keep the so-called secret of these shows is a shit-wit. So let's give them things they've never even thought about before, eh?"

Accordingly, when Lady Redhead turned and smiled up at him, he nodded, stepped forward, and announced simply, "'Caladrius,'" and effaced himself to his side of the stage.

"Once there was a great white raven, a solitary raven, a lonely raven called Caladrius, that kept to itself, not mingling with its kind."

The tale went on to describe the bird in detail, and as Jeska spoke the lines, Mieka fashioned the huge snow-white raven and set it to preening itself where it perched on a castle windowsill. It was a very pretty bit of magic, that slender stone tower and arched window, and Cayden was very proud of it.

The first half of the story had Jeska gradually sprawling into a chair—a real one, which Mieka disguised as a one-armed sofa covered in plain blue silk—sickening unto death, increasingly hoarse-voiced. He wore his own splendid face and form; Mieka and Cade knew without having to mention it that Jeska's looks would have every woman in the audience just that much closer to tears as he failed and faltered. So young, so beautiful, and dying . . . When the white raven rose up and flew in a great circle round the whole pavilion, the ladies all gasped. It came to rest on the end of the sofa, tilting its head as Jeska grated out words of despair—and sudden hope, as he recognized the white raven for what it was: the Caladrius, bird of healing. Should it look away from him, he would die—but if it gazed steadily into his eyes, the malady would be taken into the bird and flown to the highest heavens to be burned away by the sun.

"Look at me," Jeska pleaded, "look at me, I beseek, and do not look away!"

Shining gold eyes regarded him for a long, long moment. The audience held its breath, trembling as Jeska trembled, afraid to hope—and then crying out with happiness as the wide wings spread and the yellow-orange mists of the illness seeped from Jeska's eyes into the bright eyes of the bird. Then the white raven launched itself into the air, spiraling upwards and vanishing into a wayward cloud.

Cade was pleased with that cloud, too; he and Mieka had worked on it for hours, while Rafe experimented with increasing the sensations of well-being as Jeska "healed" and finally leaped from the sofa, shading his eyes to look at the place where the white raven had flown up to the sun.

But where most tregetours would have ended it there, simply telling the legend of the Caladrius, giving the audience pain and fear and then joyous relief, Cade had different ideas.

Jeska turned back to the chair, and in the time it took him to sit down he had acquired the smug face and dark green robes of a respected physicker with a thriving practice. He used one finger to twirl the point of a fussy white beard—crimped, scented, edged around his cheeks and

lips with excruciating precision. After the delighted relief
of healing that still lingered in the air, the amused condescension he emanated brought a few low mutters from
the audience. Cade hid a grin. Men or women, it didn't
matter who was watching; the reactions were the same.
Touchstone was that good.

"Oh, have they started?"

Piercing as a swordthrust to the magic as well as the
ears, the woman's voice echoed off the copper ceiling
and off every single one of the thirteen columns. Cade
pushed his fury into a box and locked it, frantically assisting Rafe in the redistribution of energy and sensation
Mieka had only just conjured. Jeska's guise didn't waver
for an instant, and he gave a casual, commanding gesture
that drew people back into the playlet, but the flow of
mood was ruined. As Cade helped Rafe reestablish the
environment, he was marginally aware of the rustle of
gowns and the scrape of chairs as the woman found a
seat proportionate to her importance.

Cade knew who she was. It had been over seven years,
and she was masked now as she had been then, but he
knew her by the flower she wore: not a real flower, but a
famous and fabulous jewel worn sometimes as a cloak
pin, sometimes as a pendant necklace, and tonight as a
decoration in her coiled black hair. Each petal was a
pearl—not the round or teardrop shape favored by other
ladies, but eight long, thin, curving chunks tinted the yellow of a ripe pear. In the center was a thumbnail-sized
yellow diamond. The whole was set in a spray of gold and
silver leaves. It was well-known of her that she couldn't
resist wearing this flower, even when supposedly in disguise, for she would never tolerate being treated as anything other than what she was: Princess Iamina, the
King's sister.

Cade helped Rafe and Mieka use the time she wasted
finding a chair to rebuild the atmosphere in the pavilion.

At length she was seated to her satisfaction. One of her attendants lifted a gracious hand in a *Do go on* wave. Touchstone would now be allowed to continue.

Jeska fiddled with his beard a little longer, then spoke into the almost-silence. Gently, as if speaking to a backward child, but scarcely able to hide his scorn for such superstitions, he explained that if the sick man sees the white raven and the bird turns its head away, the person is thus filled with despair and loses hope, and with it strength, and sickens worse, and dies.

"Yet should the Caladrius look keenly upon him with its bright golden gaze, will the sick man not take heart, and strengthen, and heal? So you see, the question is: Does the white raven heal the man, or does the man heal himself through what he believes about the white raven?"

The physicker settled his robes about him, smiling an insufferable smile. As he did so, from the clouds flew the white raven, and a voice called softly from thin air:

"But what if the malady is blindness? What if the sick man is blind? What if he cannot see hope and healing perched beside his bed? Tell me that, good scholarly man—tell me what happens then!"

"Blind? That's not in the story. What's all this rubbish about being blind?"

Control your temper, Cade told himself. This would be good practice. He glanced a warning at Rafe, felt him clamp down on the flow of magic from the glisker's bench—where Mieka was seething, those eyes nearly black. Jeska, having just enough magic of his own to nudge a working if needs must, stripped himself of the old physicker's countenance, stood, and looked down his perfect nose at the place where the princess sat.

"Certain sources," he told her—intimately, confidingly, as if they were alone in all the world, "mention that the white raven actually *can* cure blindness."

"Really," she sniffed. "And how does it do that, masquer?"

"Oh, very simply." He smiled his sweetest smile, like an Angel in a High Chapel window, and said slowly and distinctly: "Eat its shit."

Lady Redhead suddenly jumped to her feet and began to applaud. The rest of the ladies did likewise. Cade went over to Mieka's glass baskets, collecting Rafe and Jeska with a look. When they were all together—the Elf still with murder in his face—Cade whispered, "Let's not give them 'Purloin.' She doesn't deserve it."

"Who the fuck *is* that?" Mieka demanded. Anger whitened his face, making the livid bruise on his cheekbone uglier even beneath the makeup.

"Princess Iamina," Jeska said. "Or somebody just as rude who stole her flower. I'm surprised you didn't recognize it. I thought everybody knew."

While Mieka was squinting to get a look at the jewel, Rafe said, "How about 'Troll and Trull'? She deserves that one, if anybody does."

Cade mentally ran through their folio, wanting something pointed but not lethal. There was magic enough in the withies he'd already primed—more or less specific to "Purloin" but with a few tweaks he could adapt them. But to which piece?

"We'll give 'em 'The Dragon,'" Mieka snapped. "And send the firebreath right up her skirts. Everybody else has been there, why not us?"

"Oh Gods," Jeska moaned softly as Cade turned to do some fast work on the glass twigs. "Did you *have* to put that image in my head?"

*   *   *

As IT HAPPENED, Cade didn't make it back to the lodgings that night.

Waking just at dawn, he lazed against lavender-scented

pillows and traced with his gaze the graceful flow of red hair across Lady Torren's naked shoulders. Not losing his temper, he reflected with satisfaction, had unexpected rewards. Torren had been deeply impressed that he had only shrugged off Iamina's rudeness—but in truth she had been furious enough for both of them. She'd waited until they were safely hidden in a luxurious little grotto seemingly constructed of ferns and mosses before giving vent to her outrage. That night he learned an interesting aspect of anger that he'd never encountered before: that passionate feeling was passionate feeling, and could be expressed in ways infinitely more pleasant than punching a fist through a window.

Or exploding a glass withie.

He knew the ladies felt cheated that they hadn't seen Touchstone's trademark. Cade hoped that meant there would be another invitation to a "secret" late-night performance, but it didn't really matter to him one way or another. It hadn't been until halfway through "The Dragon" that he realized that Mieka Windthistle in a rage was dangerous. The flames were fiercer, the Dragon bigger and nastier, and Cade could sense Rafe working harder to temper the emotions surging on waves of magic. Tonight the Prince wasn't just troubled by the prospect of having to live up to his ancestors' exploits: he was also resentful, and rebellious, and angry.

Jeska adapted, as he always did. But tonight he kept hold of the spent withie Mieka had thrown to him as his "sword," refusing to toss it back at the end of the piece. To shatter one of the withies still in the baskets, one that still contained even a trace of magic, would be a colossal stupidity even Mieka wouldn't risk—though when he leaped off the glisker's bench and joined them to take their bows, he was furious at being deprived of his flash. Rafe's elbow in his ribs and nod to the audience mollified him a little, for Princess Iamina was still white-faced and shaking. Mieka had sent the Dragon's fiery breath right at her.

Gazing up at daybreak through the screen of green leaves, Cayden stretched on the bed of pillows and blankets and reflected that whatever the Elf had done with the residue of his rage, he didn't want to know. Lady Torren had approached him while he was packing the crates, and he'd lost track of everyone else at that point. A woman could do that to a man, he mused. Girls were one thing; women were quite another. And Torren was definitely a woman. He suspected that this wasn't the most profound insight of his life, but it was certainly the most recent.

He hadn't lied when he told Mieka he was fifteen, his first time. What he hadn't said, and what he wouldn't have admitted if someone set him alight with real fire, was that the first time had been a disaster. The second had been much worse. But because at fifteen a boy could be randy and scared or randy and determined, but randy above all else, the third time had been rather wonderful. It had remained warm in his memory until he discovered the girl was spreading word amongst her friends that the legendary correlation of the length of a boy's nose to the length of other appendages in the predominantly Wizard male was in fact no legend, and she could attest to it of her own experience.

After that, he'd decided that he was willing to be as emotionally shallow as any girl ever born, because the good Lord and Lady knew no girl was ever going to want him for his looks. If they closed their eyes, their minds, and their hearts while they were with him, so much the better. It meant that he didn't have to see, think, or feel, either.

Done often enough, of course, *shallow* became very easy. By his eighteenth year, this began to worry him. Not worried enough to puzzle out what to do about it, but concerned nonetheless. He began to wonder what it might be like to have what Rafe and Crisiant had together. It would be nice, just once, to find out what it was to be with a girl and have his eyes and mind and heart wide open.

Not that this was apt to happen. The beard he'd been struggling to grow—which, on Mieka's wise advice, he had shaved off—had done nothing to hide or improve the rest of his face. At nineteen he was still getting taller, and ever more awkward in the arrangement of arms and legs and hands and feet that seemed to have no correlation to each other. He remained what his mother had always said he was: someone's horrid joke on his handsome parents.

But Lady Torren hadn't seemed to think so. And he'd seen, by the light of a trio of tiny lamps she asked him to ignite so she could look at him, that she kept her eyes open the whole time.

And this time—well, both times, actually—had been better than wonderful.

He stretched again, and reached a finger to stroke the smooth line of her back. His touch woke her. She blinked drowsily up at him, and smiled, and in the golden dapples of early morning sunshine he saw the freckles scattered across her nose, and the flecks of brown in her green eyes, and that even without lip rouge her mouth was a lovely shade of peach.

"What most ladies say at such a moment," she mused, "is 'I must look a fright.'"

"You don't," he replied. "And you're not 'most ladies.'"

"As it happens, I'm not," she agreed.

Cade laughed silently. He was about to suggest that, since he wasn't "most men" either, they might find a way to prove their uniqueness to each other again. But then she said something that left him blank-brained with shock.

With a fingertip she traced the line of his jaw from ear to chin, scratching gently at his morning stubble, and murmured, "You're nothing like your father, you know."

After a moment he heard himself say, "I know." But he didn't want to hear a catalog of the differences. He most particularly didn't want to know if his father had auditioned her for Prince Ashgar. Giving her a smile that was nothing more than a stretching of his lips from his teeth, he sat up and reached for his clothes. The new gray-blue jacket was hopelessly wrinkled, as was his shirt; he'd have to beg the Trollwife at their lodgings to steam the creases out before the performance tonight. Ah, yes—the performance. The perfect excuse. The performance before the King and his nobles . . . and Prince Ashgar and his attendants . . . including the First Gentleman of the Bedchamber.

"I really ought to be going," he said.

{"Oughta be goin'," he mumbled as he struggled into his shirt. "Workin' t'morrow."

"There's no hurry."

He shook his head and gulped half a glass of brandy, not wanting to look at her. He buttoned his shirt up wrong, and had to redo it.

"You're very drunk."

He waved away her concern. "Been drunker'n this an' played 'Windows' from start to finish. Great reviews the next day, too."

"Oh, top score tonight, if that's what you're asking. Both times."

His jacket was around here someplace. Ah—here on the floor, sprawled atop a garish bright rug, black-bordered shapes like a demented stained-glass window. "You should come to our next show," he managed.

"I don't think so."

He looked up. "Why the fuck not?"

She raked long dark-blond hair from her eyes and

regarded him with something that wasn't quite contempt. "Who do you think you are?"

He swept her a sardonic bow that nearly toppled him. "Cayden Silversun, Master Tregetour of Touchstone."

"You wear that like the scars on your hands. And speaking of your hands—that ring. It's like a tag pinned to your shirt so people know where to return you, when you go lost."

Don't worry about going too lost, Quill, I'll always come find you.}

"You needn't leave so soon."

He looked at his hands. No scars. And no parchment, either, with scribbled directions and that promise to come find him. He blinked down at the girl, confused. None of the colors were right—her hair was red, not blond, and the blue curtains were green leaves, and the gaudy rug was nowhere to be seen. And everything, including him, reeked of lavender. He supposed that was better than stinking of brandy.

"It's just dawn," she coaxed. "Surely you can stay a little longer."

He shook his head to clear it. "We've another show tonight. For the King." He concentrated, and envisioned the colors of the sea-green and silver ribbons, the brown wax seal on the invitation. The parchment that didn't promise that Mieka would come find him. "And—and we still haven't decided what we'll do. I have work, priming the withies for my glisker. I'm beholden for last night, Lady, forgive me for hurrying off."

The path back through the castle grounds was long and frustrating, and rather sweaty, for the softer mornings of spring had given way to the full sun of summer. Before he reached the gates into town he was longing for that huge bathtub in the garderobe of their lodgings, and was half-tempted to plunge into the moat, or maybe the river, except that he couldn't swim. He checked his pockets for coin enough to have the servants carry up water to fill the tub. But it turned out that his wish had been anticipated.

Mieka was sitting in the kitchen, making himself useful with knives and whetstone while he gossiped with the Trollwife. He smiled when he saw Cayden, and broke off a conversation about Prince Ashgar's dreary matrimonial prospects to say, "Mistress Luta made muffins! They're in the warming oven, ready for when you finish your bath."

"My—?"

"You're in rather fragrant need of one, Quill. Though I must say, the lavender perfume is rather intriguing. The little redhead, I take it?"

The Trollwife shooed Cade out of the kitchen. "Go on with ye, laddie! Take that jacket and shirt off first, they're wrinkled as a raisin."

Half an hour later, it was Cade's skin that had started to wrinkle. He was just about to pull the plug that let the water drain down to the elm trees when Mieka strolled into the garderobe.

"Oh, that's much better," he announced after taking a deep, experimental breath. "I don't know what Mistress Mirdley puts into that white soap of hers, but it's much nicer than the lavender stink you were wearing when you came in." Cocking his head, he watched Cade's eyes for a moment before asking, "So you're feeling better, now you've washed the scent of her off you?"

There may have been possible replies to this; Cade couldn't think of any at the moment. So he shrugged and said, "Tell me what I owe you for the bath."

Mieka waved it away. "'Twas for me own comfort, not yours. How could I work tonight with you over there by the curtains, whiff as the Royal Gardens? Want something to eat? I brought tea and muffins."

"You mean you didn't eat them all on the way up-stairs?"

"I thought about it," he replied seriously. Then, gaze roaming down Cade's chest, he added, "But Mistress Mirdley will string me up by me poor fragile little ears if you come home even skinnier than when you left." He caught up a towel and tossed it to Cade. "Rafe has a mind to do 'Feather-heart' tonight, so you've some adjusting to do on the withies—" All at once, he snapped his fingers and cursed, digging into a back pocket. "This came for you this morning, early. Lord Coldkettle's office, looks like, by the seal and ribbons."

"But we already received the Court invitation. Do they want us to do a second show?"

"This is for *you*, not Touchstone. Open it!"

He did, not caring if he dripped bathwater onto it, because he recognized the handwriting. "It's from my father."

"Really?" He half-turned from examining his fading bruise in the mirror. "That's right nice of him, to congratulate you on First Flight of the Winterly."

"He doesn't have anything to say about that. We're to be particularly good tonight, and do 'Hidden Cottage,' because the Prince is entertaining ambassadors from six different countries."

"I've heard it muttered that there might be an exchange of players next summer, diplomatic goodwill and all that."

"Nothing to do with it. Ashgar is shopping. We're supposed to be extremely impressive tonight so they'll see that it's a refined, cultured kingdom their princess or duchess or whatever would be queen of one day." He tossed the letter onto the tiled floor and levered himself out of the bath.

"Cade . . . d'you think your father was the one as got us the booking tonight?"

"Does it matter?"

"Yes."

He wrapped the towel round his hips and reached for another to dry his hair. "Why?"

"I don't care to be beholden to people who don't—" He broke off, then finished in a rush, "I mean, how can they not understand how lucky they are, to have you for a son?"

Had he been thinking only recently that Mieka could enrage him more swiftly and more easily than anyone else he'd ever encountered? Looking down into those troubled, resentful eyes, he had to smile. "My father had nothing to do with it. I found out last night from Lady Torren. She commended us to Lord Coldkettle herself."

"She told him to book us *before* you bedded her?" He whistled between his teeth. "Gods, Quill, how good *are* you, that they favor you before they've even known your favor?"

"I do all right. And it wasn't a bed, exactly," he confided. "A few blankets, a lot of pillows and ferns."

Mieka laughed and threw him another towel. "And she didn't even give you breakfast? Scandalous! Wait'll I tell Blye!"

"Don't you bloody dare!"

When Cade was dried and dressed and fed, and Mieka had stolen only one of the muffins, he leaned back on his bed with a pillow between his spine and the wall and frowned at the Elf. "You're in a mood this morning. I was sure you'd go find Princess Iamina after the show and—"

"—mend her manners for her?" He shrugged. "Auntie Brishen understands there are many sorts of emergencies. 'Twas only the thought of a greenthorn kept me out of the castle quod. Though I find I like the purple better. One doesn't get quite so silly. We were to have a discussion, weren't we, about that? Tonight, p'rhaps, after the show—if you haven't already promised Her lavender-scented Ladyship a repeat performance."

"A one-night special engagement," Cade replied.

"Good. You'll like thorn. It'll be fun, Quill."

It wouldn't be like going lost all by himself. Mieka would be with him.

Thirteen

DURING THE TEN days of Trials, the presence of any particular nobleman depended on a variety of factors. Relationships—if any—to or with the royal family; ability to afford the journey, the clothes, and the lodgings (an invitation to stay at the castle could be more expensive in the end than hiring rooms in the town); the current political climate; whether or not other nobles with whom one had been at daggers drawn for generations would be at Seekhaven; and, last on the list for almost everyone, a liking for the theater.

Since reaching his majority at the age of sixteen, the Archduke had never taken into consideration anything but his own enthusiasm for a good show. Early on, when he was scarcely more than a child and his regrettable father was dead, the royals had decided to be magnanimous towards the boy, and invited him to Trials every year. What harm could there be, after all, in a five-year-old—especially when all his tutors and servants were in the royal employ? Much better to be seen as generous and forgiving, and to impress on the child that his future and indeed his life depended on loyalty to the king who had vanquished his father.

That they were all cousins had something to do with it. Not because of any sentiment; His Gracious Majesty was not a fool. He was a student of his forebears' actions (which happened to be one reason Touchstone had done so very well at Trials; their speculations on what it must be like to be continually reminded of one's ancestors' valiant deeds had impressed the king very deeply, and he had let his appreciation be known to be judges). King Meredan decided to follow a many-times-great-grandfather's plan, and keep the enemy's son close, so that when the opportunity arose, the boy could be married into the royal family, merging the different lines and negating all other claims to the throne. This would have worked out admirably, except that Princess Iamina had done the stupidest possible thing by running away to marry Lord Tawnymoor, a thing she regretted within three days of having done it. The Archduke remained unwed, though not for lack of offers both subtle and blatant. What precisely he might be waiting for, no one could have said, but though his preference was unambiguous—he liked women, the blonder and curvier the better—no lady had yet snared his lasting attention or his genuine affection.

Informed speculation was that the Archduke was biding his time until Prince Ashgar finally chose a bride, and that his plan was a match between the next generations. But when Cade glimpsed both young men in the audience that evening, he decided that whoever was doing the speculating was not as well-informed as rumor had it. Though ambassadors from eight different Continental nations were indeed present, not all of them clustered around the Prince.

The piece Touchstone performed in Fliting Hall for the gentlemen of the Court was one they usually did for a laugh. Tonight they played it straight, though Mieka could be seen to roll his eyes every so often as Jeska declaimed the stock phrases from that most sentimental of romances, "The Hidden Cottage."

The plot could have been predicted by a child of three.

Beautiful maiden (pastoral variety) with ambitious mother. Handsome young lord (poverty-stricken variety) with avaricious father. Could anyone doubt the inevitability of a marriage contract agreed upon by the respective parents, especially as the girl and the young man had never even met? Throw in two jealous sisters, a kidnapping, the young man's rebellious flight on the day of the wedding, a cottage deep in the forest . . .

The opportunities for comedy were endless. Jeska had a particular fondness for giving the young lord a dreadful sense of direction, and his clumsy wanderings gave Mieka plenty of scope for creating whimsical scenery as the mood took him—and sometimes he took the young lord halfway around the world before allowing him to blunder upon the cottage. (His rendition of certain landscapes was perhaps less than accurate, but every time Cade insisted that none of the books mentioned lilacs in any of the newly explored deserts, Mieka defiantly made the flowers bigger, brighter, and smellier.) The mutual love-at-first-sight sequence, the discovery of their true identities, the return to the girl's home to find the nastiest of the sisters had married the young man's father and they were making each other magnificently miserable—it was the low comedy of "The Sailor's Sweetheart" with more characters and on a more lavish scale, and audiences howled with laughter.

This night, however, every time Mieka looked as if he might indulge himself, Cade fixed him with a glare. He sulked, but kept his sense of humor under control while providing Jeska with the most innocently lovely of young girls and the most nobly handsome of young lords.

With all those emissaries to entertain, Prince Ashgar wished to present himself as a sensitive, cultured, kindhearted man who, like the young lord of the playlet, would fall instantly in love with whichever girl was lucky enough to become his bride. And indeed, as the lights glowed brighter in the glass globes over the doors and around the ceiling once Rafe allowed all the magic to fade, the Prince could be seen brushing a tear from his cheek.

Cade rather thought he might vomit.

No sooner had the applause begun than Mieka started their next piece, a rollicking Mother Loosebuckle farce that had everyone roaring with laughter. Cade and Jeska had debated whether or not to include the more obscene puns, then shrugged at each other and decided to keep them. Explaining colloquialisms to the foreigners wasn't their problem.

But whatever any of these men had heard about Touchstone—indeed, if they'd heard anything about them at all—Rafe made sure the evening was remembered. At the playlet's raucous conclusion, before Mieka could lay a finger on a spent withie to toss into the air, Rafe had blasted carefully controlled spurts of magic at half a dozen of the glass globes over the doors. After some shocked gasps, the applause and laughter were even more enthusiastic. Touchstone had given them the show they'd come to see.

Cade, who was watching Prince Ashgar, barely noticed. For a fleeting turning of time he saw a young blond girl of about sixteen, not quite a woman, with the promise of striking beauty in her high-boned face. Tall and long-limbed, she gripped her skirts in her hands as she ran across a plowed field towards a manor house, wild excitement in her deep blue eyes. Cade glimpsed a range of sawtoothed mountains looming above a thick pine forest, white peaks stabbing into a painfully blue sky.

Then it was gone: the girl, the field, the manor, the mountains, all of it. Mieka was perched atop the glisker's bench, ready to leap over the glass baskets as had become his habit; Rafe was coming out from behind his lectern; Jeska was waiting for them and for Cade so they could take their bows. Hastily he tucked the vision away in his mind and joined his friends, and even though both Rafe and Jeska knew about him, neither saw in his face or his eyes what had just happened.

It was Mieka who frowned a little as he looked up at Cade, thick brows quirking a question that Cade answered with a smile and a shrug. No answer at all, of course—and the boy knew it. Soon, Cade knew, he would have to explain at least some of it. But not yet.

Touchstone left the stage to the Shorelines, who performed their signature piece, "Breakers and Blue," which they'd been doing so long that everybody knew every nuance. Cade lost interest halfway through and left the wings for the artists' tiring-room.

Rafe was already there, propping up a wall with one shoulder, gazing skeptically down at a squat, Gnomish young man whose every extravagant gesture endangered a thirteen-light brass candelabrum taller than he was. For the second time that night Cayden was reminded of his Fae heritage. This time it wasn't a turn but the memory of a foreseeing dream. He'd seen this little man before. He'd been waiting for him to show up.

Rafe caught his eye and nodded him over. Cade paused along the way to snag a glass of ale, then approached, heart racing. This man would be important to Touchstone, he knew it. He *knew* it.

"—organize your travel schedule, keep track of the equipment, see to it that portions of your earnings are regularly distributed to your families, all that sort of thing. And set up bookings not just for your time off but for your return to Gallantrybanks before Trials next year. That will be important—"

"I know," Cade interrupted. "The Shadowshapers played a show at the Kiral Kellari last month, to try out new material and keep their name current in the city. Cayden Silversun," he added by way of introduction.

"Kearney Fairwalk. Your servant, sir."

It was a standard politeness, that. But Cayden had never had it spoken to him by a lord before. All the years of grim practice at keeping his countenance served him well when he heard the name. What the man hadn't mentioned, and didn't need to, was the ancient lordship that went with Fairwalk Manor. There was an expression of mingled embarrassment and gratification on the nobleman's round, dark face. It was as if he took pride in the name, knew very well that everyone recognized it, and appreciated the doors it opened for him. Yet in other ways he regretted the instantaneous judgments inherent in so illustrious a name and title. Cade realized at once that Fairwalk's situation was closely akin to his own: a desire to make the name known because of his own efforts, not any prior associations. This thought made him smile as he held up his palm. It was a greeting unused amongst any but the nobility, one to the other; Cade's antecedents allowed it, and his own pride demanded it.

Fairwalk matched his own stubby fingers to Cade's long, thin ones for a moment, then lowered his hand. All at once he flushed up crimson beneath a shock of carefully arranged sandy curls that had already wilted in the summer heat, and looked anywhere but at Cade. "Your fettler and I have been discussing—I mean to say, don't you see, I thought I might offer my services and connections. Not that I've any more experience than yourselves, really truly," he added with a rueful shrug. "But I do know most of the people whose lands you'll be visiting, and all that sort of thing. Mention of my name has at least a bit of meaning. They won't try to cheat you out of a performance fee—and so many of them do try, it's frightfully shocking!"

Cade nodded. "I'd heard as much from Rauel Kevelock. Romuald Needler takes care of all that for the Shadowshapers." He eyed the man for a moment, a rather nasty part of him enjoying the nobleman's flusterment. Fairwalk wouldn't be the first theater enthusiast to lose his composure in the presence of players he admired. "Are you offering the same sort of managing services, my lord?"

"If it's agreeable to you. I've seen your work both here and back in the city. You're not just good, you're going to be great."

"Ah," Rafe said, looking over Cade's shoulder. "The girl with the tray of whiskey." And without a by-your-leave, he abandoned them in favor of another drink. Rafe had scant regard for lordships. Not that Cade did, not really. But, unlike Rafe, he'd grown up in a household where such persons were not uncommon as visitors, and his mother's conversation was such that he couldn't help knowing who was rich, important, or both—and who wasn't.

Lord Fairwalk was very rich, extremely important, and from the bashful eagerness on his round and ruddy face, completely mad for the theater. "P'rhaps we might meet and discuss the idea while you're resident in Seekhaven?" Fairwalk ventured, running his fingers fretfully through his limp hair. "Or I would be tremendously pleased to call upon you in the city, of course, if your time here is already otherwise occupied."

A brief vision of his mother's expression on being introduced to Lord Fairwalk danced gleefully in Cade's mind. But there'd be no business done once she got him into the drawing room, only gossip and gamesmanship. So he said, "If you're not busy tomorrow afternoon . . ."

"Splendid! Excellent! I'll come by your lodgings right after lunching, shall I? I know where you're staying—" He broke off, flushing even redder. "That's to say, I asked about, just to know, you understand, in case you—"

"It's fine," Cade assured him, amused.

"Until tomorrow, then—much beholden, and frightfully chuffed, don't you see," said His Lordship, and effaced himself.

Judging by the applause, the Shorelines had finished. The four of them entered the tiring-room a few moments later, and Cade grinned to himself on seeing Mieka trailing along behind their glisker like a frolicsome puppy. He supposed he'd have much the same expression on his own face if he ever met up with the players he'd first seen, who had made so fierce an impression on him that he'd known instantly what he wanted to be when he grew up. Odd, he mused, how almost every player he'd ever met said the same thing: that they'd known right away, no questions, no second thoughts. Awareness of the theater wasn't enough; one had to experience it for oneself, that kick in the backside that changed the direction of one's life forever.

But he'd never again encounter the young men who'd shown him the path he wanted to take. The Mazetown Players were all dead now. The very day after Master Emmot had taken Cade to see them, they had chosen to shorten the journey to Gallantrybanks by hiring a boat instead of a coach. The trawler had been lost at sea. Cade still remembered the pieces they'd done: the old standard "Shamblesong" and an original playlet meant for children, a work of charm and whimsy that the tavern audience hadn't understood. But Cade had known what the tregetour had been aiming at, and hadn't cared that he'd drawn attention to himself by applauding madly when almost no one else did. The masquer had pointed him out to the tregetour, and they'd smiled at him. Even as Cade smiled back, though, he promised himself he'd never give an audience any cause to sit on their hands the way those people had. No work of his would be presented until it was perfect.

The wonder of it was that he'd more or less kept to that vow. Not his fault if their gliskers had been substandard. The pieces themselves had been as good as they could get. And now that he had Mieka—

He was briefly startled to realize that with the probable addition of Lord Fairwalk, he had it all. A brilliant masquer. A solid fettler. The best glisker in the Kingdom. A reputation. First Flight on the Winterly. And now a likely manager.

The real money wasn't on the Circuits. It was in the private performances. Nobility, wealthy merchants, the various guilds—all would pay for an evening of theater, and pay very well indeed. Add to those performances the bookings in Gallantrybanks while not on a Circuit—not just at taverns or the few small theaters, but in private homes—and a group could make the sort of money that had allowed the Shadowshapers to buy their very own luxurious wagon with their name scrawled across the side.

Cayden refused to trade on his father's name. As a major official of Prince Ashgar's household, Zekien Silversun knew everyone. The trouble was that everyone knew him, too. As for Lady Jaspiela—her connections would be useless, even if Cade was of a mind to try using them. They would blanch with shock should anyone even suggest that they acknowledge a traveling player as kin. The ancestor who'd been a poet, he was marginally respectable. At least he'd done his scribblings in decent privacy. They would admit to him, but only if bluntly asked. The hopes that had come with Lady Jaspiela's marriage to a wealthy Master Fettler's son had died long since, vanished with the money Zekien Silversun quiddled away. They would never acknowledge Cade, let alone help him. And anyhow, they were all much too busy making sure nobody remembered anything about Lady Kiritin to want any name associated with that of Highcollar or Blackswan put into the public consciousness.

No, Touchstone needed Lord Fairwalk or someone like him. The Shadowshapers had Romuald Needler, and he'd done very well for them. But although he had a vast network of relationships with the guilds in each city and town, he wasn't directly linked to any of the noble families, let alone one with the ancient name of Fairwalk. If His Lordship was efficient about organizing private bookings, if he could get them paid on time and in full, if he could arrange their travel and lodgings and equipment and so forth, then he would be worth the ten of every hundred pence they'd have to pay him.

It didn't even occur to Cayden until late that night to consult the others about Fairwalk. He was sitting out in the back garden having a final drink with Mieka and Rafe—Jeska having found a local lovely without murderous males lurking nearby—when Rafe asked idly if Fairwalk had said anything interesting. Cade wasn't abashed that he'd forgotten to mention it. He had always made all the decisions. He mentioned tomorrow's proposed visit, and Mieka sat bolt upright so fast, he nearly splashed his drink onto the lawn.

"What did you sign?" he demanded.

"Nothing. And what d'you care, anyway? As long as you get paid—"

"What do I *care*?" He rounded on Rafe. "Did you hear that? What the fuck do I *care*?"

"Rein up, Mieka," the fettler advised. "We'll all be there tomorrow to listen in—" He broke off with a smirk. "Well, all of us, if Jeska gets bored with the girl."

"So we get to 'listen in,' do we? Lovely! Perfect!" He sprang to his feet and snarled down at Cade, "Listen to this, then: *Fuck off!*"

The garden gate had clanged shut before Cade could find his voice again. "What just happened?"

"Bit too much tonight, I think," Rafe assumed with a shrug. "His head's made of solid iron, but it's an Elf's body attached to it, innit?"

"What's *that* mean?"

"Ever take a look at his arms? Right inside the elbows. He spikes quite a bit of bluethorn, Cade. More than you ever guessed, I think," he added as Cade's jaw dropped. "Usually he's pretty careful to balance the liquor, but—oh, for the love of the Angels, mate, have you never noticed? There's nights I can barely keep my hands round the magic, he gets so wild. Jeska and I, we feel it more than you do, but I would've thought . . ." He peered at Cade's stricken face, then shrugged. "It doesn't happen that often. He's excited. Success like this . . . I think maybe he thinks with part of him that it can't really be real, y'know?"

"How often?"

"Not very. He'll be fine by tomorrow. Not that he'll remember any of it—and won't believe you if you tell him." Rafe pushed himself to his feet and stretched, then gathered up the empty glasses. "I'll just put these in the sink for Mistress Luta. Dream sweet, Cade—if you dream at all, that is."

He sat there long into the night, shock and anger gradually resolving into worry, and then a snort of disgust at himself. He'd no right to judge Mieka. It had taken him quite a few months of experimentation to discover the exact amount of alcohol it took to mute his dreamings. And before he'd discovered blockweed, he'd started to need more and more to drink. About a month before that booking in Gowerion, in fact, he'd got so drunk after a very bad show with a very bad glisker that Rafe had practically carried him back to Redpebble Square and he'd woken in the stillroom, his cheek cradled on the stiff straw of a broom. He hadn't dreamed that night—or if he had, he remembered none of it.

Master Emmot had had a lot to say about the effects of drink on a gift like his, mostly to caution against overuse. But if Cade had learned anything in the years he'd spent at the Sagemaster's academy, it was that Emmot's experience of Longseeing was a fingertap on the cheek compared to the kick in the face foreseeing was for Cade. Or perhaps age made one tougher, more resilient. Cade didn't know. There had been times he'd almost hoped he wouldn't live long enough to find out.

"Poor Wizardling!" the familiar voice jeered in his head. *"Such a trial and such a penalty to be you!"*

It remained that if Mieka sometimes misjudged the proportion of liquor to bluethorn, so too Cade knew what it was like to overestimate how much he could drink. This was his first encounter with the Elf in that state; it took no prescience to know it wouldn't be the last.

Rafe was right: the next morning, Mieka behaved as if the scene in the garden had never happened. As far as he was concerned, it hadn't. When Cade cautiously mentioned that Lord Fairwalk would be coming by to discuss a possible contract, he nodded his interest and continued shoveling eggs and toasted cheese into his mouth. Evidently an overindulgence in bluethorn and liquor gave him quite an appetite.

They were just finishing the meal when Mistress Luta sloped down the kitchen steps into the garden, a sealed and much-folded piece of parchment in her broad hands.

"For you," she said, handing Cade the letter.

No ribbons. A thumbprint served for a seal in the wax. He smiled, knowing who had sent this. The smile died as he scanned the opening sentence. "Oh no—poor Blye!"

"What's wrong?" Mieka demanded—rather indistinctly, around the last mouthful of egg.

"Master Cindercliff died last week."

After swallowing, Mieka said, "I'm truly sorry to hear it. But he was suffering, wasn't he? I s'pose it was his time, and no kindness for him to linger."

Jeska took the letter out of Cade's hand without a by-your-leave. "Day after we left," he said, frowning as he worked out the words. "Dery says she didn't want him to write and tell you before Trials but now he—what's this word?"

Rafe in his turn grabbed the parchment. "She'll go to my mother, won't she? Of course she'll go stay with my mother."

"Sure as shit she won't be staying with mine," Cade growled. "I wouldn't be surprised if Her Ladyship is responsible for this."

Mieka's eyes blinked wide. "I know your mother's not exactly the most wonderful woman who ever lived, but—"

"No, you idiot—the offer for the glassworks!" He sprang to his feet, pacing a few steps towards the garden gate. "I knew this would happen, I just knew it!"

"Offer—?" Mieka echoed. "What offer? Rafe, let me see!"

"They won't do anything for another week at least," Rafe began.

Cade shook his head. "It's midmonth for the payment. It's always midmonth. She won't be able to get at whatever money he left her for weeks and weeks, you know how the courts are when a woman inherits. They have to make a show of searching all over the Kingdom for the next male heir, no matter what it says in a will—"

A piercing whistle startled him into silence.

"Much beholden," Mieka said rudely. "Now, would you care to explain all this ranting and raving?"

"Her father's dead. She's a girl, and by law she can't inherit until they've made a search—which she has to pay for, can you believe it? The money her father's been borrowing comes due midmonth every month. It doesn't need saying that she hasn't got it on hand, nor anywhere near it. Even when it's all sorted and they let her have legal title, she can't carry on the glassworks herself. She'll have to hire a man for appearances' sake."

"You mentioned an offer?" asked Jeska.

"Dery's not sure," Rafe said, scanning the letter. "But

I'd wager Crisiant's wedding necklet somebody's been waiting for just this to happen, and the offer will cover the loan and nothing more. Not even half what the business is worth." He read through to the end, and finally handed the letter to Mieka. "Dery doesn't say if this buyer has a name."

"It doesn't matter." Cade flung himself back into his chair and began stabbing the wooden table with his fork. "She'll lose everything. If only he'd been able to hang on, just until I'm twenty-one and—"

"You're not thinking of *marrying* her?" Mieka exclaimed.

"Of course not! For one thing, she wouldn't have me. At twenty-one my grandsir's legacy comes to me, and there's nothing my mother can do about it. She tried," he added bitterly. "Right after Dery was born. Father about had a seizure the night she brought it up."

Rafe reached across the table and plucked the fork from Cade's restless fingers. "And I'll wager my own wedding necklet that *she* almost had a seizure about a minute later."

"Too right," Cade agreed. When Jeska and Mieka looked puzzled, he explained, "The only way to disinherit me would be for him to express formal doubts about being my father. The legacy comes through his side of the family."

Mieka gave a crow of derisive laughter. "Now *that's* something I'd pay to see! Lady Jaspiela, ravaging her own reputation! The Whore of Redpebble Square!"

"But what am I going to do about Blye? She must be frantic."

Mieka tilted his chair back, folded his hands behind his head, and announced, "Blye is *my* glasscrafter, and mine she stays. I'd marry her meself, but I doubt she'd overlook my sordid past. Pity, too," he mused. "I think we'd have very pretty children, she and me. But if she won't take me, at least she'll take my money." His eyes found each of them in turn as he said, "And yours, and yours, and even yours, Quill—and her pride be damned."

Jeska, whose mother depended on his income, and Rafe, who wanted desperately to marry Crisiant, nodded at once. "We've enough for the loan payments," Jeska said. "This month, next month, however long it takes for the court to hand over what's rightfully hers. There'll be enough bookings between now and when Winterly starts. And we'll pay the fees for the searching, too."

Rafe went on, "Which means we'll own half the glass-works. She can pay us back by making the withies. The guild won't let her have a hallmark, and her father's will be formally destroyed by the time we get back, but her work has always been good. She can get by on plates and such for a bit of a while—"

"Oh, not that long," Mieka said serenely. "Just until I convince Chat that he needs better than what he's been using, and Blye's the one to provide."

"Who's he got now?" Rafe asked.

"Master Splithook."

"The best in Gallytown!"

"His withies cost a bloody fortune and they're half of them rutilated," Mieka replied flatly. "Chat was grumbling about it on the way here, weren't you listening? Splithook's been living off his reputation much too long. Time and past time he goes back to spinning simple little witch spheres, and leaves the finer work to those as can do it right."

Jeska had begun to copy Cade's stabbing gesture, only he was using a knife. "We get away with it," he said slowly. "Using Blye's withies, I mean. They're the ones you shatter. Those her father made, with the legitimate hallmark, those you keep to bring out in case we're inspected. But the *Shadowshapers*, Mieka—"

"Chat's hands are just as quick as mine. He can switch withies for inspection. And he owes me a bit of a favor."

Cayden stared at first one and then the next and then the next of his friends, flummoxed. Were they truly willing to use their hard-earned money—?

"Don't," Rafe warned, catching his glance.

"Yeh, *don't,*" Mieka seconded. Springing to his feet, he stretched widely and brushed crumbs off his tunic and trousers. "I'm off, then. Somebody find us transport back to Gallytown—Cade, close your mouth, I thought we told you not to say it! Chat's over at the Riverbrink Inn. I'll be there and back by lunching."

"Need any coin?" Jeska was already reaching into a pocket.

"I'm fine, beholden. Chat's not much of a downdrins drinker. He won't get started until sunset. Amateur!" He winked and scampered away to the garden gate. It clinked shut behind him before Cade finally found his voice again.

"You don't have to—I mean, I can find enough money—"

"Did we or did we not tell you to keep it shut?" Rafe snarled. "We can see Blye safe, so we will." Then, head swiveling as the kitchen door slammed: "Oh, shit—Fairwalk."

Cade would have said exactly the same thing, but His Lordship was now within earshot, escorted out into the garden by the landlord—bowing, stammering, almost fluttering. And the landlord was nervous, too. No one of such rank had ever graced his premises. As Fairwalk seated himself, and Jeska politely asked if he'd care for tea, the landlord glared at Cade as if wanting very much to shriek at him for the lack of warning.

"G-good morning," said Fairwalk. "I know I'm early, scandalously early, but—I just couldn't, don't you see, really truly—"

"Nothing to signify at all." Jeska smiled his most dazzling smile. "Before we start, though—do you know anybody with a fast rig can get us home to town by tomorrow night?"

Fourteen

KEEPING HIS MOUTH shut had never been Mieka Windthistle's specialty. It wasn't that he was untrustworthy, exactly, or that he lacked respect for other people's private business. He'd found as he got older that if it was important enough, he could keep his silence, and sometimes without even having been told to do so.

It was just that sometimes he couldn't help it—it was so much fun to shock, to provoke, and occasionally to avenge himself or someone he cared about. He had a true gift for outrage, and he knew it, and usually it was enough to keep him entertained without spilling other people's secrets. But every so often it was irresistible, the prospect of revealing a not just surprising but downright shocking bit of information.

His own secrets, however, he knew very well how to keep. Life in a crowded home with all those brothers, sisters, aunts, uncles, cousins, and occasionally people he didn't even recognize, had taught him how to give the appearance of blithe and innocent transparency while clutching his real feelings close and hidden.

Vered Goldbraider had no such restraint. As Mieka waited politely in the cozy, sunlit parlor of a very nice inn on the river while a servant went to find Chattim Czillag, he heard Vered's distinctive down-province accents from the taproom. Come to think of it, he reflected, he'd rarely encountered Vered without receiving the impression that the man not only lacked several layers of skin, but that the skin he did have was always scraped raw by one thing or another. Gods, he was worse than Quill.

Rising from his chair in the entry hall, Mieka ambled towards the taproom doorway. Vered had warmed up and was now shouting at the top of his lungs. There were few people around to listen, but Mieka knew Vered wouldn't have cared if the entire Court and its collected retinues and all their miscreate children were within earshot.

"Gods be damned to him, then! Won't have him nor nobody else commandin' me words, nor yet tellin' me so much as what shirt I'll wear or not wear! D'ye be hearin' of me, then?"

Not just his accent but also his speech patterns had departed south without leaving a forwarding address, he was that angry. For a few moments Mieka thought he was railing at something Rauel had done—again—but then Rauel himself began yelling much the same thing.

"Who the fuck does he think he is, eh? Sendin' some lackey round here, tryin' to buy us—do we look like whores to you?"

A third voice, unfamiliar to him, spoke in low, soothing, yet slightly frightened tones. He didn't catch the words as he crept into the taproom. It was gloomy in here, the low ceiling latticed with heavy black oak rafters, the murk eased somewhat by a variety of leafy plants in big iron cauldrons. Mieka wove his way amongst these towards the voices coming from the far corner.

"No!" Vered snarled. "Not now, not ever, and ye take that answer back to His fuckin' Lordship and shove it up his bumhole!"

Mieka's attention was snared by a pungent odor coming from the bizarre tree at his elbow. Whatever fertilizer they were using to keep this oddity alive, he didn't care to speculate. A spindly thing, just a few feet of pale trunk with a froth of spiky leaves at the top, it looked like an imaging from one of the broadsheets Cade was always showing him so they could augment the usual scenery with strange foreign plant life.

"You heard him!" Rauel's voice had gone shrill with outrage. "There's an end to it!"

Mieka was intimately familiar with the sound of shattering glass, but it turned out that it rather startled him these days when Touchstone wasn't responsible for it. The young man who scurried past startled him even more, for he was clothed in the orange-and-charcoal livery of the Archduke. Vered came stomping right after him, caught sight of Mieka lurking behind the skinny tree, and actually bared his teeth. They looked very white and very sharp in his dark face.

"You'll be next, boy!" he sneered. "Write that down— you'll be next!"

And with this inexplicable announcement, he stalked out of the bar.

Mieka stood there, too dazed to move, until Rauel called out, "Somebody there?" and he jerked as if the sound had been a knifethrust.

"Rommy?" came Chattim's voice.

"N-no, Chat, just me." He stepped out from behind the tree. "I've come to say we're heading back to town today—"

"Did you bring any money with you?" Sakary Grainer had never been exactly friendly, not since the nerve-shredding night Mieka had sat in for Chat, but this was surly, even for him.

"A bit," Mieka replied cautiously.

"Get on in here, then. Vered took all the coin with him, and I need to get drunk."

Mieka approached their corner of the bar. The girl behind it was wide-eyed and rightly afeared of the three remaining Shadowshapers, but she also held her ground until Mieka tossed his last remaining se'en-pence pieces onto the bar. As she drew pints, he glanced at Rauel, then Sakary, then Chat, and wondered what in all hells he'd walked into.

The ale was half gone before Rauel spoke—in conciliatory tones, temper spent. "He's a quick foul drunk, our Vered, we all know that. No head for it, none at all."

Sakary pondered his glass for a few moments, then replied, "Woulda said the same if he'd been sober." Gulping back the last of the pint, he slid off the barstool and grimaced at Mieka. "Beholden. I owe you one, back home."

Perhaps recent experience of Cayden in a similarly sullen mood kept Mieka's mouth shut. He neither accepted the debt nor dismissed it as unimportant. Sakary grunted, wiped his mouth with the back of his hand, and left the taproom.

"Where to, d'ya think?" Chat asked Rauel.

A shrug. "You know them, they'll each find someplace to sit and seethe." Finishing his own drink, he glanced at Mieka. "You're heading home, you say? So early?"

"A friend's father died."

"Sorry to hear it. We would've enjoyed the trip back in our wagon, were you four there. Now—" He winced eloquently. "See you at the Downstreet, maybe, before the Royal starts."

When he was gone, Mieka turned to Chattim, suggesting, "I'll be off, then, shall I?"

"No, bide a bit, if you would. Another round, darlin' dear," he coaxed the barmaid, and Mieka dug into pockets, hoping he had a few pence stashed someplace. "I've got it," Chat told him. "I only said I didn't because the rest already had enough. Let's go sit out back."

Rightly interpreting this to mean he didn't wish to be overheard by anyone, not even the barmaid, Mieka took his first and second glasses with him and followed Chat into the back garden within view of the river. They sat at a small table, the barmaid unbent enough to bring out a bowl of spiced walnuts, and when they were quite alone with the elm trees and the river and the summer warmth, Chat heaved a sigh.

"Good thing you're leaving town, or you prob'ly *would* be next."

"For what? The Archduke?"

"Saw the flunkey, then, did you? Himself sent round to command a private word with us. Rommy's off visiting his old mum in some village south of here, so he couldn't stop it before it started. Always a mistake to let Vered drink before noon, and even worse when there's business talked of without Rommy around."

"P'rhaps all the Archduke wanted was a private performance."

"If only." Chattim ran a fingertip round and round the rim of his glass. "A scandal and a shame, it is, that we've got so soft we can't none of us direct a man to the door when he very much needs and requires direction."

Unable to contain himself any longer, Mieka asked, "But what did he want?"

"Us."

"I'm not understanding you, Chat."

"His own private theater group. Oh, we'd still be on the Circuit, but in his employ."

"I've heard he's right daft about the theater, but isn't that taking it a bit far?"

"They do it all the time on the Continent. Rich nobles buy up the contract of whatever group they fancy, and hire a manager to do the everyday things, the bookings and suchlike—"

"But why? To make money?"

"Not that much in it. No, it's for the standing. The brag. Count Such-and-So's Players, the Grand Duke's

Own Men, that sort of thing. There's a court or three that buys up a group for years, and when they get tired of them, buys up another. It's just something the nobility do, that's all." Despite their privacy out here in the garden, he lowered his voice, and Mieka leaned closer. "Nobody that side of the Flood's half as good as even the worst players in this whole kingdom. It's why I'm here and not there."

Mieka nodded as if he comprehended. And he did, in a way: better to be equal to if not better than your peers than be thought utterly brilliant amongst incompetent bodgers. "Where you come from," he suggested, "they don't have people like Cayden," then added swiftly, "or Vered or Rauel."

"Not a one that I ever met. The bloodlines are blashed—like this ale," Chattim added, directing a frown at his glass. "Watered down. Nothing like what we can do, you and I, with one eye only half-open. They manage well enough with the simple things, but—" He transferred his frown to Mieka's face. "Don't you *know*?"

Mieka shook his head.

"Where I come from—" He broke off as the girl came out again, bearing a tray with yet another round and, this time, a plate of bread and fried cheese. "Gettin' on for lunching, is it, darlin'?" Chat said, smiling his lopsided smile. "Give us another bit of a while, and we'll be gone so you can set up." When she paused and searched his eyes as if judging the honesty of the statement, he smiled even wider, his comically uneven face acquiring a wry charm—but his deep blue eyes were ocean cold. Once she was gone, his lip curled with annoyance. "Never stayin' here again, that's for certes. Rauel heard it from Thierin that it's very nearly the best place in town. You know Thierin Knottinger, right?"

"To look at, not to talk to. Rauel thinks Pirro Spangler should join up with him, I hear."

"Rauel is, at bottom, a moron. Oh, he's pretty as a Chapel Angel and he could charm the scales off a snake, an' he's clever and talented enough—but he's got the brains of a coney and the morals to match. He likes Thierin because Thierin's even more his opposite than Vered is."

Mieka didn't quite comprehend this, either, but it didn't interest him at the moment. Neither was this the time to broach the subject of Blye's withies. "Tell me what the Archduke wanted, and I'll stand you a lunching at our place if you'd care to come back with me. Mistress Luta's cooking is a foretaste of heaven."

"We've a show tonight for the ladies, and somebody's got to go find Sak and Vered for rehearsal, or I'd join you with pleasure." He eyed the glass the girl had just brought out, then seemed to think better of it and reached for a chunk of bread. "What was I saying?"

"Where you come from," Mieka prompted.

"Oh. Well, I'm not usual, not at all. That's why I'm here and not there," he repeated. "Our kind, not just Elf-enkind but Wizards and Fae and Goblins and every other sort of person with magic, we're looked at sidewise most places. Where d'you think the chirurgeons go to learn how to kag an Elf's ears or file down his teeth? The panic when one of the traits shows up—" He shook his head. "You ask your masquer sometime, he can tell you."

"Tell me what?" Mieka was more bewildered than ever.

"What's his name, then? Bowbender. Had it from his father's father, wouldn't he—and when the Archduke's War started, what did the King import from elsewhere? Soldiers. Mercenaries. Men with names nobody here could pronounce, so they put names on 'em according to their craft."

"So . . . so Jeska's father got nervous when his son turned up with Elfen features—"

"Because he'd learned how to fear from *his* father. Whatever that man had in his own ancestry, two generations of this Kingdom's girls and—" He circled a forefinger with a flourish at his own pointed ear. "And I bet you don't even know why he thought like that, do you?"

Again Mieka shook his head.

"Didn't you ever go to school? Or don't they teach what happened two and three hundred years gone?"

"If they did, I wasn't listening," Mieka conceded.

He was given a brief and shocking history lesson. Chattim talked of magical folk of all kinds, pushed into enclaves and then pushed out of countries entirely. He spoke of waves of intolerance that coincided with hard times or plague, difficult times that required someone to blame and someone to punish. He told about how if the magical folk fought back, they were only confirming the worst suspicions and fears of ordinary Humans. So they left, when and as they could, for more congenial places.

"Your King at the time of the First Escaping, he was Wizardly himself through his mother, and he gave welcome. So after that, no matter who was throned, settlements were established here where more could come when they needed to. I've heard that voyagers to the new lands across the Ocean Sea actually meet up with magical folk who originally came from all over the Continent. I've half a thought to go see for myself, if any of my long-lost kin—" He broke off as Mieka snorted with laughter. "Funny, you think?"

"You on board ship? *Very* funny, Chat, you know it is! You can't even look at a seashell without turning greensick!"

The other glisker sniggered. "Make a hobby of sailing, do you?"

"We'll all have to, won't we, if this scheme for— what're they calling it? 'Artistic trade,' that's it. If that's set up, then it's over the Flood in leaky little boats for us players, and then—" He broke off as Chattim looked bewildered. "You didn't know? There's talk all over Seekhaven of sending groups over to the Continent—"

Chattim slammed a fist on the table. The dishes and glassware rattled, and the little brass lantern jumped a foot. Mieka darted out a hand to steady it.

"I knew it! I *knew* it! Selling us like wool! Sending us places where they've never seen a real performance, not the sort we can do! No wonder the Archduke wanted to buy us!"

It came clear to Mieka then. Anyone with a stake in a celebrated theater group would have a cut of whatever was earned on the Continent if this scheme went through. Chat had been wrong about its being mainly for prestige, this ownership of players' contracts. Highborns and guilds of other countries would vie madly to present players who actually knew what they were doing; the potential earnings were enormous. But if what Chat had said about throwing out magical folk over the centuries was true, then the likes of Wizards and Elves who not only didn't hide what they were but used all the magic at their command in their work hadn't been seen on the Continent for years.

"We'll be freaks," Mieka blurted. "They'll come to gawk and gape at us like—like when the King sent samplings from his bestiary garden on tour through the provinces!"

"And we all remember what happened when he did."

Mieka repressed a shudder. At Bexmarket, one of the gigantic dappled cats had reached a paw out from its cage and sliced open the cheek of a boy who'd ventured incautiously close. The subsequent riot had resulted in the deaths of four townsfolk and the escape of the cat— who was rumored to be roaming still in the rugged mountains.

"They'll be warned off us," Chat went on bitterly,

"just as people were warned not to come near the wild animals."

"And they'll come anyway, and dare each other to bait us, poke sticks into the cage—Gods, and to think I was lookin' forward to it!"

"When I was a bantling," Chat mused, "we lived in a twenty-stride village—well, maybe thirty, if you had short legs. Been there for generations. There were the Wizards with their earthenware manufactory and the Goblins who ran the kilns for them, Trolls at the post stables and store, some mostly Humans who farmed, and Elfenbloods like us who did the leeching and the brewing and the grinding at the mill. Then the old baron died, and the new one married, and his wife bore stillborn son after stillborn son. She took it into her head that not only was the leech incompetent with his potions, but the midwife was strangling every child before he could draw his first breath, the Wizards had poisoned the plates she ate off, and the Goblins were burning corn-plaits of her babies in their fires. Oh, and the Trolls were mislaying her letters a-purpose at the post, so there'd be no town-bred Human physicker to come attend her. She even thought the poor farmers were in league with my grandsir, giving the baron's kitchens only mold-rot flour. So all of us left before the baron could gather up his kin and come kill us."

"Kill you?" Mieka stared at him. "You don't really mean they would've—"

"Killed us. And in the nasty ways, nothing so simple as a hanging or beheading. My grandsir, he had cousins in one of the big cities, so we lost ourselves there in the crowds. But when I turned up able to do what I do, there was a choosing to be made. Sell me for what the ambitious lordling up the street was offering, or lose me to him anyway for no money at all." Chat picked up the full glass of ale and drained half of it down his throat. "So you'll be seeing that I've been sold before. I don't much like it."

Mieka fell back in his chair, appalled. For the first time in his life, he regretted his atrocious career as a scholar. He should have known these things, he told himself, he should have listened.

"I bought myself back years ago." The dark blue eyes slanted a look at Mieka. "How old d'you think I am? You'd be—what, eighteen, nineteen?"

"Um . . . eighteen this summer, but don't tell anybody."

A brief smile angled across his face. "I'm thirty in a month. Most people guess early twenties, and being Elves, we all of us look the same and young for years and years without even trying. But it took me from sixteen to twenty-four, saving enough to buy myself back." He contemplated his glass again, brows twitching. "I expect those years will show up with a vengeance once I start to age like the rest of our folk." He glanced over at Mieka and shrugged. "You'd best be getting back if you're to be leaving today—and I soundly recommend leaving before the Archduke's fingers start scrabbling for *you*."

"I—yeh, I should go—" He stumbled to his feet. "See you back in Gallytown, then."

"Safe going."

He left his friend solemnly drinking in the dappled sunlight of the garden, and walked back along the river only dimly aware of where he was. When he caught sight of the twin spires of the High Chapel where everyone was supposed to attend worship again tomorrow, he hesitated a moment, then shook his head. He would find nothing there, no information and no counsel. There were the self-consciously splendid windows and self-congratulatory sculptures, and nothing that spoke to him at all.

Because what he was thinking was not that if this foreign tour scheme occurred he and everyone like him would be seen as freaks, nor that it would be dangerous to perform in places where Wizards and Elves and Goblins and other magical folk were reviled, nor even how horrifying it was that people had been chased out of their homes and countries under threat of death. What Mieka was wondering was why, if the king during what Chat had called the First Escaping had been part Wizard, he had done nothing to stop it.

Quill would be able to tell him what to make of all this. Quill enjoyed anguishing himself about such things. And with an abrupt insight into a mind that had intrigued him from the start, Mieka knew that once Quill thought about it, he'd not be writing sympathetic lines about living up to one's forefathers but instead would make each prince of dubious legend speak about striving to be better than his ancestors had been.

Turning from the cold and lofty symbol of Wizardly devotions, he hurried back to the inn. The chaos of departure had happened without him: everyone else had done all the packing, and a sprightly two-horse rig was almost loaded. The landlord was happily thumbing through voucher chits that would gain him money without his having to provide further room and board. Mistress Luta stood by with their hamper, and by her grunt as she hefted it into the carriage she had accounted for most of the vouchers anyway. Jeska was saying their farewells to the landlord's wife, and Rafe was already inside and fussing with the window latches. Cayden stepped down from the carriage, scowling, then caught sight of Mieka and waved.

"Late as always! We were about to leave without you."

"Never," he replied, giving the horses a wide berth as he jogged up to the rig. "What would you do for entertainment along the way?"

"You—you must be Master Windthistle," said a voice nearby, and he turned to find a Gnomish little man with too much sandy, curling hair regarding him with dark eyes that blinked too often. "I'm Kearney Fairwalk. I hope—I do so much hope we'll have a chance to talk, back in town, don't you see."

He supposed he really ought to accustom himself to being called *Master Windthistle,* and not feel he ought to be looking round for his father or one of his uncles or brothers. He was a player on the Winterly now. He had performed before the King and Court. He was a part of something worth being part of. "Uh—pleasure," he managed, wondering where his manners had gone, his glibness. There was something odd about this man; he knew it without knowing how he knew it. But perhaps he was being foolish, spooked by Chattim's tales of noblemen who bought groups of players or forced magical folk into exile. From somewhere he dredged up a smile and a bow. "Yes, of course, looking forward to a good long conversation—"

"Mieka!" Rafe bellowed. "Get in here!"

Cade stood aside as Jeska climbed into the carriage, then came forward to shake Mieka by the scruff of the neck. "Now!" was all he said, but the shake was affectionate, and Mieka grimaced an apology at His Lordship before scrambling into the rig.

There was barely room for the four of them. The hamper of food and the empty whiskey barrel were on the floor. Mieka propped his feet on the latter and look around at what would be his home for the next long, wearying while. Surprised by the softness of the dark blue leather upholstery, impressed by the ornate wrought iron firepocket (even though they wouldn't need its warmth), he was delighted by the rack of glassware and bottles—and amazed by the shelf of books, each one bound in blue leather and stamped in gold with a design of oak leaves.

"His Lordship's own rig," Jeska affirmed. "We've hired him."

Mieka leaned out the open door of the carriage to call out his gratitude, but forgot his manners again as Cade bent down to hear whatever it was Fairwalk was saying to him. He could see only Cade's long, thin back, but the nobleman's face was turned upwards and there was a look in his dark eyes that Mieka recognized instantly. He'd seen it directed at himself, from men and boys and women and girls alike, since he was fourteen years old.

Not that it shocked him. He didn't care one way or the other what anybody else did in bed. But another flashing instinct told him that Cayden would never identify it for what it was. For all his learning and his brilliance, Quill was rather touchingly innocent in many ways.

Which reminded him of something else Cade was innocent about, and he looked round the carriage. "Where's me things?"

"Luggage boot." Rafe eyed him knowingly. "You'll have to settle for drinking Lord Fairwalk's liquor."

Mieka gave a shrug, annoyed that Rafe had guessed so accurately that he'd been looking for his wrapped roll of thorn. "Fine by me—but I hope the rest of you don't get thirsty."

Fifteen

"EARLIEST WE GET there is dawn tomorrow," said Lord Fairwalk's coachman, "so you might's well relax. His Lordship's orders are to get you to Redpebble Square as quick as may be, and that's what I'll be doing. We stop for naught but changing horses. No pissing out the windows—splash the paint, and you'll be licking this rig clean with your own tongues. Need the garderobe, you'll have about five minutes—His Lordship keeps his own horses at the post stations, and the ostlers know to be quick about the changings. The seats fold down into a nice big bed if you've a mind to stretch out and don't mind rolling about a bit. Sheets in the compartment next the bookshelf. If we get a wheel stuck, it's all of you out to help push. And I don't answer questions. Right. We're off." He slammed shut the little door just behind his seat, and true to his word the carriage surged forward after a whistle to the horses.

Mieka looked round at Rafe, Jeska, and Cade. "Sheets?" he echoed faintly.

Snuggling broad shoulders back into the padded seat, Rafe grinned. "Rather like being able to run people over with my bed."

Sometime after midnight, at their third very quick stop to change horses, Mieka had had enough of scrunching himself into a corner while Rafe sprawled across the folded-down seats and snored. Jeska was similarly asleep, though in a much tidier fashion. Cade practically fought Mieka in a scramble to the door and outside into the fresh cool air.

The coachman was limping slightly as he paced around the carriage to check the wheels. Mieka offered him a swig from a bottle of Lord Fairwalk's excellent peach brandy, but he shook his head regretfully.

"It's as much as my place is worth for anyone to smell anything stronger than onions on my breath when I get back to His Lordship's stables. Beholden for the meat pies, by the bye, lads. Usually I'm choking down whatever lukewarm swill's left over from supper at these places." He nodded to the closed and darkened tavern, his lip curling.

"No trouble," Cade said. "If you'd like a breather, I can drive for a while."

Mieka squinted in the dim light from the stable lamps. "Drive? You?"

"Oh, I've all sorts of peculiar accomplishments."

"Gods! I can't even ride!"

"Nothin' to it. I'll teach you one day."

"No, you won't!" he replied fervently.

The coachman was chewing his lip as he scrutinized Cade's face. "I can't deny I'd like an hour's rest. And you wouldn't be putting yourself or your friends in danger just for the fun of whipping the horses to full gallop—you're not that sort. Oh, I know the look," he added. "Saw it often enough in His Lordship's father, didn't I?" He leaned in close, sniffing. "How much did you drink tonight?"

"Glass with supper, about sundown," Cade replied promptly. "Nothing since."

Mieka thought of the other bottle of peach brandy, now empty, and kept his mouth shut—a thing neither he nor Cade had done while the bottle was still full.

"Well . . . come up on the box for a bit, and I'll see if you know what you're about."

It took the coachman ten minutes to assure himself that Cade did indeed know what he was doing. They stopped to allow him to climb down and settle himself in Mieka's corner of the carriage—which Mieka vacated in favor of joining Cade up top.

"But don't you let that Elf touch those reins," the man warned.

Mieka's best big-eyed-innocent look was lost in the dimness. He perched happily beside Cayden as the rig moved off again, throwing his head back to enjoy the breeze in his hair.

A few uneventful miles later, Cade said, "It's good of you, Mieka, offering to help Blye."

"It's more than an offer. It's a promise." He paused. "How d'you know she wouldn't have you? Bespoken, I mean, and married."

"Because I asked." There was a soft chuckle. "We were eight years old at the time."

Mieka nodded. That was all right. As long as it was nothing more recent.

"I wish she would," Cade fretted. "She'll be all alone now, and—"

"—and if there's any woman in Gallantrybanks who can take care of herself, it's our Blye," Mieka finished for him. "You were about to say something silly about protecting and providing for her, Quill, and you'd best not say anything like that to *her*."

"She'd only laugh at me. Or slug me a good one."

"Or both!"

"You're right, though—we have to look out for her the only way she'll accept, and getting her to accept it will be a misery."

They were quiet for a while, and Mieka peered out into the darkness beyond the carriage lamps. Forest now, though soon enough they'd come out onto the Tincted Downs, so called because with almost every month in spring and summer a different sort of flower bloomed and painted the rolling grassy hills yellow or pink or blue. One day, he told himself, he'd have to come see them in the daytime, and not go rattling through by night.

All at once Cayden said, "I can't help wondering . . ."

He glanced over, wishing the side lamps directed more light in Cade's direction than onto the road. "Yes?"

"Forgive me for being blunt, but—why don't you just ask your father for the money and buy the glassworks outright?"

Slumping back against the seat, he nodded to himself and took a pull from the brandy bottle. "Been wonderin' when you'd get round to that."

"You knew I'd take note of the address you gave the hack driver that night. Waterknot isn't what anybody would call a slum, now, is it?"

"Might's well be, for all the coin we've got. You want to know all of it, don't you?"

"Doesn't it fall under the category of 'entertainment'? Tell me a story, Mieka."

"I owe you one, I s'pose, for all the tales you think up for me to play. The short of it is that my grandfather married somebody *his* grandmother didn't much like. The Waterknot house is entailed to the eldest son, but the money she could do with as she pleased, and it pleased her to make Grandsir into a man with a bleedin' great barracks by the river and not a single penny of the Windthistle money. Still pleases her, in fact," he added thoughtfully.

"Your great-great-grandmother's still alive?"

"Well, that's the thing, innit."

"I don't understand."

"She's Elfenblood in six of her eight great-grandparents. That's about as pureblood as anybody gets nowadays. Likes to pretend it's eight of eight, the rotten old horror. And considering she's past a hundred, it might's well be eight of eight and she'll live for-fuckin'-ever. Her only son died young, and left only my grandsir. When he married a girl with barely enough Elf to give her the right sort of ears—" He waved a hand lazily. "—there went the money."

"So your father's the eldest son, and he inherited the house. But your elder brothers—they're all Human to look at, you said?"

Mieka laughed. "Makes the old besom grind her last three rotting teeth every time they're mentioned— because they're named after her grandfathers. She had high hopes when Fa married, because Mum's a Staindrop *and* a Greenseed *and* a Moonbinder. Thought it would cribble out the blood, y'see, a proper little sieve. Get rid of the Wizard and Human and Piksey and so forth, make for the appropriate number of sweet Elfen children, all with sharp little teeth and big pointy ears. Me grandmum—the one who started all the trouble by not bein' the one grandsir should've married—she had eleven children."

Cade whistled softly through his teeth; the horses' ears pricked up and he cussed under his breath, holding tighter to the reins. "Quite a crowd."

"Great-great-grandmum thought it was just plain vulgar. But I'm told she was actually thinking of coming to Gallantrybanks for Jed and Jez's Namingday—until somebody worked up the spittle to tell her that the high and mighty Sharadel Snowminder had two redheaded Humans for great-great-grandsons."

"So you and your parents and brothers and sisters—"

"—all live in that echoing old pile of rock by the river, with assorted aunts, uncles, and cousins. And all of us who're old enough either work in the house, not so much to keep it clean as to keep it from fallin' apart, or go out to earn what we can." He hesitated, then finished, "Fa makes instruments, y'see. Lutes, mainly, though he's done a harp or three in his time. Couldn't play to save his own life, but there's somethin' about his fingers and a lovely plank of spruce. . . ."

"Like your fingers and a withie?"

"The same," Mieka said, pleased that Cade understood. "Not much money in it, 'specially as he's picky about who he sells to. Sends packing all the simpering maidens and lovesick swains wanting to learn just that one perfect all-purpose song for wooing. You really have to be able to *play* before he'll sell you something to play on."

"Let me guess. There's magic in them."

"He can't help it. It's not in the strings, it's in the wood."

"Like it's in the glass, what Blye does."

"Exactly! I knew you'd feel that, when you made those withies." He paused a moment, then decided it wasn't the right time to talk about what else was in those glass twigs of Cade's. "In the hands of somebody who knows what he's about, a lute of me old Fa's crafting makes a sound like an Angel come down from the clouds."

"Your father has no patience for amateurs."

"Less than none. Nor for deceit, neither. You should see how he treats the ones who come round pretendin' to be actual musicians!" He paused in uncorking the bottle. "He'll like you."

Cade snorted. "You have this idea of me that's all wrong, y'know. Leaving aside my character or lack of it, look what it is I do. I make up stories. That's professional deceit."

"But there's truth in those stories, Quill."

"Of a sort." Cade adjusted his grip on the reins, long fingers suddenly fretful. "I don't know, Mieka—getting to a truth by way of guile and trickery—"

"Don't you bloody dare start," Mieka warned. "You talk that kind of talk with Rafe or whoever's interested. But not with me. We give an audience things that are unreal, but that doesn't make them any the less true."

"Oh, I'd like to set you loose on Master Emmot, I would!"

"Is he the one taught you to grow a garden maze in

your own head and then try to puzzle your way out of it without a map?"

"That's one way of putting it. So your Fa will like me, eh?"

"Of course. You're making sure I'm doing what I want to do." All his parents had ever wanted was for their children to be happy. Easy enough to say, but Mishia and Hadden Windthistle really meant it. He knew Cade wouldn't believe it until he saw it for himself, though.

Cade was still chuckling. "I can't even begin to guess how many things you found out you *didn't* want to do. But I know very well how miserable you made everyone while you were doing them!"

"Oh, and I can just see *you* dancin' happy off to work in a shipping office, with a million pieces of parchment to keep straight and tidy!"

"They wanted *you* to be a clerk?"

Mieka laughed softly in the darkness. "It wasn't as bad as the whole long horrible week I spent workin' for me own brothers. Jedris and Jezael, they've a good business going, especially after Lord Coldkettle's house nearly collapsed over in Spillwater. They spent so much time while they were growing up climbing the rafters and crawling the spaces betwixt the walls of our poor old Wistly Hall, by now they know without knowing how they know what's needed in any building they walk into. They'll tell you it's the listen and the smell of a place, but *I* think it's a bit of magic showing up—odd, for certes, but there it is." He paused for a swallow or two, then asked, "Anything definite in your little brother yet?"

"He's only seven this summer. So you worked for your brothers for a whole week?"

"Give me a withie, I'm an expert. They're even callin' me 'Master Windthistle' now, right? But hammer or saw . . ." He shuddered.

"Is that how you know so much about the way things are constructed, then? At the Downstreet, I mean, with the ceiling timbers. And you didn't have any trouble at all with that copper roof."

"Think you're the only one with peculiar accomplishments, do you?" A moment later, as Cade laughed aloud, Mieka heard himself say, "I wondered if you could do that, you know. When I first met you."

"Do what?"

"Laugh. I thought it might be something else you only did in private, like the writing."

There was no answer for a long time, and Mieka began to worry that he might have overstepped again. But then Cade said, "It's something you do, isn't it? Make people laugh. I'm no more proof against it than anybody else."

But he'd been quite the challenge—though Mieka didn't tell him that. "Doesn't make for regular work, though, does it—except in doin' what we do onstage. I helped out Mum's father, too, for a summer. He's by way of making everybody's gardens lovely. That makes it nice when Jed and Jez get a job of work. They find a way to mention him, casual-like, and there's Grandsir arriving the next week with five cartloads of fresh new soil and a dozen trees to be planted, and everybody makes money."

"And you not knowing a rose from a daisy!"

"Do so! The daisy's the one lacks thorns. And speaking of which—"

"Been wonderin' when you'd get round to that," Cade said in deliberate echo of Mieka's earlier words. "There won't be time when we get back home, y'know. It'll have to wait."

"Once we get Blye's troubles sorted," he agreed. "And *that* takes us to His Lordship. What did he offer, and what did you make him take instead?"

"You don't mind that I did the negotiating for all of us?"

"Better you than me, Quill. Oh, and before I forget, I was wanting to tell you I didn't have the chance to talk to Chat about Blye—he was all full of what the Arch-duke wanted from the Shadowshapers, which is a story in itself, and led to another story I want to ask you about. With all the books you've read, p'rhaps you can clear up a few things for me, about history and—"

Cade suddenly caught his breath, shoulders flinching. Ahead in the road, lit by the side-lamps, was a small, cowering dark shape, its eyes glowing eerily green. Mieka barely had time to identify it as a fox when its luxuriant tail flashed white and the animal streaked across the road to vanish in the underbrush. One horse skipped a stride and the carriage lurched as the other one stumbled. But there was no firm hand on the reins to settle them back down: what Mieka could see of Cade's face was dead white, eyes staring, lips parted on a gasp. The carriage picked up speed as the horses broke into a gallop.

Mieka hung on with one hand to the ornate railing, hearing Jeska's startled exclamation, Rafe's sleepy growl, the coachman's string of curses. He told himself to reach for the reins—though he hadn't a single clue what he ought to do with them besides yank as hard as he could—when the tall body beside him gave a sudden jerk. Slack fingers clenched, Cade leaned back, gradually slowing the horses. After a dozen more strides they steadied. But the look on Cade's face . . . Mieka realized he'd seen it before.

"Quill? What—?"

"You bloody fool!" bellowed the coachman. "Stop this rig right now! You hear me, boy? *Now*!"

The carriage had scarcely rolled to a halt before the driver was out and ordering them down. Mieka dropped lightly to the road and said, "Sorry—it was me. I'd a fancy to give it a try, and—"

"I *told* you—" the man began furiously as Cade climbed down.

"No, no," Mieka hurried on, "he'd naught to do with it, I grabbed the reins—it's my fault, I'm ever so sorry—"

"Shut it, Mieka," Cade snapped. "I'm sorry, sir, he's lying, it was me—"

"I don't give two shits which of you it was! Get in and shut up!"

Within moments the furious driver was back on his bench, and Mieka and Cade were back in the carriage. And Cade, Mieka told himself silently, was *back*. Rafe had conjured a bit of light to the interior lamp, and by the look in Cade's eyes Mieka knew that this was exactly the same thing that he'd witnessed before. Yet he didn't ask. He knew none of them would tell him. Angry and frustrated, he curled into his corner, folded his arms, and prepared to pretend to be asleep.

The lamp was doused and in the darkness Cade asked quietly, "Why did you say that, Mieka? Why did you try to tell him it was you, not me?"

He could say that mayhem in his general vicinity was almost always his fault anyway, so why not take the credit for it and add to his legend? Less charitably, by putting it onto himself, Mieka was indebting Cade to him. Yet the truth, which he knew could be quite different from what was honest, was that he'd wanted to spare Cade being shouted at while still in shock. If the look in those gray eyes had been any indication—and Mieka knew it was—then Cade couldn't be held responsible for what had happened. Deflecting the coachman's anger onto himself had been a protective instinct. It rather surprised him.

"Mieka?"

He responded to the irritable prompting with a shrug lost in the darkness. "Seemed the thing to do."

"What, lie? Was that the thing to do?"

"To people who aren't us? Yeh." He couldn't help but add, "Something you might think about, next time you go elsewhere and won't tell me what's happening to you."

"I haven't the least idea what you're talking about."

"*Now* who's lying?"

"Shut it, both of you," Rafe muttered. "Get some sleep."

Wedged into his corner, Mieka brooded and wished he had access to Auntie Brishen's wyvern-hide roll of thorn for all occasions. He knew he was right about whatever had happened when Cade saw the fox in the road, he *knew* it. Why wouldn't anybody tell him what was really going on?

He'd been gnawing on this for quite some time when he heard the whisper and rasp of someone sliding across leather. He sensed the warmth of Cade's body and smelled the combination of brandy, ink, shaving soap, and—annoyingly—just a hint of the lavender used by that girl with the red hair. Or perhaps that was only his imaginings.

"Don't lie to me," Cade breathed, barely audible. "I'll brook the drinking and the thorn and the foolery, and even the tricks onstage, but don't ever lie to me. Because I'll always be able to tell, Mieka, always."

"Same back to you, Quill," he muttered.

* * *

THEIR FIRST STOP in Gallantrybanks was not Redpebble Square, or even Criddow Close. They directed the coachman to Rafe's house instead, where they were sure Blye would be under the kind care of Mistress Threadchaser.

She wasn't. She was still at the glassworks.

"I tried! Lord and Lady witness that I tried!" exclaimed Rafe's mother. "She'd have none of it."

"She's working, isn't she?" Jeska asked. "Trying to make enough to pay off the next part of the loan when it comes due."

"That she is, day and night. Silly child, I told her she was welcome, that we'd take care of her—"

Mieka didn't cast a significant glance at Cayden; he'd decided he wasn't speaking to or even looking at his tregetour until an apology or an explanation occurred, preferably both.

Cade wouldn't have noticed if Mieka had grabbed him by the shirtfront and shook him. He was swearing in a low, fierce monotone, and went on swearing all the way to Criddow Close. It was something of an education, actually. Mieka had heard most of those words at one time or another, but not strung together this fluently and embellished by fists slammed at intervals against the uncomplaining leather seats. Upon reaching the glassworks, Cade transferred the pounding to its outer door, and the cussing resolved into a single bellow of rage: "Blye!"

A titled lord's elegant if dust-covered carriage was not the most common sight in Criddow Close. Doors opened all down the narrow street—including the back door of the Silversun residence. But the door of the glassworks and its shop stayed shut. Mieka had just followed Rafe out of the rig when Derien came hurtling up to them, talking so fast that not one word was intelligible. Mistress Mirdley was right behind him, alternating exclamations of relief that they were home with admonitions to Dery.

"We weren't looking for you until tomorrow—will you *shoosh*, boy!—but it's a blessing from the Old Gods that you're here so quick. She's grieving and worried sick and I don't know—Master Derien, if you don't quiet down—"

Rafe caught the boy up in his arms for a hug. "It's all right, bantling, settle down and breathe. That's the way." Over the child's head, he collected Mieka and Jeska with his gaze. Cayden was still yelling.

The door finally opened, and Blye—dirty, disheveled, hollow-eyed—began screaming right back at Cade. "What d'you think you're doin', eh? Shrieking outside my door at this hour! Damn you, Cade, put me down!"

For he had wrapped his arms around her and lifted her right off her feet, just as Rafe had done to Dery. "Why didn't you send for me when it happened?" he demanded. "I would've come home, you know I would've come home—"

"Why d'you think I didn't tell you? Let go of me!"

Rightly judging that this argument would go on for a while, Mieka turned to Mistress Mirdley. "Can you and Dery go get her things?"

"She's coming back to my house with me," Rafe added.

Dery wriggled his way down, breathing hard but coherent now. "She wouldn't let me write to Cade, but after the man came and asked all those questions I knew he had to know and I knew you'd come back and—"

"What man?" Jeska asked, frowning.

Mistress Mirdley looked up at Mieka. "She won't do it. She won't leave."

"Oh yes she will," he muttered.

He strode past Cade—still holding the struggling, spitting Blye—and into the glassworks. It took him a few moments, but then he saw them on a corner table: a dozen new withies spread out for polishing. Grabbing one, he slid the crimped end up his sleeve, keeping a few inches of it concealed in his palm. Turning on his heel, he went back to the shop, estimated the distance between himself and Blye—back on her own two feet now, and shouting at the top of her lungs, standing too close to Cayden.

Unpolished though the glass twig was, still he sensed the magic she had used to create it, familiar to him by now and comfortable. Comforting. Nothing of Cade's work was in it, but that it had been fashioned for him was unmistakable. It was as if her thoughts about him while she'd worked, her deep understanding of his character, had imbued the glass. Here was his rigorous intensity, his striving, his passion, his need to be not just better than he was but to be the *best*. Yet there were other things, too, sparkles of humor and recklessness, and an entirely different sort of intensity that was arrogance and uncertainty in the same glints of magic. These things were himself, Mieka realized; Blye's knowledge of *him* infused the glass as well. None of the others she had made up until now had reached him until Cade had done his own work. Now he could sense what made this withie his just as much as Cade's. He was swept with affection and gratitude for Blye, and used these emotions as she finally stalked far away enough from Cade for Mieka to do what he knew he must.

Gently, he awakened the withie. Unprimed, untouched by any magic but Blye's, with nothing inside it he could use as he used onstage, yet it was a conduit just as it always was. Mieka held out his hand, trying to be casual about it, but nobody was looking at him and he could have waved the thing as he pleased. He kept it discreet, though, the magic he used to calm her down. He took nothing from her, not her grief or her anger, and he changed nothing about what she was feeling. What he did was ease feelings, not create them. He gentled her anger and her fear.

It was how he had first figured out he had the makings of a glisker, this ability to affect others. He'd always thought it was his wit, his looks, his charm, his big innocent eyes. But he'd been working people's emotions on instinct, even though before the withies and his training it had been unfocused and unreliable, quite weak in its effects—especially compared to what he could do now.

Blye stopped yelling. She was shivering a little, arms

wrapped around herself rather than waving furiously in the air, but she was calm. Mieka slipped back into the glassworks, replaced the withie, and went back outside in time to see that Cade had wrapped Blye tenderly into his arms and was smoothing her limp blond hair.

Satisfaction put a smile onto Mieka's face—until he happened to look at Mistress Mirdley. She knew. Muted as the magic had been, she had sensed it. They went on staring at each other as Rafe and Jeska unloaded Cade's things from the carriage and Lord Fairwalk's coachman drank gratefully from the huge cup of tea Dery gave him, and at length the Trollwife nodded slowly and Mieka could relax.

Within the half hour, Cade and Rafe had taken Blye off to the Threadchaser home, and Jeska had departed for his own house on foot, grateful to stretch his legs after the long hours in the carriage. Mieka had elected to stay and explain as much as he knew—and discover if he could get explanations for what he didn't know. Settling in the kitchen with breakfast enough for three piled onto his plate, he cheerfully stuffed himself and between bites, sips, and swallows managed to convey the gist of what Touchstone had decided to do.

"—and that way, we'll own the glassworks just like your grandsir did, Dery, with our very own crafter working for us—and for a few select friends," he finished with a wink.

"More tea," said Mistress Mirdley, and poured from a fresh pot without further comment. She wouldn't look Mieka in the eyes.

"Do you really think Blye will let you do that?" Derien asked, frowning.

"Well, it's not just that she hasn't much other choice. It's for the best all round, she'll see that eventually. But it has to be presented to her in just the right way, and I hope your brother isn't babbling like a blatteroon when she's in no fit state to hear above one word in ten. It'll wait for tomorrow or the next day."

"I can help," Derien offered. "It was me paid for the post courier, but I've still some left of what I've saved."

"What you paid the courier counts as a share in the business," Mieka told him. "You can be special communications commissioner, and whenever we need to send a letter quick-like, you can arrange it with His Lordship."

"Whose Lordship?" the boy demanded, wide eyed.

"Lord Kearney Fairwalk." He grinned as he announced the name and Mistress Mirdley dropped a spoon. "I'm not sure of all the details yet—Cayden had the arranging of it—but he's to take charge of our bookings, see to the equipment, make sure we have decent lodgings on the road and get paid on time and—"

"So long as it's understood," Mistress Mirdley said severely, "that it's Touchstone he's working for and not the other way round."

Derien sniggered. "This is Cade we're talking of! He'll see to it, no worries! Who else is going to use Blye's withies, Mieka?"

"I'll tell you if you tell me about the man with the questions."

"Thought you'd snag on that," said the Trollwife. " 'Twas the morning after the death, and then again two days after that."

"Blye didn't see him, not either time," Dery contributed. "I was outside waiting for the Good Brother, and Mistress Mirdley was upstairs helping Blye ready her father's body. It was a lot of questions he had, and thought I was stupid enough to answer."

"Such an adorable, innocent little boy as you are!" Mieka teased.

"So p'rhaps I don't need lessons from you after all!" Dery retorted. "He was the stupid one, wearing a cloak to his boot-tops, and hot as the glass kiln outside at not even noon. Did he think nobody'd notice?"

"It's the foolish arrogance of high nobility," Mistress Mirdley observed. "Thinking nobody but them has two wits to rub together. It seeps down into their servants as well."

"What did this man in the cloak want to know?"

"Well, he told me at first he was from the Guild," Derien said, "but the things he asked, he was lying about that, because the Guild already knows names and merchandise and shipping agreements and all that, don't they? I asked him if he thought I looked like a business clerk."

Mieka pretended to examine him head to heels. "No, can't say you do. There's a decided lack of ink on your fingers—from lack of doing your schoolwork, no doubt. What else did he say?"

"That he supposed the shop was popular, and did a lot of trade. I told him I wasn't a tariff inspector, either."

"Snide child," Mieka said sorrowfully.

"Cade's a terrible influence," Dery agreed. "The second time he came round, Mistress Mirdley and me, we were just setting off to bring Blye something to eat, and there he was in his cloak again." He paused a moment, brows knitting over a nose that would never even begin to rival his brother's. "There was a breeze that day, Mieka, and it blew his cloak aside, and he was wearing a dark gray tunic with orange piping. That's the Archduke's livery, right? Those colors?"

"You must have mistook it," Mistress Mirdley said. "Why would the Archduke be interested in a glassworks?"

"I told you before, I didn't make a mistake!" Dery exclaimed, shoulders stiffening in the same stubborn way Cade's did. "I know what I saw!"

Mieka had by this time lost all impulse to laughter. He

chewed his lip, trying to add a proposed purchase of the Shadowshapers to an inquisitiveness about a glassworks whose owner had just died. He couldn't do the sum without more information, but he was in no doubt he wouldn't like the total.

"I believe you, Dery," he said. "I'll tell you why when Cade gets back. But I do believe you. It was quick of you to notice."

Derien accepted this with dignity, but couldn't repress a *See? Told you!* glance for Mistress Mirdley. She harrumphed with a sound like a blocked drain.

"Time you got some ink onto those fingers, isn't it?" she asked pointedly. "Unless you want another scold. How many would that make this week?" When he had slumped off to his neglected work, she turned to Mieka. "That was a kind and gentle thing you did for her. But I hope you have a care with it, boy."

He didn't pretend ignorance. "I don't use it like that— not often, anyway. Truly."

"It was soft enough that no one else suspects. Make sure no one ever does. Onstage is one thing. It makes you good at what you do. Off . . . it makes you dangerous, and you know it."

Which was precisely why he didn't use it. Not often, anyway.

Sixteen

IN HIS FAVORITE and most private little nook of the vast house on Waterknot Street—a hideaway he was fairly sure not even his eldest brothers had ever discovered—Mieka could escape the noisy commotion of everyday life with his family. Cayden and Rafcadion had their personal eyries on the top floors of their parents' homes; Jeschenar had hollowed himself out a warm, dry cave of a place in a corner of his mother's leaky cellar, where he could memorize his lines or enjoy his latest girlfriend. Mieka's refuge was halfway between these extremes. A deeply eccentric ancestor had tacked onto the house a series of triangular turrets overlooking the river, jutting like spines on the back of a recumbent dragon. His excuse had been that he wanted a clear view of whatever fleet of foreign Wizards came sailing up from across the Flood or down from the wild hills of the Westercountry to attack and pillage Gallantrybanks. The last time either of these things had happened had been about a thousand years ago. Mieka knew that much history, at any rate. But whatever his great-great-whatever-grandsir's quirks, and however dodgy the continued acquaintance of some of those turrets with the walls had become, he was grateful to the old fool. One of those six turrets, the one with the best view of the Plume, had a little chamber at its base that nobody except Mieka knew about, accessed by a trapdoor in the room above. In winter it was cold; in summer it was stifling hot. A stolen firepocket alleviated the chill; if the summer breeze was right, the chinks in the wooden floor above drew air from the two square windows overlooking the river. If the space became more cramped as he grew older and grew up, he didn't mind. It was quiet here, and solitary, and these were two things rarely to be had at Wistly Hall.

Over the years since he'd found it—quite by accident, playing Seek-Me-Find-Me with his twin sister—he had embellished the little room with blankets, pillows, the fire-pocket, and stolen placards of famous theater groups. Very soon now he expected to take all the latter down and stick up a placard advertising Touchstone instead. But he would keep the big parchment sign he'd made shortly after seeing his first playlet: *Mieka Windthistle, Master Glisker*.

He had spent many long hours in this lair: dreaming, practicing with imaginary and then real withies, watching tall-masted ships sail to and from the merchants' docks, wondering what famous or infamous persons might be in the pleasure barges plying the river below the Plume. But he never wished himself onto any of the boats, for he was as useless on water as he was on horseback—indeed, his few experiments in either activity had had similar endings: abrupt and uncomfortable. He remained unconvinced that landing in the water, which at least was a bit cushiony, was better than landing on his bum on the hard ground. He had no desire to repeat either experience.

Six days after Touchstone's return to Gallantrybanks, he sat cross-legged on a pile of pillows purloined from various parts of Wistly Hall and stared at the two groups of withies arrayed on a threadbare counterpane nicked from the refuse bin in back of a draper's shop. A pile of used buffing papers and glossing cloths lay nearby, and he surveyed the gleaming results of last night's hard work with satisfaction. Persuading Cayden that he was perfectly capable of the maintenance required on older withies (tiny scratches and scuffs left unattended could become problems) and the polishing necessary for new ones hadn't been easy, and he'd had to pretend to lose his temper. Two dozen of the withies were of Blye's making even though—most illegally—they bore her father's hallmark at the crimp. These were the last that ever would; the Guilds were always prompt, whenever a master crafter died, in seizing and destroying his coveted stamp. A living of sorts could be made in glassware, ceramics, metalwork, weaving, and so forth without an official chop, but exportation was illegal and there was excellent money in the Kingdom of Albeyn's ever-growing trade.

Mieka ran a fingertip lightly down one of the slender glass twigs. He was used to these in performances now, accustomed to the sensitivity of Blye's magic and the way it so knowingly created the structure for Cade's. Last week, though, snagging up a just-made unpolished withie to use surreptitiously on her, was the first time he'd realized how well she knew him, too. He had no idea how she did what she did, and didn't want to know. Finding things out, learning the why of them, usually took away just one more bit of mystery from life. He was grateful for her giftedness, and impressed, and that was sufficient.

Six more withies lay to his left. These were the ones Cade had fashioned even more illegally. He'd been told that these were the ones he'd have to use as the shatterings. But he didn't want to destroy them. They were . . . different. Special. And, fully aware that this was unlike him, he wanted to understand why.

Cayden, he told himself with a rueful grimace, was gifted, too: at messing up Mieka's hitherto predictably chaotic life.

He'd spent his first two months with Touchstone alternating between a burning curiosity about the brilliant, grumpy tregetour and a total terror of misjudging just how far he could go in making him laugh. A pair of big puppy-dog eyes and a large collection of cheeky wisecracks disarmed most people's annoyance if he sneaked a toe across the line (well, leaped right over it, mostly), but he hadn't been sure about Cade.

He still wasn't. He knew he was now an irreplaceable part of something worth being part of, but there were times Cayden flummoxed him. He thought he had several good ideas about why—that Harpy of a mother, for one thing, and his morbid sensitivity about his looks. This last was ridiculous as far as Mieka was concerned: Hadn't Cade any idea how beautiful his eyes were, or that he'd grow into that face as he got older? Mieka's own looks, he was well aware, were of the pleasing, pretty sort— quite nice while they lasted, but ultimately a bit insipid. Cade's face, for all his beak of a nose and long jaw and sharp chin, would never ever be boring.

There was something about these withies of Cayden's making that perplexed him just as much as their maker did. He sensed their power even now, even drained of the magic Cade had primed them with for Trials. They had nothing of Blye within them. They felt of Cade because he had created them, not just because he had enhanced them after they were made. His emotions were inside the glass. What bothered Mieka wasn't the stubbornness or the ambition or even the trace of reckless defiance linger- ing from the night he'd made these. It was the fear. He hadn't sensed any of it after Cade had primed them for his use, but now that they were empty again the feel of them worried Mieka. He supposed it might be echoes of Cade's concern that he might get caught. Lady What's-her-name's grandson fashioning his own withies, never mind how harmlessly, would have the authorities apoplectic. But Mieka knew the fear wasn't because of that.

Minster chimes up and down the river added their re- minder to the sudden growling of his stomach: time for tea. He stowed the withies into their velvet bag and hauled them and himself up into the overhead room, smiling as he remembered all the years when he'd needed a stepladder to reach the floorboards for a good grip. He shut the trapdoor and pushed concealing boxes and broken planks across it. The turret was no looser in its moorings than usual, but he frowned to see that the iron pegs showed another winter's wear in rust. He'd miss his cubbyhole, once he had coin enough for lodgings of his own. Jumping the foot-wide gap between the turret's wooden floor and the stone stairs, he shut the rickety old door—habit, really, because nobody came up here—and started down the steps. A detour to his own room for a quick wash and a fresh shirt was followed by a stop in Jinsie's bedchamber so he could scrutinize his reflection in the only uncracked, unspotted, untarnished full-length mirror in the house. Judging by the design of the gilt-wood frame, it belonged to about the same period as the mirror over the fireplace in Lady Jaspiela's drawing room—lots of carved swirls and curlicues, and a single undecorated fingerspan of space at the bottom where the owner's name or badge or symbol or something was supposed to go. Lady Jaspiela's had a black swan painted in, and a very grouchy-looking bird it was, too. This mirror was unmarked, though Mieka assumed it had come down in the Windthistle family for a few generations. As he snatched up his sister's comb to run through his hair, he wondered briefly how this looking-glass had survived the periodic spasms of *What else can we sell?* that sent everyone exploring the house yet again for hitherto overlooked treasures. He couldn't help a little bounce of excitement at the thought that soon now, very soon, nobody in his family would ever again have to ransack the premises for salable objects. He was a Master Glisker now, and Touchstone was going to be rich. Well, after they settled everything with Blye and the glassworks, anyway. Angling the mirror towards the window for better light, he grimaced at the beginnings of a blemish on his chin, and poked through his sister's dressing table for Auntie Brishen's secret-recipe skin salve.

"Mieka! Hurry it up, they're here!"

Jezael had always been the loudest of the family, but bellowing orders to workmen thirty or forty feet overhead had taught him whole new levels of thunderous. "Coming!" Mieka yelled back, scowled again at the spot, and ran out of the room, the velvet bag of withies cradled carefully in his arms.

They were Touchstone, invited to tea at Wistly Hall. Mishia and Hadden Windthistle had decided it was time and long past time they met their son's partners. It was a glorious summer's day and tea was set up on the back lawn that sloped down to the river. Away from much-mended upholstery, scarred tables and wobbly chairs, worm-eaten rafters, and the occasional crumbling bit of stonework, Mieka could almost believe that his old pus-blister of a great-great grandmother wasn't really hanging on to every pence with the iron fist she didn't bother to put inside a silk glove. If the cups didn't match the plates, let alone the saucers, who would even notice when the view of the river was so fine? If the teapots were chipped, who would care once they were lounging on blankets and pillows on the sun-flooded grass? And if it took Mistress Threadchaser's mocah cakes and walnut muffins to fill out a somewhat sketchy selection of tea-time treats, who could possibly be embarrassed once Rafe explained that the Windthistles would be doing his parents a favor by giving their opinion of these new recipes?

And besides all the other distractions that made one forget the decaying splendors of Wistly Hall, Blye was wearing a skirt.

Mieka was so astonished by this when he saw her that he simply gaped for a moment before recovering his manners and sweeping her a bow. A wry smile crossed her tired face as she acknowledged the salute with a mocking little curtsy.

"It was very kind of your mother to invite me," she told him later as they lazed on the grass, plates and cups empty at last. "I wasn't going to come, but . . ."

"I'm glad you did. Can I get you anything else? More tea?"

She shook her head. "I'm fine. I'm here because you haven't been round to Criddow Close lately and I want to say how beholden I am to you for—"

He held up a warning finger. "Not a word. Not one word. It's purely selfish of me, Blye. There's no one else as could make the withies for Cade and me. Your work is what got us to Trials and onto the Winterly, so I'll hear no more about it."

"But, Mieka—"

"Did I tell you or did I not?" He gave her his best glare, with knitted brows and jutting chin, and at last she smiled.

"Good show the other night at the Downstreet," she said. "Meaning it's one that will keep me making glassware for days!"

"I do love to know someone else is working even harder than me!"

"Work? You?" Jinsie plopped herself down beside them, munching on an apple. "Blye, we're off to Narbacy Street tomorrow for something to wear to the Kiral Kellari. You'll come, of course?"

Blye gasped. "You got the booking? Why didn't you tell me you got the booking?" Half-turning, she yelled, "Cade!"

He looked round from talking with Hadden Windthistle—whom he topped by head and shoulders. "What?" he called back.

"Kiral Kellari?"

A smug grin spread across his face. Pausing to excuse himself to Mieka's father, he ambled over. "Rauel commended us to the owners, but 'twas Kearney who settled the deal. Nice, not to have to talk me throat dry negotiating."

Jinsie pulled a face. "'Kearney' now, is it? Haven't *we* got grand!"

"'Lord Fairwalk' to you, child," Mieka admonished. She stuck out her tongue at him; he pretended to snatch it out of her mouth; she howled in imitation agony—and quite unexpectedly a child's voice rose in a wail. Mieka turned to see his youngest sister standing nearby, tears streaming down her cheeks. "Oh, Jorie, sweeting, 'twas only foolery!" He scooted across the grass towards her. "Jinsie's just fine—look!"

The child insisted on an inspection. Satisfied, she forgave Mieka with a pat on the arm and toddled off. When he returned to the blanket where Blye, Jinsie, and Cade waited, he found Jorie's twin, Tavier, earnestly presenting Cade with a seemingly endless collection of worms. He kept reaching into his pockets and giving over squirmy black or gray things of varying lengths; Cade kept accepting them, solemn-faced.

"So is that what you want to do when you grow up, then?" Jinsie was asking. "Gather bugs and such and help Auntie Brishen in her brewing?"

Mieka hid a grin as Cade's gray eyes widened; he knew Quill was suddenly wondering just exactly what might be in various thorns.

"No," Tavier informed her. "I want to be a dragon."

"Hmm. That's interesting. What sort of dragon?"

The boy gave the question due consideration. "A *bad* dragon."

"With lots of teeth," Blye agreed as Mieka fell over laughing.

"And breathing fire, don't forget the breathing fire part," Cade reminded her. "Pity none of these are primed," he went on, gesturing to the velvet bag on the blanket.

"Your brother could show you the dragon he made for the King."

"That's just pretend," Tavier scoffed. "I want to be a *real* dragon. They grow from worms."

Jinsie's eyes rounded. Tavier wandered off, presumably to find more worms, and she whispered, "You don't think he's—oh Gods, Miek, he couldn't be *eating* the awful things, could he?"

"Not big enough," Cade said, placing the handful of forlorn little worms onto the grass. "But I'm sure he'll keep looking." Then he glanced at Mieka and laughed. "And there's us humbled, right enough! 'Just pretend'!"

"Where's Fa going?" Jinsie asked, shading her eyes with one hand as she squinted towards the house.

"I think I heard something about a customer." Mieka shrugged. "Could be a good sign, him coming round at teatime. Nothing more suggestive of a real artist than bad manners."

"What's *your* excuse, then?" his sister demanded. "You're the rudest person I know!" Pushing herself to her feet, she said, "I think I'll go have a look. I'll come find you later, Blye, about the clothes."

And then it was just the three of them, and Mieka knew exactly what they were about to discuss.

He had told Cade about the man in the Archduke's livery coming round twice to Criddow Close, asking about the glassworks. Cade had discussed it with Dery, then spoken with Lord Fairwalk, who had promised to look into the matter. Blye had received formal notice from the Guild that there was a buyer—not Touchstone, someone else—and been informed that it was understood that after the search had been made and no male heirs found, she would be selling up. She took the greatest pleasure in informing them that there was another offer and she would be taking it. The Guild had had no opportunity to be offended, for it was Lord Kearney

Fairwalk who had formally presented the petition for the proposed sale.

To get the subject started, Mieka asked, "Any word from the Guild?"

"They've signed off on our deal," Cade said. "They couldn't not sign off on it, not with His Lordship staring them in the face."

"He thinks it's madness." Blye began toying with the ragged fringe on a pillow. "I'm not sure I don't agree with him. No group owns their own glassworks."

"My grandsir did," Cade reminded her with a weary patience that told Mieka this must be roughly the hundredth time he'd done so.

"I know!" she snapped, her tone causing Mieka to adjust his estimate upwards by about a thousand. "It was *my* great-grandsir as was his glasscrafter, wasn't it?"

"A fine thing, family tradition," Mieka announced before they could really start sniping at each other. "The Windthistles have several, not all of them illegal, and it looks as if Jed and Jez are about to carry on with one of them." He pointed to the little wooden pavilion down by the water, where the two tall redheads had finally yanked open the door that *would* stick no matter how they tried to mend it. "Anybody else for a swim?"

Cade shook his head regretfully. "I've nothing to wear."

"Wear? Swimming?" Mieka laughed. "Although now I think on it, there's company present so they might be polite and at least pretend they're mannerly, refined, modest—"

"And therefore completely unrelated to *you*," Cade remarked. "Your parents are wonderful, Mieka. Cilka and Petrinka seem nice, civilized girls, and so does Jorie—and aside from a partiality for slimy little things best left wriggling underground, Tavier's a good lad." With a narrow, pensive look: "Are you sure you weren't adopted?"

Mieka yawned.

Jeska had followed the eldest Windthistle twins into the pavilion. The trio emerged wearing nothing at all and plunged into the water, yelling at the chill. Mieka waited for Blye's attention to return from the view, and finally snapped his fingers in front of her face, laughing when she blinked in surprise.

Cade was grinning. "It's wearing a skirt what does it, I'm convinced. Reminds her she's a girl."

She gave him a withering glare. "The Guild doesn't seem to require reminding. Even though it bowed its collective head and tugged its collective forelock before the noble Lord Fairwalk."

"What about the other buyer?" Mieka asked.

Cade spread his thin hands and grimaced. "Whatever Dery saw in Criddow Close, Kearney says there was no trace of the Archduke or any of his people. If he was really interested, he'd've had somebody show up to present his own petition, wouldn't he?"

"I wasn't there to see this man," Blye said slowly, "so I don't know. But Dery had to've been mistook. I mean, what would the Archduke want with a glassworks?"

"What would he want with a theater group of his very own?" Mieka challenged. "I know what *I* saw, and it was that gray and orange livery on the lackey Vered Goldbraider sent streaking off like a scalded cat. Oh, and I keep forgetting to tell you, Blye—Chat would like to know when he and the others can come by for a consultation." He smiled as she caught her breath. Turning to Cade, he went on, "Just look at her! For us, she shrugs. For them, she goes all fluttery!"

"I've never 'fluttered' in my life!" she exclaimed.

Cade, eyeing her sidelong with a wicked glint in his gray eyes, said, "I think you're right, Mieka. A definite flutter. Though that, too, might be just the natural result of wearing a dress for a change."

Blye looked murderous. Mieka hastened to say, "And right lovely she looks in it, too. Shut up, Quill."

But Cade kept teasing her. "You'll be wearing it for the Shadowshapers when they visit, won't you?"

Mieka realized that whereas Cade had been amused when he caught her staring at Mieka's brothers and Jeska, he was jealous that she was indeed impressed by the prospect of such illustrious new clients. An instant later—remembering that not two hours ago he'd been telling himself how well she knew both him and Cade —Mieka wasn't entirely sure he didn't feel the same. She'd have to learn a lot about the Shadowshapers, wouldn't she, to make their withies just as good as the ones she fashioned for him and Cade. This would quite probably make the Shadowshapers even better in performances than they already were. And *this* would make them just that much more difficult to beat at Trials. That Touchstone would one day triumph over all comers and gain First Flight on the Royal Circuit was something Mieka had never doubted, not since that first night in Gowerion. But it only now occurred to him that in helping a friend, they would also be quite literally placing an advantage in the hands of rivals.

He decided that the challenge would be fun. Almost as fun as teasing Cade. "Oh, Blye and Jinsie will find something stunning at the Narbacy Street tailor just for the occasion, the Shadowshapers bein' not just *anybody,* y'know. And before I forget again, Chat says at your convenience, Blye, and do you like toffee—he lives just over a confectioner's."

"He need only bring his friends and his custom," she replied. "And a nice disregard for a hallmark, of course."

"*And* an ability to keep their mouths shut," Cade added.

Crafters of all kinds had spent a long time getting control over their own professions. Mieka had heard his father complain about it more than once. In the old days, before the upheavals of the Archduke's War had unsettled everything from Albeyn's magic to Albeyn's trade, the highborns owned all the tools of production, charged a skilled craftsman for their use, and claimed a portion of the products. This system still prevailed in parts of the land, in things such as blacksmithing and flour milling, but the City of Gallantrybanks had a royal charter stating that only the Guilds could decide who owned a workshop, who made the goods, and who could sell them. Only the Guilds could authorize a hallmark, and anything without a hallmark sold so cheaply that it was scarcely worth making. Blye, of course, would receive no hallmark from the Glasscrafters Guild.

"Jeska helped me do some totting up," she went on, "and I think I can make basic expenses with what I've always done—plates and utensils, things that don't require a Master's hallmark. Even if the Shadowshapers like my work, it'll take me some time to learn their style, so there won't be much coming in from them for a while, not until I can make their withies as easily as I do yours." She folded her burn-scarred hands in her lap, and stared at them for a few moments. "This is assuming, of course, that no male heir can be found."

"Stop fretting," Cade told her. "I never heard your father mention anybody else by way of family—"

"Be glad you're not stuck with this lot," Mieka interrupted, gesturing expansively from wall to crumbling wall of the garden. "Just look at all this herd roaming the pasture—horrifying, innit? With us, it'd take a hundred clerks a hundred years to figure out whose claim comes first. There's all the marriages to consider, for one thing— who brought the Greenseed or Flickflame or whichever pretentious prehistoric line back into the Windthistle fold. Of course, there being not much to claim, there wouldn't be much competition," he reflected.

"I can't imagine growing up in a family like this," Blye said. "It was always just me and my father."

"There's times," Mieka confided, "I'm not sure which of 'em I'm actually related to, which ones married in, and which ones just showed up one day and nobody ever bothered to ask!"

"Can't tell just by looking, can you?" Cade remarked. "Nobody'd ever believe you're brothers with those two great hulking redheads."

"Jedris asked about windows," Blye said suddenly. "You didn't put him up to it, did you, Mieka?"

"Windows? No. What about them?"

"They've a project going, I gather, and can't find someone to make the windows at a reasonable price."

Mieka looked at her for a long moment, then said quite seriously, "If that's what he said, that's what he meant. Something you have to understand about my brothers, Blye—neither of them could lie if his own life hung in the balance. I used to think it was because Mum used her truth-tell hex on them a bit too powerful when they were little—oh, she has one, and it's vicious!" he added when Cade's brows shot up. "You don't ever want it directed at you, believe me! But it's not that, with Jed and Jez. It's that they've neither of them imagination enough. They're the kind who hear pattering on the roof and look outside to be sure it's raining—but it would never occur to them that possibly it's mice."

"Or Tavier, the baby dragon?" Cade asked, smiling. "It's not charity, Blye. They need someone to do the work."

She shrugged. Whatever she might have said was lost when a short, stocky, extravagantly Elfen personage stumped across the grass towards them, snarling Mieka's name.

"Oh Gods," he muttered. "Brace yourselves, it's Great-Uncle Breedbate."

A nickname, of course, one that was never used in his presence. One of the eleven affronts to great-great-grandmother's pride, Barsabian Windthistle had spent his life determined to prove himself more Elf than any Elf ever born. He wore ridiculous clothes, the kind always seen in centuries-old depictions of Elves: dagged-hem tunics, wide-collared shirts, trousers that bloused at the knee over pointy-toed boots. He used the most archaic words he could dig up out of musty old books—which he read not for their literary or scholarly value but solely to find such antiques. He cast nasty spells whenever the mood struck him, confirming the worst that was ever said of Elfen mischief. And it was the great tragedy of his life that somehow, even though his ears and feet were classics of Elfen perfection, he had a lovely set of straight white teeth.

"You there, boy!" bawled Uncle Barsabian. "What're you doin', collifobbling with the likes of him?"

"And a good afternoon this beautiful day to you, too, Uncle," Mieka returned with a wide and, he hoped, beguiling smile. "Did you enjoy your tea? Permit me to introduce you—"

"To a *Wizard*? Not bleedin' damn likely, boy!" Glaring down at Cade, he shouted, "Why they let scroyley things like you walk free is past my understanding! Swanning round as if you owned the world and all the stars besides!"

There was more in this vein; much more. Everyone had learned ages ago simply to let the old man talk himself done. Arguing was pointless, and any protests that he might consider the feelings of those he screamed at were countered with the entire list—and it was lengthy—of incidents proving that Wizards *had* no feelings. The best that could be hoped for was that someone would come to the rescue—which Jedris and Jezael did, fresh from their swim and wrapped in sheets too threadbare to be used on the beds anymore.

"Uncle! There you are!"

They each took an elbow, preparing to haul the old man off. But, though interrupted in his usual tirade against Wizards, Uncle Barsabian pointed a gnarled and knobby finger at Blye. "And a Goblin flyndrig besides! Who let *you* out of your cave to associate with decent folk?"

Mieka scrambled to his feet, shaking with rage. "That's beyond enough, you scabby old horror! Get him out of here!"

"Gladly," said Jedris, and together the twins lifted Uncle Barsabian off his feet and carted him away, with the old man yelling all the while, "Put me down! Unhand me! Gleets, the pair of you!"

"I'm so sorry, Blye," Mieka said, dropping down to the grass again, fists still clenched. "He's addled, of course—always was, so I'm told—but that's no excuse. I don't know how he got out. Usually Mum's careful to see that he keeps to his room when there's guests."

Blye shook her head. "Plenty of Elfenkind his age hold a grudge."

"He oughta keep it to himself. Bleedin' old pillock."

Cade was frowning. "What in all hells is a 'gleet'?"

"I don't like to say, not around a lady. He's always been a one for what he thinks are the old ways and the old words, and bein' more Elf than the first Elf that taught all the other Elves how to be Elves." He paused, then decided they deserved to know why Uncle Barsabian was the way he was. "There's just the one exception to his Elfenness, and that's how he went peculiar. He refused to show fear, y'see. Five days he was in a black cellar before he gave them the satisfaction of—well, you know." He shrugged. "Not that they broke him. He just made them wait for it. When he finally got out, he claimed there was a family of Goblins down there, and making all sorts of light with their iron-forge, 'cept that whenever the Wizards came to see if he'd finally conjured the fearing fire, they'd shut their rock wall and hide. So you see he doesn't much like Goblins, neither."

"Five days?" Cade looked appalled.

"Somebody at the time sneered at him that he must be more Human than he looked, not to react the way a real Elf would. So he set out to be the most Elfenly Elf who ever lived."

"Poor old man," Blye murmured.

"The bulk of the family isn't quite that mad," Mieka promised, then added, "the family I'm sure I'm related to anyway. Gods, how I wish that didn't include Uncle Breedbate." Who, he didn't say, had a nose for finding previously unnoticed valuables, which was probably why Mum kept him around.

Blye rose to her feet. "I think I'm for another cup of tea. You?" When they shook their heads, she smiled and went up the sloping lawn to the terrace.

After she was out of earshot, Cade said, "The Archduke talked to Rafe at Seekhaven, right after our show."

Mieka felt his eyes widen almost out of his head. "What? Rafe never said anything about—I didn't even *see* him!"

"All sorts of charming compliments, deeply impressed, hopes to see us on the Winterly—shoveled it on, according to Rafe." Cade pleated a corner of the blanket. "Irked me some, that he went to Rafe 'stead of me. But after I heard what he said, and how much Rafe disliked him . . ."

"But why would he talk to—?" It hit him like a cudgel to the head. "He was shopping! Ha! Vered and Chat both said we'd be next, after them—I can't wait to tell them we were *first*!"

"Don't say anything to anybody, Mieka. I've been

thinking about what Chattim told you, and trying to fit it into this offer for the glassworks, and until I understand it, I don't think we ought to let on that we even know he was interested in buying it."

He chewed his lip, then nodded. "All right. I'll keep quiet. Oh, stop lookin' at me in that tone of voice! I can keep a secret!"

"It'll be interesting, watching you prove it. I—" He broke off, his attention caught by something or someone up at the house. His gray eyes lost all light; his face lost the flush brought by the sunshine. He looked, in fact, much the way he'd looked those times when—

No. This was different. This wasn't what Mieka had begun to term the *Elsewhere* look. This was . . . recognition?

Mieka turned, and saw his father standing at the tea table with a tall, lean, awkwardly dressed young man who was cradling a lute in his arms as if it were his first-born son. Heavy reddish-brown curls framed an almost golden face that wore a pathetically grateful expression. Mieka's initial reaction was delight that Fa had found someone worthy of his work and had made a sale. But then he glanced at Cayden again, and this time he was sure he saw a remembering in his eyes.

"Know him?" he asked as if he had no interest in the matter at all.

"What? Oh—no, he just seemed familiar for a moment, that's all."

Mieka wanted very badly to remind Cade of that little lecture he'd had the cheek to give about lying. But Blye was walking towards them, digging into the pockets of her skirt, and as she knelt beside them on the blanket she held out two small boxes made of clear glass, one for each of them.

"I made these for you. I already gave Rafe and Jeska theirs."

Mieka cradled the sparkling little box in his palm, examining the thistle etched onto the top half. "It's beautiful," he whispered.

"They're for your medals," she explained. "Rafe's got a spider on his, of course, and I put a drawn bow on Jeska's, and Cade's is a falcon—but turn them over, and there's a dragon on the bottom. To remind you."

Most players kept their Trials and Circuit medals in a little bag or a drawer or a wooden box. Chat's girlfriend had sewn his into a needlework framed on his wall. For some, the medals were all they would ever have to prove what they used to be. Not Touchstone; he knew that with something stronger than magic.

"Beautiful," he repeated, and on impulse leaned over and kissed her right on the lips.

"Oy!" exclaimed Cade, laughing again. "A flutter, a definite flutter!"

She threw a pillow at him.

Seventeen

THE SUMMER PASSED in a blur of performances, both in and around Gallantrybanks. Their schedule of shows was both grueling and lucrative. The Downstreet's owner (more to the point, his wife) was ecstatic to have Touchstone break as many glasses as possible, for as many nights as possible, and agreed to whatever Lord Kearney Fairwalk stipulated by way of payment. Blye's loan was taken care of for the next three months with just the trimmings. Fairwalk himself was paying for the heir search.

Despite professional success and the personal satisfaction of helping Blye, Cayden was a wreck. He appeared to have misplaced his sense of humor. Mieka began to think that all the times he'd seen Cade laugh were naught but the delusions of a stronger than usual bit of thorn. Vicious during rehearsals; locking himself for days in his fifth-floor room during fits of what Mieka assumed was creative vehemence; ruthless with his criticisms after each and every show—even their triumphant first appearance at the Kiral Kellari (oh, the delights of smashing all those lovely little mirrors!); demanding, dictatorial, he hadn't even joined them to celebrate the Guild's reluctant acknowledgment that there was no heir to the glassworks other than Blye. Rafe and Jeska had experienced his moods before, and most of the time simply shrugged when he sulked. But Mieka was rapidly losing what little patience he'd ever had. What in all hells did it take to make the man happy?

In midsummer, on one of Touchstone's rare days off, Mieka took his twin sister and two eldest brothers on a little expedition to visit Blye. He'd thought to nip up to the fifth floor of Number Eight, Redpebble Square, to ask Cade if he wanted to use up a bit of the previous night's trimmings on a nice evening out. There was a new tavern over by the Plume that sounded fun: a spectacular view of the waterfall, outdoor tables beneath a canopy of twinkling lanterns, and an exotic bill of fare promising authentic tastes of faraway lands.

But Mistress Mirdley shook her head. "He's in another of his mopes, and will welcome no company. It's my thought that he can barely tolerate his own."

So back Mieka went to the glassworks, annoyed, and busied himself inspecting a dozen new withies while Blye demonstrated how a big glass platter was made.

"Y'see, with flint glass, you work it at a lower temperature, and it's easier to get rid of trapped air bubbles. . . ."

Mieka glanced up from the withies. "Did you hear something?"

". . . and you get a brilliant, sparkling effect with every facet you cut, because the light is reflected all through the object, whether it's a plate like this or—"

"Oy!" he said. The knock at the shop door sounded again.

"Could you do that with a window?" Jinsie wanted to know. "It'd look splendid in a window, wouldn't it, Jez? West-facing, to catch the sunset."

"But if you get the melt wrong the glass will crizzle—that means lots of little cracks—"

"Blye," Mieka said loudly, "I think there's somebody wanting into the shop."

"That's a fine word, that is, crizzle—I'm expecting Cade to steal it any day now—"

The knock became pounding. "Blye!"

At last Jinsie turned to him. "*Will* you stop yelling?"

"There's somebody thumping the shop door down."

"Probably Cade." Blye shrugged. "Go let him in, won't you, Mieka? Beholden. Anyway, as I was saying, once this cools I'll let you hear how it rings. You can always tell lead crystal from plain glass by the ringing of it."

"Master Glisker on the First Flight of the Winterly Circuit," Mieka muttered as he opened the connecting door from the glassworks, "and now I'm playing footman. Keep yer hair on, I'm comin'!" he hollered as the pounding started up again. And then it occurred to him that Cade would call out—loudly and impatiently these days, his voice as well as his temper flayed raw with nerves about the Winterly. Slipping into the shop, he lifted the window's heavy parchment shade a trifle and swallowed a yelp.

They all stared as he came running back into the works and snatched up all the illegal withies.

"Guildmasters!"

"Quick!" Jinsie opened and presented her sizable shoulder bag—whatever did girls keep in such things, that they required so much room? he wondered stupidly, shoving the withies inside.

"Anything else needs hiding?" Jezael asked.

Blye's silver-blond hair came loose of its tie as she looked frantically round the works. "I don't know—I don't think so, just the withies—"

"Done," said Jinsie. "Jez, go open the door to them. And then go find Cayden." And, after rummaging about in the bag with a clink and clatter that made Mieka wince, she pulled out a comb and a clean scrap of silk, leaving him in charge of hiding the bag.

"What can they want?" Jedris asked.

Blye winced as Jinsie wielded the comb through her tangled hair. "I haven't done anything!"

Mieka gave her a sardonic smile. "And that matters?"

By the time Jezael escorted the two Guildmasters into the glassworks—and then departed to fetch Cade—the smudges had been cleaned from Blye's face and hands, and her hair was smooth. Mieka was all affability and charm, performing introductions, saying that he and his brothers and sister had just been watching the artist at work.

"Beautiful, isn't it?" he finished, gesturing to the platter—two feet long and a foot wide, clear flint-glass and curved ever-so-slightly at the edges.

"Competent," grunted one of the Guildmasters, a Goblin from his crooked yellowing teeth to his long, grasping fingers.

"Your pardon for the intrusion, Mistress," said the other, whose height and heft and large thick hands would be more suited to a blacksmith than a glasscrafter, "but as you have recently been declared the inheritor of these works, it's our responsibility to inspect the premises."

"What for?" Jedris asked, a smile on his broad-boned Human face but the chill of Snowminder Elfenblood in his gray-green eyes.

"Violations," said the Goblin, and, clasping his hands behind his back, began taking tiny, precise steps around every inch of the glassworks.

"Have any been reported?" Mieka asked innocently.

"No," the tall Guildmaster admitted. With a glance at Blye, he added, "But she is, after all, a woman."

Nothing could be more calculated to put sparks into Jinsie's eyes. This was not the time for one of her lectures. Mieka scowled furiously at her behind the Guildmaster's back, and stood aside to watch as the premises were scrutinized.

Blye had recovered the powers of speech, and answered whatever questions were put to her. Mieka listened absently; he was alert for the sound of the shop door opening again, glad that Jinsie had thought to send for Cayden. But long minutes went by, and longer minutes than that, and still Cade didn't arrive.

Blye's voice lost its nervous shakiness as she spoke. Yes, almost all her father's pieces had already been sold. It was part of the Guild's agreement allowing Blye to run the glassworks that everything bearing her father's hallmark be got rid of, so that no one coming into the shop would think that any of the wares were anything but of her making. This meant that all the goblets, glasses, cups, bowls, and anything else hollow—including withies— were gone from the shop now. Those of her father's things that remained were in the back room, waiting for Blye to sell them—and if she couldn't, to give them away.

Yes, she now made plates, mirrors (Mieka hid a smirk on catching that word—after the Kiral Kellari show, Lord Fairwalk had negotiated the contract to replace the mirrors Touchstone had broken), windows (Jed attested to their quality), bases of goblets (it was allowed for an apprentice to make these, so Blye did, and sold them for hallmarked crafters to add the hollow glass on top), and coiled-glass flat-topped candleflats (unsuitable for narrow tapers because there was no socket, but perfect for wide pillar candles). Mieka noted the absence of the word *withie*, and with his heel nudged Jinsie's bag a little farther under the workbench.

Yes, she adhered to the Guild's specifics for the content of the glassware. Mieka heard words like *flint* and *limestone* and *quartz* and *soda ash,* and edged towards the connecting door to the shop. Where in all hells was Cade?

The Goblin Guildmaster had finished his investigations. He stood before the worktable where the newmade platter had cooled by now, scowling at it as if it had done him a personal injury. For a moment or two he fingered the embroidered badge of office on his plain brown jacket. Then he glared at Mieka.

"Door!"

Mieka jumped to open it, even more annoyed with himself for the obeying than with the Guildmaster for the ordering. Footman, for certes. The Goblin stirred not a step from the table.

"Boy!"

Unsure who was being addressed, and pricklying in spite of himself, Mieka nearly jumped again as a strange and scrawny shape darted past into the glassworks. No taller than Mieka's elbow, there was Goblin in the boy's long fingers and ragged teeth, Troll in his oversized nose, Light Elf in his white-blond hair and pointed ears, and his very white skin had a bizarre bluish cast that could only mean Westercountry Piksey somewhere in his lineage.

"Bottle," growled the Goblin.

Cheap white wine was opened and poured onto the platter, enough to reach the slightly curving rim. Mieka looked his bewilderment at Blye; she seemed surprised but not worried. Then her eyes went wide, and as a familiar flowery scent touched his nostrils Mieka knew before he turned his head that the woman sweeping past him into the glassworks—almost certainly for the first time in her life—was Lady Jaspiela Silversun.

Cayden was right behind her: grim-faced, steel-jawed. He gave Mieka one imperious, silencing look before following his mother to the main workbench.

"Cayden," said Lady Jaspiela, "you may make these persons known to me."

"I would do so, if I had the least idea who they are."

The arrogance was breathtaking. All Mieka could do was watch, dimly aware of his brother Jezael standing beside him, equally awestruck.

The Goblin Guildmaster met Her Ladyship's look with a sneer that almost matched her own. Almost; not quite. His colleague made the sort of bow one gives to a societal equal, which earned him the eloquent arching of two pairs of aristocratic eyebrows.

Mieka didn't catch the next exchange. Jez had poked him in the ribs and bent down to whisper, "Did you stash the withies?"

Horror hollowed his chest. Lady Jaspiela was standing half a foot away from Jinsie's shoulder bag, where Mieka had shoved it under the worktable. He kept his gaze strictly on the spread of her blue silk skirts until he could be reasonably confident that he could control his expression. Then he looked at the Goblin, who was still regarding Her Ladyship with resentful scorn.

"And so for some reason best understood by yourselves," she was saying, "you considered it necessary to overrun these premises, disturbing everyone else at their homes and occupations in the meantime, and block Criddow Close with your rig. It is my wish that you conclude your business here as rapidly as possible and then be gone—within, I suggest, the next five minutes."

Before his companion could speak, the Goblin snapped, "Impossible."

"Indeed?" asked Cade in a silky tone Mieka had never

heard him use before, and wouldn't care to have used on him. "Why might that be?"

The other Guildmaster hastened to explain. "There are still questions to be answered, and an inspection of the shop and any back rooms, and the apprentice quarters—"

"What apprentices?" Blye asked, very nearly keeping the cynicism from her voice. "Who'd apprentice to a *woman*?"

"All the same—"

Lady Jaspiela interrupted, "It is *not* 'all the same' to *me*."

"Or," Cayden put in, "to the people on this street who look to my lady mother for their welfare."

This told Mieka how he'd got his mother into this. Oh, he was cunning, was Cayden Silversun. Lady of the manor was a part she'd adore to play, even if the manor was naught but a block of shops and homes in back of her mansion.

The Guildmaster was stubborn. "And there is the matter of the flint glass."

Before anyone could ask, the Goblin snapped his fingers and the boy handed him a thin strip of what looked like heavy rag paper tincted dark green. "Lead," he announced, and slid the paper into the wine on the platter.

Everybody was drawn towards the table, everybody but Blye, whose cheeks had drained of all color. So had the slip of paper.

"I'm most dreadfully sorry," the tall Guildmaster said, looking it but not sounding it. "But until every other piece of flint glass here can be similarly tested, we must order this shop closed."

"Nonsense!" snapped Lady Jaspiela. "What can you mean?"

"It's the lead content," Blye managed in a faltering voice. "What makes flint glass sparkle can leach into acidic liquids."

"Causing all manner of insalubrious results," finished the Guildmaster.

"But—but it takes *hours* to happen, and the caution is for storage, not for goblets and things—and anyway the melt I used for this platter—it's the same as my father used, and there was never any problem—"

"Perhaps my predecessor in this position was not as diligent as he ought to have been," was the smooth reply.

"Twenty-four parts out of a hundred," Blye was insisting, with more vigor now, "and the Guild allows up to forty in drinking vessels—"

"The policy has come under review. Were you a member of the Guild, you would know that."

"She's a *woman*, remember?" snarled Jinsie.

"Uh, just a thought," Mieka said, holding up a hand. "But was anyone really contemplating taking a drink off that platter? Looks a rather awkward gulp to me."

"That's not the issue."

Cade addressed Blye. "When was this platter made?"

"Just now," Jedris reported. "We watched the whole process."

"And the materials were taken from where?" When Blye pointed, Cade asked the Guildmaster, "Is there a test for the lead content of that sand?"

"Irrelevant," said the Goblin.

Cade looked down on him. "Perform it."

This involved weighing and measuring and other things Mieka found uninteresting compared to watching Cade. For it had occurred to him that it must be something exceptional, to know that a brain and a heart like that were always there to defend you.

Jinsie's voice caught his attention, something about moving out of the Guildmasters' way, and she paused to sketch a brief curtsy to Lady Jaspiela while on her way past. At the main workbench, she casually crouched down to retrieve her bag, rising with no indication that it was much heavier than it ought to have been. Settling the bag at her hip, she joined Mieka.

"Nice curtsy," he whispered.

"She's a one, isn't she?"

"You've no idea."

"Twenty-four," the Goblin announced suddenly.

"We've no guarantee," the other Guildmaster stated, "that the melt used for the platter is the same as—"

Jezael took a step towards him. "Are you calling my brother a liar?"

Lady Jaspiela held up a manicured hand. "Surely not—isn't that right?" she inquired of the Guildmaster, who pursed his lips but said nothing else. Her voice was a dousing of pure venom as she went on, "Then there must be something amiss with your little papers, mustn't there? Perhaps you're not as diligent as you ought to be." With a magnificent sweep of silken skirts, she turned to the door. "Your five minutes are now two. Cayden, see them to their conveyance." With a nod to Mieka and a definitive clicking of her heels, she left the glassworks.

Her elder son drew himself to his full height. "You're finished here. Next time, bring a smaller carriage—and don't park in the middle of the road." Something resembling a smile stretched his lips. "My lady mother dislikes it when anyone inconveniences the neighborhood."

Mieka waited until both doors had shut behind Cade and the Guildmasters and the boy. Then he demanded of Blye, "How close was that?"

"Close enough," she answered grimly. "They can inspect anybody anytime they like, of course. But I didn't expect the bit about the flint glass. You're not supposed to sell decanters without a caution label against storing wine in them."

"But plates and platters are all right, aren't they?" Jedris asked. "And goblets?"

"Food or liquid doesn't stay in contact long enough to

absorb any lead. Even so, Da always used the least possible to get the shine. But that paper—it turned as if that platter were made from forty-of-a-hundred melt."

"So Lady Jaspiela was right," Mieka mused. "There *was* something dodgy about—"

The crash of an opening door announced Cayden's return—and in full voice, too. "Bastards! Cullions! Do you know what I saw when they got into their rig? You know who was in there waiting for them?"

"Somebody wearing the Archduke's livery?" Blye's tone was mild, but her dark eyes blazed brighter than her kiln. "C'mon, Cade, it's obvious, innit? He couldn't buy the glassworks, so he's punishing us by trying to shut it down."

"Nice bit of fakery on those testing papers, then," Jinsie remarked. "Or the wine."

Mieka shook his head. "It was corked and waxed, and opened right in front of us."

"Trust you to notice everything about the alcohol and nothing about anything else!"

"You wait till Kearney learns of this," Cade said. "You just wait till I tell him!"

Jinsie approached him, put a hand on his arm. "Do you really want to pit him and the Archduke against each other so soon?" she asked quietly. "Out in the open before anybody's even sure what's really going on?"

"Don't do it, Cade," Blye said. "A blunt challenge wouldn't be at all wise."

"Why not? Why not expose him for a liar and a cheat and—"

"And what?" Mieka asked pointedly. "It's just mischief. He's the fuckin' Archduke—your pardon, ladies—who could possibly pin anything onto his splendid silk coat? If he likes, he could have us kicked off the Winterly, Quill, you know he could. We don't know what he wants," he insisted as Cade looked mutinous. "A glassworks, a theater group of his very own—from the things Chat was saying, it's not for the prestige, or even the money, once the tours of the Continent are put through. It's something else he's after and we don't know what, and until we do . . ." He finished with a shrug.

After one stinging glare, Cade turned on his heel and swept out of the glassworks in a manner that reminded everyone whose son he was.

"Such an affable young man," Jinsie remarked. "Polite, personable, and all the winsome charm of a nest of angry wasps."

"Oh, shut it," Mieka told her. "There's a lot on his mind."

There were things on Mieka's mind, as well, and about a week later he decided he'd had enough of Cade's tantrums, and went once more to see Blye.

He brought along Chattim Czillag. This was in advance of the appointment with all the Shadowshapers. Reasoning that Blye wouldn't have the chance to get nervous (fluttery, to use Cade's word), would appreciate having a friend there with her (once she stopped being furious at the surprise, of course), and would like Chat anyway, he'd chosen a day when the wind off the river blew some freshness through the summer heat. Persuading Chat to a little excursion was easy; getting Blye to open the door was much harder. But he prevailed, as he always did, and they sat in the cool, glittering dimness of the shop, drinking the iced fruit juice Mieka had brought along and talking of anything but glass for at least an hour.

At length, Chat helped wash up the goblets and said, "So I'm told that withies can be made that actually allow this pillock here to be mistook for a real glisker."

Before Mieka could do more than pull a face at him, Blye laughed. "I can't wait to find out what they'd be like in the hands of somebody who knows how to use them."

Aim, draw, and clap i' the clout o' the target, Mieka told himself, perfectly happy to be maligned to his face if it got him what he wanted, and left them to it. He'd scented delicious things cooking in the Silversun kitchen on his way past earlier, and intended to whine his way into an ample share of them.

Cade and Dery had escorted their mother to the horse races on the grounds of the Palace, and wouldn't be back until nightfall. Thus the two footmen and the maid were taking their ease in the kitchen while Mistress Mirdley worked her own magic on sausage pies and a salad that took superb advantage of the farm carts that glutted the city with ripe fruit. It was with the greatest reluctance that Mieka declined a third helping of everything and went to see how Blye and Chattim were getting along.

He found her alone, and rather stunned.

"Three dozen to start," she said. "He didn't even wait to have me meet the others. He wants three dozen. And he offered three-quarters what he was paying Master Splithook. I know, because I asked round. He says the joys of not having to compensate for rutilations are worth having to lie about who makes the withies for him—"

"Three-quarters times three dozen?" He didn't bother to attempt the calculation; he was hopeless with numbers. "That's a tidy little sum, Blye."

"I didn't take it. Oh, pick your jaw back up! I told him half, until I get to know them all well enough to fit the withies to them like I do you and Cade."

"I hope you told him that when that happens, it'll be Splithook's full price!"

She snorted with laughter. "You don't know when to quit, do you?" Then, suddenly and most unexpectedly, she gave him a frown. "Except not as much, lately. Especially around Cade."

Not knowing how to respond to this, he shrugged.

"He said so, the other day. Wanted to know what was wrong."

"Nothing's wrong."

"But you're not as—forgive me—unmanageable as you used to be."

"Maybe I'm growing up. About time, innit?" He gifted her with his most disarming smile. "After all, I'm comin' up on me eighteenth Namingday this summer." Realizing what he'd revealed, he almost slammed a frustrated fist onto the counter and remembered just in time that he'd probably overset every glass on the shelves above.

"I knew it! I knew you were still underage!" Blye laughed at him again. "Don't worry, I won't let on. Besides, you're the type who'll look about eighteen until you're eighty."

"And then it'll all catch up with me," he finished with a shudder.

"Cade says your great-great granny is still alive. What is she, something over a hundred?"

"A hundred and four, with bonelock in every finger and wens all over her face, and a lucid thought p'rhaps once a year," he retorted. "I'd slice me own throat first."

"Is that the only thing that scares you, then?" she asked, her voice and her eyes very much softer. "Is it growing old, or growing old so sudden, the way Elves do?"

"The sudden of it," he admitted. Then, because he avoided this sort of conversation devotedly, he countered, "And what is it *you're* most affrighted of? I told you, so you have to tell me. It's only fair."

"Not of growing old," she replied quietly. "Growing old alone."

"Nothing for you to worry about," he announced. "You've us, haven't you?"

She eyed him thoughtfully. "Anybody else would've

said something about getting married and having lots of children and grandchildren."

"If you want to, I'm willing." His reward for this was a smack on the arm. With any other girl, he would have followed with a long, affronted tirade about those who'd leap through fire at the chance, and didn't she think he was good enough for her, and he was crushed that she didn't like him after all, and similar outrageous nonsense. But this was Blye. "Marriage is the usual extent of a girl's ambitions. Nothing 'usual' about you, Blye." Then, in a further flush of awkward sincerity that startled even him, he added, "And it's not the only thing I'm afraid of. For one, those withies of Cade's. There's fear in *those*, I can feel it every time I touch them. If it's not betraying him, can you tell me what he's so scared of?"

She took a while to answer. "He hasn't told you. He should have, before this. I don't know if I ought—but I think you deserve to know. I think you've earned the right."

And slowly, groping for the words, she described dreams and visions that beset Cayden sleeping and waking, taunting him with glimpses of futures that might come to pass—that *would* come to pass if changes went unmade. He never knew what those changes must be or what might further result from them, which decisions would prompt a better future and which would awaken even worse. The worry of it, the grinding uncertainty, the paralyzing fear of doing anything at all—

That afternoon Mieka came to understand that it wasn't an *Elsewhere* look he'd seen in Cade's gray eyes, but *Elsewhen*.

"He used to tell me almost all of them," Blye murmured. She still wouldn't look at him. "About seeing himself older, working at things he had no intention of doing, and then fixing it so whatever it was got closed off, and wasn't any part of any future anymore. I think the first one, when he really began to understand what it is that goes on inside his head, was when his father got the appointment at Court. Prince Ashgar turned eighteen, and a Household was set up for him. Zekien put his name up for Private Secretary, but Cade knew at least a week before the official letter came that he'd got Bedchamber instead. He let it slip to me, bragging a bit. First Gentleman is supposed to run the private chambers, supervise the servants, all that. Nobody knew back then what Zekien would be called upon to do, or that he'd do it so well," she added sourly. "When the letter came, and everyone but Cade was surprised . . . that was the first time he realized, I think. He wasn't quite eleven. Over the next year and more I got to recognizing a particular look on his face, and pester him to tell me. He had to tell *someone,* it was gnawing him up inside, knowing what was to come and thinking he was helpless to change it. But then he found he *could* change it. And that's when he went off to Sagemaster Emmot's academy. After he got back, he wouldn't tell me as much as he used to. But I can still see it in his eyes, even hours after he's had a dreaming."

"He had a waking dream on the way back from Seekhaven. There was a fox in the middle of the road, at night, and he—"

"I know. He did tell me about that one." She hesitated, and finally met his gaze again. "No specifics, but it was concerning you. You fretted him at first, you know—you never showed up in any of the foreseeings, but then you just appeared out of thin air in Gowerion and he expected to start seeing you more and more often. But it's only glimpses he has of you, a few moments, a few words."

"But if seeing the fox was about me—"

"You weren't listening. Not that it was *about* you, but that it *concerned* you. There's a difference."

"Is that what makes him afraid?" Mieka demanded. "What I'm feeling in those withies of his—something about me in the future scares him?"

"You'd have to ask him that. If you dare." It was said with wry sympathy, for they both knew very well that to confront Cade could produce any reaction from cold, flat denial to raging fury. "But I think you're right," Blye went on. "I think there's something about any number of possible futures that scares him, in regard to you. I don't know what he sees, but it's not pleasant."

"And I was the one as told him his dreams are important," he murmured. "I told him he had to keep dreaming."

"What do you mean?"

"Nothing." When she frowned, he amended, "Nothing much. This Sagemaster Emmot—did he teach Cade how to—Gods, Blye, how *would* you control such a thing?"

"You can't. There's things to do afterwards, to get all of it organized and analyzed inside your head, pick the visions apart to try and figure out what's most important, what might be changed. There's things he can do to calm himself, if the dreaming is too disturbing. But it's worried me ever since he started in the theater, because there are so many more people that get brought into his view, people he has to interact with. It's routine that quiets him, settles him. And there's nothing quiet or routine about traveling a Circuit. Rafe and Jeska know about this, but I don't know that they'll be able to help him the way you could."

"Me?"

"If the dreams he fears have to do with you, then doesn't it stand to reason that you're the one can reassure him?" She was almost begging for this to be true. "Stay near him, sleep in the same room if you can, so that if he wakes affrighted he can see that you're still there. Give him some kind of an anchor, a connection to what's really real. What already *is*, I mean, not what *could* be, according to what he sees in his dreamings. Is this making any sense?"

Mieka nodded, and not just to make her feel better. "If I'm what worries him, then I'll stop worrying him as best I can. I'll be what's really real, there with him every day—and every night, too, because I think you're right about having me there if he wakes from one of those dreams."

"But don't change who you are," she cautioned. "Don't be different around him, don't—"

"Don't stop playing the fool?" He managed a smile. "Blye, darlin', *that's* how I'll reassure him. I can't be aught but what I am, and he'll find that a reality to hold on to. And *that* sounds as if it makes no sense at all—"

"—but it actually does," she finished for him. "Which makes us both either very, very clever, or quite, quite mad, y'know."

"Mad *and* clever, that's what I am and what I'll continue to be. The inconstant constant, the predictably unpredictable."

"This is sounding worse and worse!" But she was smiling again.

"It's what he expects of me, and if I become somebody different, that would worry him even more."

"Just—just have a care to him, won't you? And when he finally tells you about—"

"I won't mention that I already know."

It would be interesting, he reflected, keeping Cayden's secret, because he would be keeping it from Cayden himself. Clever and mad . . .

Eighteen

HAVING LEARNED AT last why those withies of Cayden's felt like fear, Mieka spent the rest of that afternoon pondering over what Blye had told him, and what he'd promised. That such a gift of magic existed, he had no doubt. Plenty of people had flashes of twice-seen, and it sometimes indicated Fae ancestry. Being predominantly Elfen—notwithstanding all those strains of who-knew-what flooding the family bloodstream—Mieka didn't know much about the Fae, but he did know this: They actually *could* foresee the future. They were capricious about what they revealed because they disliked looking upon evil and so reported only what pleased them. Nobody trusted a Fae's predictions; nobody's future was made entirely of rainbows.

Mieka knew without thinking about it that even with this Fae foreseeing inside him, Cayden was unflinchingly Wizard enough to look upon any future in its brutal entirety, and stubbornly Human enough to want to do something about it.

He also knew that his instinct had been right: those dreams were important.

Yet whatever else it was the dreams revealed, the ones that frightened Cade were about Mieka. Or, rather, *concerned* Mieka, as Blye had corrected him. Unable to think what sort of actions of his might prompt futures that terrified Cade, Mieka decided that the only thing for it was to keep his promise: to be near Cade if he woke scared, and to be both clever and mad.

Thus resolved, he started off to the Downstreet that night in a serene mood swiftly spoiled by the weather. The cooling breeze had died away, and it was a thick and sultry evening that got worse inside the confines of the tavern. They'd just finished one of the sillier Mother Loosebuckle farces, and Jeska was snatching up the coins almost as fast as guffawing patrons could throw them. Mieka was in the midst of catching his breath and wishing for a tall drink of anything as long as it was icy-cold when he glanced over at Cade. The smirk on his tregetour's face wasn't quite the one that came after a particularly good performance; indeed, he'd been picking nits with everything lately. Tonight there was the triumph of a fine show in his cloud-gray eyes, but something else as well. His attention was fixed on someone in the audience with a look of recognition Mieka realized he had seen before, when the young musician had come to Wistly Hall to buy one of Fa's lutes. Squinting, he tried to locate whoever it was Cade was staring at with so smug a grin. But just then Cade slipped from behind his lectern (recently presented to him by Lord Kearney Fairwalk, a gorgeous thing of rosewood inlaid with curlicues of carved and polished dragon bone) and approached the glisker's bench.

"Let's give them 'The Dragon,' shall we? I know we were going to do 'Caladrius' and there isn't much room for you to spread out, but—"

"You didn't give me enough to work it with," Mieka replied, irritably mopping sweat from his face and neck with one of Mistress Mirdley's dish towels. "Have mercy, Quill—all we lack in this furnace is a fire-breathing dragon!"

Cade moved round behind him, grabbing up a fistful of withies on his way. "Here. This should be enough."

"Change of plans?" Jeska asked, coming over to empty his hands and pockets of coins into a new little glass basket Blye had made just for the purpose.

"He wants to do 'The Dragon,'" Mieka said.

"Scale it back a bit—no pun intended," Cade told them. "We haven't done it since Seekhaven, but we ought to leave a chavishing behind, once we're on the road, about how lucky they were tonight to see what the Court saw."

Jeska crooked a finger at Rafe, who sauntered over. "'Dragon' instead of 'Caladrius' all right with you?"

Wide shoulders shrugged. That was his only comment.

"Helpful," Mieka snapped.

"It won't take me more than a few minutes to prime these," Cade soothed. "C'mon, Mieka, it's important."

He was about to invite Cade to explain precisely *why* it was important when he caught another almost gleeful glance at the audience. A quick look at Jeska and then Rafe told him they'd noticed nothing, or if they had, and understood, they weren't letting on. Mieka chewed on his lower lip for a moment, then nodded.

It could have been a disaster. It was a piece they'd last played in an outdoor pavilion, with five times the room for conjuring the Prince and the Dragon and their epic battle, and to cram it into a tavern with a dodgy arrangement of ceiling rafters was risky at best. But they did it, and by its ending Mieka couldn't hear the shatter of glassware for the uproar of applause. The coins were thrown so enthusiastically that a few almost hit him, all the way back at the glisker's bench.

Eager as he was for a cold drink—and a fresh shirt—he stuck close to Cayden after they'd taken their bows and left the stage. The tavern owner tried to pull him aside to express the extent of his raptures, but Mieka smiled and sidestepped him, arriving at Cade's elbow just as he paused before a table in the far corner of the room.

"I'm told you want to meet us," he was saying to a startled young man wearing a dark blue shirt—to minimize the splotches of ink, Mieka realized, that so abundantly decorated his fingers.

"I do indeed. Tobalt Fluter, *The Nayword*. You'd be Silversun?"

As drinks were handed round, Mieka thought he might understand. The weekly broadsheet was gaining a reputation for being the first to report the latest trends in everything from the cut of a coat to the style of a poem. Naturally Cayden would want to see an article on Touchstone in *The Nayword*. Someone must have tipped him about the man's presence tonight, and that was why—

No. Mieka was certain of what he'd seen in Cade's eyes.

He exerted himself to be charming and funny—and an exertion it was tonight, after all that work in all this heat—giving Tobalt Fluter some excellent material. He had to keep reminding himself that he wasn't supposed to know that whereas Fluter was meeting Touchstone for the first time, Touchstone's tregetour had undoubtedly seen this man before. Talked to him, perhaps; come to know him as a friend. Or would do so; or *might* do so. Or something. This shaded Mieka's reactions to the writer: wanting to impress him, predisposed to like him because Cade probably did—or would, or might—he began to see how insanely confusing life could become for someone who had prescient dreams. When he read the article a few days later, he was pleased that not only had all their names been spelled correctly, and his jokes cleverly conveyed, but Tobalt also seemed to grasp most of the subtleties of their work. The instant he thought this, he wondered if Cade had known it all in advance.

There was another memorable night during Touchstone's summer run at the Downstreet. It started out dismally. Mieka had had a little too much to drink at the family's early evening celebration of his and Jinsie's Namingday, and had pricked a little too much bluethorn to invigorate himself for the night's performance. Thus he was acutely aware that except for absolute essentials, none of his partners was talking to him. Nothing but a nod or two when he arrived; nothing but a terse reminder of what playlets they'd chosen. He was edgy and fretted during "Caladrius," and then when it came time to masque Jeska as the Sweetheart, he made the gown golden and the hair green for just an instant before correcting his mistake. He sensed Rafe exert iron restraint on the magic after that, and cursed himself. None of them would look at him when they gathered up front to take their bows.

Cade left the stage first, closely followed by Jeska. Mieka looked imploringly up at Rafe and said, "I'm sorry—it was only for a second, nobody noticed—"

A quirk of one brow and a twist of his mouth beneath his beard were all the reply Rafe gave. When he jerked his head in what amounted to an order, Mieka trailed along behind him, torn between misery at his blunder and a growing defiance. Had none of the others ever slipped up before? Had Jeska never muddled a line, had Rafe never faltered in his control, had Cade never left out of a withie a bit of magic specific to a piece?

He followed Rafe past the packed tables towards the stairs, confused when the fettler began the ascent to the next floor. Mieka hadn't been up here since the tavern keeper's wife had shown him her Lady Shrine months and months ago. Oh Gods, he was about to be scolded, and roundly—and on his Namingday, too. At least, he told himself glumly, they were considerate enough to yell at him in private.

Rafe flung open a door to the left of the landing. It was dark as a wyvern's maw inside—and then a blaze of light erupted from a trio of six-branched clear glass candleflats framing a pyramid of pastries. Blinking at the glare, all at once he saw his parents and Jinsie and Blye, Jedris and Jezael, the Threadchasers and Mistress Bowbender and Crisiant, and even Mistress Mirdley and Derien, all laughing and cheering as Cade and Jeska bellowed, "Happy Namingday!"

Never had he passed from wailful to joyful so quickly in his life, not even with the finest of Auntie Brishen's thorn in him.

He gave Jinsie one of the candleflats and put the other two in his under-the-turret lair. They would always hold pride of place in whatever home he made for himself later on—but for the time being he wanted them hidden where scavenging relations of the Uncle Barsabian sort couldn't find them while he was away on the Winterly Circuit.

And then one early autumn dawning he was in a coach, clattering out of one of the Palace's lesser court-yards, and the Winterly had begun.

There was no one to see them off except Lord Kearney Fairwalk, and it turned out that he wasn't there to see them off but to accompany them. Mieka wondered when this had been decided, then shrugged. He didn't much care whether His Lordship came along for the ride or not. And perhaps Cayden's mood would improve, what with Fairwalk chattering away as usual about how clever Cade was at rearranging and rewriting lines, and urging him to work up some truly original things soon. This was what Mieka had been demanding forever, with not much result. If Fairwalk could manage it, he wasn't going to complain.

His Most Gracious Majesty had fastidious notions about the behavior of his players while on a Circuit—even when in the privacy of the coach he provided. It was, after all, *his* coach. Framed on the door just beneath the window was a set of printed guidelines for comport-ment.

Abstinence from liquor is requested. But if you must drink, let it be no more than one bottle each day, and shared amongst you.

No unsanctioned passengers are permitted. This

includes relations, friends, acquaintances, business associates, strangers, flirt-gills, and all manner of trulls.

At all stops, refrain from the use of rough language in the presence of ladies and children.

Blankets and carriage-robes are provided for your comfort. Do not abuse the privilege by hoarding the majority of them to yourself. The offender will be made to ride with the coachman.

Do not snore loudly.

In the event of runaway horses, remain calm. Leaping from the coach in panic will result in injuries and leave you at the mercy of the elements, highwaymen, and hungry wolves.

Should the coachman judge a passenger guilty of any of the following offenses, that person shall receive chastisement as the coachman determines.

1. *Foul language*
2. *Drunkenness*
3. *Incivility*
4. *Indecency*
5. *Incorrectness of attire*
6. *Damage to His Gracious Majesty's property*
7. *Endangering the horses, the coachman, the outrider, fellow passengers, the citizenry, or the peace of the Kingdom*

Rafe read the whole of it out loud as the coach pulled away from the Palace gates, and finished with, "They musta known you were comin', Mieka."

It instantly became Mieka's objective to pull off each and every one of these infractions and get away with them unscathed. He kept his resolve to himself for the moment, however, because Cayden would simply have murdered him.

Cade's temper had not significantly improved with the waning of the summer and the preparations for the Winterly. Well, they were all nervous. Rafe kept fidgeting his fingers with the bracelet of heavy copper links Crisiant had recently given him; he'd be writing her ten letters a day, Mieka was convinced of it. Jeska had spent the first hour of the journey trying to read the folio of playlets he had memorized long ago, then given it up when the swaying of the coach began to upset his stomach. Cayden wore an expression as if just last night he'd seen an Elsewhen that included six months of lice-infested beds every night, ice-encrusted shaving water every morning, horrible food, and blashed beer. Fairwalk occupied himself with the itinerary, making notes and muttering into his lace-frothed neck-band. He would be traveling with them until word got round that anything but the finest treatment given to Touchstone would distress His Lordship most severely. Nobody said anything to anybody else for three solid hours.

Mieka was bored.

Thus he simply couldn't pass up the chance to mark off one of the Rules when it presented itself.

The coachman had called a halt beside a summer-parched stream so that the passengers could stretch their legs. On a walk round the vehicle, he found that one of the leather lashings that secured the boot had flapped loose. Cade blanched; his precious glass baskets and withies were packed in there. Mieka took one look at the coachman, who was puce in the face and speechless with fury, and saw his chance.

"Who the unholy fuck was the fritlaggering fool back at the Palace who did this?" Mieka snarled. "Is this the King's best coach and the King's best driver, or is it not?" And then he let loose with a string of insults, invective, abuse, and just plain profanity regarding the sanity, antecedents, personal habits, and sexual practices of whatever idiot was responsible for securing the straps back in Gallantrybanks.

Mieka's cussing vocabulary had been faithfully gathered since the age of six. His sources included everyone from dockworkers to his own brothers, with contributions from his father (when referring to Great-great-grandmother) and even Uncle Barsabian. He used almost all of it in the space of two minutes. It was Auntie Brishen's view that a gentleman ought to be able to swear fluently that long without repeating himself. Mieka did her proud.

Then he conjured up a look of absolute horror, turned to the coachman, and began stammering apologies.

The man smiled all over his weathered, snub-nosed face. "Not a worry be in your head about it, lad. That's the best I've heard since me brother caught his wife with the stable boys."

Mieka's turn to stare. *Boys,* plural? The impulse to inquire further was squelched when Cade yelled, "Mieka! Shut up!"

After assisting in securing the boot, they all climbed back into the coach. Everybody was staring at Mieka. Perfect.

"Cade," he asked sweetly, "lend me your new pen?"

Lady Jaspiela Silversun, giving in with surprising grace to the inevitable, had gifted Cayden with a beautiful new writing instrument that owed nothing to any duck or goose or swan ever hatched. It was a slender, elegant thing made of golden oak, and instead of the sharpened end of a feather, at one end was a silver nib to dip into an inkpot. It was absolutely the latest innovation, according to Prince Ashgar, who, according to Lady Jaspiela, had suggested it to her husband as an appropriate present. (Mieka knew the instant she said it that the gift was to please the Prince and not her son; he kept this to himself, and his opinion about persons who gave presents only when prompted.) Dery's contribution had been heartfelt: a leatherbound book of blank pages to fill with ideas.

Mistress Mirdley had brewed up the blue-black ink in her stillroom, and Blye had provided the bottles to keep it in.

Once the mystified Cade had produced the requested pen and ink from his satchel, Mieka crouched on the floor beside the Rules and crossed out the words *Foul language*.

Rafe was suddenly howling with laughter. Jeska, shoulders shaking, put his head in his hands and groaned. Lord Fairwalk looked bewildered.

But it was Cayden's face Mieka watched as he slid back into his place on the brown leather seat. A confusion of emotions played over the long, tense face, tightening wide mouth and thick brows, bunching the muscles of jaw and forehead. Finally—*finally*—he gave a great roar of laughter.

Satisfied, Mieka folded his arms and beamed at them all. "One down, six to go!"

Quite mad, yes; but he also congratulated himself on being very, very clever.

* * *

THERE WERE MANY good things, several bad things, and a few really great things about being on the Circuit. Best of all was the traveling. Worst of all was the traveling. Or perhaps the best was performing—although that could be the worst, too.

First Flight had many privileges: the newest of the traveling coaches provided by the king, the most experienced driver, the earliest schedule, which allowed Touchstone to miss—with a conspicuous lack of regret—the long slog round the north slope of the Pennynine Mountains in the middle of winter. The coach was fairly fast, too, so they spent fewer days cooped up on the road. Granted, they had to play more shows than the Crystal Sparks (Second Flight) and the Wishcallers (Third), but they also had more days off than the required one-after-every-fifth-performance. And the break so generously provided by Lord Rolon Piercehand at his lovely little Castle Eyot would be fully seven days long, as opposed to the five and four accorded the other Flights.

Mieka had grilled Chattim at length about what to expect at each venue. He'd wanted to know what the halls were like, of course, before setting foot in each for the first time, having no wish to present Touchstone as floundering amateurs. But he'd also asked about what there might be to see and do, which taverns had the best drinks and food, and most especially where the prettiest and most willing girls could be found. Chat had eventually given up talking and given him a list. Cade had a list, too, assembled from books about history and famous sites and scenery; thoroughly typical of him, and to Mieka's mind thoroughly boring.

He'd guessed going into this that boredom would be his major concern. He was right. The excitement of travel wore off rather swiftly. He regretted that; the first weeks of swaying about in the big, leather-suspended coach had been quite fun, because there was always something new to see, someplace new to explore, and the prospect of an audience to amaze. After those first few hours of nervous silence had been broken, conversation didn't lack, either. If they weren't discussing the shows just finished or the shows soon to come, they were laughing at Fairwalk's gossip about the nobility. They shared stories about their families and their childhoods, swapped lies about girls, and Jeska could always be counted on for salacious balladry. More important to Mieka, he was learning more about how Cayden's mind worked and his ambitions for Touchstone. As for his own ambitions—after a week in the coach, these dwindled to procuring a wagon as comfortable as the one owned by the Shadowshapers.

Four days out of Gallantrybanks, they might have been in another world entirely. The great city's reach extended farther than Mieka thought possible. There were long stretches of road between towns and villages, and grand swaths of land with manor houses plopped in the middle, yet the grasp of the capital was almost a physical thing. Traffic in produce and people was constant, and the roads well-maintained.

But on their fifth day of travel, he sensed a loosening of the hold. Conversation at inn-yards and taverns was of local matters, not what was going on in Gallantrybanks. They were just as far from the city as they'd been at Seekhaven, but the feel was entirely different. Especially when it started to snow.

That fifth day, which ought to have been an easy ten miles to Shollop, a ridiculously early storm mired the roads and sent them to the boot for blankets and carriage rugs. Extra time was built into the Winterly schedule for bad weather and other mishaps so that canceled shows were uncommon, but everyone knew that luck would play a large part in whether or not they fulfilled their engagements on time.

Luck, and Jeschenar's skills at weather-witching. It was only one of the things Mieka was now discovering about his partners, these three young men he'd thought he'd got to know rather well by now. He'd found out, for instance, that Jeska's family history was pretty much as Chattim had described it. His grandfather had been from some foreign land and sold his skills with the bow to the king, and took a name that matched his profession when he married a very pretty girl of scant education and no outward signs of magical forebears. Fortunately for the next two generations, her family insisted that his prize money be spent on a house. A hired soldier being of little use in a Kingdom no longer at war, he had become a teacher, mainly of his expertise with the bow and occasionally of his language. His wife died bearing her fifteenth child in nineteen years—none but the eldest, Jeska's father, had survived—and after that Bowbender vanished into the intricacies of Gallantrybanks' worst districts, resurfacing when his only son married. He lived long enough to pay a chirurgeon for the kagging of his grandson's deviant Elfen ears, then died in a tavern brawl. Jeska's father succumbed a few years later to a shortage of gainful employment and an excess of drink. His mother, left a widow at twenty-three, supported herself and her son as best she could, somehow earning enough to keep them in the small house and keep him in school. She turned out to have a minimal knack for weather-witching, but poverty and exhaustion sapped the meagerness of her magic and for the last six years she had been an ordinary charwoman. But Jeska had picked up some tricks from her, which he used now to the gratification of his friends, Lord Fairwalk, and their coachman.

Mieka had known nothing of Jeska's history. Neither had he known that the masquer had turned twenty the previous spring and had a three-year-old daughter. The mother had married someone else because Jeska hadn't been able to support a wife and child. He saw the little girl every so often, and she was acknowledged as his—she could hardly be anyone else's, Rafe had remarked, not with those golden curls and squared-off cleft chin—but now that Touchstone was on the brink of making important money, Fairwalk was worried that the mother might apply to the courts for a share of it.

Not that Jeska told all of this at one go. The revelations came over several days. It was Fairwalk who delicately coaxed their life stories out of each member of Touchstone, with many apologies for prying, saying that he needed to know their pasts so he could plan their futures. Mieka knew this to be something of a lie. The only one who truly interested him was Cayden, and not just because he was the tregetour, the source of ideas and the magic that could bring them to life.

He never let on that he knew Fairwalk's fascination with Cade was not merely that of a theater fanatic for a significantly talented player. Neither did he ever hint that there was a much better source of information about their futures available. Many, many futures.

The first stop on the Winterly was the university town of Shollop. Very pretentious, very grand, and very full of students who, after a month in classes after the summer holiday, were more than ready for renewed carousing. There were artists of all sorts, from painters who relied solely on paint and painters who worked with magic, to musicians, sculptors, imagers, poets, and crafters and designers of everything from glassware to jewelry. Added to these were scholars of history and literature, languages and the law. Cayden was, predictably, intimidated. This did not sweeten his temper. By the night of their performance before the Shollop Marching Society (a private show arranged by Fairwalk; the official venue was the Players Hall on the university grounds), Mieka had once again had enough of his tregetour's sulks.

So instead of breaking a withie or two, he decided— with Rafe's amused connivance—on a more interesting approach.

The Marching Society's venue had at one time been a greenhouse where the university's naturalists and the university's cooks battled constantly over how much space would be given to the exotic plants brought back for study from distant lands and how much to vegetables. Then an obscenely wealthy nobleman had left his entire fortune to Shollop for "the Health and Comfort of the Kitchens." Gleefully in possession of a large new winter gardening location, the cooks had abandoned the old greenhouse to the naturalists. These worthies had petitioned the king, saying that this precedence of scholarly bellies over scholarly brains was an outrage. So His Gracious Majesty, who at the time had just begun his fascination with plants and beasts (and, eventually, people) from faraway regions, "encouraged" his nobles to contribute to the cause.

Thus the old greenhouse had been abandoned, and the Marching Society had bought it up for practically nothing, and the only reminders of its previous function were the odd-looking plants in crumbling pots scattered about amid the tables, and a lingering odor of fertilizer.

When Touchstone investigated the venue on the afternoon of their show, Mieka formed the opinion that the place needed a good airing out. Rafe agreed.

So at the end of the riotous "Troll and Trull" they shattered one wall's top row of glass panes.

The students loved it. The authorities were not as pleased. It was left to Lord Fairwalk to adjudicate the matter—and keep Touchstone out of the local lockup—while Cade, Mieka, Rafe, and Jeska were treated to as many free drinks as they could swallow.

Mieka fell into bed shortly before dawn, quite drunk and entirely delighted with his success, for Cade had lost his diffidence around these young men—his own age, most of them—who knew so much more about so many more things than he did. He'd actually enjoyed himself. Just like old times—if *old* included a few months ago. Not that Mieka had understood five words in twenty of most of the conversations Cade had been drawn into. But it was enough for him that the drinks were free, and excellent, and that Quill had had a good time.

He hadn't reckoned on the next morning's hangover.

They were due to depart for Dolven Wold that afternoon. Rafe always woke early by long habit, professing himself incapable of sleeping much past the usual hour when his parents began the day's baking. He was hoping to get over it. Jeska, now that he no longer had to fit bookkeeping into his days whenever he could, was catching the knack of sleeping in. Since leaving school at the age of fifteen, Mieka never got out of bed until late morning unless physically yanked from the blankets. But even he was up and about before Cade that morning.

The rest of Touchstone had gathered in the empty taproom, waiting for Fairwalk to tell them it was time to pack up and get ready to leave. Rafe was, predictably, writing to Crisiant. They'd been gone only fifteen days and this had to be at least his fifth letter to her. Mieka had every respect in the world for the girl, and liked her as much as she'd let him, but it just wasn't decent for even a bespoken to have this kind of stranglehold on a man. Jeska was playing a rousing game of slapcards with the innkeeper's daughters—aged six and nine, giggly around this young man they already recognized as stupendously good-looking. Hells, any female out of nappies saw it. Mieka kept eyeing the bar. His breakfast ale had worn off and he was just about to head back upstairs for the bottle in his satchel when Cayden stumbled into the room.

Bleary-eyed, colossally hung over, snarling on his way to the kitchen—Mieka tried to make himself as small and unobtrusive as possible in his chair. Except for last night, Cade in general had been surly; today he was likely to be insufferable.

"What th'fuck d'ya mean, there's no breakfast?"

Rafe glanced up from pen and parchment. Jeska missed slapping the table and hit his own thigh instead.

"Closed until *dinner*?"

The kitchen door swung open in time to hear the innkeeper's condescending reply: "We get up in the *morning* around here, son."

Cade erupted from the doorway. His pale eyes fixed on Mieka. "Let's go!"

"Cade—" Rafe began.

"Find Kearney and tell him to order me a bath!"

Mieka traded winces with the fettler and scrambled after Cade out into the bright sunshine and muddy slush of the street. A block later they were outside a dry goods shop. Cade yanked open the door and snapped, "You got money? Go find me some milk."

"Er . . . Cade, what d'you want with—?" But the rest of the question stuck in his throat when Cade glared at him.

So he went up the street, peering into each shop window, and finally located a place that sold cheese. His request was met with blank looks, and a lot of time was wasted as he explained he really did want the raw material, not the finished product, but eventually he emerged with milk (he had to pay for the covered jug, too). Cade was pacing outside the dry goods store, a heavy burlap sack in his arms.

Mieka caught him up, careful not to spill the milk. "Cade, what're you—?"

"Shuddup."

Back at the inn, they blew past Fairwalk on the stairs. His Lordship mumbled about a hot bath waiting, but there was scarcely time because they really ought to leave, don't you see. Mieka scrambled up the stairs after Cade to the second floor garderobe's lovely big bathtub, filled as requested with steaming hot water.

Cade ripped opened the bag, dumped the contents into the tub, and pulled a spoon out of his pocket. The bag slapped to the tiled floor. Mieka saw the label for the first time: ten pounds of Bellytimber's Best Porridge Oats.

" 'Twas the milk what made it Art," Mieka told Rafe and Jeska and the baffled Lord Fairwalk once they were in the coach. "Anybody else woulda been content with eating a few spoonfuls of plain porridge—even me!—but not Quill! Gods, it was *beautiful*!"

Rafe and Jeska collapsed, howling with laughter. Cade sat with arms folded, cool as a cloud.

His Lordship frowned. "But you don't mean to say— that is, he didn't actually—I mean—"

"Oh yes he did!" Mieka crowed.

"You! Stop! Stop at once! Don't you dare move those horses one step!"

It was the innkeeper, arms waving wildly, covered to the elbows in congealed porridge.

"I thought it would harden faster," Cade remarked.

Mieka shouted out the open window to the coachman, "Drive!" Then, with a polite, "Do pardon me an instant," he turned, and as the coach jolted forward unhitched his trousers and presented his naked backside out the window to the infuriated innkeeper.

This time Cade brought out pen and ink without being asked, and personally crossed off the words *Incorrectness of attire.*

"That's two," he said, and grinned.

Nineteen

MIEKA KNEW HIS luck in finding himself, at so young an age, part of something worth being part of. He knew himself to be not much more than a young man of substantially Elfen blood who was damned good at glisking, drinking, making mischief, and making love, and asked little else from life other than to do at least two of those things—preferably three, and ideally all four—every night. But he was also beginning to realize, mildly intrigued, that Touchstone, and especially Cayden Silversun, had the potential to make him so much more.

After those first acts of rebellion against the King's

little list, he behaved himself. More or less. Not only did he have many more months to accomplish his goal, but he decided he'd best space things out for the times when he got too bored or Cade succumbed again to the sullens.

He had given up trying to persuade Quill into an evening of sampling thorn. For a time he considered slipping something interesting into Cade's drink, the way he had with Rafe, but refrained. Bearing in mind how perplexed Auntie Brishen had been about the reaction to blockweed, Mieka decided that experiments ought to be cautious, and at Cade's own request.

Life improved with Cade's disposition, though there was plenty about the Winterly Circuit to strain everyone's temper. Still, memory of the porridge-and-milk morning could make Mieka smile even when the coach wheels were mired in mud and they all had to get out and push while Jeska attempted to dry out the road; even when the "beds" they'd been promised turned out to be one blanket and a smelly pillow each on the floor of an inn's upstairs storage room (swiftly remedied by His Lordship, bless him); even when he wanted to have a girl so desperately that he couldn't get to sleep without redthorn. By the fourth week of the Winterly, the sexual drought was getting beyond desperation, and even his promise to Blye, and to himself, could no longer keep him from emulating Jeska—who somehow managed to find himself a girl almost every night. Rafe had announced that in his opinion, any girl foolish enough to marry the masquer would have to bring a straw mattress and a stable blanket to the wedded bedchamber if she ever wanted to enjoy her full marital rights: *"Can't get it up anymore without the smell of hay and horse, can you, lad?"*

Being conscientious about sleeping in the same room with Cade seemed sillier every day—especially on those nights when a pretty barmaid winked at him. Rafe seemed not to notice girls at all, possibly because he knew any dalliances would be reported back to Crisiant but probably because he simply wasn't interested. Mieka thought this bizarre. First of all, as long as a man didn't bring home a pox, what business was it of his woman's who he slept with while away from her? But second of all, and much more telling, Crisiant was Crisiant, which pretty much explained everything even if Mieka couldn't put it all into exact words.

As for Cayden . . . he was just too intense about the Circuit, and performances, and arriving on time, and the equipment, and . . . just *everything*. They had Fairwalk to deal with all the arrangements now, so what did he have to anguish himself about? Mieka supposed he'd been at it so long he couldn't just stop. But although after that riotous night in Shollop he usually joined in the celebrations after a performance, and was merry enough when he did, not one glance of speculation or outright suggestion from a girl ever registered with him. And glances there were, despite his conviction that no woman would look even once at him when Jeska and Mieka were there to be appreciated. Mieka thought this ridiculous, too.

Late on their last afternoon in Dolven Wold, third stop on the Winterly, they went to have a look at the outdoor venue where—with luck, good chavish, and another triumph at Trials—they'd play next summer on the Ducal Circuit, possibly even the Royal. Dolven Wold's indoor hall was a tricky one, long and rather narrow, with a bounce off the sweeping curves of the staircases at the far end. Chat had warned Mieka about that, and the unholy chill of the place that made firepockets necessary at regular intervals amid the audience. The magic needed for warmth, minimal though it was, could always be felt, and they'd had to make allowances for it. But the outdoor site—ah, *there* was a place where a glisker and a fettler and a masquer could stretch full out. The "seats" were terraced rows cut into the side of a hill; the "stage" was an intricate pattern of flagstones that matched the red walls and towers of the ancient, abandoned castle. Rose Court, the theater was called, and as Jeska and Cade meandered its snowy breadth, Rafe and Mieka climbed all the way to the top tier.

"This will be *spectacular*!" Mieka yelled down into the curving bowl of the theater.

"Everybody else does 'spectacular' at Rose Court!" Cade called from the stage, startling Mieka with the just-beside-him quality of the sound. "We'll be *fantastic*!"

Rafe was hopping back down from snow-step to snow-step, laughing, arms flailing madly, and all at once Mieka had a sort of foreseeing of his own: a string of children, bundled up in winter clothes, jumping along behind their father. Imagination, he knew. But lovely to contemplate. He'd be Mad Uncle Mieka, and they'd all come over for tea and swimming at Wistly Hall—

And then imagination flared like a sunglint off the snow as a trill of laughter sounded behind him. He turned. The girl was small and dainty, her long blond hair braided with blue ribbons. The green of her cloak matched the green of her eyes. She stood just beside a knobbly old pine tree, like a forest Sprite about to welcome him to her home.

"Where'd you come from, darlin'?"

"Mieka!" Cade shouted. "C'mon, let's get back!"

"You go!" he replied, sauntering towards the girl.

"Mieka!"

"Later!"

The girl smiled at him. It took no special talent for dreaming the futures to know that his weeks-long drought was over.

It turned out that she lived with her sister in rooms

above a shop selling household goods. The pair spent their days tending the counter and making or repairing brooms and brushes of all shapes and sizes. He liked the rough feel of their hands.

His way back to the inn lit by a full moon, he had no trouble locating the squat little structure close by the old castle walls. Fairwalk, who seemed determined to educate them about each stop on the Winterly, had related how Dolven Wold had started life as a fortress, expanded into a fair-sized town with the fortunes of its owners, become a royal residence when Princess Veddie married the foreign Archduke Guriel and took a fancy to the place, and had somehow survived the ravages of the war that had seen the castle itself largely destroyed. The present Archduke never visited here, the place where he'd been born. The citizenry usually shrugged at the mention of his name. But even now players on all Circuits were ordered to include at least one of the Thirteen at every show they gave—just as a reminder.

Mieka crept up the back stairs and slipped into the hallway. No creaky floorboards here; the whole inn was built from solid rock taken from the demolished red sandstone castle walls. Letting himself into the room he shared with Cayden, he leaned back against the door and grinned to himself as he began peeling off his gloves. The girls truly had been delightful. Just what he needed.

The shutters shafted thin strips of moonlight across the floor, not touching either bed. What guided him to Cade was the sound of shifting blankets and a whimper of his own name.

Several times on the journey he'd come half-awake in the middle of the night, vaguely aware that Cade was looking at him. Once the man had been standing next to his bed. Mieka had always gone back to sleep and the next day Cade had been fine. But this time the whole damned bed was shuddering. As Mieka approached, the covers twisted around the long body as Cade fought whatever was going on inside his head.

Mieka froze. Ought he to let this play out, so Cade would wake and see him and know that whatever he'd dreamed, Mieka was all right? Or ought he to wake him up? Blye had never said anything to the purpose. She had never seen Cade during one of the sleeping visions.

As he stood there, unsure and beginning to be as frightened as Cade, a violent movement knocked Cade's arm into the cabinet between the beds. The pain woke him, and he cried out.

"Quill? It's all right, everything's fine, you were just—"

"Mieka?"

That thin, splintered plea shook him. "It's all right," he repeated, knowing very well that it wasn't. "You were sleeping," he said stupidly, then flinched as bluish fire glared from the candle on the little cabinet. "Gods, you look awful," he blurted.

The gray eyes caught at him. In the next instant, with an effort that tightened every muscle in his face, Cade looked away and said, "Sorry. Get some sleep. Early start tomorrow for—for—"

"Sidlowe," he murmured.

"Yes. Of course." Another struggle produced something resembling a smile. "Nice evening?"

Yes, very—but not worth this, was what he wanted to say. "Bit of an exertion. She had a sister."

"No mother lurking about?"

So casually spoken that Mieka was certain the answer was important to Cade. "No, they're on their own." He tried to ignore the wince back from him as he gathered up blankets and sheets. "Here, it's cold. You'll turn into six feet three inches of ice."

"Six feet two," Cade corrected, huddling gratefully into the covers.

"Not according to those tatty old brown trousers of

yours." When Cade blinked up at him, he smiled. "The ones you bought before we left are still long enough, but those brown ones—honest to all the Gods, Quill, it's an embarrassment to be seen with you every time they come untucked from your boots." When he still looked bewildered, Mieka chuckled. "You've grown about an inch taller since they were made. All leg."

"Oh."

"That's me Quill," he teased, "eloquent at any hour of the day or night! Close the light and go back to sleep. Everything's fine."

Mieka stripped in the darkness and got into bed. He stayed awake quite a while, listening as the rhythm of Cade's breathing became slow and even with sleep, wondering why he hadn't asked to be told about the dream. Just a gentle query about why Cade had said his name might have done it. Just a friendly commiseration over the spiciness of the stew they'd had for lunching being cause enough for a nightmare . . . anything, *anything* to give Cade an opening to tell him about how and why he dreamed.

How long was Mieka supposed to pretend he didn't know?

He couldn't ask. He couldn't force Cade's confidence. Cade had to choose the time and the place and the reason for telling him. Mieka would just have to wait. That this would require patience—not a conspicuous feature of his character—afforded him a wry amusement as he finally drifted off to sleep. Clever and mad, those he could manage without inconveniencing himself at all. Patience . . . that was another thing entirely.

The next day was one long test of his forbearance. Short on sleep, rousted out of bed at some loathsome hour of the morning, curled once again into a corner of the coach so Rafe could stretch out his long legs to the opposite seat, Mieka tried to distract himself with ideas about breaking the rest of the Rules. Drunkenness he could manage without even thinking about it; no fun there. The trick was to avoid angering the coachman. The man seemed to like him, but who knew what punishments he might think fit if Mieka broke any of the Rules in a way that pushed him too far?

He figured he had a way to cross off *incivility* without too much risk. Likewise property damage. He'd have to see what sort of opportunities presented themselves, though, for the ones about disobedience and endangerment.

If *Do not snore loudly* had been on the list proper, he would have turned over Rafe to the coachman's tender mercies anytime since they'd left Gallantrybanks. Unfortunately, the coachman wasn't in a position to mind. The fettler snored like a trumpet announcing the imminent arrival of the most august of personages. No one below royal rank would merit such a thundering great noise. Jeska didn't so much snore as snort, in sharp little gasps like a cat trying not to sneeze. Lord Kearney Fairwalk could only be said to snore *delicately*. A soft buzzing sound would escape his open mouth, and then, as if even in sleep he was afraid of giving the slightest offense, he would clear his throat and subside into silence.

Cade didn't snore at all. With that nose, it was unnatural that he didn't. But he didn't. There were times when Mieka found this even more annoying than Rafe's trumpet blasts, Jeska's sniffly little snorts, and Fairwalk's dainty whirrs combined.

Mieka, of course, had never snored in his life. So it was a good thing it wasn't on the list. He'd never be able to accomplish it.

A nice tankard of strong brown ale at lunching was just about to put him to sleep when he heard a noise somewhere between a honk and a rasp, and Rafe growled something that sounded like *For the love of all the An-*

gels, will somebody shut him up? Knowing he must be referring to someone else, and rather indignant that Rafe of all people should complain about snoring, Mieka snuggled more deeply into the carriage rug and kept his eyes closed.

All at once he couldn't breathe.

He woke with a splutter, jerking away from the fingers that had pinched his nostrils shut, and bumped his head against the window.

"*Much* beholden," Rafe said feelingly.

"Don't mention it," replied Jeska.

"What—why—how come you did that for?" Mieka demanded.

"You were snoring."

"I was not!"

"Were so."

"I *don't* snore!" Mieka insisted.

The rest of Touchstone traded eye-rolls. Fairwalk looked embarrassed, and looked out the nearest window.

"The windows rattled and the horses nearly took fright," Cade said solemnly. But his eyes were dancing with laughter.

"Why d'you think we make him take the same room as you, when we've two rooms instead of just one?" Rafe asked.

Jeska answered before Mieka could open his mouth. "Because *he* doesn't need eight hours of sleep. Have to be at me best for every show, don't I?"

Mieka retorted, "Since when have *you* ever been in a bed for eight hours at a stretch if there wasn't a girl in it with you?"

"A touch, old son," Cade told Jeska. "You're in the local hayloft half the night most nights, no denying."

Jeska waved it all away. "Fact is, Mieka snores like grinding papers on a thousand withies, and there's an end to it."

"He does, that," Cade said. "Though it's rather more like a tortured goose, don't you think?"

"Gosling," Rafe corrected. "He can't be full-grown yet, can he? I mean, look at him. Scrawny little thing."

"Cullions," Mieka muttered, hunching himself into his corner. A few minutes later, he said, "I do *not* snore."

Whether he did or not had nothing to do with where any of them slept that night. Though Gallantrybanks' reach might extend far into the countryside, for a hundred and more miles around Dolven Wold memories stretched even farther. Part of the Kingdom now, to be sure, not the Archduke's domains; but there was no mistaking their loyalties during the late war.

"Nubboddy say'd nuddin' 'bout no Elferbludded," drawled the innkeeper, placing his considerable self in the main doorway of the only lodging within twenty miles.

"I'm afraid I don't understand," Fairwalk said, stubby little fingers gripping the itinerary page. "This is the specified accommodation on the Winterly Circuit, is it not?"

"Not fer his like."

Touchstone stood shivering in the gloom and mud of the stable yard, exhausted after dawn-to-dusk in the coach. They were cold, hungry, thirsty, and cramped, and the day had been bearable only because of the hot meal and warm beds supposedly waiting for them here in this lonely roadside inn.

When the proprietor eyed him ears to boots, for the first time in his life Mieka knew what humiliation meant. He was an Elf, and he was unwelcome here. Elfenkind had declared for neither King nor Archduke; thus they were considered to have dishonorably eluded all responsibility. Sometimes in Gallantrybanks someone obviously Elfen would get stared at, and Uncle Barsabian claimed to have been spat upon. This innkeeper was regarding Mieka as if he were more foul than the shit decent folk scraped from their shoes. Mieka felt his cheeks burn. Then pride stiffened his bones and he deliberately shook his hair back from his face, giving the man an even better view of his ears. The man's lip curled, and he looked away as if the sight of those pointed ears was too disgusting to contemplate.

Rafe's spine cracked as he drew himself to his full height. "You've had theater groups here before, on the Circuits. You've seen Elves. What's your problem?"

The innkeeper was thoroughly unintimidated. "New contract, innit? Shifted from the old Lamb 'n' Lark t'me this year."

"We'll go there, then."

"Try, if'n ye like. Burned down, the place did. Was Elferbludded what diddit, so it's said, when a room got denied him. Fired it to the floorboards with his stinkin' magic. No welcome fer such most places 'round here, now."

"But surely," Lord Fairwalk protested, "*surely* you know that all gliskers are substantially of Elfen stock! I mean to say, there's not a group of players in the Kingdom without an Elf—have you never been to a performance?"

He sniffed and spat. "Wuddint catch me in reach of that sort."

"How in all hells did you get this contract?" Rafe demanded.

The coachman spoke up for the first time. "His will be the only beds between Dolven Wold and Vasty Moor, now. I hadn't heard about the Lamb. And it's not true that Squimmie didn't let Elves under his roof. Been drivin' the king's coaches these fifteen years, haven't I, and there was never a breath of a word spoken—"

"Squimmie died this summer past," said the innkeeper, with a certain degree of relish. "Him as inherited was a right-thinker, same as me, and paid fer it with the loss of his 'stablishment." Then, looking at Mieka again, he warned, "Don't *you* be thinkin' nothin' at all, Elferboy."

There would be no blithely assuring the man that *"Thinking only gets in the way! Me, I never allow a thought to linger longer than I can recognize it and throw it right out me brain!"* There would be no charming his way into food, drink, and a bed tonight. There would be no deployment of what his mother called The Eyes, no winsome smiles, nothing of his usual tricks for getting what he wanted. This wasn't the first time his wiles had failed him, but it was certainly the most important. It wasn't just him disconvenienced, was it? Because of him, his friends would suffer.

The coachman shrugged, surveying the place from the dark, narrow upper windows to the cresset torches set at intervals along the inn-yard walls. "Never been here before. I didn't know. Sorry, lads."

"Not your fault, not at all," said Fairwalk. Then he reached for his purse. "Perhaps we might come to an arrangement with this good man, don't you think?"

Cade grasped his wrist. "No."

Mieka began to back away. "It's all right, I'll sleep in the hayloft tonight, it doesn't matter—"

"No," Cade said, even more forcefully. Using the clipped highborn accent Mieka had last heard in Blye's glassworks, he went on, "Suppose we address a few words to the Master of the King's Revelries."

"You're a long ways from Court here, case you hadn't noticed," the innkeeper sneered. "Ain't never been an Elferbludded under this roof and never will. I've rights as owner and freeholder and if that boy wants a bed he can make himself one in the sty, where the likes of him belong."

Jeska started forward, fists clenched. Rafe put a cautioning hand on his arm. "Not *yet*," he murmured, and the innkeeper turned brick-red.

The coachman glanced over his shoulder, squinting at his horses, then shook his head. "I'd say drive on and find another place, but there's another five miles in them, and that's all."

"Stable them," Cade said suddenly. "And get yourself to a bed. This is our matter to resolve. Perhaps a bit of illumination?" he suggested—and suddenly every torch ringing the yard blazed to life with brilliant blue flames three feet high. "You'll note," he said pleasantly, "the color. That's not Elf-light, that's Wizardfire. It's rather uncommon, and I'm rather good at it."

"I'll have the law on you!"

"*I'll* have the price of our rooms and food for the night," Cade snapped. "Now!" The fire flared emphasis.

"Wizardly threats," the innkeeper blustered. "Do as you like—you'll have no beds, no dinner, and no coin from me! And you'll not be the only one a-writin' to the King!"

"Foreigner, ain't you?" Jeska said all at once, and the man swung towards him with a snarl. Pointing to the inn's sign, nailed above the door, the faded colors glowing eerily in Cade's blue fire, Jeska continued, "That'll be a Huzsar's cover, all that tall fur and a gold chinstrap. What name was it your father took on after he was paid to ride in the Archduke's cavalry? It'll be something to do with horses—bridle, stirrup, saddle, reins—c'mon, man, what're you called?"

"Prickspur," Mieka said. "It's there, in small letters, at the bottom of the sign. See?"

"And what of it? I'm born and bred here, same as you, and I've rights!"

"Of course you do," Lord Fairwalk soothed. "We don't look to interfere with them, we're only asking you to fulfill your contract."

"Contract says naught 'bout puttin' up Elferbludded in my inn."

"Thing of it is," mused the coachman, "it probably doesn't. That's all understood."

"In this case, deliberately misunderstood," Cade observed. "The coin. Or it's not Elfen magic you'll be worrying about. It'll be *mine*."

The blue flames spread, torch to torch, creating a solid ring of fire around the muddy yard. Muffled screams came from behind the shuttered upstairs windows. The innkeeper's face turned an even deeper crimson as he dug into his pockets and flung two handfuls of coins into the muck.

"And not the barn, neither!" he shouted. "Ye'll sleep in that great ugly coach and be out of here by daybreaking!"

The door slammed behind him. Iron rasped on iron as a heavy bolt slid home. Mieka gulped and crouched to pick up the coins.

"Don't touch them," Cade ordered, and as Mieka snatched his fingers back, said, "Rafe? Which spell, d'you think? Vomiting? Purging?"

Jeska shook his head. "What if he sends somebody else out to get them?"

Cade chewed his lip for a moment before nodding. "Right. How about what we did to Master Plerian's switch?" When Rafe grunted softly, Cade gestured to the coins, glinting dully in the mud. "They hold the imprint of the last hand that touched them—and when that hand touches them again—"

"He'll wish he hadn't," Rafe finished.

Jeska pulled Mieka to one side as the pair of Wizards hunkered down on their heels. "That switch Cade talked of—it was tin, and three feet long, willow-supple, and Rafe still has scars on his back from the last time it was ever used."

"What did they do to it?" Mieka whispered.

"Bespelled it so that the next time the man touched it,

it burst into flames. I heard that he wore bandages for a month. You can't put the fire out with water, and it burns until there's nothing left but a lump of metal."

"How old were they?"

"Twelve or thereabouts. Sneaked in after school hours to do it. Don't ask where they learned something like that, I couldn't tell you. But that much magic, that young . . ." He ended with a shrug.

Implication understood, and it staggered him: Cade and Rafe could have been anything, chosen any Wizard-crafting they fancied. Their magic was powerful enough to get them into any academy in the Kingdom, even university at Shollop or Stiddolfe. Yet they were players, tregetour and fettler, here in this mud-thick inn-yard, casting a schoolboy's vengeance spell because someone had refused to let Mieka sleep under his roof.

Back in the coach, they arranged themselves and all the blankets and carriage rugs as comfortably as they could. Everyone was thinking about it, but Fairwalk was the only one who spoke longingly of his own rig with its fold-down seats. Before bundling himself up in his cloak, Cade got out his pen and ink.

"Which is it?" he asked. "Were we uncivil, or did we damage His Gracious Majesty's property?"

"The coins are still coins, right?" Rafe shrugged. "Will be until sometime tomorrow, I reckon."

"After we're long gone," he agreed. "*Incivility* it is, then." But he hesitated, and glanced over at Mieka. "Unless you had something more interesting planned for that one?"

Mieka shook his head wordlessly. A part of something well worth being part of, he reflected, huddling with them under the carriage rugs that night, and fell asleep hoping he wouldn't snore.

Twenty

ON ARRIVING AT the next stop, the only inn serving a
tiny market town, Touchstone stayed hidden in the coach
with the shades drawn until Fairwalk could be sure
there'd be no repeat of the previous night. For certes, it
all looked much the same. The yard was just as deep in
mud-slush, and the sign above the door bore the name
STRINGFELLOW below a depiction of a drawn bow. But
after a tense few minutes, His Lordship returned smiling
to the coach with the innkeeper himself in tow: a dark-
skinned man whose ears had obviously been kagged.

Touchstone was made welcome—so much so, in fact,
that after an excellent supper and fortified by herb-flavored
home-brewed ale with an astonishing kick to it, out of
sheer gratitude they played a rather cramped but still
satisfactory version of "The Sailor's Sweetheart" for free.

His Lordship had spent half the day mentally compos-
ing his letter to the Master of the King's Revelries. It
took him an hour in a corner of the crowded taproom
before dinner to write it out in a flamboyant hand, with
all his names and all his titles at the bottom, plus his personal seal marking the yellow wax that affixed the yellow and green ribbons. Mieka announced himself awed
by the brass-bound wooden box that unfolded into a
traveling writing desk with all the embellishments, including a selection of silver-nibbed pens like the one
Cade's parents had given him. Then he sneezed.

"Bit smoky in here," he said, not wanting to admit
that his head was beginning to feel stuffy. Last night in
the coach he'd been warm enough to fall asleep but not
warm enough to stay asleep very long. He absolutely refused to catch his usual winter sniffles, the Old Gods'
annual snide reminder that whereas he had enough Hu-

man in him to drink, use almost any sort of thorn he pleased, and grow a beard, he was also helpless when it came to a head cold.

After the show, as they mounted the stairs to their room, Fairwalk mentioned that he'd hired a lad to carry the letter back to Gallantrybanks by way of Dolven Wold, where a second letter would warn the next group coming through. They could adjust their travel to bypass Prickspur entirely, or adhere to the itinerary and forget about sleeping in real beds that night. The Second Flight was the Crystal Sparks. Although Elfenblood didn't show in their masquer, their tregetour and glisker had very pointed ears.

Sidlowe was a port town, inland on a river Mieka didn't know the name of and didn't care about. The place fascinated Cade, though, for it was here that the tenth of the Thirteen Perils had actually happened: the loss of a fabulous treasure. He spent his free hours tucked away in the Minster library or talking with old-timers who might remember something their grandsirs might have said that was real about the event. He even wanted to dig it out of their folio and present it at least once, but Jeska dissuaded him.

"And what if we get a reputation for doing it one way, the way we planned in case we got it at Trials, and eventually you find out that it happened another way? Leave it for when you're sure."

Thus neatly sidestepping the issue of how lethally dull the tale was. If "Dragon" was mostly flash and gimmickry, "Lost Treasure" was nothing but talk, some rain, more talk, a few bursts of lightning, yet more talk, thunderclaps, and somebody yelling that there'd been a mudslide and nobody could find the treasure. After all this time somebody ought to have spiced the thing up a bit. The truth Cayden seemed determined to find was probably even more boring.

Fairwalk, who was returning south now that Touchstone was duly launched, reminded them that Sidlowe would be a good place to buy and send Wintering presents back to Gallantrybanks for their families. With ample coin in his pocket, Mieka indulged himself for days in shop after shop, and along the way learned that Rafe could give a magpie lessons in acquisitiveness. He could also haggle from half to two-thirds off the price of just about anything. The packages they gave Fairwalk took up most of the boot of the post coach and the equivalent of another seat, to the irritation of the three other passengers.

Mieka had watched for further indications of Fairwalk's intentions towards Cade, but nothing suggested anything other than admiration for great talent and a wish to be friends. Still, Mieka knew what he knew, and figured the nobleman was simply biding his time. Considerate of him, not to try to distract Cade on this, their first Winterly, when he had enough to do and enough to think about. Once one got used to his rather prickmedainty ways, Fairwalk was all right. And he encouraged Cade to write his own works, not merely rewrite other people's; for this alone Mieka would have put up with just about anything from him.

After Sidlowe came the long, snowy trip to Scatterseed, where they played nine shows in nine days: four afternoon performances and five evening. That last day, with two shows ahead of him, Mieka could hardly get out of bed. He hadn't consulted Auntie Brishen's wyvernhide roll of thorn very often, but he knew today he'd need it. His head had a fuzzy sort of ache and his nose felt raw inside.

Afterwards, he admitted (but only to himself) that mayhap he'd used a little too much. Either that, or he should have stuck to beer and not had those two—or had it been three?—hotted-up whiskeys. Whichever, by the time the Minster chimes sang out seven and they were ready to go onstage at Scatterseed Grange, he was bleary and twitchy all at once, and nearly tripped over his own feet on the backstage stairs.

"Mieka?" Rafe grabbed his arm to steady him. "Are you all right?"

"Fine, fine." He wanted very badly to ask what playlets they'd decided on for tonight, because suddenly he couldn't remember. He was hoping someone would say something pertinent before Cade made the actual announcement of the titles.

"You don't look fine."

Wrenching his arm away, he laughed. "What, frustled up in me second-best shirt that matches your jacket and Cade's tunic and Jeska's neckband? We're all of us gorgeous, no arguin' with it—"

"What's wrong with him?" Jeska demanded from behind them.

"Nothin' a-tall," Mieka said, hoping his voice didn't sound as slurred to their ears as it did to his own.

"Paved," Rafe announced, shaking him. "Can you work? Answer me honest, Mieka, I won't have you endangering—"

"*Paved?*"

Cade snarled, "As in your face hitting the pavement because you're drunk!" It was as abrupt as it was frightening, the sight of that face looming over him, furious as only Cade could be furious. He saw a hand raised in a fist and waited for it to connect with his cheek or his jaw. He couldn't move, not even to flinch.

Then, just as swift and twice as terrifying, the gray eyes no longer saw him. *Elsewhen.* Mieka knew it. There was no anger in Cade's eyes anymore, only fear. It sobered Mieka like a drenching of ice water.

The fingers unclenched, and for an instant he thought Cade would slap him. Then his jaw was seized in a grip that wasn't quite cruel.

"Don't ever do this again, Mieka." His voice shook. "Do you hear me? Not ever again."

Even if he could have found words, he couldn't have spoken them. All he could manage was a tiny nod. He'd feel the imprint of Cade's fingertips for days. He'd feel the frozen shock of Cade's terror for the rest of his life.

It turned out that being scared out of his wits was an effective treatment for too much alcohol and too much thorn; the fear had gone through him like a dose of salts. They got through the show with no one in the audience the wiser. But Cade didn't speak to him and would scarcely even look at him for two whole days.

What should have been a long journey to New Halt was made shorter and easier by a lack of fresh snow. A trade convoy had been through a day ahead of them, and the line of wagons had cleared the road nicely. Jeska's weather-witching was needed only to melt snow that had tumbled down hillsides since the wagons had passed. When he was feeling charitable, Mieka decided that Cade let Jeska do the work because it was one of the few bits of magic he could actually perform off the stage, and allowed him to feel himself their equal; when he was annoyed with the tregetour, he was positive it was only because Cade was lazy—and a Wizard, and therefore a snob. They reached New Halt a full day ahead of schedule—just as well, for Mieka's head was splitting and it was all he could do not to cough every other minute.

An extra day of rest, plus some assistance from Auntie Brishen, worked wonders. But a vicious wind knifed off the Ocean Sea, right through the rough streets of the harbor, through every crack in the walls of the inn, even through the seams of Mieka's clothes. Cade was acknowledging his presence again, though he might have preferred to be ignored a while longer—the fussing frayed Mieka's already raw nerves. *Take it easy, don't try for anything spectacular tonight, don't wear yourself out, just put the withies in easy reach, you needn't dance about like you usually—*

"Will you shut it? Do I tell you how to prime the bleedin' things? All right, then. *You* don't tell *me* how to use 'em. If standin' on me head and wavin' 'em from between me toes is what makes the audience see what you want 'em to see, then that's what I'll be doing. And if glass twigs blown with farts collected from the Archduke's own bumhole is what gives me what I need to do it with, then I'm ready an' willin' to sneak meself and a couple of pig bladders into his garderobe an' hold me nose, an' squeeze the things meself while Blye works the glass— awkward it'd be, but I'm sure we could work something out—"

By this time Cade was grinning, exactly as Mieka had intended. Pity he couldn't beguile a head cold the same way.

He gutted his way through their first five engagements at New Halt, every show at the Mariners Guildhall packed with sailors—and trollops dressed as sailors, prompting a lot of grumbling from Cade about why *nice* girls weren't allowed to attend the theater. It certainly would have filled out the audiences at some of the shows at Sidlowe and Scatterseed. Weather, roads, and distance sometimes made it difficult for those in outlying districts to travel, even for the only entertainments they'd see all winter. The schedule tried to accommodate important market days or local festivals, when people would be in town anyway, but that wasn't always possible. Once, in Scatterseed, the crowd had been so thin that it had hardly been worth doing the show. They gave it their best effort anyway. Not only had some of their audience saved all

year for this break from grim winter, but Touchstone was
in agreement that every performance was a step closer
to perfecting their craft. (Though more and more often
Cayden was beginning to call it *art*, which amused Rafe
no end.)

What ought to have been their mandatory day of rest
after five shows at New Halt was instead taken up by a
private performance. The shows of the kind they'd done
so far had been for students at Shollop, guilds in Sidlowe
and Scatterseed that had been outbid for sponsorship of
the Winterly, and a group of a hundred ladies who had
been their most difficult and discerning audience yet.
Mieka had expected them to spend an hour settling down
from giddy giggles at their daring in actually watching a
play; afterwards, he learned that they hired the warehouse
every year at a nominal fee (one of the husbands owned
it and valued marital harmony) when the First Flight was
in town.

This private performance outside New Halt was different. It took place in the vaulted stone undercroft of an
ominous old mansion, and it was for an audience of one.
Trading confused, speculative glances when they entered
to find only a single plain chair in the middle of the
damp cellar, by the time they'd set up lecterns and glass
baskets, the chair was occupied by a bulky personage so
enwrapped in blankets, woolen scarves, gloves, and a
bedrobe made of six colors of fur that there was no telling its age or even gender. They reined back the intensity
of the performance, not wishing to overwhelm, but it
seemed to Mieka that whatever they gave was somehow
sucked out of the chilly air and they had to work harder
to fill the space. It was perhaps more exhausting than
creation and control of their performance under the copper roof at Seekhaven. He began to worry that he might
run out of magic to use before Jeska ran out of lines to
speak.

"Weird," was how Rafe summed it up later, as they devoured a lavish meal upstairs. There was a huge table, whining under the weight of platter after laden platter; there were a dozen different bottles, some of them on ice, all of them expensive, according to Cade, who'd once worked for a wine merchant; there were no servants. During their whole time in the mansion, they had seen only one person: their audience.

"Give us a look at that note," Mieka said, extending a hand to Cade. "Nothing but instructions?"

"And the request for 'Silver Mine,'" he replied, tossing over the card before returning his attention to dismantling his second quail of the evening.

Mieka sipped white wine as he read again the simple message. A carriage for their comfort, the favor of a particular piece, dinner afterwards, much beholden. "Definitely weird," he said. "Any ideas who it was?"

"One of Kearney's friends, p'rhaps. He didn't really say when he showed me the invitation back in Dolven Wold."

"I hope he has more friends with as much money to spend," Jeska said, admiring a solid gold three-pronged fork and the slice of roast pheasant at the end of it.

"Forgot to mention," Cade went on, "we've been invited to Fairwalk Manor for a bit of a holiday before Trials." He began sorting feathers with one hand while he ate with the other—the pheasants, the grouse, and the quail had been redecked in their own plumage before serving, just as if this had been the King's own banqueting hall. "It's s'posed to be quite the parkland. Miles of pasture, more miles of forest, three lakes, a river—and the house has twenty-six bedchambers, three dining rooms, a conservatory, and a kitchen hearth big enough to roast two sides of venison at a time. I'm not sure if Kearney eats off gold plate on a daily basis, but it should be reasonably comfortable."

Jeska gave a snort. "Silk sheets, velvet blankets, feather

beds—and padded garderobe seats for that bony bum of yours."

Cade grinned. "*And* padded saddles, I hope. He's got one of the finest stables in the Kingdom." Selecting the best of the pheasant tail-feathers, he stuck it in his cap. "Oy, Mieka, I'll teach you how to ride!"

Definitively: "No, you won't."

"How about 'how to not fall off'?"

"Nor that, neither. Pass the brandy sauce."

They never learned the identity of their audience of one, but none of them cared once they saw the four drawstring pouches waiting in the main hall on their way out. Each little black leather purse contained an amount of money approaching the truly astounding. Blye's loan; Crisiant's High Chapel wedding; a whole month seaside for Mistress Bowbender this summer; Wistly Hall's new tiled roof—well, the most important bits of it, anyway . . . Mieka wished he could send the money on to his family that very instant. A much better Wintering present than the embroidered shawls he'd sent his mother and Jinsie and Auntie Brishen, hand-carved toys and dollies for his younger siblings (a dragon for Tavier, of course), and bottles of upcountry whiskey for his father and Jedris and Jezael. Touchstone had gone in together on Blye's present: a brand new pair of dragon-gut gloves. With the coin weighing down these purses, they could've bought her the whole damned dragon.

Mieka had swiped the bottle of apple brandy off the dinner table, and upon their return to their lodgings detoured to the stables to give it to their coachman. His generosity would, he hoped, be remembered when he decided which of the Rules to break next. Coming out of the side door, he stood for a moment looking up at the night sky, irresolute. With a bellyful of fine food and excellent liquor, he felt quite equal to the task of charming that sweet little kitchen maid who'd been eyeing him sidelong for three days now. But he also felt the throb of a headache and a rasp in his throat. Deciding that he was too tired to do the girl justice tonight, and still puzzled by the way one person had seemed to consume everything he could bring from his glass twigs, he was halfway to the inn's back door when he nearly got run down by an arriving coach.

"Oy!" he yelled, scrambling for the shelter of the porch.

The coach clattered to a stop, the horses shuddering, the coachman howling with laughter. "Said I'd get here in two days from Cranking Vale, dinnit I?" he called into the little window behind his bench. "That's another hundred you owe me, lads!"

Wonderful, Mieka thought; a gang of roisterous highborns with nothing to do. He'd encountered their sort in Gallantrybanks, with their fancy carriages and blooded horses and jeering laughter as common folk scurried out of their way. He knew from experience there'd be no apology, not for the likes of him, so with a curse spat in their direction he tugged open the heavy iron-bound door.

A glance into the dining room showed him the kitchen maid wiping down tables. In the interests of tomorrow night—she was very pretty, with brown hair and big hazel eyes—Mieka helped her stack chairs. She hadn't much conversation, but he preferred girls who kept to themselves whatever thoughts they might have. It saved a lot of time better spent not talking.

There was a small sitting area on the second landing where guests at the inn could legally have a last couple of drinks after curfew rang. Cade was there, and Rafe; Jeska had undoubtedly found himself a girl, as usual.

"Thought you were tired," Mieka said as he draped himself on the sofa beneath the window.

"You'll never guess who just drove in and swanned on up the stairs." Cade was chewing his lip, always a bad sign.

"You mean the cullions who about ran me down in the stable yard?" He sat up a little straighter. "Wait—you don't mean to say they're staying here? Noblemen like that, they'd be in the best inn New Halt can offer."

"Not bleedin' noblemen," Rafe grunted. "Players."

"Seems your friend Pirro has found himself a group," Cade said. "They're calling themselves Black Lightning, and they're taking over for the Wishcallers on Third Flight without ever having performed at Trials."

Severely confused, Mieka looked from one to the other of them before deciding to address the information in sequence. "Pirro's here?"

"Just said so, didn't I?"

Ah, of course; his mistake. Cade wouldn't care about anything except that this Black Lightning had never been judged at Trials and yet somehow had secured a place on the Winterly. "What happened to the Wishcallers?"

"Couldn't really say," said a light voice from above them, and sloping down the stairs came a tall, lean, strikingly beautiful young man Mieka recognized at once as Thierin, the tregetour that half the Shadowshapers liked and half did not. He'd never caught the man's last name—and there was an arrogance in those very dark eyes that assured everyone who looked into them that the name once heard would be remembered.

"All I know," Thierin went on as he lounged elegantly against the final post, "is here we are, on our way to Scatterseed the back way round. We'd a contract in Lilyleaf for a few weeks, you see—but what could the Master of Revelries do other than buy us out of it?"

Nobody seemed inclined to say anything. Mieka didn't like the sound of the quiet. "Where's Pirro?"

"Already asleep, I'd wager."

That reminded him. "Talking of wagers, how many hundred do you owe that coachman for getting you here so fast?"

Thierin made large, puzzled eyes, looking him down and up. Then, with exaggerated surprise suitable only for the broadest of farces—onstage or offstage; good thing he wasn't their masquer, he'd be jeered out of the theater—he exclaimed, "Oh! It was you, outside in the yard?"

Cayden rose, and Rafe, and together they loomed over the younger tregetour: Cade topping him by three inches and Rafe outweighing him by at least twenty pounds.

"That was *my* glisker you nearly trammeled," Cade said, soft-voiced.

"Awf'ly sorry."

"Black Lightning," Rafe mused silkily. "Bit of an odd image, that. Black in a black sky—makes you rather invisible, doesn't it?"

The dangerous gleam in Thierin's eyes acknowledged the sarcasm. "Exactly right. You'll never see us coming. G'night."

He slipped past them down the stairs. Mieka glanced up at Cade. "Don't much like him, do you?"

"Not much to like, is there? Did you note the way he stands? As if his cock's so big he can't get his legs any more together than that."

"Maybe he's just bowlegged," Rafe drawled.

"Or he stuffed one too many pairs of rolled-up stockings in his crotch?" Mieka suggested.

"Wool stockings," Cade contributed. "It's winter."

"Scratchy," said Rafe, shaking his head.

Mieka sniggered. "Fleas!"

Laughter took some of the sour taste from the encounter—never see them coming, indeed—but as they started up to their room, two voices resonated up from the bottom of the stairwell, purposefully loud.

"Hafta watch the dining room clock tomorrow at breakfast, right? Time it, to see fer sure."

"You watch the clock, Kaj, I'll watch his nose," Thierin

answered, "and we'll see how long it takes the rest of his ugly face to catch up to it comin' through the door!"

Cade had turned crimson. Before Mieka could do more than turn, Rafe's big hands had closed around his shoulders. "Damn you, Rafe, lemme go feed that miscreated pillock his own teeth—"

"We'll hit them where they'll feel it most," Rafe said quietly. "I promise. If you go about breakin' those knuckles on other people's bones, how're you gonna flourish a withie and make a dragon that'll claw right down their throats?"

"They'll be at our show tomorrow afternoon, count on it," Cade murmured. "We'll get them then."

Mieka woke the next morning feeling as if the coach really had run him over. Even the stubble on his chin ached. He lay there wondering how he could be barely eighteen and feel more ancient than Great-great-granny Windthistle. If this was what it was to get old, he'd do his best to avoid it.

"I knew we shouldn't've done that private show last night," Cade fretted as he brought in a tray loaded with local remedies. All of them smelled foul, and considering that Mieka's nose was stopped up like a bad drain, that he could smell them at all wasn't a good sign. "Here, this might do some good."

He bit both lips together, squeezed his eyes shut, and shook his head.

"Oh, don't be such a baby. Drink it."

"Just lemme have some bluethorn, I'll get through the show fine."

"Miek? You in here?" Pirro walked in through the open door, broad and brawny, despicably healthy. "Gods, you look like shit. What's wrong?"

"Head cold," Cade said.

"Top of me head to the bottom of me feet cold," Mieka corrected.

"And you've an afternoon performance today? That's not good."

Mieka squinted up at him. "Out with it," he demanded. "I've been knowing you since the first time you stepped on a withie with those clumping big feet. You didn't come here just to—" A coughing fit interrupted him, and Cayden saw his chance: the drink he gave Mieka to soothe his throat was full of a mixture vile enough to put fur on a wyvern's hide. When he finished spluttering and was reasonably certain he wouldn't yark it all back up again, he turned a bleary gaze on Pirro again. "Just say it and get out and let me die in peace!"

The glisker looked abashed, apologetic, and defensive all at once—an impossible confusion on his usually placid, pleasant face. "They asked me to come talk to you, Miek. I would've come anyway, to see how you're feeling, but—they wouldn't put it this way, of course, I'm s'posed to act as if we'd be doing you a favor when actually it's you who'd be doing a favor for us—"

"Favor?" Cade asked sharply. "What kind of favor do you need, after getting onto the Winterly without Trials?"

"That's just what I mean. We need the experience." He tugged at the silver ring decorating the tip of one ear. "I don't know what happened to the Wishcallers. We were settled in Lilyleaf, a whole month of shows, but then Thierin got the note from the Palace—"

"Favor?" Cade repeated, his eyes like frost on a steel dagger.

"We could open the show for you," was the blunt reply. "It'd be one less piece for you to get through, Miek, people would get the show they came to see—"

"Would they?" Rafe inquired from the door. "Sounds to me as if you're none too sure of yourselves. And without a rating at Trials—"

"The Master of Revelries wouldn't have hired them,"

Mieka objected, "if he thought they were awful." He
glanced at Pirro. "*Are* you awful?"

"No!"

Rafe eyed them both. "What about the other groups
at Seekhaven? The ones who were in direct competition
with us for the Winterly?"

"They really *were* awful," Mieka reminded him. "The
Nightrunners?"

"There were others," Rafe said stubbornly. Turning
his head, he called down the stairs, "Jeska! Put that girl
away and get in here!"

Pirro sat at the end of Mieka's bed. "I'll be honest with
you. They'd kill me for it, but—we *are* good, we just
need seasoning—"

"So does the average everyday soup," Cade snapped.
"If we let you go on as opener, everyone will think that
we think you're good enough. We've never even seen all
four of you in the same room!"

Pirro said, "If it's the money, we don't want it."

"I don't give a damn about the money!" Cade glanced
over to the door. "Black Lightning has a proposition for
us, Jeska."

As he explained in the nastiest terms possible, Mieka
slumped back into his pillows and thought as hard as his
thumping head would allow. Several times on the Winterly there'd been someone to open the show—usually
a musician of some sort. But this was another group of
theater players, not some local lutenist.

Pirro was cringing, Rafe looked annoyed, Cade was
very near to a rampage, and Jeska's face had gone un-
naturally still. Finally the masquer said, "I think it ought
to be Mieka's decision."

"You do?" He sat up a bit. "I can't deny I'm not up to
strength, but—"

"Please." Pirro was looking desperate now. "Just one
show."

Mieka glanced at each of his partners in turn. No help
there. They really were going to make him decide. "We
go back a way," he told Pirro. "If you say you're good,
then you're prob'ly not bad. One show."

"Beholden, Miek, absolutely beholden!" And he bolted
from the room as if afraid Mieka would change his
mind.

"A favor," Cade said in a dangerously soft voice.
"He called it a favor."

"They'll owe us, whether they want to admit it or
not," Jeska observed. "I'll go talk to the theater manager,
shall I?" And thus made his escape, neat as in a play.

Cade turned to Rafe. "What d'you think about this?"

"I think Mieka's too sick to work two pieces today.
I think he can probably get through one. But that's all."

Mieka couldn't disagree with him. Even with bluethorn,
he'd be wrung out afterwards—and there was another
show tomorrow night before they left for Castle Eyot
and a seven-day rest. "Quill," he pleaded, "Pirro's a friend."
And then, because he was too weary to argue it out, he
used The Eyes.

A cynical smile told him that not only did Cade know
what he was doing, but also that it had worked. "We
go on at three. You'll sleep until two if I have to knock
you over the head."

As it happened, he could have slept right through until
an hour before the show the next night. Black Lightning
weren't awful. They were loud, blatant, and derivative,
but they definitely weren't awful.

And the audience of sailors and trulls dressed as sailors wouldn't let them leave the stage when their playlet
was done.

Touchstone could do nothing but stand in the wings
and fume. The theater manager, outraged at first but coz-
ened into consent by Jeska that afternoon, was delighted
with Black Lightning and intended them to open for

Touchstone the next evening. When informed of this, Touchstone left the theater.

Oddly, it was Rafe who spent the whole walk back to their lodgings muttering obscenities into his beard. Cayden was simply too furious for speech. Jeska mentioned something conciliatory about its only being what they themselves might've done in similar circumstances, caught the glare Rafe threw him, and thereafter joined Mieka in keeping his mouth shut.

Back in their room, Mieka wrapped himself in blankets and curled on his bed. Jeska had stayed downstairs, and Rafe had lingered in the little sitting area on the landing to mutter into a pint of ale. Cade paced for a while, and finally burst out, "Did you hear that line of theirs? 'Open things, and things will be open to you!' Oh, that's bloody profound, that is. Open it up, and—oy, look, it's open! What a concept! What an insight!"

Stifling a sigh, Mieka rolled over and figured he might as well get it over with and encourage Cade to express himself. Otherwise he'd be griping under his breath the rest of the day and half the night, and Mieka wouldn't get any sleep at all. "I was wondering what they meant by it."

"It didn't *mean* a fuckin' thing! It's the sort of pompous drivel that makes people think they're hearing something deep and insightful."

"Now I *really* don't understand."

"These are players, right? They're supposed to be creative types. Thinkers, even. Some tregetours knot things up so complicated that nobody understands what's going on—probably not even them. People who consider themselves fairly smart, when they don't understand a line or even a whole playlet, they think that the tregetour must be *really* smart—so he gets a reputation for being wise when it's naught but intellectual tricks."

"Could you untangle that for me, please?"

"You know exactly what I'm saying. If it's so complicated nobody understands it, then it must be profound, right? But these sapskulls, they go the opposite direction. 'Open things, and things will be open to you.' Gorgeously simple, innit?" He snorted. "Gorgeously simpleminded!"

Mieka had been listening to this with a smirk teasing the corners of his mouth. Now he grinned. "Quill, you're a snob!"

"You bet I am," he shot back. "Get some rest—because tomorrow night we're gonna explode Black Lightning right off the fuckin' stage!"

"Find me an Elfen healer," he countered, "and I'll explode them into the middle of next week. I'll not be swallowing that swill again, not if you tie me up and pour it down me throat!"

Cayden scoured the streets of New Halt, finally returning for dinner with the assurance that he had found not only an Elfen healer, but even one who knew Mieka's Auntie Brishen. The next day a tiny, shriveled being limped into their bedchamber at a repellent hour of the morning, chattering in a reedy voice about how if he'd had the courage years ago, he would have courted Mistress Brishen Staindrop, he would, and quite an honor it was to treat her nephew. Mieka squinted up at him; the man looked old enough to have courted Great-great-grandmother.

Mieka groaned as he pushed himself upright amid the pillows and blankets, then flinched as a sudden shriek nearly fractured his already aching head.

"Never call up fire around the brewings, boy! Good galloping Goblins, there's things as pick up any stray magic and turn into you don't want to know what!"

"Sorry," Cayden said from over by the door. "I only thought a bit of light might help—"

"Keep yer fire to yerself, Wizard! Go on, out with

you!" When the door snicked shut, the healer leaned very close to Mieka, peering at him. "Yes, yes, there's a look of the Staindrop about you. But Human enough for a nuisance like this, aren't you?" Poking and prodding in unlikely places with fingers sharp as glass thorns, the old Elf kept talking. "Yes, yes, got a swelling here, and a tender spot there—nose running, head stuffed with sheep's wool, coughing fit to choke—"

"I need to work tonight."

"Tonight?" Brittle shoulders twitched beneath layers of wool and fur wrappers. "Well, there's ways and ways, if there's no overdoing. After, it's plenty of sleep and quiet—"

"Just get me through tonight."

A little while later the old Elf had departed. Mieka had submitted to a prick of a rather large thorn containing a mixture of obscure powders. As it made him more and more sleepy, he reminded himself that bluethorn would be necessary tonight as well, even though the healer hadn't mentioned it.

Explosions had been promised for that night at the Mariners Guildhall, and explosions there were: one not-quite-spent withie and Jeska's temper. It was uncertain which was more dangerous.

Mieka, full of an excellent dinner, two pints, and various medicaments, worked the glisker's bench like a madman, wringing sensation out of each glass twig until the things almost bled. The glass baskets shivered on the padded bench as he reached for withie after withie. Mindful of the way Pirro had bludgeoned the audience, nothing subtle about Black Lightning at all, Mieka instead used Cade's magic to coax and cajole, knowing that each physical and emotional nuance would be exquisitely controlled by Rafe. If the dragon didn't actually snap people's heads off, there washed through the audience again and again the fear that it might.

He knew Black Lightning was watching. They'd done a repeat of the "Open things, and things will be open to you" playlet, a ramshackle piece as far as Mieka was concerned, essentially a series of poems about windows, bottles of brandy, virgin girls, and finally a casket. He gathered that this was supposed to be the profound part. As the four players exited stage left, Pirro threw him a grateful smile, which for just an instant softened his irritation. But when Thierin Knottinger and his masquer, Kaj Seamark, paused to grin insolently at Touchstone, and Rafe actually growled, Mieka's resolve to make this a show to remember became a determination that Black fucking Lightning would have this show thrown in their smirking faces whenever Touchstone was mentioned.

But at the end, with the entire hall on its feet and screaming its collective lungs out, and Jeska tossed him the spent withie that had been his "sword," Mieka wasn't quick enough to catch it. Groping frantically for another, his fingers closed around the wrong one, one with some magic left inside. And when he flung it in the air and shattered it, flashes of magic stung the air and the glass shards cascaded down and one of them got Jeska in the shoulder.

The yelp of startled pain was lost in the renewed tumult of applause. Mieka stumbled in his jump over the glisker's bench. Rafe had Jeska by one elbow and was talking rapidly into his ear. Cade grabbed Mieka's wrist and they took their bows half the stage apart.

"Not one fucking word!" Cade yelled as he dragged him into the wings.

"I'm sorry—I'm so sorry, Quill, I—"

"Shut it!"

Halfway back to their lodgings, Mieka had had enough. He shook off Cade's iron grip and snarled, "I got you what you wanted, didn't I? Nobody in that hall will remember that Black Lightning ever played tonight!"

"You could've done it without thorn! I know that look by now, Mieka, I recognize it! You don't need—"

"How do *you* know what I need?" When Cade's hands reached for him, he backed off. "Don't you fuckin' touch me!" Not that he really thought Cade would hit him; he'd seen the Elsewhen look the last time he'd raised a fist, and was certain that whatever it was Cade had seen, it scared him too much ever to allow that fist to connect.

But this was rage, and beyond Cade's power to restrain it. Mieka felt his shoulders taken in fingers like steel spikes, and he was shaken until his teeth rattled. "What if that shard had hit him in the head? What if it'd sliced his face open? What if—"

"What if he'd fuckin' moved out of the way!" Mieka shouted, and fought him off again, and ran ahead to the inn.

He could hear Pirro's woefully off-key voice in the bar, singing some mournful ballad or other. He paused long enough in the doorway to yell, "Fuckwits!" and then took the stairs two at a time. The wild energy of bluethorn sustained him all the way into the bedchamber, where the little fireplace was spitting violent sparks every color of the rainbow.

Jeska turned, one hand holding a bandage to the bleeding cut on his shoulder. "Cayden told you don't ever do it again. I just made sure you won't."

In the fire lay the green wyvern-hide roll of thorn.

The roar that came from his throat belonged to some feral creature. He went for Jeska with both fists.

He woke up lying in his own bed, fully clothed, covered in a quilt, the left side of his face burning with pain and the towel-wrapped snow that was supposed to ease it.

Rafe was the only one in the room with him, sitting by the fire rereading a letter from Crisiant. He glanced over when Mieka groaned, and said mildly, "That was foolish. You're lucky, though. He won't be adding one of your teeth to his collection. You fell down before he could really get started."

The next day, before the coaches left—one going south, the other north—Mieka cornered Pirro in the empty taproom. He spoke three words: *"You owe me."* Ten minutes later he pocketed a single glass thorn and ten little paper twists. They would do him while he sent to Auntie Brishen for more. He didn't need it for a show—they would be on the road for a few days and then at Castle Eyot for a seven-day rest. But he did need it.

Twenty-one

ONCE IT BECAME clear to everyone that the trip to Castle Eyot would be infinitely pleasanter if no one in the coach sulked, brooded, pouted, or otherwise sat around feeling sorry for himself, they began speaking to one another again. By late afternoon, Jeska had even volunteered to jump out of the coach and replenish the snow in the cloth Mieka kept pressed to the left side of his face. But he didn't apologize. Nor did Mieka. Neither Rafe nor Cade was stupid enough to believe that either of them ever would.

They were all on civil if not friendly terms by the second night. Even had they not been, it was only good manners to make the effort. The designated stop in Cloffin Crossriver was run by an elderly couple who had gone to a great deal of bother to make them welcome, astonished that they'd forgotten the date.

Thus it was that Touchstone spent Wintering in a weather-beaten old inn. The holiday was strictly family-friends-and-home; no one was interested in the theater on Wintering Night, even if there'd been a place in town suitable. For a group of players on the Circuit far from their homes, it could have been a lonely evening of increasingly morose drinking, but it would have been churlish not to join in the songs and feasting laid on for them by the kindly old man and his fussing, smiling wife. The childless couple treated their four young guests and the coachman as family—which only emphasized for Mieka how much he missed his own home, especially at Wintering. Knowing it was ungrateful of him, he was just as glad to have the excuses of a black eye and a stubborn cold, and as early as possible went up to bed.

The other three lingered downstairs a while longer. Mieka could hear them, and the festivities at the Minster down the road, as he lay there in the half-moon darkness waiting in vain to get warm. The thick, heavy quilt ought to have been adequate. By the time Cade finally came in, Mieka was still shivering.

He pretended to be asleep. He even managed a snore, which prompted a stifled snigger. Eventually he could stand it no longer. Teeth chattering, stuffy nose still stinging from the sharp scent of the pine boughs decorating the bar downstairs, he gave in and gave up and got out of bed.

"I'm freezing, Quill."

He could practically hear Cade think about refusing, but only for a moment. Wordlessly he twitched back the blankets, and Mieka plunged between them.

"Don't worry, I won't steal the covers." His back to Cade, he curled around himself to conserve whatever warmth there might be.

"I'd only steal them back. I think it's colder here than it was in Scatterseed."

There was a brief silence. Then, because it was dark and Cade had been sympathetic, he said softly, "I'm sorry. About Pirro, and Black Lightning, and especially for not being more careful of that withie."

"And for the thorn."

"And for the thorn," he echoed dutifully.

"I know Jeska's sorry for throwing your little hoard into the fire. He'll probably never say it, but . . ."

"Any more than you'll ever say sorry for screaming at me?"

Another period of quiet. But he didn't regret having said it.

"All right. Sorry."

Mieka couldn't help wriggling a bit, like a puppy under a head-pat. Then he settled more deeply into the pillow and whispered, "Dream sweet, Quill."

"You, too."

Tired and unwell, he was no more aware of finally being warm than he was aware of falling asleep. But he woke fully alert an unknown amount of time later, scared without knowing why until he heard Cayden whimper. He could only speculate that the all-night celebrations at the Minster were loud enough to disturb Cade's sleeping mind. He didn't understand why. The same chants, the same songs, the same laughter, the same night of the year when people gathered for what was supposed to be gentle frivolling fun but sometimes turned to drunken carousing worthy of sailors in port after months at sea—it was only Wintering, and it happened every year, and he didn't know why Cade should be shuddering with a dream.

Yet he was, and Mieka saw that he only knew he'd been dreaming when he felt hands on his shoulders, holding him down against the mattress. The fear within his dream became stark panic, and he cried out.

"Cade! It's all right, settle down! It's just me, you're safe—"

The last light of the sinking moon was enough to show him Cade's white, frightened face. Then he slumped back into the pillows and turned his head away.

"Don't you dare apologize," Mieka said all at once. "You can't control what you dream. Nobody can do that, not even you."

"I should be able to. I should've learned by now." A brief hesitation, and then: "I don't have the sort of dreams most people have."

Mieka watched, holding his breath, convinced that the truth was about to be admitted at last. Gray eyes studied the cracks in the wall plaster, the decaying lathe slats beneath. A chill seeped through them into the room.

"Look at me. Please, Cade."

He turned his head unwillingly.

"I know I said your dreams are important, but not this kind." He waited a while longer, silently urging, *Please, please—*

The sigh might have signaled defeat. "It was about something that happened a long time ago."

"You're only nineteen years old—how long ago can 'long ago' be?"

He smiled a little. "All right, then, how about this: I try very hard to *make* it be a long time ago."

Mieka met his gaze steadily. "Tell me?"

"You don't want to hear it."

"Haven't you learned yet not to tell me what I want and don't want?" He settled into the covers, tugged them up to Cade's chin. "Tell me," he repeated. "You have to, Quill."

He didn't, not really. They both knew it. But whereas Cade didn't lie to him, neither did he reveal what Mieka already knew to be the truth about his dreamings.

He was an accomplished teller of tales, was Cayden Silversun. Mieka could see and hear and feel all of it. Eloquent words, yet impersonal, as if detailing the proposed plotline of a new and original playlet. Mieka had been wrong about the defeat in Cade's sigh; it was Mieka who had lost, yet again.

But he listened. He would always listen.

On the night after thirteen-year-old Cade spilled a pot of ink all over the workroom floor—it was supposed to go into the printing press, but his hand "accidentally" slipped—Number Eight, Redpebble Square, was graced by the presence of a very distinguished dinner guest.

Sagemaster Emmot had spent many years with the stern brethren of Culch Minster, and it showed. Just what he had done for the Archduke during the war was unclear, but whatever it was, he had served his sentence, the brethren had pronounced him cleansed, the Crown had forgiven him, and by the summer evening of his visit to the Silversun home, he had been teaching young Wizards for ten years. It escaped no one who saw him, however, whether they knew his name or not, that he had indeed been detained at the pleasure of the Crown, and for offenses relating to misuse of magic. For it had also pleased the Crown to lop off his thumbs.

Neither did anyone know why Emmot was allowed to teach. Most people assumed it was because he had proven convincingly that he had rethought his position on various issues, and was being given a second chance. The brethren at Culch Minster vouched for him. Some suspected a wealthy and influential but anonymous patron. There had been rumors at one time that he had been permitted an audience with the King, before whom he had promised on his knees and on pain of instant death that he would teach nothing that might ever be used in war. (This was discounted as absurd; Emmot had never been important enough in the Archduke's forces to merit personal royal attention.) A few considered it part of the amnesty granted those who had fought on the losing side, a demonstration—cynical or not—of the Crown's generosity.

Whatever the circumstances or the reasons, Sagemaster Emmot had been freed, had become a teacher, had established his own academy in a tiny seaside village, and had arrived at Number Eight, Redpebble Square, for dinner.

Cade was never permitted to come downstairs when there were guests. So he was caught unawares when Mistress Mirdley called up from two floors below that he was to get dressed in something clean and present himself in the drawing room at once, and don't forget to comb your impossible hair! Scrambling off the bed, where he'd been reading an old copy of Twenty-two Troll Tales, he skittered into the drawing room just as his mother was pouring wine for a tall, skeletal, bald old man who took the stem of the glass between the first and second fingers of his right hand.

"Master Emmot," said his mother, catching sight of Cade in the doorway, "this is my son. Come in and make your bow, Cayden."

He did, unable to keep his eyes from the maimed hands. Master Emmot seemed not to notice his rudeness, and nodded kindly when Cayden gave a gawky version of the Court bow his father could perform with such effortless grace.

"Done service at Wintering, have you?" the old man asked.

"Once," said Lady Jaspiela. "He was eleven."

Cade felt every muscle in his body constrict, as if instinct ordered him to make himself as small as possible. He remembered that night.

"His looks, of course," she continued, apologetically. "His father had to plead with the Good Sister, and even then he was only allowed in the back hallways. We had thought to set him on the path to the Minster, or at least a place at a Chapel somewhere, but . . ." She ended with a shrug.

"Ah."

The silence lingered, and Cade stole a glance at his mother. She seemed caught between attitudes, she who was always perfectly secure in whatever pose she selected. Honored, but also nervous, as if she didn't quite know how to behave to this formerly caged Wizard. But there was also something of excitement in her eyes, and Cade didn't understand it at all.

"My husband sends his regrets," Lady Jaspiela said at last. "He's detained at Court tonight."

"I'm sorry to have missed him." He kept looking at Cade with eyes so dark a blue they were almost purple, like irises.

"Prince Ashgar often keeps Zekien with him for those long, involved conversations men so adore—"

"Your pardon, Lady," the Wizard interrupted, "but I was given to understand you've another son?"

"Why, yes. A year old. His name is Derien."

"Then you don't really need this one."

Cade could have told him that.

"The point being," Master Emmot went on, when it became obvious that Lady Jaspiela was having trouble finding words, "that he needs me. I've established an academy. I think he might do very well there."

Cade held his breath. To leave here, to escape, to learn magic more resonant and complex than the simple spells of the local Wizarding school—

—but to leave here, the only home he knew, to leave Mistress Mirdley and Blye and Rafe—

—but . . . magic—

"Tuition will be waived, of course," Master Emmot said. "And I'm certain we can settle on a reasonable charge for room and board."

"I'm certain we can," said Lady Jaspiela.

"In a year's time, then."

"No!" Cade exclaimed. "I want to go now!"

"Cayden! Be silent!"

"Why do I have to wait? Why don't you want me now?"

Master Emmot arched a brow at him, then turned to Cade's mother. "He's only thirteen."

"I'm tall for my age—and I know things, I can work spells other boys can't—please, let me go now, Mother—"

Careful of the fine glass, Master Emmot set down his wine. "With your parents' permission, boy, and if you truly want to—"

"Please, Mother—" As she hesitated, he warned recklessly, "I will if you say I can or not!"

"Don't dictate to me, boy," she snapped. "Get to your room. Now!"

He did. He packed. Huddling in a shadow by the ridiculous rose-filled urns that marked the entrance to the house next door, he waited until a hire-hack drew up outside his own front door, hoping Master Emmot would be a gentleman and discourage Lady Jaspiela from escorting him outside. When he heard the door open and shut, he peered between the roses and saw the old man making his way alone to the hack. Straightening to his full height, he stepped from behind the urn and presented himself in silence.

"Said your farewells, have you?"

He nodded. A glance in his baby brother's room, a quick hug for Mistress Mirdley—who swept everything edible she could find into a knotted string bag and thrust it onto his arms—that was all. He felt bad about Blye and Rafe, but he'd asked Mistress Mirdley to explain.

Sagemaster Emmot gestured with a maimed hand to the door of the hack. "Climb in."

They were well on their way north to the seacoast before the old Wizard spoke again. "You'll be wondering why, of course. I've seen you. Not in the way most people see, or mayhap I ought to say 'look' because so few peo-

*ple really see anything at all. Once I was sure, I came to
find you. But the decision had to be yours. You'd either
make the break yourself, as you did tonight, or stay and
never learn, never develop. Never become what you most
truly are. Tonight you overcame whatever fear you have
of leaving familiar surroundings, of parting from the
people you love and who love you. You also overcame
your fear of the depth of magic you know very well
you'll be learning. Tonight was, in fact, your first lesson.
It's in your power to shape the future. To make it happen."*

He couldn't take his eyes off the old man, the crags
and furrows of his face emphasized by the light of candles within glass chimneys mounted either side of the
door.

"For example, I saw you coming out of Master Honeycoil's shop, and looking very pleased with yourself, I
might add." For the first time, Cade saw a smile twitch
the gnarled face. "What exactly was it you did to earn his
wrath?"

"Mixed up an order on purpose."

"I waited a while, to make sure it wasn't a quirk, but a
few weeks later I saw you again, and a few weeks after
that as well. Time was required to make arrangements—
I'm not a wealthy man, but recently I received a most
agreeable donation. And now here you are. And of your
own choosing, which is the most important part."

Mieka didn't relinquish Cade's gaze even once during
this story. The silver moonlight was almost gone by the
time he finished. The room was colder now. A freshening
wind outside fingered the pines and reached in through
the cracks in the plaster. He pulled the covers more
closely around them, burrowing down.

"Master Honeycoil?" he said, trying to prompt the
words he'd been waiting for these many months.

"I—I worked for him, for a while. He's a wine

merchant. It ended the same way the bookbindery job ended."

"You made a mistake on purpose." He waited, but the words did not come. The words of honest confession did not come. He nudged a little more. "I don't understand. Why would something like that, dreaming about what happened that night, make you so afraid? You were shaking in your dream, Quill, I *know* you were scared."

"It's what came after that . . . when I had to tell him what had happened at Wintering, when I was eleven. . . ."

"You don't have to tell me." *Please tell me, please tell me. . . .* That he didn't want to was clear in his eyes. Mieka put a hand on his shoulder, confirming the tremors that had come back into the long bones. "Some other time. It's too fuckin' cold." He smiled as Cade relaxed beside him. "Want me to warm us up?" Not waiting for an answer—answers were things he wasn't going to receive tonight, if ever—he sneaked a hand out from under the blankets, gesturing at the second bed. "Hold your breath," he advised, "and hope we don't suffocate before I sort it out. Never had the benefit of a really good school. Not that I would've paid any attention anyways!"

Cade spluttered an apprehensive protest. A moment later suffocation was indeed a possibility, for not just the blankets but the mattress zoomed over and fell on top of them. By the time they struggled out from under, dumped the second mattress onto the floor, and wrapped themselves in the quilts, they were close to suffocating again, this time from laughter.

In a little while they were warm. The moon was gone, and it was dark and quiet in the bedchamber. Mieka inhaled softly of Cade's scent: his breath that smelled of whiskey and his skin that smelled of Mistress Mirdley's pure white soap scented with sage, the same scent that clung to his nightshirt. There was a faint tang of clean sweat, and a hint of woodsmoke in his hair. And perhaps an elusive touch of paper and ink, though that might have been his imagination making an instinctive association. Eyes closed, Mieka breathed him, and slowly realized that to him, Cade smelled like magic.

"What scared me first," Cade murmured, as if there had been no interruption in the conversation, "was something he said later. I guess I dozed off, because suddenly I was awake again and he was talking. He said I'd shown myself willing to turn my back on what was familiar, the certainty of a roof over my head and food in my belly, on whatever love and friendship home could offer, so that I could chase knowledge. He told me that I'd already discovered that the learnings of the mind are more important than the promptings of the heart."

Mieka couldn't help but interrupt. "That's not true, Quill. People need both. And he was wrong about you, anyway, you'd never—"

"Wouldn't I? That night, I did. I turned and walked away. Derien, Mistress Mirdley, Blye, Rafe. . . . I left without a moment's hesitation."

"But that's not abandoning them, you just—"

"I sent Blye a letter. I'm fine, hope you're well, off to school, see you next summer. She sent it back to me inside an envelope, in shreds."

"I just bet she did!" Mieka couldn't help a snicker, and struggled not to end it on a coughing fit. "I'm surprised she didn't shred *you* once you got home."

"I didn't go home for almost two years."

He considered this. "Were you lonely?"

"I was too busy learning to be a great Wizard, just like Lady Jaspiela wanted."

The self-mockery angered him. "Anybody can be a great Wizard. You're a great tregetour, the best, and soon everybody's gonna know it. Even your mother."

"What's important to me and you doesn't mean anything at all to her. Or my father. I think my grandsir would've been pleased, though."

"The fettler? The one who left your father that mirror?"

"Yeh. It's been dead even longer than Grandsir has."

Mieka wasn't so sure about that. He didn't like glancing into that mirror over the Silversun hearth, because whenever he did, he felt as if his teeth itched. "I'm glad you didn't become the kind of Wizard your mother wanted. If Master Emmot's idea of being a great Wizard was to teach you how to walk out on whatever or whoever got in the way of what you want—"

"But it's in me to do that, Mieka. I proved it that night."

"*Would* you do it? Could you turn away from me and Rafe and Jeska? When you look at us, is all you see just three people who are useful to you?"

"No, of course not!"

"All right, then." It spoke well of Cade that being told such an awful thing about himself had scared him. But Mieka didn't say so aloud.

"After that was when he made me tell him about Wintering."

Mieka wanted badly to see Cade's face. But he knew that the prospect of being watched while he talked would shut Cade up quicker than the front door on a beggar at a Spillwater mansion. So he didn't ask for a bit of light brought to the bedside candle. What he said was, "That was the first time he saw you, wasn't it?"

"Saw me?"

"You told me he'd had glimpses of you. He was a Longseer, wasn't he?" Again he gave Cade the chance to clarify, for Mieka was fairly certain Master Emmot had come to Redpebble Square because he had the kinds of seeings Cade had.

"That's one of the things he could do."

The disappointment was so severe that Mieka felt the sting of frustrated tears behind his eyes. He wanted so much to be trusted by this man, to be told what Jeska and Rafe already knew. It just wasn't *fair*—

"He hadn't seen me inside the Minster, though. Just outside in the yard, emptying slops."

Mieka bit both lips together to keep himself silent as the story unfolded. Cade certainly knew how to organize a narrative, he thought bleakly, even when the story was his own. Mieka truly became that eleven-year-old boy, trimmed and garnished in velvet clothes, the elegance so laughable a contrast to his homely face that not even his mother's triumph at finally seeing her son in service at Wintering could survive the sight of him. Mieka saw her expression wane from pride to dismay, saw her wave him out of the house as she would a stray insect. He felt the cobbles under the soles of thin shoes as he walked across Redpebble Square to the waiting hire-hack, smelled horse and leather and the pine bough for luck that decorated the driver's bench, saw the lights of the Minster loom bright and then brighter and then so brilliant that his eyes hurt. He knew the humiliation of being banished to the back halls, to fetch and carry for the boys, the good-looking boys, who were allowed to serve at table.

Everyone else was stealing tidbits off tray after tray of delicacies, but he had no appetite. The other boys were sneaking drinks, too. When dinner was over and the entertainment began in the hall, he was the only one not staggering drunk. So he saw it all, from the sparse shelter of a half-closed door, peering through the gap between wood and stone, unable to move, unable to look away.

"They all wore costumes, disguises. Some of them not very good—I recognized several of my mother's friends. I even saw the King's sister. That's when I knew why Lady Jaspiela wanted me to serve at that particular Wintering.

"Do you know what really goes on there? Most people don't, not unless they're invited to a Minster for a highborn celebration. They send the boys home once dinner is over. But one of the cooks ordered me outside with a cauldron of slops, and it was very heavy, and I spilled some as I was emptying it. The clothes I had on were borrowed, so I had to clean up as best I could. By the time I got out of the garderobe, everyone else was gone. I couldn't find anyone to tell me how I was to get home. I heard the singing still going on in the hall. But I'd only opened the door partway when the procession began.

"Their costumes represent all the races. Harpy, Gorgon, Faerie, Elf, Pikseys and Gnomes and Goblins. Even Trolls, though they're hard-put to convey the concept while still looking as elegant as possible. They wear wings of gold or silver tissue, and false coverings on their teeth, and twist ribbons of all colors together to make a Gorgon's hair. I even saw one couple dressed as Merfolk— they had to carry them in chairs, of course, because the costumes ended in fishtails and they couldn't walk. Everybody circled round and round the hall. I think there was music, but I don't recall the tunes.

"When they're all arrayed along the walls, that's when it happens. The Woodwose is shoved in, and—"

"The what?"

"The wild man of the woods, all covered in hair—"

"I know what it is," he said impatiently. "What's it doing at Wintering?"

Distracted from his story, Cade asked, "Elves don't celebrate that way?"

"Of course not. How barbaric! We banish the old year by singing and dancing. Just before the feast, the lights all go out, one by one. That's the old year dying. Then somebody comes in dressed as Spring and lights everything up again, and hands out flowers—"

Skeptically: "In winter?"

"Preserving flowers is a specialty of the Greenseed Kin. How else d'you think Rafe managed to have roses sent to Crisiant for her Namingday last week? Told you I had connections, didn't I?"

"I cry your pardon, exalted one," Cade said dryly. "What happens next, at an Elfen Wintering?"

"We eat, drink some more, dance some more, and stagger home around dawn. Oh, and we take our flower along, and everybody has a vase at home to put it in, and we keep track of how the petals fall."

"I've heard of that! Isn't there somebody who comes by to interpret?"

"If you haven't any Earth kin in your line, yeh. We've never had to pay anybody to come read for us—Mum's quite good at it, and her mum before her, and my sister Cilka looks to be in the way of such things herself."

"It's too bad you're missing that, this year."

He shrugged. "So what happened at that Wintering? Why the Woodwose?"

For the first time since the blankets had warmed them, Cade shivered. "This one was a criminal—a murderer, I think, because his head was shaved beneath the costume. Robes made of hair, real human hair, stitched or woven onto burlap or something and then all knotted up and tangled with leaves and twigs and such. He was pushed into the middle of the hall, and stumbled about a bit—he looked drunk. But he was frightened, too. As if he knew what was about to happen."

Mieka tugged back the covers enough so he could look at Cade. There was just enough dawnlight filtering through the windows to make him wish he hadn't, and whatever he'd been about to say fled his brain. The gray eyes were colder than the snow outside, and for the first time Mieka glimpsed the possibility that Sagemaster Emmot had been right.

"I'm told," Cade said, staring up at the ceiling, "that at other Wintering celebrations for highborns, it's just play-acting. The Woodwose is young and good-looking, and he doesn't have to do much—just caper about, and they all snatch handfuls of hair or ribbons off his costume until he's naked. Everyone laughs, drinks some more, and eventually they go home, and he gets paid quite a bit.

"But this particular Wintering was attended by the King's own sister, and things were different."

Mieka reviewed what little he knew of Princess Iamina, and decided he'd best prepare himself to hear absolutely anything once Cade started talking again. This took some time, but finally—tregetour to the deepest veins in his body—he was compelled to finish the story.

"As I said, he was a criminal, a murderer. They tore up his costume, and then they tore him to shreds. I watched them do it. They actually ripped him apart—and Iamina was right in the thick of it, laughing the whole time. Not that it took long, poor bastard."

Mieka slid down into the covers again. "What did they do when they found you?"

"They didn't. I hid. For the longest time, I couldn't move—but then the blood started flowing towards me, just a little rivulet along a seam between the stones, and I stood there watching it get closer and closer. Thickening, as it began to congeal. Then somebody came over with a shawl or a scarf or something, and knelt to mop it up. He took it back to the Princess, and wrung it into her gold winecup. I can still see the flash of that jewel she wears, the yellow pearl flower, as she tilted her head back and he poured into her mouth.

"I started running down the hallway. I'm not sure how I got outside. I ran all the way home. Mistress Mirdley was waiting up for me, and put me to bed—she never asked a single question, bless her. I never told my parents, of course. You're the first person I've told since Master Emmot, that night in the hire-hack."

"What did he say, when you told him?"

"That I'd provided him with a very valuable piece of information about Princess Iamina, and we must keep it to ourselves for it to remain valuable."

Was it still valuable eight years later? Mieka neither knew nor cared. Nothing mattered except that Cade trusted him with this, thought enough of him to tell him the truth. Not all the truth, not about the Elsewhens, but enough for now. Mieka recognized the gentle adjustment inside him for what it was: someone else began to matter to him more than he did.

The rising sun brought no warmth with it. The wind had picked up outside, seeking through the cracks, and even with two beds' worth of blankets atop him, Mieka started to shiver again. Wordlessly, Cade coaxed him onto his side and spooned himself against Mieka's back, wrapping his arms around him. It felt very safe. Not like a hug from his father or brothers, or even what he felt huddled in his little turret lair. It was both those things, and more. He didn't understand it, but he didn't matter right now.

"So that's the sort of thing you dream," Mieka whispered. "No wonder you liked blockweed. Quill, when you said you ought to've learned how to control your dreams—I know I said it already, but nobody can do that, not even you."

"Sometimes I can, though. It's just—I hate being so helpless."

"What're you gonna do, teach yourself to live without sleeping because you don't like what you dream?"

There was a smile in Cade's voice as he suggested, "I could nap during the performances."

Mieka elbowed him, but gently. "Shut up. And—dare I say it—go to sleep."

Twenty-two

NOW THAT CADE had trusted him with at least some of the truth, Mieka daily expected the rest of it. Not that he was waiting for a casual, *Oh, and by the bye, when I dream I see what might happen in the future—pass the toast, won't you?* Being the Master Tregetour he was, Cade would find some dramatic opportunity, fraught with feeling, wherein he could anguish himself to his heart's content while finally revealing all of the truth. Mieka didn't mind that sort of thing; indeed, such were the emotions he mined for performances, his own and those of everyone around him. In a way, he didn't even feel that bad about the Prickspur incident. He now had an experience of genuine humiliation to add to his arsenal.

But no confession was forthcoming. It was as if that long talk in the darkness on Wintering Night had never occurred.

Perhaps he wouldn't have minded so much if he hadn't been in that stage of illness when he wasn't getting better fast enough. This year's cold had lasted a long, long time, exacerbated by travel and work and, he had to admit it, a bit too much thorn of one sort or another. He wasn't used to being this sick for this long. By the afternoon of their arrival at Castle Eyot, his temper was a match for Cade's at its worst.

New and luxurious surroundings didn't help. Castle

Eyot was, as its name suggested, situated on a small island in the middle of a river. The castle's crenellations
towered over a snowy little valley so pristine that it seemed
someone had flung white velvet across the ground. There
was a jewel box of a chapel just across the eastern bridge,
and across the western bridge the usual garnishes of
workshops and cotes for those who served a nobleman's
needs but were not lodged in the castle itself. The view
from Mieka's bedchamber was exquisite, the food and
drink were superb, and he'd never been so bored in his
life.

Cade fussed. He hovered. For two solid days he
brought books from Lord Rolon Piercehand's considerable library to Mieka's room and sat reading by the fire,
ever alert for any indication that Mieka might exert himself to do anything better done by the small army of
servants—such as pour water into a glass or push the
curtains aside to look at the mountains.

On the third morning, Mieka kept his door locked
until he'd washed and dressed. Cade did not appreciate
this and told him to get back into bed. Mieka slipped past
him and went exploring. Well, not so much exploring as
escaping down any hallway that presented itself, until he
was hopelessly lost. He wandered about a while longer,
gradually coming to the conclusion that if this was what
Wistly Hall had once looked like, when the Windthistles
enjoyed practically limitless wealth, he much preferred
his home as it was. Gilt mirrors and gigantic porcelain
vases, carved wooden chairs and elaborate tapestries,
plus souvenirs from His Lordship's exotic travels—not
his sort of place at all.

He meandered through, more and more lost, encoun-
tering whole walls of imagings that featured landscapes
both beautiful and frightening, and stained-glass windows depicting personages who seemed to peer down at
him as he passed. He was making a face at a stodgy old

stained-glass scholar when he turned a corner and yelped, stumbling over a thick rug as he backed away from a massive display of mounted stuffed animal heads. Most of them were posed with jaws agape, vicious teeth gleaming. Once recovered from the initial shock, he crept forward, fascinated in a sick sort of way by the trophies—until one and then three and then the whole wall started snarling at him. He tore out of the long hall and ran smack into Rafe.

"I thought I heard your sweet voice raised in song," he said. "Met our fellow houseguests, have you?"

"What the fuck *are* those things?"

"One of His Lordship's collections. There's a roomful of musical instruments, and another of clocks, and on the other side of the castle there's a hallway devoted to wood carvings from some island kingdom someplace. Most of them," he added musingly, "are quite indelicate."

"There oughta be signs posted. C'mon, let's have lunching. I'm thirsty."

There was a packet of letters waiting for them at table. At every performance stop on the Winterly, a packet had arrived with letters. Crisiant had organized this. She went round to the Threadchasers, Jeska's mother, the Windthistles, and the Silversuns to collect whatever they wanted to send their boys, stuffed everything into a large envelope, and posted it in time to reach them. It worked the other way round, as well: though Rafe was the only one who wrote regularly, whenever the others had a letter he would include it with his latest to Crisiant, and she would deliver it. Mieka had taken advantage of this exactly twice, both times with a short note for Jinsie to tell her everything was fine, we're a smashing success as usual, don't worry, love to all. Rafe, of course, wrote pages and pages; Cade had written to Blye and Derien several times; Jeska merely trusted Crisiant to give his mother all the news, for he was as inept at writing as he was at reading.

Mieka sat down at table, relieved that Cade had something to distract him from the inevitable scold—worse than Mieka's own mother, he was, and with a much nastier vocabulary. All the letters were in response to Wintering gifts, which was surprising since it hadn't been that many days since the holiday. The Royal Post must be getting more efficient, Mieka thought, tearing open the seal on a letter from his mother. This proved to include a note from Jinsie and drawings from Tavier and Jorie. These he passed round the table, and when a servant whispered a suggestion that perhaps he might like the items framed, he readily agreed. It would be a lovely reminder of home from now on, to take from his satchel pictures of the dragon Tavier intended to become and the big vase of Wintering flowers Jorie had arranged herself, and place them where he could see them.

"What's Blye have to say?" Jeska asked, and Mieka looked over from his own letter from Jinsie to see Cade's deep frown.

"Somethin' we already knew, mainly. Black Lightning. Pirro came to see her about having withies made." He slanted a look at Mieka.

"Did she sell him any?"

"Not a one. He brought Thierin along."

Rafe nodded. "She doesn't like him, either. Good girl."

"If they're taking over for the Wishcallers," Jeska said, "that means they'll be at the Castle Biding Fair, right?"

"And exhausted." Cade smiled as he tucked Blye's letter into a pocket and helped himself to more pigeon pie. "Lilyleaf all the way to Scatterseed, back down to New Halt, prob'ly only a day or two here to rest before Bexmarket, Clackerly, and Coldkettle—that's a lot of traveling and a lot of shows."

Mieka shook his head. "You've got it all wrong. They'll prick just that much more thorn, and the performances will get even wilder."

"How do you know they're using?"

"I know Pirro." But it was Kaj Seamark as had the look about him: skinny as a stick, pale and edgy, living on bluethorn instead of sleep and food. That was what happened to you, Mieka reflected, when you didn't know what you were doing with thorn, or when the thorn you were using wasn't as carefully prepared as Auntie Brishen's.

He received an unwelcome demonstration of this latter truth on the fifth night of their stay at Castle Eyot.

Lord Piercehand was absent from his favorite dwelling, off exploring some remote shore to find further curiosities to embellish his home. The servants behaved as if each member of Touchstone was His Lordship's dearest friend. This sort of thing made Jeska fidgety; he was as unacquainted with being waited on hand and foot as the rest of them, but where Rafe seemed unimpressed by it, Cade took diffident advantage of it, and Mieka fairly wallowed in it, it simply made Jeska nervous—probably because his mother was herself a servant. Yet he was also the most polite and thoughtful of any of them, and it was his suggestion that they express their gratitude to the staff by giving them a brief performance.

Without Mieka.

They argued about it from lunching until tea. Cade was adamant: Mieka was almost well, and nothing was going to jeopardize that, certainly not the strain of a show they didn't even have to play. A mildly loud discussion turned into a shouting match, which ended only when Mieka flung himself out of the room in a fury. An hour later he was back, armed with his own contentions: he was perfectly fine, by now he could work "The Dragon" in his sleep and Cade had never done the glisking for it at all, it wasn't fair not to give these people the best show they could offer—

"No," Cayden announced, and went back to his reading.

Mieka went back to his room.

Preparation was simple, really. Light a candle and pass the thorn tip through the flame three times. Empty a twist of powder into a spoon, and hold it over the heat until it liquefied. Wait a bit until it cooled some, then carefully drain the liquid into the wide end of the glass thorn. And then choose a vein.

Some people would sit back and wait for the first effects—the soft flush of heat, the building sense of strength and awareness—but Mieka had been strictly taught by Auntie Brishen to use these minutes in tidying up. He burned the paper twist in a little bowl on the dressing table. He rinsed the spoon in water and then poured a bit of brandy into it, which he then emptied into the bowl. His next task was to similarly rinse the glass thorn; he'd toss the liquor into the garderobe later. His attention caught by his own gaze in the dressing table mirror, recognizing the way his eyes had turned the familiar blue-green, the first slight contraction of his pupils, the rush of blood to his cheeks. This must be powerful, he thought, to work so fast. Usually he was all finished with cleaning up everything and was sitting back with a tot of brandy before he really started feeling it. Suddenly fascinated by the spread of rosy color across his cheekbones and down to his throat, he watched his own face in the mirror while groping absently for the glass thorn so he could wash it with brandy and put it away.

It bit him.

In the next instant he realized there was no blood on his finger. "Silly," he muttered. It did look like a tooth—one of those nasty sharp teeth displayed downstairs on a wall he hoped he never saw again in his life. He cleaned

the thorn, packed it in its little wooden box, smiled at
Jorie's framed drawing of Wintering flowers on the dressing table, and went looking for Cayden to show him he
was perfectly fine, had energy and to spare for a performance of "The Dragon" tonight.

Humming to himself, he hopped down the back stairs
two and then three steps at a time. At the bottom was
a rug patterned with flowers that disguised a mud pond
so deep that he sank to his ankles and nearly lost his
balance arms flailing body twisting to keep upright and
mud sucking at his boots and—

But the floor beneath the rug was solid stone, he could
feel it underfoot.

What in all hells was in this bluethorn, anyway?

Whatever it was, he could maintain for the length of
a performance. No trouble at all.

So when the huge porcelain vases either side of the
garden door sprouted stubby legs and began to march in
place, he only grinned. When the hanging lamps in the
hallway over his head grew spindly limbs and crawled
across the ceiling like big silver spiders, he stuck out his
tongue at them.

Rafe appeared around a doorway. Oh, bless all the
Gods for Rafe, he'd know where Cayden was. He opened
his mouth to ask, but all that came out was, "Quill?"

"Over to the entrance hall. We're using the stairs for
seating. I think he's primin' a few withies." He paused,
came closer. "Mieka? You all right?"

"Fine!" Maintain. Maintain. Even though Rafe's black
hair and beard had turned to running rivulets of tar that
dripped down the white front of his shirt to the floor.
This wasn't bluethorn. He must've misread the label.
Had there been a label? He didn't remember.

He had to find Cayden. He'd be safe with Cayden. He
remembered feeling safe with him. Warm in the darkness, with good smells of soap and whiskey and ink and

paper and woodsmoke and blood from the cut on his finger where the glass thorn had bit him—

Mieka was lost, and he needed finding.

He searched the mansion warily, not wanting to come upon that wall of heads, frightened that if he did, they'd grow bodies and leap down from the wall and come after him. Bad enough that things kept changing colors, that his finger was bleeding again, that flowers were growing up from the carpets and the spaces between the tiny gardens rippled like white water so he had to leap from rug to rug and the flowers were dropping petals that turned into blue and pink and yellow spiders and skittered across the floor and then finally he saw Cade.

He nearly sobbed with relief.

Cade looked up from the glass baskets with a smile, and it was the most beautiful smile Mieka had ever seen. Why did he worry so about the way he looked? It was a magnificent nose he had, and wonderful eyes the color of silver raindrops.

"Well? Are you speaking to me again?"

"What? Oh. Yes. Speaking." He knew how bizarre he sounded by the quirking frown on Cade's face. Turning away, he walked around the hall. No carpets, so no flowers. Black marble floor, not a single rippling wave. He was safe. He was with Cade. Looking around the vast space, he said, "Big. Weird ceiling bounce, yeh?"

"I've been thinking, and if you're really feeling better, then—"

"Me? Fine!"

Cade frowned more deeply as Mieka danced over to his side and picked up a withie. It felt cold, like a twig of ice. As if there was no magic in it and never had been and never would be, poor dead little thing—

"Mieka?"

The cold and lifeless withie wriggled in his hand, coiled around his fingers, up his wrist, hissed at him.

With a frightened cry he shook it off him, dropped it, and it shattered.

"Mieka! What the fuck did you do that for?"

The glass baskets were full of glass twigs and they were all writhing, spiraling up to cant their crimped glass heads at him and he had to smash them, smash them all before they saw Cade and wrapped around him and squeezed the breath from his lungs and the foreseeing Elsewhen dreams from his mind—

He slipped on the slick black marble floor. Cade caught him around the waist, lifted him off his feet, yelling in his ear. The withies were scary blue and viscous green and the dark thick red of blood, poisonous colors he'd never seen Blye make for him, and they *hissed*.

He struggled against Cade's restraining arms. Somehow he got free. Lunging for the glass baskets, he grabbed a handful of withies and flung them to the floor. When they shattered, he laughed.

"Mieka!"

Magic had escaped. He could feel it, flying around the hall, all the magic he used to make scene and scent and sound and sensation winging madly from stairs to ceiling to doors to window glass that splintered and shivered onto the black marble floor. Frigid snow-smelling wind roared through the empty windows, whipping at his hair.

"Mieka!" Cade bellowed, and he looked up, and this time he knew the fist raised to hit him would connect. Blye worked so hard to craft those withies, Cade worked so hard to put the magic into them, and now—

Yes, fear was a quick way back to near-sobriety.

His legs gave out and he fell to his knees. Staring up at Cade, so tall above him, he saw stark rage and welcomed the pain he knew was coming, hoping he would be knocked out the way Jeska had knocked him out so he wouldn't have to see anything more—

But the fury was gone from the gray eyes, and the fist

unclenched, and he didn't understand at all. He deserved it, didn't he?

"Why dinnit you hit me?" he mumbled.

"What?" Cade crouched beside him, a hand on his shoulder.

"You were gonna hit me. Why didn't you?"

"You're not going to remember any of this, are you?"

It seemed perfectly reasonable to say, "Not if you don't want me to."

"I didn't because—because I was afraid that if I started, I wouldn't stop."

"You mean you've seen it?" When Cade looked horrified, Mieka said, "Your Elsewhens. Your dreamings."

"Oh Gods," he breathed. "How did you—?" Then he broke off and pulled Mieka to his feet. "I'm taking you back upstairs. You need to sleep this gone, whatever it is. Though where you managed to find—"

"Pirro," he said, leaning comfortably against Cade, tucked beneath his arm. He was right. Safe. Even with what had almost happened just now . . . safe. What had almost happened just now was *proof* that he was safe.

"Did it ever occur to you that he might've tricked you, given you something that wasn't what he said it was? If you pricked thorn before a performance, and acted this wild, you'd put everyone in danger the instant you picked up a withie."

Mieka shook his head. Pirro wouldn't do that to him. Cade went on talking, but the words didn't matter as much as the sound of his voice, the softs and grims of it, the risings and fallings, a curious music but music just the same. Eventually they were up the stairs and in Mieka's room, where Cade coaxed him onto the sofa next the fire.

"Just rest. Close your eyes and rest."

All at once he was incredibly tired. "Stay?"

"Of course. Sleep it gone, Mieka. We'll talk when you wake up."

He woke up in the high, big bed with its luxuriant covers tucked to his chin. The tapestry curtains had been drawn shut all around him, but through a rift came the red-gold glow of firelight and the low, soft voices of his friends.

". . . found the thorn-roll. I'll keep it in my things from now on, so he can't get at it. We can have somebody look at it and find out exactly what Pirro gave him."

"Cade," said Jeska, "d'you have any idea what it was?"

"None. The packets are all the same, though—blue ink along the edges of the paper. I'm assuming that means 'bluethorn' but who knows?"

"Little shit-wit," Rafe muttered. "It hasn't made him sicker, has it?"

Mieka thought that over. He felt remarkably well, his head clear now of thorn *and* the lingering remnants of his cold. He could've used a drink, though.

"Not that I can tell. We'll keep an eye on him."

"We'll keep six eyes on him," Rafe corrected.

"Pity the next stop isn't Lilyleaf. We could toss him into the waters there for an afternoon. I'm told it cures anything from a hangover to bonelock."

"Does it cure stupidity?"

Mieka almost blurted out a protest, but Rafe's next words made him glad he'd kept his mouth shut.

"I'm surprised tonight turned out as well as it did. Even without the flourishes—yeh, I know you did your best, Cade, but I never knew Jeska was that good."

"A lot can be done just with the voice, y'know. It's the tone, the speed, the rhythm of the words. Cade's are good to begin with. I just had to put some extra into it tonight. I can get a rhythm going that makes people—I dunno, it's like their breath and heartbeat keep time with the words. Not quite music, but close."

"I gave you the backdrop," Cade said musingly, "and

most of the costuming and even a few of the sounds. Rafe kept it all steady, just like always. But what you did tonight—it wasn't just the voice. Whenever I caught a look at your face—that was amazing, just amazing."

Jeska said something about there really being only seven basic facial expressions, but Mieka had turned his back and pulled a pillow over his head.

They didn't need him. That's what they were saying. All he'd ever wanted in his life to be was a good—no, *great*—glisker, and he was, he knew he was, and they had discovered tonight that they didn't need him.

"Fuck *that*," he muttered into the blankets. He'd show them, he would. He'd be better than ever at the Bexmarket shows, leave the yobbos gasping, and they'd tell everyone they knew that the glisker for Touchstone was the best ever seen.

Didn't need him? They'd find out—

"Mieka?"

The whisper startled him out of feigning sleep. He rolled over and blinked at the firelight through the open bedcurtains. "What?" he snarled.

"Feeling better, then. Good." The mattress shifted as Cade sat down, his back to the fire so that Mieka couldn't see his face. "You remember what happened this afternoon?"

"Yes."

"All of it?"

"Yes." To prove it, he asked, "Why did you say that? About not being able to stop if you got started?"

Cade caught his breath. A moment or two passed before he said, "Because you can make me more furious than anybody I've ever known in my life. That driver—your Auntie Brishen's man who drove us back from Gowerion? He was right. You're all kinds of trouble, aren't you?"

"But worth it."

"You heard him say that?"

Mieka laughed to himself. Sometimes Cade was so easy to trick. "No. But I'm certain sure that's what he said."

"You just never stop, do you?"

"Not until I get what I want." He punched a pillow and put it behind his back. "I didn't mean for you to know that I know. About the dreams. I wanted you to want to tell me."

Low-voiced: "I nearly did, Wintering."

"Why didn't you?"

"I'd already said quite enough, I thought. Who was it told you?"

"Blye. Don't blame her, Quill, I pestered her. And you know what I'm like when I pester." Wishing he could see Cade's face, he went on, "What is it you see about me in the future that bothers you so much?"

"I can't tell you. No, Mieka, I'm serious. It's mine to sort out. What if I told you, and it was the exact opposite of what you really wanted, who you really are, and you changed just because of me?"

"If you see me on horseback galloping over the edge of a cliff, I think I'd like to know so I can avoid riding lessons!"

Cade laughed a little. "If it was something like that, I'd tell you!"

"Oh, the intensity of my relief!"

They were quiet for a time. Then Cade murmured, "My own life, that I can change with a clear conscience. But I can't ask somebody else to rearrange himself just so I can sleep at night. Do you understand? And why do you believe me, anyway? What makes you sure this is the truth?"

"Blye," he said simply. "She'd never lie about something that important. You used to tell her about the dreams—"

"Not after I started learning from Sagemaster Emmot. He let me work it out for myself, that it wasn't right or fair to expect anybody to live life according to what made me comfortable. He made sure I understood that before I went back home the first time."

"So you didn't hit me, because you've seen yourself do it and not stop." Not that he believed that, not really. "It's something *you* can change. Something *you* have control over. Do I ever hit you back?"

"No."

"Because that's something *I* control, isn't it?"

"Yes."

"And that means you have to trust me to make the right choices." He paused. "But you *don't* trust me, do you?"

"It's not that."

"So tell me. Explain it to me."

"Not tonight."

"When?"

"Soon enough. It's tough to explain."

"I'm not stupid, Cayden."

"It'd be easier if you were," he retorted. "But you'll want to know everything, won't you? Every detail. Can't you just accept it, and be like Rafe and Jeska and Blye, and leave me alone—"

"No," he said flatly. "The Elsewhens don't have to do with them. They have to do with *me*. You'll tell me, you won't be able to help yourself."

"Want to bet?"

"You'd lose. I never stop until I get what I want."

Cade stood and pulled the bedcurtains shut. "Dream sweet," he added in a voice sharp with irony.

"Quill!"

But the door snicked shut, and he was gone.

Mieka scrunched down into the pillows again. So he could make Quill angrier than anybody else, could he?

Well, the feeling was mutual. Just when he thought he'd learn everything at last . . .

And as for that part about not wanting to control him—Gods, what a load of chankings. *Get to bed, Mieka, get some sleep, Mieka, don't tire yourself out, Mieka, you won't be working the piece tonight, Mieka*—and that reminded him that they thought they didn't need him, and that made him even more furious.

"Tell me what I'll do and not do," he grumbled, "I don't bloody think so! Do it or not do it because his dreams will show him whatever it is they show him that's so awful it scares him silly—and he won't even *tell* me—the hells with that!" He'd do as he liked and as he pleased, and those stupid Elsewhens weren't going to stop him. "I'll learn to ride, I will," he decided aloud, not quite clear on what had prompted the resolve but liking the way it made him feel. *"Dream sweet"*—he snorted, and rolled over again, and went to sleep because he wanted to, *not* because Cade had ordered him to do it.

Twenty-three

WINTERLY WAS TURNING out to be nothing like Cade had expected.

The traveling was worse, though the drinks were rather better. The performances were more exhausting, though getting easier as they gained experience to match their instincts. The accommodations ranged from their own coach that night outside the Prickspur establishment to the opulence of Castle Eyot. Thinking that he knew Rafe and Jeska very well indeed, he discovered that you never knew anybody until you traveled with them day after night after long snowy rainy muddy cooped-up-in-a-confined-space day. He'd anticipated having time to work on several original ideas for playlets—the more fool he. When he wasn't readying the withies or his group or himself for a performance, he was in the middle of a performance, or downing enough ale or whiskey so he could sleep well after a performance, or worrying about the venue for the next performance—or trying to find Mieka before or after a performance.

Now that the Elf knew his secret, Cade thought there could be real openness between them, real trust and friendship. Instead, there was less.

Cade had to admit to himself that he was partly to blame. What bothered him wasn't so much that Mieka knew; it was that Cade had found out that he knew, and if he could keep that a secret from Cade himself, whose secret it really was, then—he felt himself getting confused, which was pretty much his usual state around Mieka these days. What it fined down to was that he felt a kind of defiant justification in keeping the rest of the secret: the contents of his foreseeing dreams.

That wasn't what really bothered Mieka about all this, he felt sure. He kept remembering that resentful *"I wanted you to want to tell me."* He did feel a bit guilty about that. But whenever he considered apologizing, he also remembered that arrogant *"I never stop until I get what I want."* Cade felt a morose certainty that this would prove to be true.

Now that he had recovered from his illness, the Elf was as madly entertaining as ever on the road and as madly intense during the performances. Bexmarket, Clackerly Minster, Coldkettle Castle, Lilyleaf, and half a dozen private engagements besides—Mieka was their cornerstone, as an elderly and distinguished lordship told Cade one night over a late supper. *"I've been knowing the theater these sixty years and more, son, the last fifty of 'em here in my own manor, Winterly and Ducal*

*and Royal every year coming to play for me and my
guests. And I tell you to your head, son, for as good as
you are even at your age, and as great as you're going to
be and your masquer and fettler with you, that Elf is the
cornerstone of your art."*

Cade had managed a smile instead of a flinch, and told
himself to appreciate that the old man had called it *art.*
But *cornerstone* made other words echo in his mind:
"When the *Cornerstones* lost their Elf, they lost their
soul."

It wouldn't happen. He knew it. He was certain sure
of it.

At least, whatever had happened to the *Cornerstones*
wouldn't happen. There was so much else that could. He
could never make Mieka understand. He was certain
sure of that, too.

Kearney Fairwalk had been waiting for them at
Lilyleaf. It was his custom to take the waters there every
winter. Indeed, much of the nobility could be found loll-
ing in the baths or sprawling in the assembly rooms this
time of year. The town had two venues: Lilyleaf Theater,
a gorgeous place barely a decade old built by subscrip-
tion and filled to capacity every night, and Old Bath
Hall, a cramped structure with terrifyingly steep tiers of
stone seats, with the players down at what felt like the
bottom of a well. Those unfeared of heights preferred
Old Bath Hall, for the intimacy of the place and the so-
lidity of the stone made for an intense experience, especially if the players were less than cautious with their
magic. Cade, surveying it the afternoon before their first
performance there, wondered if this was where Black
Lightning had made their reputation.

Kearney brought with him two young men, one of
them familiar. Tobalt Fluter had been meaning to go to
Castle Biding for the great annual late-winter fair; His
Lordship's invitation to tag along to Lilyleaf had been

gratefully accepted. *The Nayword* was doing very well, but circulation and advertising revenues were not yet so large that its editors would turn down a free ride.

"Not that he'll be soft on you, not at all," Kearney warned them the first morning of their stay. "This will be your first big interview—please do keep civil tongues between your teeth, won't you?"

Mieka bared his teeth in a grin, his tongue gently clenched between them.

"Do try, Mieka," His Lordship urged. "It's important."

"Who's the other one?" Rafe wanted to know. They'd all seen a wispy youth follow Tobalt up the stairs, carrying a leather-bound folio half as tall as he was.

"The imager. I've brought new things for you to wear—he'll want several poses—"

"They're going to print our imaging in the broadsheet?" Cade felt his stomach begin to ache. Apart from a single instance when he'd sat still for a small fraction of forever while his schoolmate Arley Breakbriar had practiced on him, he'd never had an imaging done. What that excruciatingly accurate rendition of his face had shown him was even worse than what he shaved in the looking-glass every morning.

Mieka angled a look at him, and Jeska was about to say something soothing, he knew it. Rafe's laughter distracted them all.

"You honestly think you're going to get Mieka to hold frozen for more than the space betwixt two breaths?"

"I'll practice, shall I?" the Elf said at once. He stuck his tongue out, lifted one hand in an obscene gesture, and held the pose as Rafe began a mocking count. He was up to twenty when Mieka collapsed in giggles.

"Case settled in my favor, damages and court costs to be determined," Rafe announced.

"I coulda done it if you hadn't been making faces at me."

"You'll have to do it," Kearney said severely. "This is *important,* Mieka."

The new clothing was . . . interesting. Kearney had decided to dress them in black, white, and two shades of gray. They met downstairs the afternoon of the interview and laughed at one another for a good ten minutes.

The shirts, trousers, and sleeveless jackets were of more or less the same cut, but in differing combinations of colors. Rafe was in black with a charcoal jacket; Jeska in pale gray with black; Mieka in white with light gray; Cade in charcoal with white. All four of them flatly refused to wear the neckbands. Rafe said the pleats looked like pie-frills and Jeska decreed that the white lace edging was absolutely outside the limit.

Kearney was frantic when they wouldn't even try the things on. "But it's the latest fashion, and it will soften all the stark lines of black and white—"

"It's dead hideous, and I won't wear it," Mieka said, tossing the neckband to the table where Tobalt waited with a grin on his face. "What're *you* lookin' at?" he demanded in a growl. "You like it, it's yours!"

"My wife would love it. Beholden." He bunched it up with scant reverence for the pleated frill and shoved it in a pocket. "Now, if you're all frustled to your satisfaction, if not Lord Fairwalk's, shall we get started?"

"Not just yet." Mieka raised his head and his voice, and shouted, "Croodle! Four ales, my darlin', from the goodness of your heart!"

Mistress Ringdove was their hostess here in Lilyleaf. No one dared term her an alewife; her husband had been a sailor who brought her home from the Islands, took over his father's old tavern in the seacoast town of Frimham, and promptly died. She sold up, moved to Lilyleaf, and on the strength of her home brew—said to be as beneficial to the health as drinking the rather smelly waters here, and tasting infinitely better—had within a few years purchased this inn all on her own. She was nearly as tall as Cade, her skin was as black as the soot that wouldn't dare come within miles of her pots and pans (from which came the most delicious food), and when annoyed she planted her fists on her hips and roared like a guards captain, but with an even more shocking vocabulary. This was why everyone called her Croodle, the cooing of a dove being the very last thing she sounded like.

"Only four ales?" Tobalt asked a bit forlornly. "But I'm thirsty, too!"

"You'll stay sober and write what we speak." Mieka grinned at him. "Now. What are they saying about us back in Gallytown?"

"Not much—yet."

Rafe gave his usual taciturn answers to the reporter's questions about life on the Winterly Circuit, then sat back with his ale and listened while Jeska elaborated. Not only did he have something complimentary to say about each locale but each compliment was different. Cade was frankly amazed until he recalled an evening up in Scatterseed when the masquer had been debating the attractions of six different girls, trying to decide whose bed to embellish with his presence that night. The astonishment of it was that he'd conducted this discussion with a seventh girl—the one he'd intended to and in fact did end up with—and hadn't had an unkind word to say about any of them. She thought him the sweetest, dearest man in the world. Quite the line of patter, had Jeska, adaptable to any occasion.

Mieka told several very funny tales of their travels. Some of it was even true. Then it was Cayden's turn.

Tobalt asked a single, simple question: "Why is it, do you think, that men go to the theater?" Mieka groaned and signaled for another round. Cade glared at him, and then began his answer.

"I've thought a lot about this—"

"And talked even more about it," Mieka interrupted.

"—and it seems to be that it's the same reason they go to bear-baitings, musical concerts, and Chapel. They can be part of a group, all experiencing the same thing. They feel connected to each other—not just for the duration of the show, but in the future, when they meet up with someone who was there and they say, 'Oy, remember that night we went to see Touchstone?' There's a sense of belonging, a connection to the rest of the audience that comes during a performance, and this is given back to the players through energy and applause—"

"And money?" Tobalt said with a grin.

Cade forced a smile and took a swig of his ale. Beside him, Mieka was chortling quietly. Rafe looked amused; Jeska looked bored. But this was important, it addressed the whole concept of why there were players and plays and theater to begin with, and—

"So no matter what the composition of the audience," Tobalt was saying, "whatever their ages and station in life, their work, their other experiences, at the theater that night they have this one experience in common?"

"Yes. And that's another reason why it's so unfair that women aren't allowed to attend the theater. It deprives them of that chance to feel that connection with other people. To have those kinds of experiences in common with the rest of society. They're part of society, a hugely important part. They cook our food and sew our clothes, they take care of our families, clean and organize and—and make sure everybody gets to Chapel on time!" He smiled, thinking of Mistress Mirdley. And then he thought of Blye. "They do other things, too, things that it used to be only men were allowed to do. Even what's tolerated these days, and it's *barely* tolerated in most cases, it's not officially approved. There are women who are crafters and run businesses and shops, but they can't join the guilds who're supposed to represent them and have a care to their rights—as far as the guilds are concerned, they *have* no rights. I think it's unjust, that they're excluded from so much, and I'd like to see them *included* in the theater experience."

"Onstage?"

Cade blinked.

Mieka laughed aloud. "Never thought about that one, eh, Quill? Give him another couple of months to talk it out with himself—and any poor lout within hearing range!—and he'll have an answer for you. But he'll need some time to—"

"Yes," Cade said suddenly. "Absolutely. Onstage."

Now Mieka looked awestruck. "Oh, they'll be talking about us and nothing else back home after this is printed, and no mistake. What a scandal-maker you are, Cade Silversun!"

"I think I've got what I need," Tobalt agreed. "Just one thing, if you would, Cade. You talk about the communal experience of Chapel or theater—what about executions? There's always an awfully big crowd at a hanging."

While Cade was flailing about for something to say, he saw a look of wicked glee cross Mieka's face, a look he had grown to dread. But before he could open his mouth, the Elf spoke.

"And lots of women there, too. Isn't that right, Cade?"

Goaded, he retorted, "And there's the contradiction! How is it that society forbids women to watch a play, to protect them from I don't know what, and yet doesn't bat an eyelash when they come to watch a man gasp his life out at the end of a rope?"

Tobalt's pen scratched so quickly it nearly tore the paper he was writing on. Mieka succumbed to a fit of giggles, mischief accomplished beyond his wildest hopes. Cade wanted to wrap his arms around his head and moan.

Instead he smiled as the reporter got to his feet, and said, "You'll owe me a drink for the increase in sales."

"I'll owe you half a wine shop. See you at Castle Biding, then. And I think the imager's ready for you now."

Lord Fairwalk, who had been hovering in the taproom doorway this whole time, now came forward and fussed over their clothes and their hair. Then he led them to the front parlor—Croodle ran a classy inn—where the two lecterns and a glass basket of withies waited for them, along with the imager—who looked rather ill. The watery greenish eyes were as unfocused as Mieka's could be on thorn, he was pale as a corpse, and he kept mumbling to himself as if in a fever. He stood, swaying a little, behind a wide table on which the huge portfolio had been opened. At least a dozen short, colorless withies lay to his right, and a large glass of whiskey to his left.

"Here's what I want," said Kearney, and proceeded to pose them much as they arranged themselves onstage. Cade and Rafe behind their lecterns, Mieka in back, a withie in each hand, Jeska in front. It was so utterly uninspired that the four of them traded eye-rolls and grimaces.

"This will be the first one," His Lordship said, standing back to survey the effect. "Nothing behind them—I don't want anything to distract. We'll see how this one comes out before we try the next."

"It's only for a bleedin' broadsheet," Jeska muttered, "not to hang on a wall at the Palace!"

"Shush! Hold still! He's about to start!"

They became petrified as the imager gave a sudden whimper. It was the oddest damned thing, watching him work: the vagueness and torpor turning to a crisp precision (though he kept mumbling). It didn't take as long as Cade thought it would, not nearly as long as Arley's agonized process. From a corner of his eye he could see Mieka, frozen in place but clearly desperate to break free. No imaging could come close to portraying him unless that imaging moved and danced and flung withies into the air and shattered them as he laughed behind the glisker's bench. And Jeska—how did a motionless picture in a broadsheet capture the subtleties of voice and face and movement that were his artistry? The brief show they'd done at Castle Eyot, with Cade able to provide perhaps half of what Mieka did, had nonetheless been a success, and because of Jeska. Ever since then Cade had been toying with the notion of doing a playlet without any magic transforming his masquer at all, using nothing but that expressive face and voice to draw the audience in, to move them. It would relegate Mieka and Rafe to providing and controlling the backdrop and physical effects, but Cade didn't think they'd mind very much. In point of fact, he didn't care if they minded at all. It was an idea that excited him, not just because it was different but because it would be a challenge. Art was about challenging oneself: to do better, to be better. Sagemaster Emmot would have said, *"So is life, boy,"* but Sagemaster Emmot's voice was figuring less and less in Cade's contemplations these days.

Lord and Lady and Angels, when would this man finish? Cade knew the cramp threatening his shoulders was merely nervous tension: the annoyance of having to hold absolutely still was starting to make him twitchy. He didn't see the need for any of this anyway. There would have to be placards to advertise their performances in Gallantrybanks before and after Trials, but imaging was expensive and wouldn't give anyone a real idea of what Touchstone looked like. Rafe, whom he could just see beyond Jeska, was the only one that an imaging could fairly portray—but only if it caught him with that glint in his blue-gray eyes and that sardonic turn to his lips. As for himself . . . he'd rather not think about it, beholden all the same.

Finally the fourth withie dropped to the table and the

imager drew in a wheezing breath before groping for the whiskey. Mieka took that as a signal to howl his release. He hurtled for the taproom door, yelling for Croodle to save his life by pouring him a drink.

"Excellent, excellent," Kearney murmured, standing at the exhausted imager's shoulder. "For the next—and take your time recovering, dear boy, there's no rush—I want something rather different. But we can discuss that once you've rested a bit."

Cade followed Mieka into the taproom, found him gratefully gulping down ale. Ordering another, he sat at the bar beside his glisker and undid the top two buttons of his collar.

"You forgot your falcon," Mieka said. "But it probably wouldn't've shown up anyway. If he does the next one close-to, you have to wear it. Dery will be in transports, to see it on you."

He nodded, ashamed of himself for not thinking of it. Again he wondered how Mieka could be such an infuriating, impossible little smatchet one moment and so gentle and thoughtful the next. All Elfenkind were capricious, but Mieka—

"And you were wrong, y'know," he went on. "There's men as go to the theater to escape everything around them, including the rest of the audience."

The abrupt turn in subject left Cade a step or two behind—another of Mieka's irksome qualities.

"They don't want to feel 'connected' to anything but what's happening onstage. It's their own little world they retreat inside, and they let us in but they don't let any of their own feelings out. Remember that night in that empty old house in New Halt? Whoever was sittin' there, he sucked up everything we had and then some. You can't tell me *he* wanted some kind of 'communal experience' or to be part of anything. Lookin' back on it, makes me feel a bit of a whore."

There was the other thing about Mieka, Cade thought helplessly: Just when you wanted to wring his neck, he'd come up with something shrewdly instinctive that rearranged Cade's brain the way a foreseeing did.

"And as for protecting the ladies from theater but letting them watch a hanging—oh, but here's His Lordship, come to haul us off to imitate statuary again." Mieka sighed, and finished his drink, and called, "Oy, Kearney! Wait a bit while Cade gets his little silver falcon out of its cage, right?"

The second imaging took much longer than the first, because it was of their heads and shoulders only and thus required more and finer detail. The young man, sufficiently revived but still muttering under his breath as if rendering incantations, had them each sit before him in turn, stared without blinking until Cade marveled that his eyes didn't water like fountains. He seemed determined to capture inside the withies each hair in Rafe's mustache and beard, every faint freckle on Jeska's nose and cheeks, the exact furl and point of Mieka's ears. Cade didn't want to know what feature of his own face occupied the man to the point of obsession. Or, rather, he was sure he knew: his nose.

His was the last imaging to be completed, and when he was finally told to go, he discovered his friends were a drink ahead of him. The ale kept coming courtesy of Croodle, whose heart had been melted days ago by one glance from Jeska's limpid blue eyes. Not that she flirted with him; no, she had decided that he, and by extension the rest of Touchstone, were exactly the little brothers she'd wanted but never had. Mieka initially pouted a bit, that he hadn't been the one to win her over. But as long as it got them free drinks, he'd evidently decided that Jeska could have the credit.

They were discussing the next night's performance, which would be at the Old Bath Hall with its dizzying seating and oddly sunken stage. Jeska was worried about having to play up, not out and to each side; Rafe was worried about bouncing all that magic back down into the well. Mieka scoffed at them both. Full of liquor and full of himself, he turned to Cade all at once and said, "Don't listen to 'em. You can put the usual magic into those withies, y'know. Hells, gimme some extra! Cram 'em up till they won't take no more. I can handle it."

"No," Cade said quietly, "you can't. And even if you could, there's Rafe and Jeska to consider."

"And the audience!" he said stubbornly. "The place must seat four hundred!"

"No," Cade said again.

"Coward." He raised a piteous face to Croodle, who chuckled and drew a whole pitcher. "Oh, beholden, sweet darlin'!"

"Cheeky li'l ol' thing, you be." She grinned. Then, spying the beginnings of a fight at one of the tables, she surged out from behind the bar, bellowing, "Oy! Under my roof, you raise your fist and you lose it at the wrist!"

Cade decided that a return to their conversation was necessary. "Rafe does just fine spreading the magic so everyone feels it. Even in a theater as odd as that one. I can't give you any more than I'm giving you right now." He heard what he'd just said and watched Mieka's mocking smile and wanted to squirm.

"Really? Pity, that." After knocking back the rest of his drink, he grabbed the pitcher and poured anew. "Y'know, Quill, you're lucky I came along to Gowerion. Without me, you'd still be playing for blashed beer in leather tankards. Instead—" He held up the glass, swirling with green like a trapped whirlwind, which Croodle said must be used for Mieka's drinks because it matched the color of those eyes when he was drunk and happy. "The best, an' all 'cause o' *me*!"

Rafe, silent until now over his drink, glanced up, a

sudden spark of danger in his eyes. Jeska merely snorted his opinion of Mieka's boasting, perfectly sure of his own beauty, worth, talent, and destiny.

Cade said, "Without my magic to use, and Jeska to use it on, and Rafe to make sure it doesn't get used badly—"

"Badly? When have I ever—?"

"My point precisely. It's him you're beholden to for that."

Mieka slammed a fist onto the bar, abruptly furious. "You'd be nothing and noplace without me!"

"Really." Rafe wasn't smiling.

"It's me they come for, I'm the one who does all the work! Who's the one talks to the reporters at every stop on the Winterly as has a piddling local broadsheet? You can't be bothered, Jeska's off with some skirt, Cade goes on and on about what this piece or that piece means and nobody gives a shit—'cept for today, when he has to go and say somethin' so outrageous, we'll be lucky to keep him out of quod for incitement to rebellion! Women on-stage! You never know when to shut up, Quill!"

"*You're* saying that?" Jeska spluttered. "*You*?"

"Those other broadsheets, all they want is a funny story or two so they can sell a few copies of their two-pager! And it's me as gives 'em what they want!"

"Good at that, aren't you?" Rafe murmured.

"Yes, I am! And you oughta be glad of it. It's for us. For Touchstone."

"Well, if we're such a chore to be around, and if we'd be nothing without you, find yourself another group of players. Go on, do it. Or—better still, do your absolute minimum next show, since we bore you and aren't worthy of your brilliance. Show us how much we need you."

Mieka turned white. "I can't do that. I won't. And you know it." Then, shrewdly eyeing Cade, who had been silent this whole time: "And you won't slack off on be-spelling the withies, either, and for the same fucking reason. Oh, you'd love to, wouldn't you? Give me almost nothing to work with, show me how much *I* need *you?* Your pride wouldn't let you do that and we all know it."

"Neither will *your* pride let you give anything less than your best," Rafe reminded him. "You say what you like to us, in private, but if I ever read anything about Touchstone that even tinges of what you said just now, I'll take you apart. Do you understand me?"

Mieka jumped to his feet, shaking with fury. "Fuck you!" he snarled, and stormed out of the taproom.

"That might have gone better," Cade observed, and buried his nose in his drink.

"I'm tired of that arrogant little Elf takin' all the credit for your hard work."

"He didn't, not exactly. And in a lot of ways he's right, y'know. We weren't going anywhere before he sat in with us in Gowerion."

Jeska was staring. "Why are you defending him?"

"Just pointing out the facts. Yes, he's an arrogant little snarge, but he's mostly right."

"That's what *he* always says," Jeska retorted.

"No," Cade corrected softly, "what *he* says is that he's *always* right." Smiling, he toasted them with his ale, finished it off, and set the glass on the bar. "Whereas all of you ought to know by now that being always right is a privilege reserved for *me!*"

Twenty-four

HE WAS A little disappointed with Mieka. The Elf seemed to have given up his self-imposed mission to violate all Seven Rules and live to tell the tale. Of course, he'd been ill or recovering from his illness for a significant bit of time, but anyone as madly clever as Mieka ought to have completed at least half of that list by now.

Or maybe, Cade reflected as the coach rattled up a paved—actually paved—road to Castle Biding, Mieka was growing up.

Certainly he took his work more seriously. Every performance seemed to be a challenge to the others and to himself: be the best. The absolute, unqualified, indisputable best. Cade had to admit that at times during this long, brutal tour, they'd got a bit sloppy, cut a few corners. Whoever would have thought that four young men, the oldest of them not quite twenty-one, would be so bloody exhausted by work they loved? It was the traveling that did it, he decided. But they couldn't let the shows suffer just because they were tired. These men had paid good money and often traveled quite a ways to see them perform; they owed every audience their best. And it was their mad little glisker who'd reminded them of it.

Out the coach windows he could see the beginnings of a fair-sized town made of tents and enclosed wagons. Castle Biding perched like a preening pale gold dragon on a small hill in the middle of it all, with winter-fallow fields on the left side of the road providing the living space for hundreds, perhaps thousands, of people who'd spend nearly a month at the fair. To the right was the fairground, already thick with garish pennants flying high above smaller tents, painted stalls, rickety wooden booths, and hawkers who could afford the entry fee but not the hire of a space. There were no fairs like this in or near Gallantrybanks anymore; the shops were too numerous and varied, and practically anything was available any time of year. The only event of the kind was the annual horse show on the Palace grounds, which combined a market with ten days of racing. But there was nothing like this fair available in the capital anymore, and for all the disdain of native Gallybankers for country folk and country living, Touchstone gaped out the windows at the sights. They were themselves objects of importance; carts moved out of the way for their coach, people waved, girls flirted with their eyes and smiles, and as the coach rolled across the bridge and began the ascent to the castle yard, and everyone stopped to cheer the newly arrived players, for the first time they had a hint of what it might be like to be the Shadowshapers, famous and beloved.

Their lodging was in the castle itself, in two rooms set aside for the players who would arrive, one after the other, to perform at the fair. Their tower chambers were high above the river that bent around the castle hill before flowing straight and swift to the south. After dinner, Cade took his winecup all the way to the top of the tower to watch the sunset. Cooking fires and the occasional bonfire spattered the tent village, randomly, not like the every-twenty-feet torches that lit the fairgrounds in a tidy grid. Wandering to the other side of the battlements, where everything was dark, he stood finishing his wine, waiting for moonrise.

"I knew you'd be here."

His fingers clenched around the pewter cup, then relaxed. He'd heard those words before, though in a different setting. The feeling, though, was almost the same. "Thought you'd be investigating the local ladies."

"They've been a touch too open about investigating *me*," he replied wryly, coming to stand next to Cade.

"That's right—you like 'em shy, don't you?"

"I like not to find their hands down me trousers before I've done more than look 'em in the eyes. More wine?" He held up a bottle, sloshing it gently.

"Please. Did you catch a look at the theater when we drove in?"

"A bit small. No wonder they have us doing two shows a day, and a waiver of the five-and-a-rest rule.

That's partly why I came up here—His Lordship's being motherly and says get to bed."

"In a while." He sipped the splendid white wine, glad Kearney was back to provide such luxuries from the Continent—and to take over the day-to-day worries about lodgings and payment again. He hadn't realized how little he'd missed having to organize things until someone had started doing it for him. "Shame the weather's not reliable enough to try the outdoor theater."

"The weathering witches can keep the ground dry and the wind from blowing the tents down, but it'd take a hundred Wizards to chase the clouds away." Mieka leaned his elbows on a crenellation, shoulders hunched. "I agree, though—a whole outside wall of the castle and the whole of the sky to play with—it'll be fun, next time we're here."

"You're assuming we'll make Ducal."

He laughed. "I'm assuming we'll make Royal!" Then he caught his breath and pointed down at the river. "Oh, Quill—look! Isn't it beautiful?"

"Moonglade," he said softly, remembering now what the foreseeing dream had shown him. He hadn't seen this, but something like it—when? Way last spring, at Seekhaven? He could scarcely credit the passage of time.

"Write me one of those," Mieka pleaded. "I don't care what the rest of the piece is like, I want to do *that*!"

"I-I actually do have something in mind," he heard himself say. He wasn't aware of making the choice to tell him. It simply happened. "Not with a moonglade, but—I dreamed once—a dreaming kind of dream, not—"

"Not an Elsewhen?"

"Is that what you call it?" he asked, amused. "Anyway, I was walking down a long hallway, just blank walls on either side—"

"How can you tell?"

"About the walls?"

"No, lackwit, about what kind of dream it is."

He considered. "I've always just sort of *known*. The feeling is different."

"How?"

"Are you going to listen to what I dreamed or not?"

"I'm always listening, Quill."

He held out his cup, and in the moonlight Mieka shared out the rest of the bottle. "I couldn't see an end to the hallway, and there weren't any doors—it was a little scary. But the instant I started wondering how I was going to get out, there were dozens of doors along each wall. All different. Plain wood, painted, iron, some with brass hinges and some with bars, a couple with windows in them. I went looking for the right one, and I don't know how I knew which it was, and I opened it, and there was a future inside. It was my own room at Redpebble Square, and I could see on the desk the book I'd been reading the night before—the night I had this dream, I mean, what I'd been reading before I went to sleep—"

"Who said there was a wrong door?"

"What?"

"You said you opened the right door. How do you know there were wrong ones? Or—no, not *wrong*, just different. Like your other dreams. You chose a door even if you didn't know you were choosing—"

"I haven't the least idea what you're talking about." *And neither do you* hung unspoken between them.

"You picked the door that went into your own life."

He turned from the beguiling moonglade to frown at Mieka's earnest face, glossed with silver in the darkness.

"All those other doors—you could have opened them, you could have at least looked or even walked inside to find out what was in them. That's the way your Elsewhen dreams happen, innit? Only you don't have a choice about opening the doors. You get thrown through them whether you want to be or not, right?"

"More or less."

"Well, *this* is a future, too. Right now, this minute. Last year or last week, *this* was a future. At some point you walked into the room where *this* happened, this moment we're in right now."

"What are you trying to say, Mieka?"

With a shrug, he muttered, "Trying—and failing."

"Just talk. You always get to it when you talk it out."

"Is that what happens?" Quick glinting grin. "I thought I just blunder on and on until somebody tells me to shut up."

"I talk *around* a thing, circling in on it, surrounding it with words so it can't get away. But you talk your way *to* a thing—your words sneak up on it and when it's there in your hands, like as not you're just as surprised as it is." He smiled at the incredulous widening of those eyes. "Don't worry. It'll make sense eventually. The words will find their right places."

Mieka was quiet for a few heartbeats, then sighed. "In that dream, you walked past all the other doors. All the other futures. You opened this one. You chose *this* door. And I think—Quill, don't laugh at me, please?"

He shook his head. "I won't. Keep talking."

"And don't be angry with me—I mean, this sort of anguishing about something, it's what *you* do, I'm no good at it—"

"You're doing fine. Just tell me."

Mieka took a deep breath. "I think what the dream was saying is that you keep choosing the same door on purpose every time you wake up in the morning. You feel in the dream that it's the one you're supposed to open, right? This life, and none other."

"Because this life is the one I want to be in?"

He nodded gratefully. "Day after day, you choose to be

here. Even if it's not the kind of life other people would want, or that they want for you, this is the one *you* choose. The door you open."

"This life, and none other," he echoed softly.

There was another small silence. Then Mieka asked, "Did I just ruin everything you wanted to use about that dream in a playlet?"

"I think you just told me what I need to write."

"Really?" He gave a little bounce of delight. Then, with a shrewd glance up at Cade: "Does that mean I'm more important than any of you will admit? And I really am worth all the trouble?"

Cade nudged his shoulder, laughing. "You arrogant little Elf!"

"Don't say that as if you just found it out!"

* * *

MIEKA WAS UP early (for him) the next morning, and woke Cade by clamoring with all the smatchety determination of a spoiled five-year-old to go see the fair. Rafe was already out exploring; Jeska, predictably, hadn't spent the night in his own bed. Cade took one look at the tidy coverlet and pillows, shook his head in a resigned sort of way, and went back to his and Mieka's room to get his coat and fill his purse. Their first performance was scheduled for late afternoon. They would have just over an hour for dinner and a drink before the evening show. Cade had already primed enough withies just after their arrival yesterday, so he felt free to spend the day as he pleased. Correction: as pleased Mieka.

It was an easy walk down from castle hill along the cobbled road to the fairgrounds. The scents of other people's breakfasts from the campsites had them buying sage-flavored sausages wrapped in flatbread and apple preserves from the first food cart they saw. Happily munching, Cade and Mieka set off to investigate the fair.

One aisle was devoted to fabric handiwork. Huge complex weavings and small embroideries; ready-made gowns, skirts, trousers, jerkins; clothes for children and clothes for their dollies; reels of plain ribbon and embellished ribbon and varying widths of lace; curtains and tablecloths and humble dish towels; pillows, bedsheets, counterpanes, and a really beautiful crib quilt in a pattern of tumbling baby blocks that Cade and Mieka bought to put away as their future gift when Rafe and Crisiant had their first child.

"Which probably won't be long," Mieka predicted as the counter girl wrapped the quilt in a length of cheap but scrupulously clean burlap. "She won't let him out of bed for a month once we get home. Oy, what do you want to bet she's carrying when they get married?"

"Do I look foolish enough to take that bet?" He tucked the small parcel under his arm. "Where to next?"

"I saw some woodworkers over there, I think."

He had indeed, a round dozen of them, selling bowls and plates and goblets, handles for all manner of bladed instrument, even lighter-weight chairs, with the option of ordering more from the crafter's catalog. There was even a selection of the new-style pens, though one had to go to a silversmith or goldsmith to get the nib made. Cade thought it rather impractical, offering this sort of thing at a country fair.

"After all, how many letters does a farmer write in a year? And it isn't as if a feather to suit the purpose isn't available right out in the kitchen yard."

"You *are* a snob," Mieka retorted. "They have to keep their accounts, for one thing, and for another, have you noticed how many traders are selling luxury goods? A farmer's wife doesn't need lace curtains in her front room, but they'd be lovely to have, wouldn't they? And besides all that, how do you know the next great tregetour won't buy one of those pens and write *you* off the map?"

Cade stuck out his tongue at him, and Mieka chortled.

They roamed through aisles featuring metalworkers (some of whom had fires and anvils going for customized items), silversmiths and goldsmiths and gemcutters, people who sharpened knives and people who mended all manner of things, all the while dodging other fairgoers and meandering singers, acrobats, jongleurs, and men who stood on painted crates declaiming classic poetry at the top of their lungs (thereby rendering the more tender passages of the love poems somewhat frightening). There was a section of glassblowers, at whose work Cade and Mieka both sniffed rather snobbishly, having been spoiled with Blye's creations, but the parcel under his arm reminded Cade of something.

"I have to write to Blye and tell her to start the loving cups for Rafe and Crisiant. If I know her, she'll fret over them for months until she gets them perfect."

"Better than anything any Master Glasscrafter with a hallmark ever made." Mieka shook his head. "I hope Tobalt gives a lot more space to what you said about women than he does to what you said about theater. At least get people thinking about it, instead of just accepting things as they are. And talking of that, the article ought to've been printed by now, right?"

"Kearney said something about right before we get back to Gallytown, for maximum impact, but—" He forgot entirely what he was about to say, and nearly dropped the crib quilt. Right ahead of him two booths were jammed together, holding each other up. One of them featured wooden flutes of every imaginable size, carved and decorated and inlaid with little polished stones. The other was packed to overflowing with books.

"Oy, and I knew the young lordship for a sensitive and learned man the instant he turned his head my way!" cried the bookseller, a Gnome-Goblin-Human-and-possibly-Troll mix who looked as if any attempt to read a book would make his brains bleed. "Collected from the finest libraries of the finest lords in all the Kingdom, bless and rest their scholarly souls, a better nor farther-ranging selection of books you'll never uncover!"

He waited for Cade to laugh at the pun. Cade was staring at a thick, heavy volume, bound in ragged leather, the spine cracked and some of the pages about to fall out. On its front, stamped into the leather, the gilt long since worn away, were two barely discernible words: *Lost Withies*.

"How much?"

"I knew it, I knew it—'tis a subtle and perceptive young lordship! That book there, that's from the ancient and cherished library of—"

"How much?"

"For a knowledgeable person such as yourself—"

He was about to snarl the question a third time when Mieka interrupted with a snort.

"The cover's a wreck, there's water damage, and I'll bet half the pages are missing! Name any price over a royal and I'll have the castle constables on you for cheating your customers!"

There followed much wailing and gnashing of teeth on the part of the seller, and much scornful jeering from Mieka. Cade could only stand there and stare at the book. He would have paid a hundred royals for it. Two hundred. He moaned low in his throat when Mieka picked it up and opened it, showing the seller how loose the pages were, flipping through it as if it was a bound folio of inferior poetry instead of the historical treasure Cade knew it to be.

"One royal and a happenny tacked on," Mieka finally said, grudgingly. "And it's a favor I'm doing you to agree to that."

"One and se'en-pence."

"One and two, and there's an end to it!" He dug into a

pocket and slammed the coins down onto the closed book.

The man truly didn't know what he had in his possession, or he would have haggled much longer and for a much higher price. Cade had been a fool to react this way to mere sight of the book, though Mieka seemed to have saved the situation for him—and a lot of money. The volume was tied together with string, and as the seller grumbled and fussed, Mieka said, "Oh, and we'll have that copy of *The Parchment Dragon* right there as well. Consider it a sweetening," he added, smiling with every single one of his teeth, "so that I don't report you to the constables."

More groaning, more wringing of hands. Eventually Cade felt Mieka slide the quilt from beneath his arm and press the heavy book against his chest. He embraced it, and Mieka snorted again.

"Subtle as a thunderstorm," he said. "All the pages are there, by the bye. While I was thumbing through it—and you were having an apoplexy—I took a good look. And for my brilliance in securing it for about the price of a bath each, you now owe me a good lunching. Wrangling the price down was hard work!"

Cade bought food and drink on the way back to the roadside, where they sat on the ground and ate while watching the traffic. More people were arriving, setting up tents, searching for their booths, lugging their wares. Cade wanted desperately to return to the castle with his book, but Mieka had plans for the rest of the money Cade owed him.

"A sign back there said there's two whole rows of ales in competition for first prize. Who better than us, with our Kingdom-wide experience, to give an opinion?"

It was a cheap way to get drunk. Cade called a halt after the dozenth quarter-pint each—not all of which they had to pay for, it turned out.

"It seems they know who we are, sort of," he mused, bewildered by the smiles and nods and free drinks. "How'd that happen?"

"Don't know, don't care. It's prob'ly me charming manners and adorable smile."

"No," he insisted, "some of them, they looked like they recognized us."

Mieka shrugged and plucked at Cade's sleeve. "Still thirsty," he whined.

"You've had enough. Lord and Lady know *I've* had enough." He fought down a belch. "Back to the castle, I think—"

Mieka suddenly gave a crow of laughter, and pointed. Down at the intersection of aisles was a big placard framed in rough wood. Cade blinked to see his own face, and Rafe's, and Jeska's, and Mieka's, looking at him. Printed in stark black on white, there were no shadings at all, which told him that either the engraving for printing plates had been done quick and cheap or that Kearney wanted the imaging to be as dramatic as possible and therefore had done away with fine detail. The placard bore four words along with their severely unsmiling faces: TOUCHSTONE running up the left side, and CASTLE BIDING FAIR at the bottom right corner.

"Look at us! We're gorgeous!"

Mieka was already scampering to take a closer look. Cade followed more slowly, still clutching the book to his chest. Perhaps it was all that ale putting a blur into his eyes, but he had to admit that he really did look rather presentable. There was a bit of an insolent glare to his eyes, he thought, that he hadn't noticed after the imager had done his work but was somehow brought out by the austere print. Thinking back to that day, he remembered that he'd been nervous about what he'd just said to Tobalt; that must be the source of the expression in his eyes. Odd; he didn't know he looked like that

when he was feeling defensive. The engraver had chosen
to include the little silver falcon that Cade had pinned to
his collar that day. He smiled, thinking that Dery would
indeed be thrilled when he saw it.

Then he realized that placards just like this one would
be all over Gallytown by now. His mother would have
six fits.

Mieka stood next to the placard, trying with inebri-
ated obstinacy to keep his face as solemnly like the imaging as possible, waiting for people to look at it and then
at him and make the connection. Cade walked up to
him, laughing, and tugged him away.

"Milk it till it moos! Don't anguish yourself, you'll
spend the next six days being recognized."

"Really? With free drinks?"

* * *

THE AFTERNOON SHOW went very well. The theater
was packed, and the applause began when they walked
onstage, something that had never happened at a first
performance before. Once word got round a Winterly
stop, they could usually count on a nice welcome for the
remaining shows. But this was the first time their first
appearance was applauded.

Cade was satisfied that they earned it. They were using
Castle Biding to run through every single one of their
pieces, to begin the process of deciding which to do for
the Gallantrybanks shows before Trials. Kearney had
engaged them to play the Kiral Kellari three nights a
week, and they'd insisted that he include a weekly show
at the Downstreet for gratitude's sake (also because at
both places there'd be trimmings, which they didn't receive in a real theater).

Mieka vanished after the show, and didn't join them
for dinner. He was on time to the evening performance,
just barely. He took off once their bows were done, with

a smile and a wave for his partners. Cade would have suspected he'd made his selection from the serving girls and maids back at their tower lodging, but all of them seemed to be accounted for (one of them by Jeska), so he must have found entertainment elsewhere.

Cade went up the stairs slowly, again putting off the pleasure of opening *Lost Withies*. This afternoon he'd left Mieka at the fair and trudged back up castle hill to their bedchamber, the book clutched like a lover in his arms, but he'd been too sleepy with the drink and the warm sunny day to do anything more than caress the cover. There was a certain delight in anticipation, especially with books, that he'd learned could dissipate all too quickly—but *Lost Withies* proved the exception. From the instant he untied the strings holding it together and opened it to the title page, he was enthralled. Mieka was right; no pages were missing. He tried to go carefully through the whole thing, to examine the woodcuts first and not stop to read the chapters, but his attention kept snagging on a description here, a detail there. He skimmed biographies of tregetours and fettlers, masquers and gliskers and glasscrafters, dipped into summaries of significant playlets, traced with wonder the diagrams describing how magic rebounded from ceilings, walls, support beams, solid rock. It was the one book his grandsir's library had not contained. There were rumored to be only a half-dozen copies left in the entire Kingdom. And he was holding one of them.

He wasn't aware of falling asleep with the cumbersome tome on his knees. But he heard it crash to the floor, and jerked awake to find Mieka standing beside his bed, a lit candle in one hand, his face as white as the linen of his nightshirt.

Or at least he thought it was Mieka. For an instant he had trouble recognizing him. The Mieka he'd just seen had looked so different—

"Another one about me, was it?"

Cade sat up, leaned over to rescue the book. It seemed undamaged. "Just a nightmare," he said. "Not one of the—the Elsewhens."

The boy said nothing until Cade had straightened up and looked at him again. His jaw was rigid, his lips tightly compressed. But it seemed he couldn't keep himself from speaking—just one word, thick with anger and betrayal.

"Liar."

After a terrible, frozen moment, Cade set the book on the bedside table and pulled up a blanket, turned his back, and closed his eyes. The dream replayed in his mind without his having called it up, without any promptings or applications of the disciplines Sagemaster Emmot had taught him to use.

It was quite large for a thatched-roof cottage, six rooms at least, with a finished upstairs, not just a loft. Smoke billowed from a fine brick chimney into the moonlit darkness, but the whitewash between timbers looked at least a year too old, there were a few cracks in the plaster of the upper floor, and the arching lintel stones were chipped.

The man was sniggering, drunk, his eyes wild with thorn. He had the girl by the wrist, pulling her not-quite-roughly through the front door, kicking it shut behind him. He tripped on a richly colored rug, swore vilely.

"You're home, are you?" The woman's voice was not quite a shriek, and it came from beyond an open doorway where firelight glowed.

"Shut it!" To the girl, he said, "G'on up, second door onna left—I'll be up inna minnit."

She balked. "You never said nothin' 'bout no wife—"

"How dare you bring your whore into my house!"

"Go on!" he roared, pushing the girl towards the stairs.

She twisted free and yanked open the door, and fled into the night. He swore again, and lurched into the golden glow of the sitting room.

The woman was throwing things into the fire. With every vicious little movement, a thin gold bracelet gleamed from each wrist. As he threw off his cloak, a similar bracelet made of heavier links glinted below his shirtcuff.

"What're y'doin'?" he demanded.

She half-turned, her face still in shadow, and in her hands was an old green wyvern-hide folio, open, with loose pages that she crumpled in her fist and flung into the flames as if avenging herself on each.

He staggered as if the sight was a physical blow. Then he gave a wail of agony and lunged for her, tore the folio from her grasp. Pages scattered onto the scuffed wooden floor. "You bitch!" he yelled, and slapped her. "That's *mine*—"

"*You're* mine, or so you said when we were wedded!" She turned, one hand covering half her face where he'd hit her. Her other fist lashed out hard, connecting with his jaw. "Seven years it's been, *seven years*!"

"You took everything else from me—by all the Gods, you're not takin' that, too!"

He struck her again, so brutally that she cried out and collapsed onto the floor. Both hands and her tumbled bronze-gold hair hid her face. There was blood on her fingers. But she struggled to her feet and when he straightened, holding the green folio, she sent her fist right into his stomach. He doubled over, retching, his curses gasping and incoherent as he fell to his knees. She stood over him, screaming at him, both hands on her pregnant belly.

Shadows shifted on the stairs. The child was perhaps five or six, a little boy, peeking out from between the railings, fingers wrapping them white-knuckled—unusual hands, the ring fingers and little fingers almost the same length—a very beautiful little boy with elegantly Elfen ears. His eyes were the dark blue of irises, and they were solemn, and old.]

It was the look in that child's eyes that terrified Cade more than anything else. They would haunt him, those eyes, forever.

He'd had trouble recognizing Mieka when he woke. But he hadn't recognized him in the dream, either. *Seven years,* the woman had said—twenty-five, he'd be, looking ten years older, the perpetual youthfulness of Elfenkind despoiled by the coarsening of overindulgence in liquor and thorn and rich living. The hollows below his cheekbones had filled out, there were pouches beneath those eyes, his shoulders were heavier, his belt and shirt buttons too tight. Worse, though, was the cruelty in the lines of his mouth, the grating rasp of his voice—the hand that had struck his pregnant wife. Twice.

It was beyond believing. It had been a nightmare, as he'd told Mieka, not a real foreseeing dream. It *had* to have been a nightmare.

He hadn't fooled Mieka with the lie. Neither could he fool himself.

He knew that bronze-gold hair, those beautiful hands that had clawed through the pages of Touchstone's folio. He still hadn't seen her face. But he'd seen the blood on her fingers after Mieka hit her. He'd seen the fury and contempt in her eyes—very dark blue eyes, the color of irises. And that reminded him of the little boy again, and he squeezed his own eyes shut against tears.

Why now? Why had the—the *Elsewhen,* as Mieka termed it—why had it come now to hack at his heart? After hearing the warm, familiar *"I knew you'd be here"* up on the battlements, after sharing the magic of the moonglade, after so much laughter at the fair, after so dazzling a start to their performances here at Castle Biding—after *"This life, and none other—"*

What had happened? What choices had been made over which he had no control? How could he fix this, prevent it, keep that look from that little boy's eyes?

The next morning, after dragging clean linen from his satchel, and gathering soap and razor and comb from the dressing table, he was about to head for the garderobe down the hall when he heard Jeska's shocked voice echoing up the stone stairwell.

"Cade! Cayden, you'll not believe it!"

The door burst open almost in his face. He stumbled back, caught his balance, glared at his masquer. Jeska didn't notice.

"Tobalt's just been here with word—the Downstreet burned to the ground last week!"

He heard someone—him?—ask quite calmly, "Was anyone hurt?"

"No, but it's gone, Cade, it's naught but ashes."

He nodded. So that was it. That, and whatever had happened yesterday after he returned to the castle and Mieka had continued wandering the fair. Had he met her yesterday? Was that it? Or would one of the nights they'd been meant to play the Downstreet be the night he met her? And now that the Downstreet was ashes, would they play somewhere else, and would *that* be the night he'd meet her?

He would never know. And there was the distinctive, specific hell of it. He would never know, and there was nothing he could do.

"We'll need other bookings, then," he told Jeska. "Get Kearny onto it, would you?"

Twenty-five

ONLY SEVENTY OR SO miles separated the two great university towns of Shollop and Stiddolfe, but over 150 days lay between Touchstone's appearance at the former and the last shows of the Winterly Circuit at the latter.

That final show on that final night caused a near riot. Touchstone's reputation had been growing all winter, and of course, the students at Stiddolfe wanted to outdo the students of Shollop in their appreciation. They did. Ardently. The largest of the bothy halls, residences where only young men were supposed to set foot, held a revelry that included as many girls as could be found willing to risk constabulary wrath. If some were unwilling, sufficient alcohol convinced them. This wasn't what Cayden had had in mind when he talked about how unfair it was that women weren't allowed the communal experiences available to men. When university officials finally acknowledged themselves helpless and sent for the constables, getting the girls out before the law could get in became anarchy. Local physickers, chirurgeons, and their medical students were busy well into the next morning, patching up cracked heads and stitching up gashes in well-educated hides.

Touchstone never made it back to lodgings at all that night. By the next noon they assembled listlessly in the front hall of the inn, wincing, greensick, and positive that the coach ride home to Gallantrybanks would finish them all off.

It didn't, though in Cayden's case it was a near thing. His headache was agonizing whether he thought or didn't think, and he couldn't stop thinking about the last few weeks. He couldn't summon up so much as a smile when Mieka borrowed his pen to draw a line through number seven on the list, saying as he did so, "I'll not endanger the horses, and I like the coachman too much to risk him, but, fellow passengers, we and the citizenry and the peace of the Kingdom barely survived last night!"

After spectacular shows at Castle Biding, they'd gone down to Frimham, a seacoast town that, after its harbor silted up, had reinvented itself as a health resort. Instead of Lilyleaf's ancient indoor baths, there were wide beaches of gritty sand where each tide refilled brick-lined pools; pleasant enough in summer, supposedly good for the constitution in spring, though nobody ever quite managed to explain the benefits of wading or swimming in frozen salt water with the rain pouring down. The sea and the sea air were much touted as worthwhile for one's health. The Atrium, Frimham's theater, was generally agreed to be the ugliest venue in the Kingdom. It was also the draughtiest. Mieka didn't bother creating a breeze during "Sailor's Sweetheart," because the hall did it for him. One afternoon, while they were returning to their lodgings after a performance, the wind decided to mock Cade by blowing loose a placard advertising Touchstone smack into his shoulder. The bruise lasted two days.

He hated this place, because Mieka was loving it so much and so obviously. He'd known the glisker was keeping a secret on that last morning in Castle Biding, when he saw him writing a letter that didn't go into Rafe's regular envelope to Crisiant before they left. Indeed, while the rest of them were loading up the coach, Cade saw Mieka give one of the servants a little package and a coin.

So he had already met her, Cade thought numbly. She and her mother had been sewing in the other Elsewhens—perhaps they'd had a booth at the fair. Perhaps he'd even seen her himself, while he and Mieka were browsing. No—he would have recognized her hair, her hands. But she might have been gone from the booth for a time, and Mieka might have gone back, looking for something to give his mother or sisters, and she had been there, and—

Useless to speculate. It had happened. It mattered for naught when or how. He found it bitterly amusing that the book he had so coveted had been the pivot point. He'd taken it back to the castle, and Mieka had gone on exploring without him. If only he had stayed, if only—

Useless. There was nothing he could do.

Mieka appeared on time for the shows in Frimham and vanished directly afterwards. On their day off, he was out of his and Cade's bedchamber before Cade woke up, and didn't return until nightfall. What time he did spend with his partners at meals or rehearsal, he sported a mindless grin that Cade wanted to slap from his face. And he wore the little charm in his ear every single day, the golden topaz that caught the elusive glint in those eyes. Cayden hadn't seen him wear it since the night of his Namingday at the Kiral Kellari.

Yes, he had met her, and she lived in or near Frimham. He knew it the way he knew Mieka would decline Kearney's offer of his country home for some leisure time before Trials. They'd have two weeks between their last show at the Kiral Kellari and the trip to Seekhaven. Cade didn't expect to see Mieka during that time.

Rafe, however, accepted the invitation with pleasure, for he would be married to Crisiant by then and it would be the perfect hideaway after the wedding. Kearney had been busy in that regard, as well, securing a lovely little High Chapel in a district near Wistly Hall. The stained glass, statues, and even the carvings over the doorways would all be magicked for the occasion by the Good Brother and Good Sister who would preside over the ceremony. Both sets of parents were in awe; Rafe's were trying not to show it. The Windthistles offered their riverside garden for the celebrations afterwards. They'd taken a liking to Crisiant, who gave them all the details of the Winterly that their son so conspicuously neglected to mention.

The final two Rules were not neglected. Their very last day on the road, Mieka chose a moment when the coachman was signing the usual voucher regarding the horses, stood at the coach doorway, unbuttoned his trousers, and pissed out the window. That took care of *Indecency.* As for *Theft of or damage to His Gracious Majesty's property*—he was the last to leave the coach in the Palace courtyard, and when he finally jumped down it was with the framed list, wrenched off the door, tucked under his arm as a souvenir.

Cayden wished he could have found any of it funny. He couldn't stop thinking about that little boy's eyes.

Cade's homecoming celebration was delayed a day because the afternoon he arrived back at Redpebble Square, he wanted nothing more than to fall into bed. It was ridiculous that a strong, healthy, almost-twenty-year-old man should be so knackered by work that he loved. He slept until the following noon, when Derien could bear it no longer and woke him up, demanding to be told absolutely everything. A quick wash, fresh clothes, and a weary trudge down the wrought iron stairs later, he walked into the kitchen to find Mistress Mirdley had made a gigantic lunching and invited Blye to share it. Of Lady Jaspiela there was, naturally, no trace.

Later that afternoon, once he'd talked about everything except what was really on his mind, he walked Blye back to the glassworks so she could show him the loving cups she'd made for Rafe and Crisiant. The usual design, whether in glass, pewter, silver, gold, or even humble carved wood, was two cups with a handle each, shaped to meet and match. There were obscene versions, of course, but the most popular form was that of a heart made whole when the cups were fitted to each other. Blye thought this inelegant. What she had designed for Rafe and Crisiant was of flint crystal, curved on the handled side but flat on the fitted side, with the deep cuts made in the crystal locking the two together. She showed them to Cade, anxious for approval. He smiled and told her they were perfect.

And wondered how soon she'd be making another set, for a girl with bronze-gold hair and a man who would knock her to the floor while she was carrying their child.

Blye knew him much too well. "I know you're tired, Cade, but I might've expected a little more—I don't know, triumph? You've just finished your first Winterly, you were a colossal success, and I can't go three blocks without Touchstone staring at me from one of those placards."

"In other words," he translated wryly, "what in all hells is my problem?"

She replaced the loving cups in their padded wooden box. "I know you're not going to tell me about whatever dreamings you had," she said, low-voiced. "But it's my guess that some of them were pretty awful."

"One or two," he allowed. "Most of the time I was too tired—or too cold!—to dream. Or at least I didn't remember them when I woke up."

"But those one or two . . ."

He shrugged.

"Cade—" Just then a piteous *Mew!* sounded at the door into the glassworks, and Blye ran to open it, returning with a tiny lump of purring white fur in her arms. "This is Bompstable," she said, "and a more dedicated cozener never begged his way into anyone's life."

Cade let the cat sniff his finger, then stroked the silky ears. "He's too pretty to be a stray."

"Jed gave him to me."

Had he been a little less exhausted, a little less heart-sore, he might have teased her. All he did was smile, and

she blushed, and that seemed to communicate everything.

But there was something he needed to say. "It's all
right that you told Mieka."

She glanced up, startled and guilty and then defiant.
"You should've told him yourself."

"I know."

Blye had been prepared for an argument. That he so
readily agreed seemed to confuse her for a moment.
"Were the awful ones about him?"

"There's nothing I can do, Blye. It's already too late."

"How do you know?"

"I just know, that's all." He ran a finger over the lid of
the box. "These really are beautiful. I knew they would
be."

"You know everything, it seems."

"I know enough," he replied stiffly.

He knew, for instance, that he'd had a flashing turn as
he got dressed earlier, just a glimpse of the girl. She'd
been sewing a short length of blue-violet silk that he now
knew was the color of her eyes. A second bit of the same
cloth, as yet unsewn, lay on the table beside her. She was
murmuring, chanting, as she worked. The words were
unknown to him, and frightening.

Over the next few days, he visited the Threadchasers,
and Mistress Bowbender, and went to have a look at the
gutted ruin of the Downstreet. There would be no decline into squalor, with Tobalt sitting at a scarred table,
saying that when the Cornerstones lost their Elf, they
lost their soul. Neither would there be plaques on the
wall to attest to all the players who'd got their start here,
and Tobalt would never say, *"But Touchstone is still together after twenty-five years."*

Sometimes at night Cayden listened to the two words
in his head, noting the vital difference. *Cornerstones*—
the first stones of a new building, holding things together

but unconnected. Tear the whole structure down, each of them would survive; pull one cornerstone out, the whole structure would collapse. But *Touchstone* was a singular. A thing they four made together, of which they were each a part. If Mieka was their soul, then Rafe was the backbone, steady and strong. Jeska: the eloquent voice. Cade himself . . . he wasn't sure. The mind, perhaps. Not the heart. He wrote from the head and sometimes the guts, but he kept his heart to himself. *"His mind's cold, but his heart's colder."* Yes, that was him, right down to the ground. The heart of Touchstone was Touchstone itself, the whole they four created together. Take away a fourth part of that heart—that part that was their very soul—and the three who were left would . . . survive.

And if there was a fleeting impression of words hastily scrawled on paper, terse terrible words he didn't want to read, and a hollow echoing voice that was his own saying, *"But I'm still here,"* it lasted only an instant.

Touchstone opened their stint at the Kiral Kellari, where the management had wisely replaced the hundreds of new mirrors on their walls with framed flat panes of glass that were much cheaper. Annoyed, because the crashing mirrors had been a wonderful effect, Touchstone shattered every glass at the bar instead. The management glared, gulped, and absorbed the loss, for Touchstone was the biggest draw since the Shadowshapers.

The Shadowshapers were, in fact, in the audience that first night, and afterwards, in the artists' tiring-room with the four blue couches, they sat and drank, and traded stories and laughed until their throats were raw. An innovation in the Kiral Kellari's program had a musician or two perform before and after a play, and when the young man finished and came back to greet them, Cade recognized him and Mieka recognized his lute. Alaen Blackpath, slowly making a name in Gallantrybanks over the winter, had also been booked at the Downstreet, and now had no idea how he would support himself. Rafe immediately engaged him to play at the wedding, both during the ceremony and after it at the feast. Cade mused on what it might be like to depend only on one's own talents, and for a few moments wished that the Lord and Lady had made him a musician instead of a tregetour.

That wish wasn't the oddest thing about that night. When Alaen first came into the tiring-room and was introduced all around, Cade felt a slow lurch that wasn't quite a turn when the lutenist's fiercely blue eyes met the equally intense blue gaze of Sakary Grainer. Cade held still, waiting for an Elsewhen to happen, and perhaps tell him why, but it didn't. After that first moment of mutual wariness, the two got on splendidly.

Not even that was the strangest thing that happened, though. Nothing could surpass the bewilderment of seeing dozens of girls outside the tavern, braving the jeers of the male patrons and, Cade realized, their infuriated parents when they got home, for none of those girls looked older than seventeen or so.

"What are they doing here?" he asked as their hire-hack pulled up in Amberwall Closure, near the ginnel that led to the artists' entrance.

"Fuck if I know," Rafe muttered. He was in a bit of a mood. He and Crisiant had had words that afternoon about his wedding clothes. She wanted him to wear one of the pie-frills that had turned out to be exactly what Kearney had said they were: the absolute latest in fashion. The words had included *Not if you held a knife to my throat, Don't tempt me, I won't wear it,* and *You will if I say you will and there's an end to it!*

"They must know that women aren't allowed inside a tavern where there's theater being performed." Cayden paid the driver as Rafe and Jeska stepped down.

Mieka had been peering out the open door, and now gave a little crow of laughter. "Trust me, Quill, they're not interested in theater. And I'd scarce call them *women*. Those, my friend, are *girls*. For all that you lived like a Nominative Brother in a Minster all during Winterly, surely you remember what girls are."

"Clearly and distinctly," he snapped, following Mieka out of the hack. "Just because I don't go running after anything in skirts, like you and Jeska—"

"Move it!" Rafe called. "We'll be late!"

Mieka had stopped to wave at the girls. He was rewarded with giggles and simpers and a few shrieks. Grinning, he fairly danced past Cade into the narrow passageway.

The plate with the spigot had been taught to recognize all four of them now, and the wall opened readily to the touch of Cade's hand. "But why are they here?"

"Us."

This made no sense to Cade. "Us?" he echoed stupidly.

"You, me, Rafe, Jeska. Touchstone!"

"I don't understand." It pained him to admit it, and pained him even more when Mieka's howl of laughter resonated through the back hallway. "We're players, we're in the theater, they can't go inside and watch, so what's the point? Why are they here?"

"Gods, Quill, are you really that innocent? Listen to me carefully now. *They are girls*. They are not here to see the show. They are here to see us."

"But we don't *do* anything outside the theater!"

"We could if we wanted to tonight—and with as many of those charming little dovies as we pleased."

"The placards," Rafe said suddenly. "They've seen the placards, so they know what we look like."

Mieka laughed again as he swung open the tiring-room door. "And now they want a much closer look—as close as they can get!"

It seemed Kearney's innovation of an imaging rather than an engraver's drawing had been true inspiration. What he deemed appropriate and even necessary to a placard advertising Touchstone's engagements allowed the female population a glimpse into the theater that they'd never even thought about before: it was inhabited by some very good-looking young men.

Cade had noted that the faces of the Shadowshapers were appearing on placards, too. Not that they needed the publicity. But no one had ever accused Romuald Needler of being slow to grasp an advantage. He had written to Cade after Tobalt's article appeared, commending his bold opinions about allowing women to attend the theater. Cade instantly understood that an increase in the audience meant an increase in the number of shows, the price of the tickets, or both. Needler had chosen his imager well, and the portraits were eye-catching. Rauel was adorably handsome, Vered looked moody and proud, Sakary glowered attractively, and Chat was endearingly homely.

But the girls outside the Kiral Kellari that night had come to look at Touchstone. At Jeska, for certes; at Mieka, absolutely; at Rafe, which would be reported back to Crisiant and earn him an hour's acid interrogation. None of the girls would be looking at Cade, and he knew it, so he was utterly baffled when, at Mieka's urging, between playlets the four of them went to a window overlooking the square to wave at their admirers outside, and one of the girls waved at him. At *him*. Looking directly up at him, smiling, eyes bright with excitement in the warm spring evening.

Of all the things he had hoped might come to him with Touchstone's success, admiration in the eyes of pretty girls had never even occurred to him. Not that he took advantage of it. Not that night, anyway.

Mieka seemed more unpredictable than ever as the

wedding approached. He fidgeted through rehearsals, was perfectly crazed during performances, and Cade would have suspected frequent indulgence in bluethorn except that it was a different sort of excitement in those eyes. He didn't understand it, and wasn't sure he wanted to.

Another lie. He understood very well what eager anticipation looked like on Mieka's face. He was waiting for something, expecting it, and it would happen the day Rafe wed Crisiant.

Unless Cade said something. Warned him. Oh, yes, he could just picture it: taking Mieka by the shoulders and telling him that this girl was a poison worse than tainted thorn. *"You'll end up hating each other, and as for what it'll do to your son—"*

It was the only thing that could make him even think about saying something. The look in that little boy's eyes.

Yet that brought up an entirely new question, one he'd never encountered before. If Mieka believed his warning, then that little boy would never be born, nor the brother or sister the girl was carrying when Mieka knocked her to the floor. If Cayden spoke, those children would never live. But only if Mieka believed him.

He might; he'd believed what Blye had told him on little if any evidence at all. He might believe this, too—

—only he wouldn't *believe* it. He'd say it was only a possibility, and now that he knew, he'd make sure it never happened. He'd assure Cade that he'd make a change here and there, decide one way instead of another, ever alert to the possibility that he could end up drunk and thorn-thralled and beating his pregnant wife.

Variations on *How can I change this?* had been torturing Cayden for years. He could cope with it. Barely. But Mieka, creature of impulse and impatience and instinct—it would either drive him mad or make him banish the whole concept from his mind when what he thought he might have to do conflicted too strongly with what he desired.

He desired this girl. Should Cade manage to convince him that it was potential disaster and he gave her up, it would remain between them the rest of their lives. And that would be poisonous, too. Mieka must make his own decisions, choices, even mistakes. His life wasn't Cade's to manipulate.

The night Cade decided this, he had the most horrible and most selfish dream of all. Mieka, sad-eyed and scared, not their lively, laughing Elf at all, hands reaching out, pleading with him: *"Don't let go—please, Quill, don't ever let go—"* His answer was to shake his head and turn away, feeling nothing. Nothing, for the one who had said to him, *"It's not in you to be wicked, Cade, nor cruel,"* who had written to him, *Don't worry about going too lost, Quill, I'll always come find you.* Feeling nothing, he could become the man who looked at stark cold words on a scrap of paper and say, *"But I'm still here."*

"His mind's cold, but his heart's colder."

And then one morning he was standing in the portico of a High Chapel overlooking the Plume, wearing his finest clothes and his little silver falcon pinning his neckband (dazzlingly white silk, plain and unadorned, unlike the embroidered and pleated extravagance knotted around poor Rafe's neck). He did his duty and cordially welcomed each guest—Threadchaser and Bramblecotte family and friends, Blye and Derien and Mistress Mirdley, Jeska and his mother, Lord Kearney Fairwalk, the Shadowshapers with their ladies—smiling and bantering with everyone as it was his role as bride's patron to do. The man who stood beside a future husband wasn't there for him: he was there on behalf of the future wife, his very presence reminding her bespoken that if he didn't live up to his promises, there was someone around who'd set him right in a hurry. This was naturally the source of a thousand jokes (and quite a few playlets, most of them obscene) and by the time Rafe and Crisiant arrived, Cade had heard all of them at least twice. Crisiant's three sisters were Cade's counterparts, who would advise her if they considered her lax in her duties as a wife. The fate of anyone daring to give Crisiant advice about anything didn't bear contemplation, but tradition was tradition.

Rafe sauntered over to Cade, who stood at the closed doors leading into the High Chapel. "Everybody here?"

"Almost. We're waiting on the Windthistles and your mother—they're probably fretting the last-instant arrangements."

"Cakes, pies, pastries, and alcohol for all this mob— remind me to have daughters, not sons. That way, all I'll have to do is show up and when the Good Brother asks, 'Who gives this maiden?'—"

"—you'll say, 'For the sake of my sanity, *take* her!'"

They were still grinning at each other when the outer door swung open and Mieka gamboled through, pausing to bow before Crisiant with a flourish of the peacock-blue cloak that covered him throat to boots. He spoke a few words that actually made her smile and blush. Hurrying over to Rafe and Cayden, he exclaimed, "I've never seen her look so lovely! Whatever did you do to deserve her?"

Rafe shrugged. "I'm me."

The Good Brother approached then, with some question about the loving cups. True to his word, Rafe had chosen Mieka to present them during the ceremony. He would also be true to his word if Mieka dropped them.

"Isn't that right?" he said, turning to address the Elf— who had vanished. "Where in all hells has he got to?"

Cade looked around.

The girl had her back turned. Mieka plucked the ivory-colored cloak from her shoulders, draped it over his arm with his own. She was a tiny thing; she could fit right beneath Mieka's chin. Twisted in the bronze-gold hair tumbling down her back was a blue-violet silk scarf, a match for the neckband tied at Mieka's collar.

"Quill!" he called suddenly, voice high with excitement. "I want you to meet someone!"

The girl turned, and met Cade's eyes, and smiled. There was no sudden curiosity, no puzzlement or shock or indignation at what he knew must be scrawled all over his face. What he felt didn't matter. *He* didn't matter. The smile curved sweetly on her mouth that was soft and innocent as a child's, and in her eyes was triumph and greedy possession as she looked at Mieka.

From within the High Chapel came the rippling notes of Alaen Blackpath's lute. The Windthistles jostled through the entry, and Rafe's parents rushed to kiss him and Crisiant, and Cade glimpsed Mieka yanking open the doors.

This life, and none other?

Any life rather than this one.

Places

Gallantrybanks capital city, seat of government; sometimes abbreviated as Gallytown; a Gallybanker is a native of the capital

Amberwall Square

Beekbacks Lane

Chaffer Stroll section of Beekbacks where the prostitutes walk

Criddow Close location of Blye's glassworks

Downstreet tavern

Kiral Kellari upscale tavern, with a real stage

Marketty Round

Narbacy Street

The Plume waterfall near Waterknot Street

Redpebble Square street address of the Silversun house

Spillwater district in Gallantrybanks

Tullyhowe Lane

Waterknot Street ritzy area of Gallantrybanks

Wistly Hall the Windthistle home

The Winterly Circuit

Bexmarket   rough industrial town
Castle Biding   site of the major chartered fair
Castle Eyot   country residence of Lord Rolon Piercehand
Clackerly Minster   even rougher industrial town
Coldkettle Castle
Dolven Wold
Frimham   seaside resort town
Lilyleaf   resort town with mineral baths
New Halt   roughest industrial town of all, and proud of it
Scatterseed
Seekhaven   the royal family's main country residence; site of Trials
Shollop   university town
Sidlowe
Stiddolfe   university town

Other Places

Cloffin Crossriver
Cranking Vale
Culch Minster   combination monastery and prison
The Flood   strait between the Kingdom and the Continent
Frannitch   country directly across the Flood
Gowerion   village outside Gallantrybanks
The Islands
Pennynine Mountains
Spoonshiner River
Tincted Downs
Vasty Moor
Westercountry

Terms

backs   street behind buildings

bantling   infant

becast   bespell

beek   to bask in the sun or before a fire

beholden   thank you

bellytimber   hearty, nourishing food

beseek   beseech

bespoken   betrothed

bind   another word for a spell; also binding

blashed   weak or watered down

blatteroon   person who won't shut up; constant talker

bodge   to fix something badly

bonding   the connection between an Elf and his or her beloved

bonelock   arthritis

bothy   hut for unmarried workmen; here, university dormitories

breedbate   someone who likes to start arguments or stir up quarrels

broadsheet   newspaper

chafferer   a vendor who enjoys bantering while making a sale

chankings   food you spit out

chapel   generic for a church

Chapel   specific church, or the religion itself

chavish   the sound of many people chattering at once

cheveril   kid leather

chirr   vibrating, high-pitched trilling

chirurgeon   surgeon

Circuit   set round of venues for traveling players; includes theaters, castles, town halls, guild halls, etc.; the three levels are Winterly, Ducal, and Royal

cloffin   to sit idly by the fire

cogger a charming trickster

collifobble to talk secretly

Colvado a type of apple brandy

corn-plaits stick figures made of corn stalks

cranking winding

cribble sort out

criddow someone broken or bowed down by age, sickness, poverty, or grief

croodle to coo like a dove

culch rubbish or refuse of every variety

cullion rude, disagreeable, mean-spirited person

downdrins an afternoon drinking session

Elf-light small flame conjured by persons with Fire Elf ancestry; also the light used in streetlamps

eyot a small island, especially one found in a river

fettler one who puts things in order

firepocket portable brazier, sometimes magically stoked

flirt-gill a light woman

flite to quarrel or brawl in words

fliting an exchange of invective, abuse, or mockery, especially one in verse set forth between two poets

flyndrig an impudent or deceiving woman

fribbler foolish, fussy man

fritlag a worthless, good-for-nothing man

frustle shake out and exhibit plumage

gallantry bank field where there used to be a gallows

ginnel a narrow passage between buildings

gleet slimy, sludgy, greasy filth

glisk subtle sensation; a slight touch of pleasure or a twinge of pain that penetrates the soul and passes quickly away

grassed informed upon; ratted out

grinagog stupid, gaping grin

hire-hack small carriage for hire

Huszar mercenary cavalry from the Continent

kag the stump of a broken tooth; in this, mutilated Elfen ears

Longseer someone who can view events at great distances

minster monastery/nunnery

miscreate illegitimate

nayword catchphrase, byword

nestcock househusband

pillock idiot; fool

pingle to fiddle with one's food, showing little interest or appetite

playlet sequence of two or three short scenes; usually lasts fifteen minutes to half an hour

Presence Lamps lit outside the chapel or minster to signify the presence of the Lord and Lady, and of their priests, within

prickmedainty man or woman compulsively fastidious about dress, appearance, and manners

quidam an obscure somebody somewhere

quiddle to dawdle or procrastinate in carrying out one's duty

rumbullion old word for rum

sapskull idiot

scroyle a scabby fellow

scuffled scrambled

smatchet impudent, contemptible child

snarge a person no one likes; a total jerk

sparge to make moist by sprinkling

stroll street where prostitutes parade

strutty boastful, conceited

swoophead a balding man trying to hide it with a comb-over

Thornlore the study of various drugs and their effects on different races

thorn-thralled addicted

tincted   stained, dyed

tregetour   originally a street magician; evolved into the word for a playwright

trimmings   tips thrown onstage to players after the show

trull   prostitute

twice-seen   déjà vu

twitchie   useless, bitchy, upper-class girl

wailful   lamentable

wistly   wistfully

yaffle   to eat ravenously while making unpleasant noises

yark   vomit

AUTHOR'S
NOTE

Muchly beholden to: Russ Galen and Danny Baror, Beth Meacham and Melissa Frain, Laurie Rawn, Mary Anne Ford, Lee and Barbara Johnson, Jay and Sonia Busby, Teresa Taylor, AshLeigh Henson, Kandice Adams, and all the other knowledgeable habitués of www.melanierawn. com for research help.

There are quite a few words herein that I stole from a perfectly marvelous book called *There's a Word for It!* by Charles Harrington Elster. (How could the English language possibly have left by the wayside the wondrous *snarge* and *collifobble* and *glisk*?) A couple of the terms I either adapted or made up myself, but as much as I'd love to claim all of them, I ain't that creative.

Turn the page for a preview of

Elsewhens

MELANIE RAWN

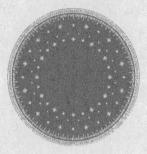

Book Two of The Glass Thorns

Available in February 2013 from
Tom Doherty Associates

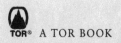 A TOR BOOK

One

HE COULDN'T BREATHE. His chest was tight, his head aching. His hands shook as he rubbed his tear-streaked face, terrified that he might have cried out and woken someone—

By the Lord and Lady and all the Angels and Old Gods, please let him have cried out and woken someone in the vastness of Fairwalk Manor.

By the time he recovered his breath and his heart stopped thundering, he knew he had stayed silent. There was no one to knock on his door, call out his name, come into his room, exclaim with shock at what he knew must be in his eyes. There was no one.

Brishen Staindrop had promised him dreams to fire his imagination and make his writing richer, deeper. He ought to've known. Blockweed hadn't worked on him the way it was supposed to; neither had this, whatever it was. All he wanted was a few hours spent someplace beautiful that danced and sparkled, someplace safe. What he got instead was horror.

And he would have to remember it, wouldn't he? It was part of him now. To tuck it all away and forget the words that unlocked it would be to lose something of himself. If he was true to his own arrogance, he would have to keep this Elsewhen as he had kept all the others.

Pushing himself to his feet, he made his slow, aching way to the hearth and half-fell onto his knees, reaching for logs to stoke the fire. There was no clock in the bedchamber—Kearney Fairwalk forbade clocks at his residences, with the splendid disregard of a very rich man for such mundane concerns as being anywhere on time. Cade might have lingered in bed and rung for a servant to replenish the fire for him, but the frantic need to see another living being had faded. He didn't want anyone to see him like this.

To be in possession of a suite of rooms at Fairwalk Manor was a privilege not accorded many. Touchstone had been invited for the fortnight preceding Trials. After their first grueling Winterly Circuit and dozens of shows in and around Gallantrybanks, all four young men were in need of time off. But rather than visit Fairwalk Manor, Jeska had chosen instead to escort his mother to a seaside town where he'd taken a month's hire on a cottage for her, and stay for a couple of weeks. Rafe and his new wife, Crisiant, had accepted His Lordship's generosity as a welcome escape after the strains of putting together their wedding celebrations. Cayden, determined on other forms of escape and certain that Fairwalk Manor was precisely the location for them, hadn't blushed a single blush when he got into a carriage the morning after Rafe and Crisiant's wedding and betook himself to Fairwalk Manor. In fact, he hadn't seen the couple at all. Not only was the tall, sprawling house gigantic, but orders had also come down from Lord Fairwalk to his servants to give his guests whatever they wanted whenever they wanted it, and do this as unobtrusively as possible. What Rafe and Crisiant wanted was exactly what Cade wanted: privacy.

Cade knew exactly how they were spending their time. He spent his exploring the library, the grounds, the stables, and the little blue leather roll of thorn he'd purchased from Mieka Windthistle's Auntie Brishen.

He'd always thought Mieka would be with him when he did this. *Don't worry about going too lost, Quill, I'll always come find you,* he'd written in the note accompanying that first little green wallet of blockweed. But Mieka was in Frimham, pretending to stay at a seaside inn while really staying with the girl whose existence made the thorn necessary.

Cade was supposed to be working on various playlets, polishing those that Touchstone might have to present at Trials and crafting his own ideas into performable shape. He arrived at Fairwalk Manor fully intending to do his duty by his group and his talents. Instead, the afternoon following his arrival, he took a long walk about the sculpted grounds, ate an early dinner, and told the servants to leave him alone. And they had done so; even if he had cried out, no one would have come. He got out the roll of thorn and stared at it for almost an hour before deciding which little packet of powder to use.

He hated what was in his mind. He had to find some way of enduring what he knew was to come. If thorn helped, then he'd use it.

Elsewhens, Mieka called them: visions while he slept and sometimes when he was wide awake of futures that might come to pass. Cade had neglected far too long the orderly categorizing of what he'd foreseen. The memories of things that hadn't happened yet were crowding his head, and he knew he had to discipline them or run mad.

The Elsewhens about Tobalt Fluter in the Downstreet, talking to some reporter about Touchstone—those didn't count now, not since the tavern had burned. He didn't have to worry about them anymore. He didn't have to think about hearing Tobalt say, *"His mind's cold, but his heart's colder"* or *"Touchstone is still together after twenty-five years."* Whatever futures Tobalt had referred to, they would be different. Cade could rid himself of the despair of the first—and the determination not to let it happen. He had to let go of the joy of the second—and the fear that now it would never come true. The futures would be different, and those dreams didn't count.

But as he went through each in his mind, reviewing them before locking them away, he noticed something strange: the lutenist in the second vision. With a soundless bark of laughter he suddenly recognized Alaen Blackpath—twenty-five years older, his reddish curls turning silver—

—just as he'd seen Mieka's black hair silvered in a single tantalizing flash, lines framing his mouth and crossing his forehead; older, yes, but still bright-eyed and laughing and beautiful.

He wanted so much to hold on to that one. It was still possible, wasn't it? Just because Tobalt could no longer sit in the Downstreet and say that Touchstone was still together after twenty-five years, it didn't mean that Cade would never see Mieka like that.

No. He had to be ruthless. He couldn't keep that one just because it made him smile, because it comforted him. He had to get rid of at least some of these Elsewhens crammed into his brain. Not that he'd ever done it before, except the once.

"Once you've learned it, the technique will in all probability save your sanity," said Master Emmot. *"If only by convincing you that there is an order to things, an order that you may impose upon them. Organization is a desirable thing. When we can accomplish it, in whatever area of life, it is to be cherished and defended. To impose order on the chaos of living, on the potential chaos of your own mind—what else is language, and the division of the world into separate nations, and even the ordering of time itself into hours, weeks, months, years? Thus, too, it*

*must be with your foreseeings. And just as words are
used to identify time, places, things, you may use a series
of words to classify each separate dream."*

To think he had actually been intrigued: learning how
to select a couple of words or a phrase that encompassed
a particular foreseeing, how to think of his mind like a
trunk with an ever-increasing number of locks, each giving access to a little compartment where a dream was
kept.

*"It's very like what men used to do when they wanted
to memorize large quantities of information, such as the
solar or lunar calendars, or an epic poem cycle. They would
construct whole houses in their minds, and furnish them
from front doorway to attic roof with items that prompted
memory of a particular thing or things. The four vases on
a table in the vestibule, each containing flowers of a different season, might be a reminder of the dates of the phases
of the moon. Perhaps the railings of the staircase each de-
pict a particular tree, like the old poem that describes the
attributes of each. Yes, I know you've read it—but could
you memorize it in perfect order and then tuck it away, to
be brought out again when you look into your mind and
see those railings? In our day, we are a literate society, so
we don't have to use these techniques to remember and
pass along information. We have only to go look it up in a
book. There are those in this world who still practice this
method of memory with images as their keys. But you are,
as we both know, someone to whom words are of para-
mount importance, so the only image you will use is that
of a large locked trunk. Make it as plain or as ornate as
you wish. The keys will not be made of brass or iron,
but of words."*

To think that he had actually found it interesting: creating the trunk, dividing it into sections according to
subject (one of them pretentiously labeled THE KINGDOM
OF ALBEYN), choosing a primary word for each section

and then more words for specific identification. He'd actually enjoyed it.

"Remember the whole of the experience, as I've taught you. Assign your key to it. Then lock it away until you wish to review it again. Or until you wish to be rid of it forever."

But he'd done that only once, just to prove to Master Emmot that he could indeed do it. His reasoning had not sat well with the old Sage.

"You tell me, Cayden, that if a man is the sum total of what he has learned and experienced, then to rid yourself of even one foreseeing would be to take away a portion of who you are. But did you hear what you just said? What a man has learned. What he has experienced. Those things are in the past. What you see is the future. Once a future becomes impossible, for whatever reason, you would be doing yourself and your overactive mind a favor by getting rid of it. Right now you are fifteen. What if you live to be eighty or ninety? Moreover, what if your turns as you get older become more frequent, or lengthier, or more detailed? They might do, you know. The brain grows and changes, and does not fully mature until the age of twenty-one or -two, perhaps longer for one of mostly Wizarding blood. My advice is to clear your mind of things that are no longer possible. Don't clutter up your life with irrelevancies. But the choice is yours, of course."

Irrelevancies—perhaps every dream he had ever dreamed was now irrelevant. Perhaps he ought to treat them as if they were.

He wanted so much to keep the one where he'd seen Mieka with those laughing eyes and that silvering hair.

But what of the others concerning him, others about him?

Watching the moonglade on a river: *"Whatever I give you, you give back to me better than I could ever imagine it. You always do."*

Watching the girl and her mother discuss their plans to tame him.

Watching himself slam Mieka against an icy lamppost.

Watching his own hand slap Mieka again and again and again.

Watching Mieka beat his pregnant wife.

Watching his own scarred fingers (when and how had those scars happened?) holding a note, reading the terrible words scrawled on it, hearing himself say, *"But I'm still here."*

He couldn't rid himself of any of it. Each of those foreseeings, and a hundred more—they were part of him. They were his memories, even if they hadn't happened yet, even if they would never happen. If he lost them, he would lose parts of himself.

"Don't worry about going too lost, Quill, I'll always come find you."

To lose himself for at least a little while seemed a very good thing. But the thorn hadn't done for him what it was supposed to do.

"I don't have the sort of dreams most people have. . . ."

This new one had come in grim sequence, like a play. Or a fire set by a professional arsonist. The scene set and surveyed. The vulnerable points identified. The progress, inevitable and devastating, to the final taste of ashes: *"Write me happy, Quill."*

Perhaps it was his own instincts, his tregetour's brain, that had given him that long plotline instead of mere glimpses. Perhaps there had been a dozen separate dreams that his trained mind had organized into a whole. Perhaps it had been the influence of the thorn. Perhaps he simply didn't dream the way other people did.

As if any of that mattered.

He'd tried to fight his way out of it, truly he had, but the thorn was powerful in him by then and it was much too late. It would *always* be too late. If he saw a possible future, it meant that something had already happened that made that future possible. He couldn't change it. He was helpless. He couldn't control what other people did or said or thought or felt.

So why bother anguishing himself about it? Things would happen the way they would happen. He had no power over futures decided by other people's choices. Yet it seemed he was constructed inside in ways that compelled him to try. If a voice sounding remarkably like Master Emmot's whispered, *"How?"* he refused to hear it.

Over the next nine days at Fairwalk Manor, he used all the different thorn packets in the roll, daring them to do what they were supposed to do. Recklessly he gave himself over to the thorn, sometimes using just before he went to sleep, other times spending the whole day lying on a deep padded sofa in the shade of an apple tree, aware that anyone seeing him would think he was drowsing. He wasn't. His eyes were closed so that the view of serene pasture and green hillside could not compete with the scenes inscribing themselves on his brain.

Always it was the same dream, with variations that never made any real difference and occasionally with elaborations that gouged pieces out of his heart. The Elsewhen infected him like a wound gone to poison, suppurating into his every conscious thought. He knew why there were no significant changes. None of the decisions that would change it were his to make. He had no choices, none at all.

But Sagemaster Emmot had always said that if he had no choices to make, he would see no futures. He'd seen this one, over and over again; therefore he must have made a decision that caused it.

On the tenth night of his stay at Fairwalk Manor, having run out of thorn, he got drunk instead. The next morning he wrote a brief letter to Brishen Staindrop, asking what other sorts of thorn she could suggest. He spent that day and the next writing "Doorways." He told himself that by calling it that, and keeping it a single play instead of the series of plays that *Broken Doors* had been in the dream, he was beginning the changes that must be made in order to render that future impossible. And as for *Bewilderland*—he vowed never, ever to write anything even remotely like it, nor use the title or any variation thereof. Senseless word, anyway.

That last night at Fairwalk Manor, he had the dream about Tobalt Fluter again.

The office was strut and brag from the carved door to the wide window overlooking the river. The walls were thick with books on shelves, and copies of important front pages and broadsheet articles framed under glass, and imagings of the famous with their signatures, all inscribed to Sir Tobalt Fluter. Little trinkets glinted on every shelf, some of them the symbols of various clans — Pheasant, Lion, Scorpion, Elk — some of them punning on the names of those who had given them: an apple made of oakwood, a circle of braided gold, a bent bow, a green glass lily leaf from the guilds of that town. A very important personage was Sir Tobalt, his influence coveted and his interest courted by anyone who was anyone or wanted to be. He sat at his desk, angled so he could see the door and the window view, and arched his brows at the young man who hunched in a severe wooden chair before him, pen and notebook at hand.

"I must've written dozens of pieces about them through the years," said Sir Tobalt. "But I'd never talked to the people around them at such length before. Gods and Angels, what some of them are saying—"

"Which people? The wives? Parents?"

A shrug and a thin, shrewd smile that crinkled the corners of his eyes. "Don't think I'll tell you my sources. All you're here for is a tickle of what the chapbook biography will contain."

"So make me laugh," the young man invited brazenly. "Set me positively howling. How much of what everyone's saying is true?"

"Nobody wants to admit to anything, especially concerning the Elf. You can't print that, by the way." He ran a fingertip along the trinket that had pride of place on his desk: a glass basket about the size of his cupped palm, with a little silver quill and a green glass withie propped inside along with a selection of the finest gold-nibbed pens. The gesture was lazy, at odds with the sudden vehemence of his tone. "Damned I'll be, though, if I include all those lies Mieka's wife told me. I hear enough of that muck from Cade." He snorted. "*Bewilderland*— that's what he'd like all of us to live in, some insane fantasy where his lies are the only truth."

"I don't understand what lying gets him. I mean, after all these years, to keep telling the same stories that nobody ever believed the first time he told them—"

"Got no choice, has he? He'd go mad, otherwise. Because he knows. He'll never admit it, but he knows. When Touchstone lost their Elf, they lost their soul."

No, Cade thought when he woke, he could never rid himself of any of the Elsewhens. They were part of him.

At last came the morning of departure for Gallantrybanks. Cade nodded to the servants, thirty of them, all lined up to bid him and Rafe and Crisiant farewell. But he didn't look directly into the eyes of any of the maids, footmen, cooks, grooms, gardeners, and sundry other staff standing there in the gauzy spring rain. He still felt too guilty. Cade's parents rarely accepted invitations to stay at noblemen's houses. His mother always begged off with the excuse that her husband's duties at Court did not permit his absence from it, and she simply couldn't think of going anywhere without him. In reality, the Silversuns hadn't the cash to spare for tipping the servants as was expected at all the great houses. Lady Jaspiela had reminded Cade several times before this trip that he must do so, especially at the home of so exalted a lordship as Kearney Fairwalk.

The housekeeper hadn't let him. "Oh no, Master Silversun, no! 'Twas our privilege and delight to serve yourself and Master and Mistress Threadchaser! We've so few truly distinguished guests, not at all like in His late Lordship's day—" She bit both lips together, as if she had said too much, then gave him a swift and sincere smile. " 'Twas our pleasure, every one of us."

As he settled into a sprightly little carriage drawn by two high-stepping grays, waiting for Rafe and Crisiant to join him, he mused on the implications of what the housekeeper had said. So he was *truly distinguished*, was he? And comparable to those who had visited in Kearney's father's time? What sort of guest did Kearney invite down to Fairwalk Manor, that a tregetour and a fettler and the daughter of a man who built chimneys for a living were *distinguished*?

The carriage door opened and Rafe handed his wife in. Cade smiled. Crisiant settled facing him, Rafe soon at her side, and as the coachman chirruped to the horses, they both looked at him for the first time in almost a fortnight.

"Too weak to shave, were you?" Rafe asked.

"It would probably be good manners to apologize," Cade said, "for not even once joining you for dinner. But I can't think of a single reason why I should. It's not as if you missed me, is it? And I knew for certain sure you wouldn't appreciate catching whatever illness I brought with me from Gallytown."

"We did wonder where you were," Crisiant said. "The servants mentioned that you seemed to like the gardens—"

"When I wasn't yarking in the garderobe," he lied with perfect glibness. He knew what he looked like: the haggard face that hadn't known a razor in a week, the circles beneath his eyes. "Kearney's people took good care of me, though, and now I'm well and ready to work." He smiled again, and winked at Crisiant. "You can have your husband from curfew bell to lunching, but there's Trials coming up so I have to steal him the rest of the day."

Rafe nodded slowly, still not quite convinced but, as usual with him, not pressing the point. "Jeska's due back home tomorrow. Mieka—"

Crisiant interrupted. "You may have to hire a regiment of retired guardsmen to drag him back from Frimham and—what was her name, again?"

"Well," Rafe mused, "the family name is Caitiffer, whatever that means."

"I thought she had a bit of a foreign look about her."

Cade glanced out the window and bit his lips against laughter. In a Kingdom where Wizard, Elf, Gnome, Goblin, Giant, Piksey, Sprite, Fae, and who knew what all else had all contributed their distinctive features— facial and otherwise—to the general bloodlines, it took a Gallybanker with Crisiant's decided views to proclaim that anyone could actually look *foreign*.

"But I don't think Mieka's ever mentioned her name," Rafe went on.

Cade said, "That's because he doesn't know it." When they both stared at him, he grinned. "Jinsie told me at your wedding that her clan is fanatically conservative, and only the immediate family ever knows anyone's given name."

Crisiant mulled this over. Rafe said, "Wouldn't make much difference in bed, I'd expect—in my experience, a *dearling* here and a *sweetheart* there usually suffice—" His wife clouted him in the arm and he laughed. "—but it seems a bit much to have to marry a girl before you find out her name."

"Mayhap that regiment can threaten it out of the mother," Crisiant said, "while they're peeling that silly Elf off the daughter."

"No regiment required," Cade assured her. "I'll just send his brothers after him."

"If you can peel Jed away from Blye," she retorted.

"I've been wanting to ask how all that happened," he said, and like every girl in possession of a happy and successful love story of her own, she was eager to detail the progress of a friend's romance. Why was it, he mused as he listened—and kept track of each incident, because he really did want to know—that when people paired off they wanted to see everyone else paired off, too? He assumed it was a generous impulse, but all he could think of was that Elsewhen that had repeated over and over, and the unknown faceless woman who would become his wife and the mother of his children, and her total indifference to the fire that had begun by illuminating his soul and could end by destroying him.

He spent so much time being afraid. Two afternoons later, when Touchstone gathered in Mistress Threadchaser's sitting room, just like always, and Mieka bounced in as blithe and laughing as ever, he began to think that perhaps he hated the Elf for not even knowing what fear was.

He sat back to watch and listen as news was exchanged. Jeska sported an enviable sun-browning from his weeks seaside; Mieka did not. This brought the inevitable teasing ("Why, whatever could you have been doing to keep you indoors all that time?"), which only made his grin all the sleeker, all the more smug, as if he'd done something very clever. Cade, sorting withies, wondered if the girl was already pregnant. Amazing, really, that she'd yielded her virginity more readily than her name. But he supposed that might be much of the attraction: the mystery of her, the wanting to possess everything about her. He banished the insistent vision of that sad-eyed little boy from another Elsewhen, grateful when Mieka turned to Rafe with mischief sparkling in those eyes, the look he always wore when about to tease.

Rafe knew what was coming. Pointing a long finger at the Elf, he said, "Make a start with me, and I'll tell Crisiant every word of it."

Mieka pretended to cower back in terror. "Gods, not that! Anything but that!"

"Can we get some work done?" asked Jeska, fidgeting with the new pages Cade had given him.

"Not before you tell us how many adoring ladies you left languishing behind you," Mieka retorted. Then, to Rafe, in aggrieved tones: "Cade was there with you at Fairwalk Manor, so he already knows everything! Won't you even tell me—?"

"We didn't see him the whole time."

"Oy, Quill! What's her name, then?"

Cade looked up from the glass basket. "Whose name?"

Mieka was making a sly, smirking face. "The lovely birdie as kept *you* busy!" Then he fell back into his chair with a look of horror. "Holy Gods—don't tell me you spent the whole while *working*?"

"Not all of it." He manufactured a smile, complete with suggestively arched brows, and tossed over a primed withie. A quick glance at Rafe showed him a frown, and too late he recalled that he'd said he'd been ill. Suddenly resentful that he was having to tell all these lies, he asked himself who cared what Rafe thought, or knew, or thought he knew?

"Speaking of *working*," Jeska said pointedly.

Mistress Threadchaser entered then, carrying a teapot and four glass mugs. The familiar little ritual of pouring out occupied them for a time. When they had settled once more, Cade wondered if they'd ever recover the easy banter, the comfortable mockery they'd known on the Winterly Circuit. All those months when they'd been far from home, with no one but each other to talk to and rely on—it might have been expected that the intensity and exhaustion of performing and the long days of boredom in the coach would have had them at each other's throats, but instead they'd grown even closer. Not a plural, like the Shadowshapers or the Crystal Sparks, but a single thing: Touchstone. A knot of four ropes that became tighter with every show they played.

Yet he'd felt that connection loosening, once they had returned home to Gallantrybanks. Onstage it had been the same. The bookings at the Kiral Kellari had been brilliantly successful. But offstage, other people began to tug. Now, after a scant fortnight apart, Cade felt the difference in the mood and it scared him. It was as if they all had other places they'd rather be: Rafe with Crisiant, Mieka with his girl, Cade with his thorn . . . of them all, only Jeska was determined to get down to it, get some work done.

So they started. A bit rusty at first, but things slowly came together. Cade had them run through bits of half a dozen pieces to introduce them to changes he'd made. When Mieka proclaimed himself hopelessly confused and threatened to smash the glass basket over Cade's head unless they were allowed to do one playlet all the way through, Cade's temper blew up like an exploding withie.

"Which particular piece of rubbish would you like to do?" he snarled. "It's all equally shitty! I hate every word of it! There's not an idea in any of it that means anything at all!"

Jeska's fists clenched as if throttling his own temper. "It's *your* writing, ain't it? It's what we've been doing for more than a year now—"

"That's the whole fucking point! It's stale and it's boring—"

"So write us something else!"

"Keep feeding the beast? I put my guts into something new and original and you suck it dry, all of you, and then the audience does the same, like a whole belfry of fucking Vampires—"

"What in all hells is wrong with you?" Rafe shouted. "This is what you've wanted since you were fifteen years old! Now you're telling us it's meaningless?"

"Yes." Mieka's voice was lethally soft. "As pointless as searching for nipples on a chicken. He's seen us work these pieces too many times. They don't mean anything to him anymore. He's not there inside them, working them the way you and me and Jeska work them. And he's not the audience, neither. *They* don't think it's rubbish."

"Audiences," Cade sneered. "What do *they* know?"

"They know enough to know we're good. Gods damn it all, Cade, we're great and everybody knows it!"

"Excepting him," Rafe growled.

"Why not join in one night?" Mieka taunted. "Watch us perform, be part of the crowd. That's what you were telling Tobalt in that interview, innit? That men want to be part of a shared experience?"

"I'm already part of something." All at once all the anger left him, and he smiled. "Touchstone. I'm part of something worth being part of."

Mieka glared at him, then collapsed back in his chair, laughing helplessly. "Oh, Quill! You're such a fraud!"

Jeska looked bewildered, but Rafe was slowly succumbing to a grin. Cade shrugged, hands spread wide in the Wizardly gesture that meant *You may trust me,* and the fettler gave a complex snort before rapping his knuckles on the table beside him.

"All right, children, that's enough. Now that we're all agreed that the three of us are brilliant and Cade Silversun is a shit-wit with delusions of intelligence, may we continue?"

And after that, everything was back to the way it used to be. Not that Cade had intended his little tirade to produce that effect—he was still wondering as he walked home just how it had happened, in fact, but was too grateful to do much analyzing. He had his group back. He was part of Touchstone, and Touchstone was well worth being part of. This *was* the life he wanted to be living.

Elsewhens and all.

TOR

Award-winning authors
Compelling stories

Please join us at the website
below for more information
about this author and other great
Tor selections, and to sign up for
our monthly newsletter!